HARLEY MERLIN AND THE STOLEN MAGICALS

Harley Merlin 3

BELLA FORREST

Nightlight Press

ONE

Harley

Fear seized me like a boa constrictor, wrapping tight around my chest. I sank back against the wall of the coven's elegant hallway and hoped nobody would see me. The shadow of a majestic dragon hid me from sight. To be honest, I'd never paid particularly close attention to them before, despite the statues being absolutely everywhere. *Talk about theming.* No one could ever be in any doubt about what the San Diego Coven's mascot was.

I smirked. Wade would've killed me for calling them mascots.

"They're emblems of our strength and fortitude," he'd have said, no doubt flashing me a withering look for good measure.

Down the hallway, classical music rang out, and my stomach twisted in knots.

Get your ass in gear. You're a Merlin—stop being a coward. I'd been giving myself the same pep talk all the way down from the living quarters. At the magnolia trees, it had taken every ounce of willpower I had not to turn around and run back up the stairs. In ten whole minutes, I'd moved ten yards down the hall. *A yard a minute... way to go.*

A few minutes more, and I'd be late.

Then again, what had they expected, leaving me alone in my room to go out-of-my-mind crazy all morning? Whoever thought noon was a good time for a ceremony was evidently out of their mind, too. I'd have preferred dawn, since I hadn't slept last night anyway. Hell, why hadn't we gotten it out of the way as soon as I'd said I'd pledge?

I wasn't really the nervous type, but this felt different somehow. I'd have to stand in front of a crowd of hundreds, with everyone staring at me, silently judging my worthiness. Having never really been part of anything for longer than a couple of years, the prospect of being a true member of the coven was as frightening as it was exciting. This was a lifetime deal, and I kept wondering when the devil was going to pop up and reveal himself. It was the foster kid in me, always expecting the good to be ripped away at the last second. Aside from the Smiths, the San Diego Coven was the best thing to ever happen to me. Here, for the very first time, I felt as though I belonged. I wasn't an addition to something... I was integral to the whole thing. A cog, instead of a spare bolt left behind in the box.

Not to mention that during the night my mind still raced with thoughts of everything that had happened in the last few weeks. I'd been at the coven for just over a month, but it felt like a lifetime. Katherine Shipton was out there, somewhere, and it was only a matter of time before she made her next move. She had the kids—I knew she did—but we had no way of knowing what she was going to do with them. Plus, she had to be pretty pissed by now. We'd knocked down three of her pawns, stalling her way to checkmate.

Emmett Ryder was dead and buried, with a simple marker above his tomb that detailed his crimes. The coven had put his body in the Crypt, deep below ground in the SDC in a restricted zone that only Alton and the Mage Council had access to. Meanwhile, Emily Ryder was stuck in Purgatory and had yet to breathe a word of Katherine's plan—or "Katie," as they'd so sickeningly called her. No person that evil could have such an ordinary name. Stalin, Vader, or Hitler, maybe, but not friggin' *Katie*. Finch was the same, stewing in staunch silence. Although, cracks had started to appear in his frosty façade, like the initial split of a heavy boot on solid ice. A bit more pressure, and he might be the first to break.

"Harley?" a voice echoed down the corridor, snapping me out of my gloomy reverie. Wade.

Maybe, if I just stay super quiet, he'll walk right by me. I sensed irritation emanating from him in spiky waves. He was *not* in the mood for my tardy antics today. Not that he ever was. Still, it didn't stop me from winding him up on every possible occasion. It was probably the most beautiful part of our friendship: the endless, sarcastic banter.

I slipped out of the dragon's shadows. Wade's deep green eyes widened for a moment. The prickling pulse of his annoyance softened into something warmer, a sudden rush of admiration, mingling with a less tangible feeling that rippled beneath the surface—something I couldn't quite put my finger on.

"I've been looking all over the place for you, Merlin! And you've been ignoring my texts," he snapped, though a note of wonder still lingered. It brought a smile to my face. "What were you doing behind that statue? Wait... you weren't *hiding*, were you?"

He looked undeniably handsome in his dark blue uniform, which shimmered strangely in the dim lighting of the hallway. The high collar was also odd—a magical stylistic choice, no doubt. Most of it ran around his neck in a band of gold. It reminded me of a chef's jacket, only way cooler. Gold buttons ran up the front, each embellished with the Latin names of the elements that gave us our magical strength—*Terra, Aqua, Aer, Ignis.* At the top, I noticed the name *Gaia* taking prime position just below the hollow at the bottom of his throat. Mother Earth, the one holding all of this together. Beside it, on the folded triangle of his golden lapel, he wore a single red gem. *Fire,* I supposed. It was a surprisingly militant look for the SDC, but it suited Wade to a T.

I crossed my arms. "I was just on my way to the ceremony."

"The great Harley Merlin, afraid of public speaking?" He sounded annoyingly gleeful. "Is that it?"

"Please. I've got bigger things to worry about than reciting some spiel. *I* was the one who talked to the Mage Council after the gargoyle incident, remember?"

Wade's expression suddenly became more serious. "You're not getting cold feet, are you?"

"I'm fine! I just wanted to take my time on the walk over. Stop making it sound like we're about to get hitched or something."

Wade's eyebrows shot up, and my face heated as the words echoed down the hall. My throat constricted, making it hard to swallow. I had no idea whether the feelings were mine or his. He had this way of muddling me, churning my mind upside down until I couldn't tell where the trail of his emotions ended and mine began.

"Come on. It's rude to keep everyone waiting," he urged, turning on his heel. His voice caught for a split second. "You look good, by the way. That shade of green suits you. Brings out the red in your hair."

"You mean I look like a Christmas ornament?"

He flashed a grin over his shoulder. "No, you look good. I'd forgotten you had arms, since I'm so used to seeing you with that leather jacket slung over your shoulders."

I shot him a look as I followed him down the hall. *How I love our little tête-à-têtes.*

My formal gown had been Tatyana and Santana's suggestion, but I was deeply regretting letting them run wild with my wardrobe. And, presumably, Wade's credit card. The emerald silk of the flowing skirt trailed behind me like liquid, while the structured bodice held me in like I was some medieval princess. Tiny embroidered flowers and vines curled across the waist and up to the bust, which showed a modest amount of flesh. After all, I wasn't out to shock my new "family." I knew I looked fierce, and it was a good feeling. Plus, no one could see my heavy-duty boots beneath the skirt, which seemed like another win to me.

"Hurry up. Everyone's waiting for you," Wade said, pausing for me to catch up. "Don't make me carry you in there, Merlin, because I will. And you won't like it."

"Yeah, yeah. The sooner this is over, the sooner we can celebrate."

The moment I stepped through the arched main doors, everyone fell silent. I could've heard a gnat fart. Already, the emotions of the gathered group were creeping toward me, threatening to overwhelm my senses. I focused on Wade standing by the door, letting everyone else and their cacophony of feelings fade into the background. He seemed proud and guarded, as though he knew what I was up to but didn't have the heart to refuse me my security blanket.

I'd forgotten how massive the Hall was, with more of the coven's scaly, bronzed mascots arching between the polished marble floor and the vertigo-inducing heights of the ceiling above me. The flickering lights of the chandeliers cast shards of radiance across the gathered audience.

My heart thundered in my chest as Wade offered me his arm and led me toward the wide, circular podium that stood nearby. I'd used the hidden back entrance, reserved for guests and, apparently, pledgers.

We made our way past the seven mirrors, their bronze edges reflecting the rusty glow of the torches along the wall. To take my mind off the swollen crowd before me, I wondered just how far these mirrors could reach and how fast one could get to a new destination through them. *Could I get to Hawai'i if I leapt through one right this second, to avoid all of this entirely?*

"Don't even think about it," Wade whispered, giving me a hard stare.

"What? I wasn't thinking anything."

All eyes were on me, and not for the first time. This place gave me an eerie sense of déjà vu. I hardly dared to look out at the sea of people, fearing it might unleash the floodgates of my Empath abilities. The last thing I needed was hundreds of feelings chipping away at my self-control, like my last big entrance here. Sure, I'd gotten a better handle on crowds, but that level of judgment, wariness, and suspicion was hard to ignore. Even so, the atmosphere was infinitely less hostile than before. There were even some smiles, if I looked hard enough.

Most of the coven seemed to be here, and they were all wearing uniforms like Wade's. The Rag Team were on the sidelines, plus Garrett, with his former investigative squad lined up sheepishly beside him—minus Finch, of course. On the podium itself, Tobe, the Beast Master, stood at the farthest edge, while the preceptors took up the chairs that had been laid out for the occasion. All six were there: Jacintha Parks, Hiro Nomura, Sloane Bellmore, Oswald Redmont, Lasher Ickes, and Marianne Gracelyn. O'Halloran stood behind them with his arms folded, looking sharp in his black uniform, while Wolfgang Krieger had taken a seat to the side, closer to Alton. Krieger seemed oddly distracted, his chair slightly turned and his clinical blue gaze fixed on one of the mirrors, as though he were hypnotized. He snapped out of it as Alton nudged him and stood for my arrival.

The preceptors and various other members of staff were to be expected. What I wasn't expecting to see were four members of the California Mage Council. Three of them I recognized: Leonidas Levi, Raffe's father, and the supposed deciding vote on important Council matters. Next to him sat Nicholas Mephiles, the revered alchemist who'd managed to turn stone into gold. He looked like he'd put on a few pounds since the last time I'd seen him, his stomach straining at his too-tight crimson waistcoat, while his jowls wobbled as he laughed at something Leonidas had said.

Then, there was the incomparable Imogene Whitehall, who offered me an encouraging smile as my eyes settled on her beautiful face. She wore a long, cream dress of delicate cashmere, buttoned from waist to neck, with a single silver bangle pushed up to the middle of her forearm. She was effortlessly stylish, her pale blond hair curving across her shoulder in a single braid. It made her look like some sort of Scandinavian goddess.

Beside me, Wade melted into a puddle of adoration, smitten to the core by Ms. Whitehall. I had to agree, she was an impressive woman who seemed to flood my mind with warmth. I just wished Wade's admiration for her weren't magnified through me. My heart beat faster and my stomach turned into a knot at the very sight of her.

I nudged him in the ribs. "Can you not do that right now?"

"Do what?" He arched an eyebrow.

"Fawn over Imogene. I can't block it out."

"I wasn't," he protested.

"That doesn't work on an Empath, remember?" I chided, feeling him trying to block me.

The last Council member was a man I didn't recognize. He was tall, in his mid-forties, but good-looking for his age. A graze of pale stubble edged across his jaw, leading down to the merest hint of a tattoo that clawed its way up his neck. His sandy hair was barely streaked with gray or white, and his caramel eyes still held a youthful vibrancy as they assessed me closely. A small *X* marked the spot beneath each of his eyes, giving him a rough-and-ready vibe.

"Who's that?" I whispered to Wade.

"Remington Knightshade," he replied. "Levi's right-hand man."

I grimaced. "And just as stuck up?"

He shrugged casually. "Maybe forty percent of Levi, if you want to look at it that way. He's part of the California Mage Council as well."

"Harley! You've made it," Alton announced, breaking up our conversation. I stared at him, trying to figure out whether that was a reference to my poor timekeeping or my induction into the coven. Judging by his flat tone and the mixture of frustration and excitement that came off him, I presumed it was a thinly veiled jab at my tardiness.

Wade let go of my arm and made his way toward the rest of the Rag Team, his emotions growing fainter.

"You've drawn quite a crowd," Alton went on, his chest swelling with something akin to paternal pride. He wore a variation of the coven's uniform, his collar and cuffs navy while the main body of his suit gleamed with a rich, golden hue. "Now, let's begin before everyone starts thinking about the banquet tables."

My stomach grumbled. "Don't jabber too long on my account," I muttered. The nerves hadn't left me, but I tried to focus on Alton as he addressed the crowd.

His soft voice somehow carried across the congregation. "We never expected to have such a strong-willed Merlin enter our ranks. It's an honor, not only because of who you are, Harley, but because of what you have done for us." He smiled at me. "That's the most important and most treasured aspect of your presence here—the selfless way in which you've risked your life, saving people you didn't even know. That is your nature, Harley Merlin, and that is the beating heart of the San Diego Coven. Everyone here is glad that you've chosen us as your family."

My eyes filled with sudden, unexpected tears. A mixture of emotions overwhelmed me—my own and Alton's, weaving pride with joy and a sense of belonging. Despite the Dempsey Suppressor inside me, and the lingering, terrible reputation that my father had left in his wake, I'd overcome. I'd proven myself more than worthy to be a part of this coven. I already knew that, deep down, but it felt so good to hear it said out loud.

"Thank you, Alt—Director Waterhouse," I said, clearing my throat.

"There's danger lurking in our city, and we will defend our home with every ounce of magic and determination we have," Alton replied. "Your presence here only serves to strengthen our resolve. We will not be defeated."

I nodded effusively, thinking of the kids that Katherine had stolen—well, that the Ryder twins had snatched on her behalf. Whatever it was she had up her sleeve, it had something to do with her endgame of becoming a Child of Chaos. How she'd do it and why she wanted to... that remained a mystery.

My gaze drifted across the gathered crowd, their emotions bombarding me like artillery fire. I let them in, and my nerves curled in frustration as I battled to make sense of the noise. I didn't know what I was looking for, but I let them in regardless. There were twenty or so that I couldn't feel. *Shapeshifters.* The rest... I couldn't help but see them in a different light now. Someone here, potentially in this very room, was spying on us for Katherine. Maybe there was even more than one mole. Either way, they'd leaked the information about the kids to Katherine and the Ryder twins—they'd had the details of each one, which had come directly from the coven's archives. There was no other way they could've gotten their hands on the intel.

Where are you, you traitors? Where are you hiding?

"Before you make your pledge to us, Harley, you must display your full spectrum of abilities so we can categorize you accordingly in our official records—you've got quite a few, after all," Alton explained, bringing my attention back around to him. "Using the information from Dr. Krieger's Reading of your blood, you have Air,

Water, Fire, Earth, Telekinesis, and Empathy abilities. Now, we ask that you begin with Air and work your way through accordingly. Does that make sense?"

Part of the pledge ceremony was my registration into the official records of the San Diego Coven. They had everything else. It basically meant adding my name to the game roster, so to speak, as an active member instead of a limited onlooker.

I nodded anxiously. "Yes, Director Waterhouse."

"Excellent. We'll clear a space, and you may begin when you're ready." He eyed the emerald silk of my gown and lowered his voice to a murmur. "Perhaps you should change your clothes first? Those who take the pledge are not usually so... formally attired until afterward."

I shot a look at Tatyana and Santana, who gave me a thumbs-up.

"This dress is surprisingly flexible," I replied calmly. "I'll be fine."

"All right. You can start whenever you're ready. Best of luck." He looked amused, but I felt anything but. My cheeks burned with embarrassment. Sure, I knew what I was doing at least half the time, when it came to my abilities, but that didn't mean I could put on a show for people.

I waited for a space to be cleared at the front of the podium—a cordoned-off semicircle, away from the mirrors, the seated preceptors, and the members of the Mage Council. That didn't bode well. Struggling to ignore the crowd, I looked down at my Esprit and let it bring me comfort. I admired the pearl and onyx of the ring and bracelet, linked by four stones—sapphire, garnet, emerald, and diamond. A wash of tentative calm shivered through my veins.

I might not have full control over all of you just yet, my pretties, but dammit, let's make this work and not embarrass me, okay?

I peered at Nomura for a moment. His curious eyes stared back—one blue, the other a rusty orange. I might not have been a particularly patient student in Nomura's school of Esprit-less thought, but his teachings about control made a lot of sense. My Esprit was supposed to enhance what was already there. Control was key to everything.

Now, all I had to do was get through the next five minutes of my Air ability without seriously injuring or maiming anyone, and I'd be just fine. *How hard can that be?*

The crowd of the packed Assembly Hall was about to find out. I could feel them bracing themselves, the room bristling with nervous energy. I lifted my hands to begin.

TWO

Harley

The diamond of my Esprit glowed, and a hush descended across the room. Whether they were waiting for me to fail or succeed, it was hard to tell. A blend of both encouragement and skepticism pulsed through the atmosphere toward me; I allowed it to feed my concentration.

Without warning, an ice-cold adrenaline rush powered through my body, coursing toward my palms. Terrified of what it might do, I reined it in and stopped it in its tracks. It shuddered straight back up my arms, seeping into my muscles and making them suddenly heavy. My breath came in sharp bursts as I paused, my body shivering from the bitter bite of Air's elemental influence. I hadn't expected that, but then again, Air wasn't my forte.

This isn't going to work.

"Alton?" I rubbed the back of my neck.

"Is everything all right?" he whispered. He looked suitably worried. I was letting him down, right in front of the Mage Council.

"It might be better if I started with Telekinesis..."

"As you please, Harley."

"Thanks."

I lifted the long skirt of my gown and tied it like an apron around my waist, shortening it to my knees and revealing the heavy-duty lace-up boots beneath. A giggle snaked through the crowd. They could laugh all they wanted. At least now I had the flexibility to move around properly, without any fear of tripping over my own dress. *Falling flat on my face isn't a friggin' option.* Alton pursed his lips, while Imogene chuckled to herself. Her laugh I could tolerate, though I didn't dare look over at my friends.

I took a fighting stance, one leg in front of the other, keeping my knees soft for balance. It wasn't necessary, but I wanted to make a decent show of things—especially on the abilities I was confident with. As I lifted my hands, the pearl of my Esprit shone vividly.

With all eyes on me, I glanced around for something to grasp at. Feeling the familiar build of energy inside me, I threw out my Telekinetic lasso and aimed for a carafe of water that stood on a small table to Alton's right-hand side. The lasso easily snatched the curved glass jug up by the neck. I held it in the air for a moment or two, before lowering it again. Concentrating intently on the invisible bond between me and the object, I tipped the jug slightly, praying the contents didn't spill out everywhere and douse the Council. As it touched the edge of Alton's glass, I let the water pour, before setting it down on the table again. Not super impressive, but I figured it was better than just lifting the carafe.

A stiff round of applause found its way around the audience.

"Well done, Harley," Alton said. "Now, if you'd like to move on to Empathy?"

I nodded and walked toward the Mage Council. They glanced at me in surprise, and a sudden spike of doubt shot through me. Was I not supposed to perform my abilities on them? My heart pounded ten times harder. *Any more of this anxiety, and they'll have to carry me out of here on a stretcher.*

"The best way to show my Empathy abilities is to share what you're feeling with everyone," I announced. "Then you can tell me if I've hit the mark or not."

No one objected, so I took that as my go-ahead. I looked at Leonidas Levi first, letting his emotional state filter into my consciousness. He met my gaze with a hard stare. Focusing entirely on him, my eyes widened in surprise. Total and utter boredom. Plus, a sour hint of suspicion and a smattering of disappointment, which stung a bit. I was doing my best here.

You just wait until I get this Suppressor out—then we'll see who's disappointed.

"Mage Levi, I hate to put you on the spot like this, but you seem to be bored with this whole thing," I stated. A splinter of panic ricocheted through me. I knew it was coming from Alton without even turning to look.

To my surprise, Levi smirked. "Very good, but you hardly need Empathic abilities to gauge that. I'd call it nothing more than a bit of cold reading. Look around, pick a person, you could say the same thing and they'd applaud you for it."

A twist of irritation coiled around my heart. Alton shared my annoyance, but I wasn't about to let Levi get away with insulting me in front of everyone. "You're also suspicious of me, and there's a hint of disappointment, too. Was I not what you were expecting?"

"Better," he commended coolly. "I have every right to be suspicious, given the weight of your surname. I wouldn't let it go to your head if I were you, however—not all of my emotions concern you. My disappointment is aimed elsewhere." He shot a casual look at Raffe, whose eyes glinted angrily.

"Do me next!" Nicholas Mephiles chimed in, clapping his hands together excitedly. The impact of his palms slapping together prompted his chin to quiver like jelly beneath his reddish beard.

I smiled. "Of course, Mage Mephiles." I focused on him. He was easy enough to read. With him, I probably *could* have guessed what he was feeling without any magical ability whatsoever. "You're very excited about cheeseburgers and sweet potato fries for lunch, smothered in the chef's famous lemon mayo, and I'm guessing you wish we'd invest in more comfortable seating because your back is in a lot of pain. I can sense your discomfort."

I could feel the cravings coming off him, getting a sense for the exact foods he was hungering after. He was focusing on them so hard that it made the emotions clearer, each one hitting me with a vivid idea of what it was that he wanted.

He chuckled heartily. "Remarkable. Yes, excellent. Right on the mark! I do enjoy a good banquet, in case you can't tell." He rubbed his belly like jolly old St. Nick, causing a button to make a last-ditch dive for survival. It landed by my feet, but nobody seemed to notice. Wanting to preserve the man's dignity, I discreetly kicked it away and carried on down the line of Mages.

"Mage Knightshade, do you want me to read your emotions?" I asked.

He waved me away. "No, no, I believe your ability."

Intrigued, I homed my mind in on his aura anyway. It was a slight invasion of his privacy, but I couldn't help it. It wasn't as though I could shut this skill off. Nervous tension bubbled beneath the surface of his Bear Grylls exterior. Being near him made me feel jumpy and oddly sad, a bittersweet sensation that was tricky to decipher. *What's your deal, Remington?* I wasn't going to get any answers from him this way, that much was clear. Expectation hung in the air above me—everyone was waiting for me to get to Imogene.

Ah, crap.

Ever since meeting her, Imogene had been one of the few people whose emotions I couldn't read. Garret was another one, plus O'Halloran and Preceptor Bellmore. The three shared one key detail in common: they were all Shapeshifters. I hadn't been able to read the psycho Ryders either, for the same reason. We'd suspected Imogene of being one, too. Still, I had my doubts about that. I couldn't read distinct emotions coming off her, but I always felt a wave of warmth whenever I was near her. A feeling of contentment and soothing light that didn't match up to the blockade I got from the other Shapeshifters I'd encountered.

"Mage Whitehall," I murmured nervously, flashing her an apologetic look that I hoped she understood.

"Please, go ahead." Her voice drifted over me like the first flurries of a winter snow. In one deft movement, she removed the silver bracelet from her forearm and set it down on the table beside her. Smiling, she waved her hand with effortless elegance. "Whenever you are ready, Harley."

Does she want me to make something up?

A moment later, I realized I didn't have to. Delicate whispers of emotion flitted away from her calm demeanor, winging their way toward me. First, a sweet ripple of intense pride that fanned out around me like peacock feathers, followed closely by a bundle of hopeful nerves. Her sky-blue eyes never left mine, and my heart seemed to swell as a glimmer of delight sparked across them. This scrappy underdog had won the favor of a freaking elf princess.

Her emotions shifted into a vein of sadness, the merest hint of a tear welling in her striking eyes as she looked at me, letting me know where her sadness stemmed from. My life, my history... the things I'd endured. I was feeling her empathy with my Empathy. I'd never known a connection like it. It was like being hooked up to pure light, the energy of it sprinting through my nerve endings.

She reached for her silver bracelet and pushed it back up to the middle of her forearm. My time in her secret world would soon be up. A tiny white light flashed for a moment, barely noticeable. Instantly, the emotions vanished, but the rush of her remained. I had no idea how the bracelet blocked anyone from reading her emotions, but she had allowed me in. Honestly, I didn't feel worthy of the privilege.

So you're not a Shapeshifter... you're just hiding your emotions from Empaths like me. People who might use them against you. Damn, as if I didn't already think you were a total badass. Imogene Whitehall, when I grow up, I want to be just like you.

I cleared my throat, aware of the wave of anticipation gathering behind me. "You're feeling pretty nervous for me, Mage Whitehall, but you want me to do well. I sensed encouragement and happiness at how I'm doing so far." I didn't want to mention the pride and the sadness I'd sensed, in case it embarrassed her. It was enough that she'd let me see it.

"Very good, Harley. I am feeling somewhat anxious for you, indeed, but you're proving your worth once again," she said, with an enrapturing smile. "You are truly doing the San Diego Coven proud. I must admit, your Empathy abilities are even more detailed than I'd thought. One has to wonder what else you sensed from Leonidas and Nicholas that you are too polite to reveal?"

A laugh ran through the crowd, Imogene's chuckle joining the masses. Levi shot her a cold look.

"Now, might you care to move on to the Elements?" Alton suggested, glancing at the clock on the wall. Evidently, I was taking my sweet time. Either that, or he didn't want me revealing *his* emotions to the rest of the coven.

"Of course," I replied with a nod. "I'd like to start with Fire."

"Certainly." His shoulders relaxed as I took up my position.

The garnet of my Esprit flickered, the red glow dancing. I lifted my hands and urged two tumbling balls of ferocious fire into my palms, forged from pure Chaos. I hurled them at the back of the room, and they smacked into the arched back of a bronzed dragon, exploding in a puff of soot and sparks. The smoke receded to reveal a melted dent where a triangular spike had once been, the molten metal trickling down the side of the beast.

Alton gave me a stern look. "You seem to have Fire handled. Let's move on, before you melt anything else."

I beamed at him. "I'd like to do Water next, if that's cool?"

"That is... cool," Alton replied stiffly.

I wandered over to the glass of water on Alton's side table and picked it up, before returning to my position in the designated semi-circle. Setting the glass down on the floor, I lifted my palms. The sapphire of my Esprit sparkled as the water shot out of the glass in a spiraling column.

As I spread my arms wider, the water followed, fanning out in one thin, cascading sheet. Every time the droplets reached the bottom of the watery pane, it meandered right back up to the top, flowing over and over in perpetual motion.

After a couple of minutes, I forced my open palms slowly together, folding the water in on itself until it created a swirling orb in the center of the podium. I watched it for a while, mesmerized, before letting it trickle back down into the glass.

"Water," I gasped, beads of sweat forming on my forehead. This magical stuff wasn't easy.

A round of applause thundered across the crowd, while Tobe wandered over to retrieve the glass and set it back on the table beside Alton. I mouthed a thank you to him, and then moved swiftly on to Earth. These last two Elements were *not* my strong suits, and I was absolutely dreading them.

"Earth," I said, for the benefit of the audience.

I cast a worried glance at Wade. He smiled wide, and I could feel the pride brimming off him, even from here. All of the Rag Team were sending me their encouragement. It billowed like a sail around me, wrapping me in an intense wash of confidence. I couldn't let them down.

Gathering raw Chaos into myself, I watched the emerald of my Esprit burn with a rich, green energy. I slammed my palms into the ground, and a crack split across the podium, right under Alton's chair. The earth shuddered beneath me, the glasses and carafes juddering toward the edge of the tables. The preceptors looked at one another in alarm, while O'Halloran moved as if to stop me. Frightened cries rose up from the crowd, the initial crack webbing out into spidery capillaries of broken earth.

"That's enough! That's plenty, Harley!" Alton shouted above the rolling thunder of the magical quake.

I jumped up, the roar and clatter subsiding. My cheeks burned as I took in the damage. "Sorry about that."

"Not to worry," Alton assured me, though his doubt flowed into me. "Just give us a strong finish."

I chuckled nervously. "Are you sure about that, after the San Andreas I just pulled?"

"You've got to finish strong to show these people what you're made of. Just make it elegant-strong, like the trained magical you are, and not doomsday-strong." He offered an encouraging smile.

I maneuvered into position once again and noticed the intense glow of the Esprit's diamond link. It pulsed with light.

At first…nothing. Then, brutal barrages of gale-force winds crashed through the windows of the Hall, drawn in from the outside garden. The hair on my arms stood on end as I saw what I'd summoned—a tornado tore through the crowd, knocking people to the side.

I struggled to regain control, but it seemed my powers had other ideas. The glass windows shattered like crystal waterfalls. The crowd ducked and scattered, but there was nowhere to hide from the twister. The doors clattered on their hinges, and the chandeliers swung above the audience, threatening to fall.

I fought to ease the winds, drawing my arms into my chest. Nomura stood, his body bent against the gale blowing in. *Crap, crap, crap, crap... come on! Cooperate!*

The tornado swept upward, surging through the chandeliers. A sickening snap rang above the din. The hinge holding the chandelier gave way, sending the glittering cluster careening downward. My eyes flew wide in a panic. Reaching for another tendril of raw Chaos, I threw out a Telekinetic lasso, grasping at the falling fixture. It froze in midair. Sweat dripped down my face. No longer able to keep hold of the tornado, I let it go, focusing my efforts on bringing the chandelier down safely. The crowd below scurried out of the way, their screams filling my ears, overwhelming my senses.

Not now. Please, not now.

The chandelier came down and rested with an innocuous tinkle on the floor.

A moment later, the winds died with a feeble whistle, revealing the devastation my errant powers had caused. The Assembly Hall was a mess, and that was putting it lightly. The tables and chairs had been hurled against the walls, and two of the main doors were half off their hinges. A sprinkling of glass, like frost covering the ground on a December morning, sprayed out from the shattered windows.

Birds sang outside in the gardens bordering this part of the coven, thankfully contained within the interdimensional pocket. Had humans from Balboa Park been involved, I was pretty sure I would've gotten an instant boot.

Nobody spoke for what seemed like an eternity. They didn't have to. I could feel their anger radiating toward me, seeping beneath my skin. There was fear, too—terror for my untrained, wild abilities. *And it had all been going so well.*

Imogene broke the silence. "Are you okay, Harley?"

I nodded, my body shaking. "I… I think so. Is anyone hurt?"

"Everyone appears unharmed," Alton cut in. At least I'd given Leonidas something to jolt him out of his boredom. Right now, his body was pulsing with pure disdain. Meanwhile, Remington and Nicholas still appeared to be reeling from what had just happened.

I put a hand over my face. "I'm so sorry."

"Fortunately, this was not a test and you have not failed," Alton replied quickly. "This was merely an opportunity to showcase your abilities… which you've done."

"And then some," I muttered, mostly to myself.

Leonidas snorted. "Almost killed us all, more like. That's what I call a liability, Alton."

"She had an unfortunate fumble, I will grant you that, but we don't deal in perfect magicals, Leonidas. She's still learning," Alton shot back. "She's come a long way from where she was a month ago. Harley might not be at the peak of her abilities yet, but she's getting there," he added, giving me a quick wink. "The San Diego Coven is here to teach and nurture its new recruits; it's not here to mock their progress. I'm sure we can all remember a time when our abilities didn't behave as we'd hoped. If we were to laugh at everyone's mistakes, none of us would be here right now." His tone held a subtle warning.

Nicholas chuckled nervously. "Yes, but I doubt any of us have almost taken out an entire room with one misplaced tornado of elemental energy. She is remarkably strong."

"Too strong," Leonidas interjected. "She ought to be in a coven that can *actually* help her to harness those feral abilities. Not here, at the shallow end of the magical pool." His near-black eyes flashed defiantly, as though daring Alton to make a move.

"The ceremony must continue," Alton urged instead, turning to the crowd. "Everyone, if you would resume your seats. This will be over shortly."

I walked over to him, feeling like complete crap. The SDC didn't need to look worse than it already did. "Alton, I didn't mean to—"

"With the Suppressor inside you… well, let's just say I didn't expect such a ruckus at noon on a Wednesday," he said, lowering his voice so only I could hear.

My cheeks flamed. "I'm sorry."

"Come now, there's no need for that," he said, his tone soft. "Take the pledge. No harm done."

I glanced at my friends and saw nothing but sympathy on their faces. Santana pressed her palm to her heart and nodded at me. They were standing with me, urging me to stand with them.

I took a deep breath. "Then I'm ready to take my pledge."

"Go to the center of the podium and speak the words," he instructed.

I walked back to my spot in the designated semicircle. Pushing away the barrage of fear and anger that drifted up from the crowd, I spoke. A hushed silence fell across the congregation, my thudding heart the only thing I could hear.

"I, Harley Merlin, do solemnly pledge my allegiance to the San Diego Coven, of the United Covens of America. I pledge my heart, body, and soul to Gaia and the Children of Chaos. May their spirit flow through me, and may the balance of the Elements, and of Light and Darkness, always rest in perfect harmony. I will not seek to tip the scales, and I will not seek to use my abilities for selfish means or at the expense of others' lives or wellbeing. Let me not strike unless struck and let me not perform what is forbidden. I promise to abide by the natural laws and rules laid out by the coven, for the safety and protection of all—human and magical alike. This, I swear." I paused, wanting to get my pronunciation perfect. "Ordo Ab Chaos."

"Ordo Ab Chaos," the hall repeated.

To my surprise, raucous applause erupted from the crowd as soon as the last words had been said, led by the rowdy whoops and hollers of my Rag Team. A grin spread across my face, my cheeks burning for a very different reason. Pride edged tentatively through me.

Only one thing could have made this moment better—if the Smiths, Isadora, and Jacob could have been here to watch me pledge my allegiance. My family was supposed to be here, but they weren't. For various and truly understandable reasons, they couldn't. Then again, the Rag Team were the best substitutes a girl could ask for.

"Welcome to the coven," Alton said, looking pleased as punch, and I felt his relief. He wore a huge smile on his face, his emerald eyes twinkling delightedly. In his hands, he carried a parcel of clothing tied up with a black ribbon. He handed it to me. "This is your official SDC uniform. We don't ask that you wear it every day, only on special occasions and gatherings… such as today." He swept an arm across the crowd, where every single coven member wore their uniform of navy and gold. "It is a symbol of unity. Wear it with pride."

I nodded eagerly. "I will."

"You've definitely earned it. Despite your earlier mishap." He winked, but then his expression shifted to a more conspiratorial one. "Before you head off to the banquet, could you spare a moment to speak with me out in the hallway? It's a rather time-sensitive matter, I'm afraid."

Great. Just when I thought I could let my hair down for a minute.

"Of course." I glanced at Wade and the others, offering an apologetic shrug as I followed Alton out of the Assembly Hall.

The coven was eerily silent as we wandered a short distance up the hallway, pausing in the familiar shadow of my favorite bronze dragon. It seemed I wasn't the only one who used it as a secret spot. He scanned the corridor, looking up and down its length with furtive eyes, before pushing down on a worn-looking scale in the dragon's armor. I wouldn't have been able to tell the difference if he hadn't pressed it. A door opened behind the dragon.

Alton ushered me inside a minuscule, windowless office with black marble walls that loomed ominously. I felt like I was in some kind of trap, where the walls would start moving in at any second. He gestured for me to sit in a high-backed armchair of deep gray leather, while he sat opposite. *Mm, goth-tastic choice of meeting room, Alton ol' pal.*

Waiting for him to speak, and feeling a bit on edge, I wondered if I was going to receive some sort of director's congratulations—a welcome-to-the-family gift or a thank-you note or something. Naïve, perhaps, but I had no idea how these things worked.

"Why the dinky, secret office?" I asked. The silence was killing me. Plus, the guy felt stressed out. Then again, there'd been a lot going on; who could blame him?

"Yeah, sorry about this. I know it's a bit cramped," he replied. "There's no time to go all the way to my office, and this is the only room in the coven, aside from my office, where I can be sure of privacy."

"Ah. Got it."

"Now, I know you've had a somewhat turbulent afternoon," he began, "and it's not in my nature to burst bubbles. However, the issue of Katherine Shipton is our top priority, especially with the Mage Council breathing down our necks, so we must not waste a moment."

My heart sank. *Back to business then, I guess.*

"The Rag Team is ready to do whatever needs doing," I assured him. They were literally down the hall.

"Well, actually, it is more about what *you* can do. Although, you'll need the help of your team. I only called you out here because it wouldn't alert any suspicions—they'll be expecting me to congratulate you privately. If I'd brought the whole group out here, there would've been raised eyebrows all around."

"Ah. And we don't want that, right?"

"No."

"So, what's the job?" I had a feeling I knew where this was going.

"You must convince Jacob and Isadora to help the coven in our fight against Katherine," he went on, his tone bordering on desperation. "Your aunt evidently cares about you a great deal, Harley. She risked exposure to rescue you and revealed her skill as a Portal Opener so that you would be safe. I know your aunt must have left some way for you to contact her."

I frowned, thinking of the update emails Jacob had sent me periodically. He was always vague about their location, but he'd let me know they were okay. "Even if she had left me some way to get in touch, they're both safer hiding out on their own," I insisted. "She can teach Jacob about his skills, in a safe environment, away from this mess. I've told you before. Why are we going over old ground?"

"Because we need their portal powers *now*."

A shiver of anxiety gripped my chest, but the nerves didn't belong to me. Alton was scared… really scared.

"Why now?" I asked.

He sighed. "I've been working day and night to secure a safe evacuation location, in the event that the San Diego Coven is completely infiltrated."

"That doesn't explain why you need the portal powers," I shot back. "Why not use the mirrors? Create a new one if you have to—a secret one, stowed away in here or something."

He shook his head. "It isn't viable, Harley. Getting everyone there by traditional means would leave us open to exposure. Katherine could watch our every move. A mirror like that is easily traceable, even if we were to destroy it behind us."

"And what? The portals are untraceable?"

"Exactly. Nobody can follow the path they take once they're closed. Who knows, perhaps Isadora is even capable of maintaining a pocket of interdimensional space—the perfect hiding place," he said. "Such an ability would ensure that we can keep the missing kids safe from Katherine, once we find them. It will ensure that we're constantly one step ahead of her."

"Can't you create a pocket for the kids, when we find them? Like this place?"

He shook his head. "Adding extra sections to the coven requires an enormous amount of energy, even for small additions. This room was created at the same time as the coven, and they are all very small. Unfit for children to hide in. To physically add more, as in brand new spaces, would only bring further attention to us. The swell of energy can be traced. Isadora's portals can't."

My Empath senses absorbed the anguish and urgency of his request. I thought of Micah Cranston, Mina Travis, Min-Ho Lee, Samson Prescott, and Marjorie Phillips. Their names were seared into my brain, though there were more we needed to save as well. It was too late for the likes of Kenneth Willow and his evil tendencies, but we could save the rest. I remembered Louella Devereaux and the cross over her face on the warehouse corkboard. It was too late for her, but we couldn't give up on the rest of them yet.

I wanted to keep Jacob safe. Selfishly, I wanted to keep my aunt out of this, too. But we didn't know exactly what role these kids were supposed to play in Katherine's wicked plans; finding all of them was extremely important if we didn't want Katherine to become even more powerful. Plus, they meant a hell of a lot to me and the rest of the Rag Team.

I stared at a filthy book on the shelf above Alton's head. *The Intricacies of Runes*. Clearly, nobody had cleaned this place in ages. Sighing, I leveled my gaze at Alton once more. "If it will truly help those kids, then… I'll do what I can to track down Jacob and Isadora."

A surge of relief flashed over me. Alton's. "You don't know how pleased I am to hear you say that. Or perhaps you do."

I shrugged. "What else can I do? It makes sense. As you say, we need them."

"Thank you, Harley. Thank you for everything you've done for this coven, and everything you continue to do," he said warmly. "I'm sorry I had to cut your celebrations short and drag you into this dinky room, as you put it."

"Don't worry about it," I said. "We can all have one massive hootenanny once Katherine Shipton is six feet under."

He chuckled. "It's been some time since I've had a hootenanny. The last time was at a gathering thrown by the Shreveport Coven… though I confess, I can't remember a great deal about it. Hexed moonshine has a way of addling the mind." His Louisiana accent thickened for a moment, as though the memory brought back the intensity of his heritage.

I arched an eyebrow. "You sure it was hexed?"

"That's the only explanation for the extraordinary hangover I had the next day." He flashed me a grin, though the twist of anxiety lingered in my gut. He was trying to cover up his fears, and I had to admire him for that.

"Am I free to head back to the banquet now?" I asked, smiling. "They've probably all started stuffing their faces without me. Cheeseburgers and sweet potato fries, remember? And that lemon mayo *is* life-changing."

"Yes, enjoy yourself." He chuckled and rose from his chair.

I headed for the door. I was halfway out into the corridor when his voice called me back.

"Oh, and Harley?"

"Yes?"

"Above all things, remain vigilant about Katherine's spies within the coven," he said. "We don't know how many we're dealing with. If anyone seems to be acting unusual, let me know immediately."

I nodded. "I'll be on the lookout."

I had no idea where I'd start my search or what type of unusual behavior I'd be looking for. But hey, I already had a few magical mysteries under my belt, suitably untangled. I could do it again.

THREE

Harley

I hurried back through the echoing corridors to the Main Assembly Hall, only to find a cleanup crew sweeping broken glass and raising ladders to fix the chandelier. Most were using Telekinesis or some version of Air to assist, speeding up the job.

The rest of the coven had dispersed. The short-lived celebrations were over. Either that, or everyone was stuffing their faces in the banquet hall. My stomach rumbled at the thought. I hadn't eaten since last night, and I was ready for something other than bitter black coffee. *Bring on the desserts!*

A few minutes later, I arrived at the dining hall. Sure enough, the folks who'd attended my pledge were sitting along the three rows of white marble tables. Delicious scents wafted toward me: brick oven pizza, roasted potatoes, herbed vegetables, burgers the size of my head, and something fruity and sparkling to wash everything down. There were desserts, too—rich chocolate cakes with a glossy finish, decadent tarts with glazed fruit and buttery pastry, and the most impressive tower of cookies I'd ever seen. It was taller than me.

Oh, the delicious calories. I may need a couple more stomachs for this.

The diners turned to look at me as I entered. A raucous round of applause erupted a second later, with feet being stomped and cutlery being bashed against the marble tabletops. I blushed and drank it in. *So what if I messed up a little? I did it in a crazy impressive way*. They'd always remember the Merlin girl who, quite literally, brought the house down. A grin spread across my face.

Everyone returned to their food, and I made my way toward the fresh batch of goodness that had just been laid out. The clink of silverware was oddly comforting as I waved to the Rag Team and kept on toward the food. If my stomach growled any louder, they'd have to put it in a box in the Bestiary. I loaded a plate to the point of no return and made my way back to my friends. They were sitting in our usual spot, their plates more or less clean.

"The woman of the hour!" Santana whooped. "Here for all your redecorating needs."

I laughed. "I just saw the cleanup crew—poor guys. It'll take ages to get everything back to normal, even with Chaos on their side. To be honest, I'm surprised Alton didn't rope us all into it."

"Me, too," Wade replied. "The moment that chandelier came down, my first thought was, 'How long are we going to have to spend picking it all up?'"

"That was your first thought?" I teased. "Not, 'Oh God, oh God, we're all going to die'?"

He gave me a wry look. "No, that was when the windows exploded."

"You got some serious power, girl, Suppressor or no Suppressor," Santana said.

"You just have to learn to use it properly," Wade added, his expression shifting into solemnity. "It's dangerous to have something so raw and not know what to do with it."

Dylan laughed as he swiped a massive hunk of bread around his plate, mopping up every last morsel. "Nomura looked like he wanted to tackle you to the ground."

"Man, I'm glad you saw that! I kept thinking he was going to lunge at me, just to get me to stop," I replied cheerfully, ignoring Wade's preachy remark. I'd learned it was the easiest way to keep out his constant grounding of me. Besides, I had no problem with being a work in progress. I *was* working on my skills and getting along pretty nicely—*thank you very much.*

"You did so well, Harley," Astrid chimed in. "You were all like, *pow,* and then *whoosh* and then *crash!* And the way you slammed your hands down on the floor like a legitimate superhero? Amazing!"

Tatyana nodded. "I admit, my favorite part was the dramatic revelation of the biker boots. Full of flair. I nearly deafened poor Wade with all my proud screaming."

Wade grimaced in agreement. "Yes, you made your pride audibly clear. I never thought I'd ever hear you shriek the way you did then, rooting for Merlin."

She shot him a brief, ice-cold glare that made me smirk. Nobody got to question Tatyana's enthusiasm, not even Wade.

"Speaking of which, I should probably get changed," I said, brushing the front of the silk dress. "Unfortunately, the party's over for us."

"What do you mean? Everyone's just getting started. There are like eight courses to get through," Dylan replied, gesturing to the room. From the looks of his stacked plates, he'd already worked his way through three. Even without my Empath abilities, the atmosphere was awesome. It felt happy and contented, a million miles away from the fear and terror that had run rampant for the last month or so.

"Not us. We've got to get back to work. Alton's orders." I shrugged, wolfing down a few mouthfuls of buttery potatoes. "Well, actually, he said *I* had to get back to work, but I figured I'd drag you guys with me."

The others chuckled, reluctantly agreeing to help. Only Raffe remained silent. He'd been quiet ever since I sat down, though I knew his sullenness had nothing to do with me; proximity to his father and the darkness of his mood appeared to be directly correlated.

"Did the Mage Council leave?" I asked, looking to Raffe.

"No idea. I imagine they'll want to speak to Alton before they go," Wade replied instead. "Lay down the law, so to speak. With those kids still missing, and everything that went on with the Ryder twins, they'll probably be fastening a noose around his neck."

"But we defeated the Ryder twins," Tatyana interjected.

Santana shook her head sadly. "Yes, but at the cost of those children."

"You think the Mage Council cares about our successes?" Raffe muttered. "They tally up the failures and stack them against us. They don't even notice the good we do. They couldn't give a rat's ass if we killed Emmett and captured Emily. Until they get Katherine Shipton in custody, the rest is meaningless to them."

Raw anger brimmed inside Raffe—a spike of frightening fury that didn't fit with the Raffe I knew. His emotions were as weirdly mixed and confusing as ever, the rage mingled with disappointment. *One of these days I'm going to find out why, buddy.*

"Okay, well, I'll get changed, and then we can bash the Mage Council in private, without the risk of eavesdroppers," I announced, tipping my head toward Garrett and his band of merry pals, who sat a short way off. I polished off the last of my plate. "Plus, there's a whole lot I've got to tell you. Where should we meet? Wade's shoebox?"

He shot me a withering look. "I'll say it again: at least I *have* an office."

"Yes, and I have *several* shoeboxes."

"Why don't we meet in the Aquarium?" Astrid suggested, hugging Smartie to her chest. "Alton said we could use it, now that we have ourselves some bigger fish to fry… if you'll pardon the pun. Plus, it's quiet and it's out of the way, and with everyone gorging themselves until they explode, nobody will disturb us."

I frowned. "The who said what now? This place has an *aquarium*? Is it like the Bestiary, but with water creatures?"

"You'll see." Astrid grinned. "I'll text you the directions from your living quarters."

"Now, get out of that dress before you ruin it with food stains," Santana chided, a chuckle rumbling from her throat.

I pressed my hands to the embroidered bodice and feigned a sob as we all got up to disperse. "And I barely got to know you, my beloved. You didn't even get to shine."

"I don't know about that," Wade said, his deep green eyes fixed on mine. "I'd say you, and that gown, will go down in coven history as the most eventful pledge ever. You did good, Merlin."

This is the closest thing to a compliment on my skills that'll ever come out of Wade Crowley's mouth, I guess. I'll take it.

Dylan nodded. "We're all pretty proud of you, dude."

"Not ashamed to be seen with me?" I arched an amused eyebrow.

"Are you kidding?" Astrid yelped. "You made us the cool kids—the ones who roll with the wild child! The Merlin who won't be tamed… and who called out Leonidas Levi in front of everyone." Laughter rippled around my circle of friends.

Even Raffe mustered a smile. "Yeah, that was awesome. His face!"

I laughed. "Glad I could be of service. Now, stop distracting me with how legendary my pledge was. I need to get changed before the clock strikes midnight and I turn into a pumpkin."

Dressed in the usual get-up of dark jeans, dark boots, a clean gray t-shirt, and my leather jacket, I followed the directions that Astrid had sent. A mindboggling labyrinth of corridors and staircases later, I arrived outside of a huge, frosted glass door. It arched upward, curving to a point like the doorway of a medieval church. Two white-gold handles were fixed in the center, both shaped like coiling fish, fitting into each other like the Pisces symbol.

Is this the place?

I'd never been to this part of the coven before. Here, the architecture was more Grecian in style, with white-gold statuettes lining the hallway in designated alcoves and a white marble floor stretching beneath my feet, shot through with fragments of silver. Ceramic pots and vases, embossed with dramatic friezes, sat on Doric plinths, each one filled with white flowers—roses, lilies, and sprays of cream buds. I felt like if I pushed the frosted glass doors open, I might find a gaggle of Olympian gods on the other side.

Instead, I found the Rag Team… and Garrett. Despite his fairly permanent position on our squad, part of me couldn't quite include him under the banner of the Rag Team. It wasn't that I didn't get along with him—we had no beef left to squash. He'd apologized profusely for hurling abuse at me over my heritage, and he and Wade were even working toward a friendship, or at least a civility. Still, he had a long way to go before he could officially become one of us, which probably suited every involved party just fine.

The group was gathered in the middle of the room. I hurried toward them and took up my spot in the circle.

"Suits you," Wade said as I moved up beside him.

"Better than the dress?"

"This is… more you." A smile tugged at the corners of his lips, and a pleasant prickle of affection danced through my veins. It was coming from him. I smiled back and stood awkwardly beside him, my limbs forgetting how to function normally. More to the point, I had no idea what to do with my clammy palms. Realizing that everyone was looking at me, I shoved them in my pockets.

"So, what is this place?" I asked, looking around in awe. "Is it part of the Bestiary?"

The Aquarium was a huge, domed hall with a curved ceiling that sparkled with sapphires. The majority of the room's light came from the enormous tanks that lined every single wall, right up to where the ceiling began to curve. A bluish glow rippled outward, a wave pattern undulating across the marble. A few of the tanks were pitch black, making me wonder what they held within.

"Think of it as an auxiliary generator," Astrid replied. "The creatures here are on loan from the Bestiary—we have them here even if the Bestiary is elsewhere. Most covens have some variation of it, as a temporary backup in case the Bestiary should fail, and as an energy booster for certain types of magic. It fuels the magical reserve within this room."

"Now that's cool." Shadowed shapes twisted and turned behind the thick glass. Unable to help myself, I wandered up to one of the tanks and pressed my hand to the cool pane. I peered deep into the water, but I couldn't make out anything. Wisps of black coiled through the liquid, like diluted ink falling into a painter's cup.

I turned around, only for a glint in the distance to catch my eye. As I whirled back to face it, a hulking shadow burst out of the blue haze and hurtled full-pelt into the glass. The impact echoed across the Aquarium, and a shiver of terror shot up my spine. I half expected the pane to crack. It reared backward and hovered in the seemingly endless azure—a gray-and-white beast that was half-fish, half-horse, with razor fins spiking along its back. Its long mane flowed with the current, while deep gills opened and closed behind the muscle of its jaw. Black eyes stared into mine.

"A Hippokampos," Astrid explained.

"Isn't that part of your brain?"

She shook her head, smiling. "It's a water creature. Half-horse, half-fish, as you can see."

"Why is it staring at me?" I whispered.

"Maybe it likes you," Garret suggested, with a wry grin.

Tentatively, I touched the glass again, only for the creature to rear back and charge the pane once more, the glass vibrating.

"Nope, I don't think it likes me." Cutting my losses, I went back over to the group. "Anyway, let's forget about water-horses. We've got a lot to talk about."

"News from Alton?" Santana asked.

I nodded. "He wants me to track down Jacob and Isadora. He thinks they might be able to help us if we need to evacuate and find a place where those kids can be safe. Something to do with the science of portal-opening and interdimensional pockets."

I trusted the Rag Team with my life. Even Garrett had proven his loyalty, though we hadn't brought him into the fold properly yet. I presumed Wade had invited him after their hatchet-burying. And if Wade trusted him, then so did I. The team needed to know what was going on, and Alton had given me the go-ahead.

"We have to find them first, before concerning ourselves with that," Wade cut in.

"I know." My tone came off sharper than I'd intended.

"Actually, we should probably attempt to do both at the same time," Tatyana interjected. "If we find the kids but we have nowhere safe to place them, then we are back at square one. Katherine and her minions will only come for them again."

"But why?" Garrett asked. "I mean, what does she want them for?"

"That's the part we don't know," I replied.

"*That* is the part we don't know?" Wade countered. "Let's be honest here. We don't really know a whole lot about her plan. We've got no idea where she is, and we have no idea how she's keeping herself so well hidden."

Raffe nodded. "We should've picked up on a hint of her whereabouts by now. It's like she's invisible."

I raised a finger, a flashbulb going off in my head. "Not invisible, but as good as."

"What do you mean?" Wade asked.

"Magicals tend to inherit at least one of their parents' Chaos types, right? Based on Finch's ability, then, I think it's safe to assume that we might be dealing with another Shapeshifter. That'd be my guess, anyway, as to how she's moving under the radar. Maybe she's got a whole armory of people she can shift into—she could be anywhere, at any time, and we wouldn't know."

"Can we find that out? Are there records?" Santana asked, turning to Astrid.

"I've tried looking Katherine Shipton up before, but most of her records have been wiped," she replied. "I don't know how, or why, but someone has done a good cover-up for her. There's barely a genealogy trail."

I frowned. "But there *is* one?"

"At the New York Coven, they should have hard copies of her family tree, if nothing else."

"Then I'll kill two birds with one stone. I'll go to New York to find out more about my father and look through her family tree at the same time—well, *my* family tree, too, I guess," I replied, enthusiasm sparking inside me. "I'll check the lineage to see if anyone else was detected as a Shapeshifter. If there's a pattern, then we'll have a clearer idea of what we're dealing with."

Garret grumbled. "Yeah, but given the stigma surrounding us Shapeshifters, it might not be the most accurate source of intel. I should know."

"It's the best we've got," Wade cut in.

"We can safely assume that Hiram Merlin wasn't a Shapeshifter, and we know that Harley isn't one," Astrid ventured, gesturing toward me. "So, by conclusion, we have to believe that Hester wasn't one either. She and Katherine were twins, yes, but they were fraternal, not identical, so it might have skipped Hester altogether."

Tatyana tapped her chin. "The maternal line may hold some answers."

"We should probably get started on some Children of Chaos research, too," Raffe said. "The one thing we're totally certain about is that psychopath's endgame of becoming one, right? So, if we can delve into some info on that, maybe we can figure out what she needs those kids for. And, maybe, we can figure out a way to stop her."

"Good thinking," I replied. "In that case, we'll have to split ourselves into a few jobs."

Wade nodded. "Finding the kids, finding Jacob and Isadora, finding out more about the Children of Chaos."

"All while attempting to stay alive," Garrett deadpanned. "How hard can that be?"

"No negativity allowed, *chico*," Santana chided.

I smiled, as Garrett looked suitably chastened. "It's a shame we don't have Jacob here now. He could probably help us out with his Sensate ability. I don't know what his range is like, but he could pick up some kind of trail."

"A human bloodhound?" Garrett snickered.

I ignored him. "We need to find the kids before Katherine poisons their minds. The others might be harder to break than Kenneth Willow, but I've got no doubt that Katherine will find a way to make each and every one of them snap, to get what she wants out of them."

"At least we know she hasn't taken them out of state," Astrid said. Everyone turned to look at her.

"How do you know that?"

"Magical state border security is very powerful," she explained. "If Katherine took the kids across state lines, we'd know about it. She's on the watchlist—one hint of her, and there'd be alarms ringing from here to Yuma."

Dylan cleared his throat. "So the kids are still hidden somewhere in California?"

"Bingo!" Astrid punched the air with overzealous enthusiasm.

Just then, the frosted-glass doors burst open and four figures strode in—Alton, Leonidas Levi, Remington Knightshade, and Imogene Whitehall. I imagined Nicholas Mephiles was still at the banquet hall, enjoying the spread. There'd be no buttons left on his waistcoat by the time he was done.

We all whirled around in surprise. Their entrance had brought the Aquarium creatures to the fore. Leonidas banged hard on the first tank he passed, sending a shockwave through the rest. Immediately, the water beasts turned on their tails—or tentacles—and swam for the depths once more. Puffs of inky fluid merged with the clear water, the creatures dispersing.

Two uniformed magicals strode in behind the quartet, dressed in black regalia. I didn't recognize them from the faculty, nor did anyone else seem to. I saw my confusion reflected back at me in the faces of my friends. *What the hell is going on?*

"Glad to see you took my advice. We've been searching for you," Alton said, breaking the tension with a smile. "You see, I didn't mean you had to get back to work *right* away, Harley. You could've enjoyed your celebration a little longer. Still, I admire the fighting spirit in all of you. Undoubtedly, we'll be eating leftovers at dinnertime, so you've hardly missed out on much."

"Indeed you haven't," Levi remarked, his nose wrinkled in disgust.

Alton ignored him, though I could feel the director simmering with irritation. *See, you piss* everyone *off, Leonidas—even one of the most patient men in the biz.*

"You'll be pleased to hear that we've actually come to lessen the workload," he continued, gesturing to the militant pair. "These two will be working with you from now on and helping out with the investigations. A job shared and all that." He laughed, but it didn't reach his eyes. I got the feeling he'd been shanghaied into bringing these two on board. "This is Stella Chan and Channing Madison, from the Los Angeles Coven."

Stella looked to be in her early twenties, with poker-straight, black hair that framed her stunning Asian features in a severe bob. Her dark eyes looked dead ahead, devoid of emotion, while her hands remained firmly behind her back. Beside her stood a giant beefcake of a dude with a sharp buzzcut. His biceps were the size of my head. Steely gray eyes stared at the farthest wall of the Aquarium, as muscles twitched in a square jaw that would've put Johnny Bravo to shame. Glancing at my friends, I noticed them gawking, too. He was almost comically muscular and looked like he might burst out of his military uniform at any moment.

"They're here to assist," Imogene said, urging them to come forward. "With so many magicals out there, looking for the missing children and setting up security measures, Leonidas thought you could use some extra hands. In these uncertain times, help must be welcomed." I could tell she wasn't entirely keen on the idea of it, either. Then again, Levi had the deciding vote. *What you say goes, isn't that right?*

Seeing Imogene again, I wanted to take her to one side to ask her about the silver bracelet on her forearm. I'd never seen a device that could deflect the powers of Empaths before, nor had I read up on any. After all, I was still plowing through the stack of books that the Rag Team had suggested I read, to get myself up to speed with all things magical. If such devices existed, I was eager to know about them. If anyone had one, of course it was going to be her. I mean, she searched the globe in her spare time, looking for rare and powerful magical artifacts—most of which ended up in the Esprit shop at Waterfront Park's hidden underworld of bars, restaurants, and stores.

An idea popped into my head. If I didn't get the chance to speak with Imogene before she left, I would find a moment to slip into that shop again and ask if they knew anything about anti-Empath charms. If they had one, maybe they'd let me examine it.

Only Remington remained quiet throughout the unexpected arrival, his gaze fixed on Dylan. A rush of strange familiarity bristled through my veins, combined with a deep-rooted flicker of nervous affection. He didn't know I was watching him. His caramel eyes glimmered with unspoken sadness, while his brows pinched in a frown. It was almost like he knew Dylan, or at least about his orphan background.

Magicals raised in the human foster system tended to generate a certain feeling of pity from coven-raised magicals like Knightshade and others. I made a mental note to ask Dylan about his biological parents, to satisfy a personal curiosity—from one foster kid to another. I'd always dreamed of a happy ending to my origin story. I obviously hadn't quite gotten it, but maybe Dylan could, for both of us. That was all any of us wanted.

"I tried to tell the LA Coven that they've already given us far too much," Alton said, making a point of avoiding Levi's gaze, "but they insisted they could spare Channing and Stella. I'm sure you'll make them feel welcome."

"The LA Coven has supplied you with ample additional security for the Bestiary. These two just happened to be left over," Leonidas replied. "Might as well put them to good use."

Yeah, by watching our every move. "Happened to be left over," my left ass-cheek. You put them here on purpose, Levi. Your poker face needs work, pal.

"I might have offered more of our people," he went on, "but you are not the only ones dealing with the endeavors of Katherine Shipton."

"What do you mean?" I asked sharply.

"It seems her influence is spreading. In the larger picture, these children pale into insignificance." He glowered at me. "There have been several thefts across the country."

"The break-ins at the Magical Artifact Armory at Fort Knox?" Alton gasped.

"Among others. These attempts at theft are taking up many of our resources. We are trying to stay one step ahead of Katherine Shipton and determine her next target. As you can imagine, it leaves us with little force to spare for something as trifling as a handful of missing kids. The Bestiary is different, as that affects us all. Two soldiers of the LA Coven will be more than enough for this task."

I gawked at him. "Katherine Shipton is stealing magical artifacts, and nobody thought to say anything? Plus, I don't think the abduction of children is 'insignificant.' Maybe to you, but to us they're innocent lives, and they're at stake here. Aren't we supposed to protect all magicals, adults and children alike?"

"She hasn't managed to steal anything yet, Miss Merlin," Leonidas snapped. "Our repeated attempts to stop her are what's been keeping us otherwise engaged. And I would ask that you don't twist my words. Children are, of course, important. I simply meant that we have other things on our minds. Matters of *national* security, rather than regional."

"Of course we'll welcome Miss Chang and Mr. Madison, Director Waterhouse, Mage Levi," Wade interjected, shooting me a look that said, "Calm the hell down." Was I the only one who felt completely freaked out by the idea that Katherine was trying to get her hands on powerful stuff?

"Is there anything we can do to help with the robbery attempts?" I pressed.

Leonidas snorted. "No. Our people are dealing with it. You would only get in the way. Now, please do as Crowley suggested and get better acquainted with your new team members. I have had quite enough of the SDC and its... quirks for one day."

Leonidas Levi was certainly full of himself, and then some. Refusing our help in such a stinging fashion was downright rude, and we deserved a little more respect than that. On the other hand, they probably had their most skilled folks dealing with this. *They wouldn't sit on their asses while Katherine tries to mug them. Fine, Levi. Have it your way.*

I hung back as introductions were made. Honestly, I wasn't sure how to feel about these newcomers. It was bad enough that we already had a mole inside the SDC. A thousand uncertainties haunted these hallways even without two complete strangers being added to the mix.

I glowered at Leonidas, who glowered back. Not that he scared me. I wasn't one to fall for his intimidation tactics. He could bring in all the hawks, if he wanted. He wasn't going to see us slip up. All this did was strengthen my resolve to catch my crazy-ass aunt and find those kids. *And when we do that, it's going to be sooooo satisfying to watch you struggle to apologize to all of us, Levi.*

Frankly, I didn't know which I was looking forward to more—stopping Katherine or hearing Levi's future apology.

FOUR

Harley

Eventually, I had to bite the bullet and introduce myself to Stella and Channing. I almost had to check to see if they had rods up their backs; they were standing so freaking straight the whole time.

"Harley Merlin, pleased to meet you," I said, offering out my hand for them to shake. I went to Stella first, figuring she was the less intimidating of the two.

"We're aware of who you are," she replied curtly. *Hmm... maybe not the less intimidating.*

"Well, glad to have you helping us out."

"It's our duty to obey the California Mage Council's orders," was all she said. It was like squeezing blood out of a particularly stubborn stone.

I moved on to Captain Beefcake. "Nice to meet you, Channing."

"Yes, it is." His voice came out practically robotic. I scanned his eyes to make sure there weren't two tiny, orb-shaped computers staring out. *Maybe there's a reset button and we can get the fun version to come out.*

"I… hope you like it here in San Diego."

He didn't respond, his gaze dead ahead.

"At ease, soldier," I teased, garnering a cold look from his gray eyes. "We don't really go in for the whole GI Joe thing here."

"No, I can see that you're less disciplined."

Was he throwing shade at me? I frowned and stepped back, letting Wade attempt to break through the icy façades of our new teammates.

I could see that Channing and Stella came from a very different type of organization than the one we had going here in San Diego. For starters, we were all dressed casually in jeans and t-shirts, except for Wade, in a suit vest from his endless wardrobe, while they were rocking full-on military uniforms, complete with what looked like medal-ribbons on their chests. San Diego loved its rules and regulations, for sure, but these guys were something else—they gave off strict, army-like vibes.

"I never thought I'd say this, but San Diego is practically horizontal compared to these guys," I whispered to Santana, who nodded discreetly.

"They make us look like amateurs," she whispered back. "Even Wade looks unprofessional compared to these two."

I looked at him to see what she meant. Wade was a head shorter than Channing and nowhere near as broad or muscular. That wasn't what set them apart, though. The way the two newcomers held themselves was totally different. They looked serious, like they meant business. We looked like we were just in this for the giggles, all of us running around playing at being magical investigators.

"It's okay, we don't bite," Wade joked. "No fangs here. Well, unless you check the Bestiary."

"There's no need for us to check the Bestiary. We have our best officers stationed there for the safety of this coven. Security has been lax and insufficient, considering the threat level," Channing replied abruptly. "Have we established a plan of action for seeking the swift return of these missing children?"

The Rag Team looked at one another in complete disbelief.

"We were in the middle of planning when you came in," Wade replied coolly.

"It seems a bit late in the day," Channing remarked. "I would've thought there'd already be a plan in place."

"Nope, but we're getting to it," I chimed in, backing Wade up. These two acted like they were the epitome of what it meant to be a coven agent. Personally, I saw two uptight snobs who were more than happy to look down on us without bothering to get to know us.

Stella cast an assertive glance across everyone. "No matter. We're here now to improve the efficiency of this… group. I'm sure we can work together toward a suitable conclusion."

Channing smirked. "There's no point trying to befriend the locals, Stella. They wouldn't know how to run an investigation. San Diego is known for its slackness; I just didn't realize *how* bad it was. We're working with a bunch of amateurs here." I noticed he kept his voice low so Alton wouldn't hear. He was standing to one side, in deep conversation with the Mage Council. I guessed they were talking about the robberies. The news had freaked Alton right out.

Wade scowled at my side. "Might I remind you that you are guests of the SDC," he said. "You might think we're 'lax' or inferior in some way, but it wasn't the LA Coven who thwarted the first wave of Katherine Shipton's plans, was it? Agreed, there have been a few bumps in the road, but we've successfully disposed of the Ryder twins and stopped Finch Shipton from causing mass chaos. Pretty good for a bunch of 'slackers,' if I do say so myself."

Stella smiled unexpectedly. "He has a point, Channing." Her eyes lingered on Wade's face. "Wade, right?"

"Right."

"Did you lead the investigative team that brought down Finch and the Ryder twins?"

He shrugged. "I had a part to play in it, sure."

"That must have been dangerous, taking on such powerful people," she said. Her dark eyes glittered as they held Wade's gaze. "I'd like to hear more about it, if you have a moment to spare sometime? It's always a good idea to get to know your enemy."

"You think I'm your enemy?"

She laughed. "No, I meant Katherine Shipton. I've read the reports, but it would be nice to hear what happened directly from the horse's mouth."

I stared at Wade, who seemed to have forgotten the rest of us were there. He smiled back at Stella and folded his arms across his chest. A flutter of self-gratification moved through me, flowing from Wade. He was flattered by Stella's attention. Irritation smothered the flattery, though the annoyance was all my own. Stella's little coven buddy had just called us all inferior amateurs, and here Wade was, enjoying her pandering.

Men.

Alton stepped forward, breaking my irritation. "Well, now that you're all suitably introduced, maybe we should get to the task at hand? This entire endeavor is of the utmost urgency." His face turned solemn. "Those children are out there, and we have to get them back. We've made promises to the parents who remain, foster and magical alike, and we've made promises to ourselves. We'll bring them into our family, where we can protect them."

"Because you did such a good job the last time?" Leonidas grumbled.

"If memory serves, *you* were the ones who told us to keep the children at their homes," Alton shot back. "I suggested bringing them all here to the coven, where we could better protect them, but you wanted to use them as bait. It backfired, and now we're cleaning up that mess before anyone else gets killed."

Leonidas frowned. "You should watch your tongue, Alton. You have yet to earn back our trust," he growled. "Do not forget that you and your coven remain on probation. The Council is watching your every move until we are satisfied that everything being done here has met our expectations. You kept your secrets from us once—you won't get to do so again."

"I'm not trying to," Alton replied. "I'm merely pointing out the facts. We wouldn't be in this situation if you had allowed me to bring the children here, as soon as it became clear they weren't safe in their homes any longer."

"Listen, Waterhouse, all I'm saying is, if you so much as sneeze in a way that I don't like, we will come down on you so hard you won't know what hit you."

"Well, I imagine it'll be you. You just said so," I said, drawing Levi's ire away from Alton.

"I'd advise *you* to toe the line as well, Merlin, especially after your little display today," he said. "You see, the surname 'Merlin' doesn't mean a damn thing anymore. It won't get you anywhere fast, unless you've got your eye on Purgatory."

Alton raised his palms as Levi and I faced off. "We're getting away from the matter at hand. This is about the children," he urged. "It isn't about the reason they're missing, or who's to blame. We just need to fix it and get them back. Astrid, what information do you have already?"

Astrid whipped out her tablet, which was connected to her brilliant Smartie AI system. "There are eleven children on our list who were specifically targeted by the Ryder twins. All of them are missing, with the exception of Marjorie Phillips, who ran away before she could be captured. She may still be at large, which puts her as a priority. She's seventeen and appears to have Air and Clairvoyance in her skillset. Some of these abilities are assumptions, based on what we've heard from parents or witness reports.

"Then we have Micah Cranston, age five, who has Telekinesis and Earth. Mina Travis, age six, with Telekinesis, Water, and Air. Samson Ledermeyer, age three, whose powers remain unknown. Then there's Min-Ho Lee, age twelve, who has Herculean and Earth abilities. Andrew Prescott, age nine, whose powers also remain unknown. We also have Emilio Vasquez, age eight, who has Fire and Herculean abilities, and Cassie Moore, age eleven, who is an Empath and a Morph."

I nudged Wade in the side. "Morph?"

"Magicals who can transfer their consciousness into animals."

"They turn *into* animals?"

He shook his head impatiently. "No, they can only take over the mind of an animal—use its body as a vessel, that kind of thing. Their human body stays where it is."

"Right, thanks." I hadn't seen it mentioned in any of the books I'd read so far. "Is it a rare ability?"

He nodded. "Rarer than Shapeshifting. Now hush. Astrid is talking."

"Then, there's Sarah McCormick, age ten, who appears to have Supersonic abilities, albeit fledgling and unconfirmed. Lastly, we have Denzel Ford, age six, whose powers remain unknown."

"What about Louella Devereaux?" Dylan asked. "Have we given up on her?"

Alton grimaced. "I'm afraid there's no use looking for her. We found her body shortly after the Ryders were captured," he explained. "Well, what was left of her, anyway. Half a leg and most of an arm, both positively identified as belonging to the poor girl."

A solemn silence hung over the group for a moment. I remembered the corkboard in the abandoned warehouse. Her face, crossed out. It had seemed unlikely that Louella had survived, but I'd been hopeful that she'd managed to get away. My heart gripped in an angry vise. They'd killed her in cold blood. *The sick bastards.*

"Any news on Kenneth Willow?" I asked, recalling the psychotic teenager with the bow-tie Esprit. He'd been the Ryders' easiest target. All they'd had to do was push the big red button in his mind, and he'd lapped it up—a readymade soldier to join their army. I knew I was supposed to keep an open mind, but Kenneth had simply been waiting for that kind of opportunity to come along. The evil in him was innate.

Astrid shook her head. "He hasn't shown up anywhere, which makes me think he's keeping a low profile. Maybe the Ryders took him to wherever Katherine Shipton is hiding. It's hard to know where he might be, but we should probably keep him on the list—see if we can find him. He might be the one person who can lead us to Katherine's hideout."

"Very good," Alton announced. "It sounds like you've got everything taken care of, and I'm sure the Mage Council members are eager to get back to their duties. How about we leave them to it, and see where Mage Mephiles has gotten to?" He turned to the other three, a polite smile fixed on his face. I sensed deceit gripping his chest. He didn't want to leave because we had everything taken care of; he wanted to leave because he didn't want Leonidas to overhear anything we might say.

Keeping secrets again, Alton? I don't blame you.

"That sounds like an excellent idea, Alton," Imogene replied, before turning to me. "I hope we will meet again soon, Harley. Perhaps I could bring you a gift from my dear friend's shop, to congratulate you on your fresh start and bright future."

I smiled, my chest swelling with pride. "I'd like that very much, Mage Whitehall. It's been a hot minute since we've chatted."

"It has been much too long. But we'll remedy that soon, I promise."

After a brief farewell, the four turned on their heels and swept out of the Aquarium, with Leonidas banging the glass one last time. In the wake of their exit, a tense calm settled over the remaining group. Everything seemed to be a competition to Stella and Channing, and we appeared to be playing the silent game.

Wade cleared his throat. "I agree about keeping our eyes peeled for Kenneth. He might be the bridge between us and Katherine. A sort of Finch substitute, since the white-haired wonder isn't squeaking a word about dear old Mom," he muttered. "Now, what kind of leads have we got on the children, Astrid? Are there any we can follow—any sightings or chatter on the news platforms?"

"If it's all the same to you, Stella and I will conduct our own investigation," Channing cut in. "We know what we're doing, and, to be honest, it doesn't seem like you have any idea what you're doing. Other than a list of names, you have nothing. Plus, it saves us bringing the rest of you up to speed on the way we conduct things in the LA Coven. You can play detectives around the city, if you want. We'll bring home the kids."

He wouldn't have dared say that had Alton still been here. *You might look like a rhino, but you're a timid little mouse in the face of authority. Coward.*

"Are you kidding? We need to work together on this," Wade insisted. "This is our case. We have the intel. We've met these kids—they know us. Do you really think they're going to follow two strangers, after being snatched by the Ryder twins?"

"A rescue is a rescue. The kids' feelings don't come into it." Channing glowered at Wade. "See, this is why we're better equipped for the job than you. You put too much weight on emotion. This is our duty, plain and simple. A task. A job. That's it. Throwing emotions into the mix does nothing but cloud judgment."

Wow, they have militarized you to within an inch of your humanity.

Wade appeared to be handling the backtalk. Throughout the

conversation, I'd barely felt any kind of emotion coming off Channing, and it wasn't because he was a secret Shapeshifter. I could sense the difference. Where Garrett's ability kept his feelings hidden, Channing just didn't feel anything. The perfect soldier.

Stella, on the other hand, appeared to be a little more human. There was no mistaking the frisson of attraction she felt toward Wade; it pulsed through me like static electricity, setting the fine hairs of my forearm on edge. I tried to ignore the sensation as best I could, though it was pretty difficult with her making doe eyes at him.

I rested my hand on Wade's shoulder. "What does it matter if they lead their own investigation, Wade? As long as we find the kids, it isn't important who goes where, or who uses what information. This is a team effort, but if they want to split into their own faction, let them. It might be easier for us to search the city without them distracting us with LA Coven procedure." I hoped they could hear the salty note in my voice.

"Harley's right," Tatyana agreed. "We can cover more ground if we split up."

"Yeah, and if they don't want to hear the leads Astrid has, that's fine by us," Dylan added, casting a subtle look at Tatyana. I didn't know what was going on between the two of them—the all-American football star and the stunning Russian ice queen—but their emotions were easy enough to read. A growing attachment sizzled between them as they stood side by side.

Channing smirked. "Glad some of you can see some sense. It's Basic Investigation 101—divide and conquer. It would appear that your fearless leader lacks basic competency."

"Watch your mouth," Raffe snapped, in a voice that didn't sound entirely like his own. He'd been so silent I'd almost forgotten he was there.

Captain Buzzcut snorted. "This coven should have trained you all better. Don't blame me for your own inadequacies."

Raffe scowled. "Don't try me, Channing."

"Why? You don't look so tough to me."

"Looks can be deceiving." A sinister flash of scarlet darted across Raffe's eyes for a moment. Channing's expression changed, his brow furrowing in a worried frown.

"Let's all just calm down, shall we?" Stella stepped in. "We'll go our way, you'll go yours, and we'll reconvene each evening to discuss what we've found. How does that sound to everyone?"

"Sounds like the best idea to come out of anyone's mouth since we came into this room," Santana said brightly. Her voice sounded oddly strained. Her concern for Raffe bubbled beneath the surface. He worried her, to the very core of her being—the worry of a woman in love, who didn't want to see that love come to any harm.

Jeez, is everyone hitting on everyone in our little group? Dylan was making goo-goo eyes at Tatyana, and she was clearly feeling it, though she was too cool to let on. Raffe and Santana were vibing off each other. Garrett and Santana used to date. And Wade and I… well, I wasn't even going to crack open that particular can of worms. *Sheesh, we're like rats in a barrel.*

"I agree. Looks like we have a plan. So, I suggest we hop to it before we lose any more of the day," I said, pushing all those thoughts of romance away.

Instead, I focused on the missing kids. Micah Cranston, in particular. I hated to admit it, but he was the kid I was most eager to find. I'd put him in the middle of this mess by insisting he stay with the foster parents who loved him. That was a rare thing to find, and I'd wanted him to have that chance at life—the chance to have a real family who cared deeply for him. Channing was right: I'd let my emotions cloud my judgment, and it had caused nothing but heartache. Micah's foster parents were dead, and that dream had died with them. All we could offer him now was the coven.

I'll make amends for my mistake, Micah. You might never forgive me, but I'll do everything in my power to keep you safe from harm.

Speaking of powers, I desperately wished I could have full access to mine. Even the display during the pledge had been a mere fraction of my potential, and right now we needed all the strength we could muster. If we ran into Katherine or any of her cronies along the way, we'd have to break out the big guns. Only, my secret weapons were squashed by this dumb Suppressor inside me.

I'd been meaning to talk to Dr. Krieger again about the surgery required to get the thing out of me, but rumor had drifted through the halls that he was sick. Each time I'd gone to the infirmary, the doors had been locked or one of the nurses had turned me away. Whether he'd been taken ill with an ordinary or a magical disease, I wasn't sure, but an ill physician wasn't a good sign for any coven.

Especially not one teetering on the brink of the terrifying unknown.

FIVE

Santana

These stone-faced *pendejos* were really starting to piss me off, coming in here and giving out orders like they owned the damn place. The dude, Channing, looked like he'd been puffed up with a bike pump. I guessed it was true what folks said about steroids frazzling guys' brains—he had the personality of a rock. Plus, judging by the outline of his ridiculously tight pants, that wasn't the only old wives' tale about steroids that was ringing true.

Meanwhile, Stella couldn't have been more obvious if she'd tried, staring at Wade like he was a tasty snack. She might as well have been licking her lips. Wade and Harley were dancing around their love-hate relationship like two snakes intertwining, but I wasn't about to have some sexy newcomer with a bob and a tight outfit snatch him out from under her. *Not that you'll* ever *get under her if you keep acting like a prize jackass, Wade Crowley. I've seen snails make their move faster than you.*

"So, can we decide on when we're heading out and then do just that?" I asked. "I'm feeling a little claustrophobic with all this testosterone flying around."

Channing shot me a stern look, but I didn't care. Truth be told, it wasn't the peacocking that was bothering me. My body ached down to my very bones, and my eyes felt like lead weights. The perfect ingredients for a snappish, intolerant Santana. I figured the events of the past few weeks were finally taking their toll. Plus, sleep had been an elusive mistress of late, taunting me with a sultry dance of oblivion, only to leave me hanging. I'd had enough of staring up at my ceiling every night, listening to my Orishas whispering about their past and my future. They loved to chat and offer words of wisdom, regaling me nonstop, but it was a killer when my mind was already distracted. The major downside of the Santeria life.

"Let's meet by the magnolia trees at dusk and run an evening patrol. See if any rats creep out as the sun goes down," Wade suggested. "Astrid, will that be enough time for you to pool everything we have together and put it all on Smartie?"

She nodded. "Should be plenty of time. Do you want me to send a copy of what I have to you, Channing?"

He looked taken aback, which pleased me greatly. "That would be most efficient, thank you."

"Cool, so we'll all meet at the magnolia trees in three hours," I reiterated, fighting with the rising irritation that slithered through my veins. "The invitation's still open to you guys, if you feel like you can swallow your pride and join us. If not, good luck with everything. You'll need it."

Harley and Tatyana cast me stunned stares, which I duly shrugged off. *So what if I seem a little... unwelcoming? If these snooty soldier-types can't play nice, they don't deserve the nice treatment. Simple as that.* Not to mention the fact that I had no reason to trust these guys. I rarely trusted new people, in general, but after all the crazy stuff that'd been going on lately, I had even less of a reason to put on a parade and welcome these rude folks. If they weren't even going to attempt to get on our side, they could stuff their LA nonsense where the sun didn't shine.

"Do you want to go grab a soda or something?" Raffe asked, as everyone made to leave. "There might still be some food left over from the banquet."

I glanced at him, wishing I could say yes. "Not right now, Raffe, but definitely another time. I need to go clear my head before we head out to look for these kids. It's all a jumble up there." I tapped the side of my head and mustered a smile.

Wade wasn't the only one tiptoeing around his feelings. About ten times a day, I wanted to grab Raffe by the face and smother him in kisses, but something always held me back. We'd never properly spoken about that kind of thing, and there never seemed to be a good time to bring it up. I sensed the feelings were probably mutual, but Raffe was a shy guy—the djinn was the one with all the confidence, though he didn't get to come out too often. No, if anyone was going to broach the subject, I knew it would have to be me.

Raffe Levi, I adore the very bones of you. One day soon, I'm going to tell you, so brace yourself.

"Do you want some company?" he asked, after a pause. He must have wondered why I was still staring at him when I wasn't saying a word.

I shook my head. "Sorry. I just need to be alone for a little bit. You know what mental prep can be like, and my nights have been a little too rough, so it's extra hard to get things to come into focus."

He frowned. "You haven't been sleeping well?"

"Not really."

"Are you okay?"

"Yeah, just a lot on my mind with Katherine Shipton and all this uncertainty, you know?"

He smiled. "Yeah, I know. Well, if you decide you want someone to talk to, you know where to find me."

"Thank you, Raffe."

"Don't mention it."

"What about you?" I wondered. "How are you feeling? I saw that little flash before—is Hyde behaving himself?"

Raffe laughed wearily. "Ah, you know how it is. Constant battle. The usual. He gets a little friskier whenever my dad is around. I think he feeds off my anger."

"Anything I can do?"

"Not right now," he replied. "Ironically, I think I might need a bit of a breather myself, to let off some steam after being in my father's presence for more than ten minutes."

"Meet you after for that soda?"

He grinned, though his eyes shifted strangely. "I'll come find you."

Exiting the Aquarium, we all parted ways. I noticed Tatyana and Dylan walking together, the sight sending a spike of excitement through my heart. I'd have to get the gossip later, once I could corner Tatyana on her own. *Harley should probably be there, too, so we can interrogate her about Wade.* It was tradition for a family member to lead a new coven pledge into the hall, but Wade had done it instead, given Harley's tragic circumstances. Presumably, he'd done it without telling her about the significance of the act. The handsome devil had done it out of the goodness of his heart, and I was eager to let Harley in on the truth. Perhaps it would give them the kick up the ass that they desperately needed.

"Where do you think you're going?" Garrett purred behind me.

I turned and gave him a sharp stare. "None of your business."

I'd tried to forget my brief fling with Garrett, but the memory still made me bitter. He'd played me for a fool, and nobody got away with that. I wasn't really one to hold a grudge, though. Let bygones be bygones, and all that. But I had a few nasty little spells under my belt, if he ever misbehaved again.

"You wanna go to the banquet hall for something to eat? We could have a drink."

I laughed. "Not a chance, Garrett."

He shrugged. "Your loss."

"You keep telling yourself that." I strode away from him and headed down the hallway. My legs felt heavy as they trudged along the network of corridors. I hadn't been lying when I'd told Raffe I needed time to clear my head. Everything inside my brain felt tinged with fog.

Before long, I found myself at the vast front doors of the Bestiary. The magic of the interdimensional pocket where the coven existed never failed to render me awestruck, the way it could mold around everything and anything. Ever since San Diego had been chosen to house the Bestiary, and Alton had surprisingly accepted, this had been my favorite place to come and be at peace. Nobody else understood why I liked it so much. After all, monsters and beasts weren't exactly soothing… but to me they were. For some reason, the Orishas quietened in there, giving me a brief respite. I adored my Orishas—they were part of me—but it was nice to have a moment to myself every now and again. A spirit-free mind.

I pushed open the giant doors and walked inside, my boots echoing on the marble floor. The guards checked my identity, before allowing me further, on the pretense of me having a meeting with Tobe. All around me, the glass boxes glinted, and wisps of shadows twisted within the misty depths. Here rested the savage product of countless magicals' Purges—the Chaos creatures thrown up and cast out, manifested from the toxic buildup of too much powerful magic.

I glanced at the charmed padlocks, feeling out the raw energy that held these beings in place. Such a small lock, yet capable of containing enormous monsters; the juxtaposition never failed to amuse me.

After the gargoyle incident, where Finch had freed a whole

bunch of the winged beasts and almost exposed the coven in the process, more people had kept their distance from the Bestiary. Not me. There were very few things in this world that scared me—Katherine Shipton being one of the rare exceptions. Nobody deserved to have that much power and influence over others. I wanted to know how she'd ended up like that, what had driven her toward megalomania. Santeria culture centered around the idea of good spirits and bad, but nobody started off their life evil. Even those who were trailed by bad spirits weren't bad by nature. Babies and children were inherently pure.

What happened to you, Katherine, to make you such a class-A psychopath?

The idea of evil spirits prompted Raffe to pop back into my thoughts. Although he'd been born with the djinn already inside him, he hadn't been born evil either. The djinn was part of him, yes, but it didn't control him. Good continued to triumph over the dark. Katherine Shipton didn't have a djinn to excuse her insane behavior. Not that we knew of, anyway.

"Santana, what a pleasant surprise." Tobe's soft growl snapped me right out of my heavy thoughts. "I thought you would still be in the banquet hall, celebrating Harley's official welcome into the coven."

I smiled as the Beast Master approached, his talons clicking on the floor. "I needed a bit of peace and quiet, away from everyone else. Insomnia is kicking my ass, and I didn't want to end up snapping at anyone. Don't suppose you've got a creature in here with some kind of sleepy breath, do you?"

Tobe chuckled, a warmth glimmering in his amber eyes. "Plenty of nightmare demons—Mara, Ogun Oru, a few Succubi, a Kanashibari or two, and a Boo-Hag tucked away at the back. All associated with sleep paralysis and inducing nightmares. Some of them will sap your energy, too, given half the chance."

"This massive museum of monsters and not a single one that can knock me out at night?"

"There is one, but she is kept in a soundproof box in the rare section of the Bestiary," he admitted. "She's an Ibong Adarna. If I were to allow her to sing, she would send everyone in close proximity into a deep slumber."

"That doesn't sound so bad."

He grinned, baring his sharp fangs. "It wouldn't be, if she didn't also turn her victims to stone, once she has reached the end of her seventh song. A beautiful creature, make no mistake. But, as with many beautiful things, she carries hidden dangers. A brutal truth, learned the hard way during my long life on this earth."

"Is that how you got to be so wise, *mi bestia gentil*?"

"I've certainly had the gift of time, in learning many lessons. For, in the end, that is all life is—a series of teachings that we may choose to accept or reject," he replied. "Mistakes and failures are guaranteed, but it is how we choose to educate ourselves after we stumble that molds who we become."

I chuckled. "I need to print that on a bumper sticker."

"Selma often spoke of life's errors as lessons. She would tell me of her own missteps so that I might use them as cautionary tales. She was, by far, my greatest teacher," he said sadly. Selma was a long-dead, ancient witch who had manifested Tobe during a Purge. He was the only good, intelligent beast to ever come out of one.

"Do you miss her?"

"I do. I have never met her equal, in all my 1,058 years—a witch so sweet and kind."

"Not even Imogene Whitehall?"

A purr rumbled in Tobe's throat. "She is, perhaps, the closest in spirit to my beloved Selma, though none can replace her."

"You're good at this, you know," I said, nudging him in his feathered arm.

"At what, Santana?"

"Putting people at ease when they need it most." I'd often come here to seek his counsel and his comforting presence. He'd been my saving grace in this place, and I wasn't sure what I'd do without him.

"I do what I can."

I perched on the edge of a glass box, a small shrew-like creature appearing at the bottom, its beady eyes staring up at me in disapproval. "How have you been feeling after everything that happened with Finch and those gargoyles? It can't have been nice, being accused like that."

"Everything was resolved in the end, and I'm not one to bear a grudge," Tobe replied. "The Bestiary is secure once more, and that's all I may ask for."

"What about all the LA snobs striding about the place like they own it? I bet they're watching you like hawks, thanks to Leonidas." I glanced around in case any of them were listening. A few guards wandered down the corridors farther back, but there weren't any here.

"I can understand their concern, so I pay it no mind. We must all be on high alert, now that we know Katherine has many contingencies in place. Finch and the Ryder twins were just the beginning of her endeavors, and we must be ready for anything she may throw at us. The more people we have here, protecting the coven, the better. Having officers here puts my mind at ease that the Bestiary will not fall, under any circumstances."

Everything about Tobe perpetuated a feeling of calm. He never raised his voice, his words always spoken in a soft, lyrical tone. He was a cool cat, and one of my favorite people. Plus, he was way cheaper than a therapist.

"They've given us two LA Coven agents to help find the kids," I said.

"I sense you are none too pleased by this development?"

"They're just so—"

"Exceedingly dull?" Tobe chuckled in the back of his throat.

"Neither of them seems to have any real personality. Honestly, it's scary. It's like they've sent us two super-advanced bots instead of actual people."

He nodded slowly. "The LA Coven is different. They view their recruits as exactly that—new soldiers, destined for a role in a formidable army. They are less keen on a soft approach, though I much prefer pacifism to outright conflict."

"Me, too."

"On the subject of potential conflict, how are you feeling about the upcoming Family Gathering?" His feathers ruffled in amusement.

I groaned, startling the shrew-like creature below me. "I'm trying not to think about it."

The Family Gathering was an annual event that took place at every coven—a traditional dinner party, complete with fancy clothes, fancy food, and fancy music, where magicals and their parents gathered over dinner and drinks. It was supposed to encourage socializing and a catch-up on what coven members had been accomplishing, but it inevitably ended up feeling like a chore. In some cases, it could also lead to unpleasant airings of dirty laundry, after one or ten too many drinks.

Then again, I'd managed to get out of it for the past four years. The Gathering happened on the same evening, in every coven across the world, with the expectation that siblings would all end up training at the same one. However, that hadn't been the case for my four brothers and me. So, my parents had done what any good parents would do and visited one of us a year. This year, it was my turn. And, to be honest, I was crapping my pants about it.

"You don't get along with your family?" Tobe asked.

"It's not that," I replied. "I love them, I really do, but whenever I speak to them… they're disappointed in me. They want me to do more with my life. They think I'm wasting my potential here in San Diego. It's not the Catemaco way."

Tobe grumbled. "They want you to return home?"

"Yeah, pretty much. They expect me to go back to Mexico sometime this year so I can end up some stuck-up, elite magical's wife and take over the Catemaco Coven with him at my side, as co-director. A tradition I'm not exactly thrilled by, as you can tell." I exhaled wearily. Catemaco was a small but vastly important hub of the magical world. As it was the birthplace and center of the Santeria practice, my family had run a tight ship in the town for hundreds of years, but my rich lineage came with certain ridiculous expectations.

"Don't you miss Mexico?"

I shrugged. "Sometimes, but I'm happy where I am. And I'd rather pluck out my own eyeballs than head back just to get married to some *tipo* I don't know. They don't understand that. They can't grasp how I can love my culture and my heritage, without wanting to live in Mexico. The thing is, I feel like I can do more good here, in the States, instead of a tiny town with no opportunities whatsoever."

"I can understand that," Tobe assured me.

"I'm glad someone can."

Across the room, Quetzi slithered into view, his gold-and-green scales shining in the low light. The feathered serpent coiled up in the right-hand corner, his white-and-fuchsia plumage shuddering like the tail of a rattlesnake, as his intense eyes watched me from afar. I'd always been in awe of him, given his link to my people. As a fixed feature of Aztec culture, he was part of my own Mexican history, once worshiped as a god for his extraordinary abilities. Once upon a time, at the height of his deification, he'd worn the *ehecailacacozcatl* around his thick neck—the breastplate of the wind—as a means to better harness the elemental forces under his control. Many of my people still wore versions of it, especially those gifted with Air abilities, though Quetzi no longer had one around his neck.

I guessed he and Tobe shared the most common ground of any creatures in this place. Neither of them was a mindless beast, banging against the glass to get out. Quetzi had been the result of an Aztec warlock's mighty Purge, and he had emerged extremely powerful and intelligent. However, where Tobe was gentle and kind, Quetzi didn't have the same inclinations. At least, that was the suspicion, based on the legend that preceded him.

"I wonder what'll come out when I have my first Purge," I mused aloud, watching Quetzi.

"You are a strong Santeria. I imagine it will be impressive."

"You think?"

He nodded, his mane bristling. "I've done this long enough to have a sixth sense about these things."

"I think my first one might be on its way," I admitted.

Tobe seemed surprised. "That is somewhat early for you, I should think. You are powerful, but you don't use your abilities as often as others might," he said. "The average is once every five years, after reaching adulthood. You've only undergone three years, if I am not mistaken?"

"Nearly four."

"At least you're not one of the poor souls who Purges every year. Still, that may be why you're having trouble sleeping. All of that toxic energy building up inside you—some internal discontentment, of mind and body, is to be expected."

I nodded. "Yep, I can pretty much feel four-ish years of toxic waste gathering inside me like a nasty ball of grime. It's like someone came in and replaced my blood with syrup."

Tobe chuckled. "I will be here to help you through it, when the time comes."

"You better." I flashed him a smile.

"I wonder how the Dempsey Suppressor will affect Harley's ability to Purge," he said a moment later. "She's rather powerful, even with that device fitted. We saw a glimpse of it today, during the pledge. There were several moments when I feared for my life, and I know I wasn't the only one."

"A big, burly *bestia* like you? Get out of here. You weren't scared."

His whiskers twitched. "Very well, I feared for *your* lives."

"Much appreciated." I laughed. "From what I've seen, Harley is determined to learn the ropes as quickly as she can, to harness her powers at their full capacity. Mind you, I know from experience that that's one hell of a way to end up with rope burn. Not that I can blame her. I'd do the same in her place. It's got to be frustrating, to have all this mojo and not be able to do anything about it, through no fault of your own."

"I imagine so."

"She's eager to have the surgery to get the Suppressor out, ASAP. It's just a matter of Krieger giving her a time and a place."

Tobe sighed. "I thought as much."

"You don't think she should?"

His amber eyes stared into the distance. "I can understand the desire, but I worry that it will make her as vulnerable as it will make her powerful. It will intensify the target already painted upon her back."

I couldn't argue with that.

Truth be told, I saw a lot of myself in Harley. We both spoke our minds and weren't afraid to stand our ground. I admired her determination to get the Suppressor out, but I worried about her too. Harley was smart as a whip yet driven by a stubborn streak that could get her into trouble. I knew it, because I shared the same streak.

Based on what Finch had said, Katherine Shipton was coming for Harley. If Harley didn't know how to properly defend herself, Katherine would finish the job she'd started nineteen years ago. An end to the Merlin clan, once and for all.

SIX

Santana

With my head still all over the place, and more on edge than I'd been before my chat with Tobe, I left the Bestiary and wandered down the hallways toward the living quarters. I had a few hours to kill and figured a nap would be as good a way as any to make the time go quicker. Besides, if I wanted to make it through the evening patrol without keeling over, I needed some shuteye. The Orishas were particularly loud today. Now that I'd spoken to Tobe, I got the feeling their increased chatter had something to do with my one-way ticket to Purgetown. They repelled the gathering darkness.

I staggered to a halt as a door swung open on the left, narrowly missing my face. Raffe, hunched and visibly raging, stormed out. He didn't see me as he strode up the hallway, his hands balled into fists. Leonidas followed a moment later.

"Get back here now!" Leonidas roared.

I ducked behind the door.

"Why?" Raffe whirled around. "You've said everything you have to say. I don't want to hear anymore."

"You will listen to me!"

"No, Father, I won't. I'm not your punching bag to lay into whenever you feel like it. You've made it very clear how worthless you think I am—I'm not going to hear any more of it. Go home!"

Leonidas squared up to his son. "Get back in this room this instant. I'm not done."

"Well, I am." Raffe shoved his father hard in the chest, sending him stumbling backward with inhuman force. Leonidas dusted himself off, but I could tell he was scared. Raffe's "condition" terrified his father—that much was obvious. As much as I hated to see Raffe warring with the djinn, it seemed like the only protection he had, the only weapon powerful enough to use against his father.

"Calm down, Raffe," Leonidas urged, his voice tight with anxiety. I had no sympathy for the arrogant asshole. It took something intensely personal to rile Raffe up to the point where his eyes glowed red. Whatever Leonidas had said or done, he'd evidently earned Raffe's fury. Apparently, it wasn't just Raffe who had serious issues with Leonidas—the djinn seemed to equally dislike him, feeding off the dysfunction.

It burned me up inside to see Raffe's suffering. If my eyes could flash red, they'd be doing it right now. An empathetic fire of fury.

"I'm calm," Raffe spat back. "Can you just leave me alone now? I don't want to be around you."

Leonidas sighed. "Very well, but this is not over, Raffe. You and I still have much to discuss. This coven is unsuitable for you, and I won't have you drag the Levi name through the dirt. I realize you feel some juvenile urge to get back at me for all the harsh lessons I've been forced to teach you, but you will thank me one day."

"I doubt that."

"Why must you resist me?" Leonidas edged around his son. "I'm asking you for very little—a bit of surveillance, in order to keep your rogue friends in check. Why do we always have to be in conflict? Why can't you just do as you are told?"

"Because I don't agree with anything you say or do."

Leonidas shook his head. "I have some business to attend to with Alton. I will leave afterward, but I will be back. This matter is not finished. There might be rules in place to forbid me from removing you from this coven, but I will figure something out in due course."

With that, he walked back into the room he'd come from. His entire body was shaking with barely concealed fear, and he wore a sullen expression. Clearly, he didn't like being sent away by his son, but he didn't dare defy Raffe in case the djinn emerged. Up ahead, Raffe remained frozen to the spot. He hadn't seen me behind the door. With rage in his eyes, he pivoted on his heel and headed up the hallway.

"Hey! Raffe!" I hissed, hurrying past the open door. Out of the corner of my eye, I saw Leonidas pacing the floor of a dark, mahogany-walled office. I hadn't seen the room before, but that wasn't surprising—the coven was massive. It'd take me weeks to check what lay behind every single door, and I didn't have the time or the desire. Still, Leonidas wasn't supposed to be here anymore. Alton had led the Mage Council out of the Aquarium with the exact intention of making them leave. Clearly, something had happened on the way out.

Raffe turned around slowly, his midnight eyes flashing a deep crimson. "Santana... sorry, I didn't see you there," he muttered. "Do you mind if we keep walking? I don't want to be anywhere near that office."

"No problem."

I followed Raffe up the hallway, turning right at an intersection. He seemed to know where he was going, but I had no idea. Right now, I just wanted to be there for him while he processed whatever had happened with his father.

"Everything okay?" I prompted.

He rubbed the back of his neck and tilted his head from side to side. "Not really."

"Your dad?"

"You heard that, huh?" he said bitterly.

"I thought he left with the others from the Mage Council."

"Nope, he decided to corner me outside the banquet hall and lead me to the Council Chamber," he explained, his features twisting in fury. "Nobody's used that stuffy office for years. He just wanted to drag me somewhere away from everyone else so he could let me know *just* how disappointed he is with everything I am, and everything I'm doing. Oh, and then to top it all off, he asked me to spy for him and told me he wanted me to leave San Diego. You know, the usual."

"I'm sorry, Raffe." I really was. My own family problems were rainbows and goddamn butterflies compared to his. "I hate seeing what he does to you."

"Nobody riles me up the way he does. He knows just how to get under my skin. I guess years of practice have made him a pro." His face contorted, revealing someone who looked exactly like Raffe but wasn't quite him. The mirage disappeared a moment later, Raffe's chest heaving with the exertion of shoving djinn-boy back down again.

He paused in front of a doorway and pulled a thin, silver chain out from under his t-shirt. A key dangled on the end. I'd never seen it before. His hands shaking, he slotted the key into the lock and turned it. A *click* sounded in the room beyond.

Glancing down the corridor, I realized we weren't far from the training halls, and yet I'd never noticed this doorway before. It practically blended into the rest of the wall, melding in a seamless camouflage. Puzzled, I followed Raffe through a narrow hallway just after the door, which ended in a spacious, windowless chamber. Sitting in the center, glowing slightly beneath a single orb of light, was a big glass box, almost identical to the ones kept in the Bestiary. Charms and runes were etched along every edge, some shimmering in the faint light. The only difference I could see was that there were several holes in the outer shell, and a thin veil of energy danced across each one.

"You should probably get out of here before things get ugly," Raffe said, turning to me with a sad expression. Every few seconds, the muscles in his face twitched, revealing the changeling version of himself that lurked beneath. He was losing the fight. Pretty soon, he wouldn't be able to hold back the swell of his foul mood, the snap of his patience giving the djinn the gateway it needed to jump through.

I'd been fascinated by Raffe's Jekyll-and-Hyde disorder ever since I'd come to the coven, though I hadn't fully understood it at first. I knew about djinns, but I'd never actually seen one attached to a person before. Not everyone knew about his condition—Harley was still in the dark, I suspected—and he didn't like to let a lot of people know, but he'd confided in me. That trust meant a lot.

"Please, Santana, you should go." He was fighting hard, sweat pouring down his face. Grasping for the key on the chain around his neck, he jammed it into the padlock on the glass box and opened the door. As soon as it was open, he hurried over to a small table at the far side of the room. He took off the key and chain and dropped them in a bowl, before pressing a button on the wall. It glowed red, piquing my curiosity.

"What does that do?" I wondered.

"It alerts Tobe to my state," he replied rapidly. "He'll come and let me out in a few hours."

"Are you kidding? You do this on your own?" My stomach twisted in knots for him, having to deal with all of this by himself. A steely resolve settled in my mind.

"I have to. Besides, I prefer it this way."

I shook my head. "Well, I'm not leaving you on your own. I'll stay and keep you company."

"Santana, you can't," he urged desperately. "I can't keep the djinn under control for much longer. He's about to manifest. You need to leave, now!"

"No, I'm staying. I'll keep my distance, but I'm staying."

"I don't want you to see me like this." He raced toward the glass box, stepped inside, and slammed the door behind him, the padlock locking automatically in place as soon as he was within the perimeter of the box. A moment later, a forcefield of some sort shot across the box, making it glow dimly. There was a small hole by the door, protected by the forcefield. I figured Raffe was meant to use it if the lock ever failed to close automatically. Until Tobe came to release him, Raffe was going nowhere. I could always let him out, but I guessed Tobe had more idea of when it was safe than I did.

"Raffe, I'm not worried about seeing that side of you. I saw the djinn when the gargoyles took over Balboa Park; it's not exactly new to me," I replied, putting on a show of confidence. He needed it right now. "Honestly, I don't care if you want me to go. I'm not leaving you. You'll be better off with some neutral company while Hyde has his moment, instead of pacing about on your own like a depressed zoo animal, with only him for company."

He looked at me with glittering eyes that were slowly turning redder. "Please go."

"Not happening."

"You're so stubborn," he muttered.

"That's what you love about me."

He smiled shyly. "Not in this particular situation, I don't."

"Tough. You're going to have to get used to it." I pressed my hand to the glass and smiled as he raised his palm to meet mine. I couldn't feel him, but it was close enough. He knew he had me here for moral support.

"Fine... but don't take anything the djinn says seriously," he warned. "He tends to get a little vicious after my dad and I have a fight. Please, remember that it isn't me. He might look like me, but he isn't me."

His words sent a chill of unease through me. Not that I was going to show it. Demons and spirits and djinns and ghouls didn't scare me... I just had to keep reminding myself of that.

"Okay, okay, I won't hold anything against you," I relented.

"Oh, but I wish you would." Raffe cackled as he slammed his hand against the glass, grimacing. I stepped away from the box, startled by the sudden change. "I'd like nothing more than to hold you against me, before stripping the flesh from your bones, piece by delicious piece."

He hurled himself at the glass, the violent impact shuddering through the ground toward me. Staggering back, he grinned a nasty grin. Every feature of Raffe's face looked wrong and unfamiliar.

"You don't frighten me... djinn." I shrugged off my initial fear, knowing the glass box would hold him.

"Want to see a cool trick?" he purred.

I frowned at him. "Not really."

"You demanded to stay here. I have to keep you entertained." He laughed coldly, the sound echoing as though it was coming from somewhere other than his mouth. It was similar to the way my Orishas sounded when they spoke through me. I guessed it was the same kind of deal.

His skin rippled, pockets of flesh bunching and swirling as though he had a snake trapped beneath the surface. It took every ounce of willpower I had not to throw up my lunch. A moment later, his entire body set alight, flames licking from his toes to the top of his skull, turning every inch of his skin an alarming shade of crimson. Fire burned behind his eyes.

"Very impressive," I choked, hoping the real Raffe was okay in there. Weirdly, no smoke filled the glass box, the flames burning clean.

"I'm not done yet," he growled. Heaving in an enormous breath that made the glass walls shake, he exhaled a violent gust of wind that extinguished the flames. Black smoke billowed around his red-tinged body, clinging to him like a magnet, before swirling upward and disappearing into thin air. Hunkering down, he tilted his twisted face skyward and let out a spine-chilling roar. It shivered through every nerve in my body, setting the Orishas on edge. They didn't like being so close to a creature like this. I could feel them wanting to rush to my aid, and it was taking a hell of a lot of energy to keep them at bay.

Through a few of the gaps in his clothes, where the heat of his body had burned holes in the fabric, I could see some of the taut muscle underneath. My throat tightened, my eyes widening in appreciation. He might've been a demon, but the body was all Raffe's. If a little on the scarlet side.

"Like I said, impressive." *The body, too. Dios mio, that's nice!*

He grinned, returning to his smokeless form. "I thought you'd like that. Besides, I needed to stretch out these pathetic limbs. Everything is wound up so tight," he murmured, shaking his body like a wet dog. "Tell me, sugar-lips, do you have any idea what kind of self-discipline it takes not to punch Daddio in the jaw when he's acting like a total asshat?"

"I can imagine."

He laughed, the sound sending a shudder through me. "I could devour you whole, do you know that? I bet your skin tastes of spice and caramel, seasoned with the baking heat of the Mexican sun." His eyes rolled back into his head as he licked his lips, a smirk twisting up the corner of his mouth.

I stared at him in complete shock. I'd only ever seen the djinn from a distance, like the day Raffe let the monster loose so he could round up all the gargoyles in Balboa Park. This was a different ballgame entirely, and I wasn't sure I liked it. The way he spoke to me... that wasn't Raffe at all. I might've wanted Raffe to be a little more forthcoming with a much-needed bit of flirtation, to let me know he freaking liked me, but this wasn't what I meant. This was, for lack of a better word, horrifying.

Everything I knew about the guy I adored, and everything standing before me... I couldn't bridge the gap between them. I couldn't make sense of it. This monster was wearing Raffe's skin, this monster inhabited Raffe's body, this monster was part and parcel of who Raffe was, but this wasn't him.

In that moment, for the first time in my life, I wanted to run away from something. I wanted to get as far away as humanly possible so I wouldn't have to hear another voice slithering out of Raffe's mouth.

Come back to me, Raffe, I pleaded. *Come back to me.*

SEVEN

Harley

Lying on the bed in Astrid's room, I skimmed the emails Jacob had sent me. A few words from this place and that place, letting me know he was okay. Never too much information, never too specific, but enough to keep me from going out of my mind with worry. Wherever the two of them were, Isadora and Jacob had each other. They were safe… for now.

Yeah, until you bring them back out into the open, where they're vulnerable and exposed.

I shook off the dark thoughts, knowing my personal feelings were getting in the way. This was for the kids and the coven. A calculated risk, for the greater good.

"Any luck?" Tatyana asked from the corner of Astrid's room. She flipped absently through a textbook on the Children of Chaos, looking for anything that might relate to Katherine Shipton's insane plan to become one.

"I keep running the emails through this program of yours, Astrid, but every single one is bouncing through a million different servers and VPNs," I replied miserably. "Isadora's phenomenally good at this. I guess being on the run for years gives you a lot of practice in covering your tracks."

Astrid nodded. "I had a feeling it might be a fruitless task. Looks like Isadora can jump through space, time, and the internet."

I chuckled. "Annoying in this scenario, but oddly comforting."

"Are you having second thoughts about Alton's request?" Tatyana asked.

"Not so much second thoughts as panic-inducing worry that Katherine is waiting for me to sniff them out so she can swoop in and snatch them."

"They'll be safe in the coven," Astrid reassured me. "We've got all these extra people guarding just about everything, and everyone is on super-high alert. It's probably the safest place for them, aside from where they are right now."

I pulled a face. "See, it's that last part that gets to me. They're already safe, but we need their skills. They'll have to put themselves at enormous risk for a coven they don't even belong to. I'd like to think they're that selfless, but we'll have to wait and see." I rolled onto my back and stared up at the glow-in-the-dark stars stuck to Astrid's ceiling. "Besides, the coven *isn't* safe anymore. There's a mole in our midst, and we have no idea who it might be."

"It might be one of us, for all you know," Astrid joked, her laughter dying on her lips. "Sorry... I shouldn't joke about that kind of thing. After the whole Finch thing, it's in poor taste."

"If we do not laugh, we will cry. Isn't that the saying?" Tatyana chimed in, setting the book down. "I think I might stretch my legs for a bit. These books are filled with nothing but fairy stories and myths."

"Is there nothing in them that might help us—a bit of subtext or something?" I asked, flipping back over onto my stomach.

"Absolutely nothing, just the usual stuff about the Children being here at the beginning of everything, forged from raw Chaos. Blah, blah, blah, blah…"

Astrid sighed. "If only we had a step-by-step instruction manual. Wouldn't that be a wonderful thing?"

"I think that'd be a terrifying thing," I replied with a tight laugh. "There'd be crazy folks trying to turn themselves into Children of Chaos left, right, and center."

"Ah, you may have a point there."

I sat up on the edge of the bed and scooped my hair into a ponytail. "Actually, I think I might stretch my legs, too. We've still got a few hours before the evening patrol. I might as well put the time to good use."

"What are you thinking?" Tatyana asked.

"I might pay the Smiths a visit, see if Jacob left anything behind. We may be able to forge a tracer spell from something that belonged to him," I replied, flashing a nervous grin. "Plus, it's taco night—it'd be rude not to go."

We'd successfully used a tracer spell to expose Finch as the Bestiary's saboteur. If we used it again to try and trace Jacob, I figured we'd have a hope in hell of finding him. Right now, our options were ridiculously thin on the ground. *This way, we kill two birds with one stone. Wherever Jacob is, that's where Isadora will be, too.*

Astrid frowned. "You haven't seen them since the incident. Are you sure you're okay visiting them? Do you want some company?"

I shook my head. "Sorry, guys, I think this is something I have to do alone. I can't keep putting it off for my own selfish reasons. I mean, they keep texting to say they miss me, asking when I'm coming around, and I keep telling them I'm busy. I can't avoid them any longer. They deserve better than that."

"I know you're used to getting things done by yourself, but you've got us now… if you ever need us for anything," Tatyana said. "You know that, right?"

My heart swelled. "Thank you. I mean it… thank you." I stood up slowly, feeling overwhelmed. "If there are any spare tacos, I'll bring them back. Fair exchange?"

"Fair exchange," Astrid replied. "Just be careful out there, okay? You're not really supposed to go anywhere on your own right now."

Tatyana nodded. "Take a cab straight there, and keep your phone on. Let us know when you're done. We'll probably be heading out on patrol by the time you've finished there, so we'll rendezvous or something. If this weather lets up, that is. Weird for San Diego, but I guess it needs a storm from time to time."

"Sounds good. I'll text you if I finish early." I'd never had any friends care so much about me before. Although, I'd never really had friends before, so I had nothing to compare it to.

I slid my phone into my pocket and grabbed my leather jacket from Astrid's coat stand, slinging it on as I headed out into the corridor. A few people wandered about, meandering back from the banquet hall. I hurried along, taking the steps two at a time, then skirted past the magnolia trees.

Not long after, I exited the main entrance to the coven and walked through an empty Kid City, making my way toward the exit of the Fleet Science Center. Against the glass, the first spatters of rain had begun to fall. I paused at the revolving doors and sent a text to Dicky's number. I didn't need the card anymore—I had it memorized. It would've been easier to put it into my phone, but I figured it was safer not to. I'd thought about driving Daisy to the Smiths, but this seemed like the safer course of action, since we weren't supposed to be heading out alone. Dicky was my loophole.

He appeared ten minutes later, flashing his headlights as he rolled up to the sidewalk. I sprinted to the cab and got in, a fine mist of rain sprinkling my hair. It was gloomy out, the sky overcast and plump with swollen gray clouds that threatened an imminent torrent. San Diego was due a storm.

"I hadn't expected to hear from you anytime soon, Harley," Dicky said after I'd fastened my seatbelt and given him directions. He already knew the house—he'd dropped me off there when I'd gone to check on Jacob—but if he recognized the address he didn't bat an eyelid.

"No?"

"I haven't heard from Isadora in a while. Thought she might be lying low," he replied. "Figured something must have happened that night I dropped you off."

I nodded. "Mm-hm. And then some."

"Don't worry, you don't have to tell old Dicky about any of it. I drive, that's it. Don't ask no questions, don't want to know no answers."

I smiled. *How refreshing.*

"Harley!" Mrs. Smith cried as she answered the door. "My goodness, I'd almost forgotten what you looked like."

My heart wrenched in my chest. The cleanup team had made her forget the Death by a Thousand Cuts hex, the wrecked house, and all the terrible things that the Ryder twins had done to her and Mr. Smith. Instead of the truth, the cleanup crew had implanted false memories about a home invasion, taking every magical element out of the equation. They'd dealt with the cuts in the only way they could, casting an illusion over Mrs. Smith's legs and plying her with numbing serums in the night while she slept. As far as she was concerned, her legs were completely fine, even though she still had a few more days of healing to do. The serums quickened the process, but they weren't instantaneous.

What hurt most of all, however, was the fact that they'd wiped all memory of Jacob from the Smiths' minds—about adopting him, about bringing him here, about everything. It had been the kindest thing to do, but it still stung.

At least they didn't make her forget about me.

"I had a few hours to spare, so I thought I'd come visit," I murmured. "I'm sorry for not coming sooner, to check on how you were both doing after the home invasion. This new job is kicking my ass."

"Language," Mrs. Smith chided.

I smiled. "Sorry. I've had a long day."

"And don't you worry about not having the time to visit," she insisted. "You're doing so well, from what you've been telling us. Homeland Security wasn't what I thought you'd do with your life, but still! It's nice to see you happy in a job. Besides, you sent us those beautiful flowers and that gift basket from St. Clair's. That's enough to win me over." She winked, ushering me inside the house. The scent of Mexican spices wafted through from the kitchen, making my mouth water.

"Still, I should've come to visit. I'm sorry I didn't."

"Enough of that. You're here now, and that's all that counts." She enveloped me in a warm embrace. I hugged her back twice as hard. *Man, it's good to see you again. I've missed you so much.* I wanted to say the words out loud, but I knew the tears wouldn't stop if I did. The defense mechanisms were firmly back in place.

Heading through to the kitchen, I tried not to look at her legs, seeking any sign of her injuries, but it was like turning away from a car crash. She must have wondered what on Earth I was doing, glancing down at her calves every couple of minutes, because she gave me a confused smile. Mr. Smith stood at the stove, mixing the taco ingredients together. He turned over his shoulder as we entered, a broad grin splitting his face. *See, they're happier than they've ever been. It's like nothing ever happened.*

"Hey, there's our high-flyer! Did they turn you loose for an evening?" he chirped, wiping his hands on a dishcloth. He crossed the kitchen and threw his arms around me, pulling me in tight.

"A couple of hours," I replied, hugging him back.

"Well, that suits us just fine. We've got plenty of food on the go—we were just wondering how we were going to eat all of this ourselves, weren't we, hon?"

Mrs. Smith rested her hand on my shoulder, as though she were scared I might disappear. "We were indeed. Ryann was supposed to come down from UCLA to spend the night with us, but I think there might be a boy in the picture. Her plans changed last minute, so you came at just the right time."

I heard the sad note in Mrs. Smith's voice. It had to be hard for them, with Ryann away at college, me doing my own thing, and no memory of Jacob. He'd been the one giving them a renewed sense of purpose. Without him, I reasoned they were bound to feel a little lost. By all accounts, many folks who had their memories wiped couldn't remember anything, but they *did* feel like something was missing. I had a feeling Mrs. Smith fell into that category, though Mr. Smith seemed quite content to fuss around his wife.

"That's a shame," I said. "It would've been cool to see Ryann. I haven't spoken to her in a while."

Mrs. Smith smiled. "She always asks after you."

"I'll give her a call sometime soon."

She brightened. "You let me know if you hear anything good!"

"I might have to invoke a vow of sisterly silence, I'm afraid."

Mrs. Smith laughed. "I do so miss having the two of you around the place. Everything seems so big, with it being just the two of us bumbling about. You'll have to come by more often… when work permits, of course. I know how busy you both are."

"I will," I promised. "I mean it this time."

"Actually, we've been meaning to talk to you about something," she went on shyly.

"Oh?"

"Well… we've been thinking about fostering another child. We have all this space, and it seems a shame not to use it," she explained. "It's all thanks to you, really. You've inspired us to try and help someone else, the way we helped you. I know there are so many children out there, stuck in the system, and we both feel that it's time we gave something back again."

My face lit up, my heart overflowing with admiration and affection. It may well have been Mrs. Smith's emotions, mingling with my own, but I couldn't have been prouder. Even with their memories wiped, and no recollection of Jacob Morales, they still wanted to make a difference in the lives of San Diego's forgotten kids. There was a bitter irony, too, considering how things had gone last time. Not their fault, of course, but Katherine had used their kindness to get to me and Jacob.

"What do you think, kiddo?" Mr. Smith chimed in.

"I think that's a great idea," I said, without missing a beat. "Any kid who ends up here is going to be one of the luckiest kids in the world."

The Smiths smiled at each other, love flowing effortlessly between them. Even after all these years, they still adored one another. *One day, I'll be one half of an awesomely sickening pair like this, still smooching after decades of marriage—still pinching each other's butts when they think no one's looking.*

"We're so glad you approve," Mrs. Smith gushed.

"Actually, speaking of lucky kids, would you mind if I headed up to my old room and had a look around? I've been looking for this journal I had from senior year, but I can't find it anywhere. It has the *only* good picture of me that's ever been taken." I hated lying to them, but there was no other way.

Mrs. Smith tutted. "Nonsense, Harley, we've got lots of beautiful pictures of you."

"Then beauty is in the eye of the very blind beholder."

"Cheeky!" A contented smile settled across her lips. "Everything's as you left it. Dinner in ten?"

I nodded. "No problem. I'll be quick."

Leaving them to their happy domesticity, I headed down the hall, only to freeze halfway. Seeing the front door from this angle brought back a wave of hideous flashbacks. The Ryder twins taunting me as Wade and I hid from sight, trying to figure out a plan of action that wouldn't get my foster parents horribly murdered. Mrs. Smith screaming as the cuts appeared on her legs, making their way up her body, the blood soaking through her pants. Mr. Smith sobbing at the sight of his beloved wife, and not being able to do anything to help her.

Shrugging off the awful memories, I forced myself to continue down the hall and up the stairs, to my old room. As I stood in the doorway, nostalgia washed over me. I glanced at the magnolia walls and remembered putting up each and every one of the artsy black-and-white photos of James Dean and Springsteen in their glory days, and a bevy of leather-clad rock musicians, while the sweet smell of vanilla drifted toward me from the reed-diffuser on the windowsill. Mrs. Smith must have put it there, replacing the headier scents that I liked. I'd only stayed here for two years, but they'd been the happiest two years of my life. *Prep school notwithstanding—they could go screw themselves.*

My powers had made themselves known throughout my childhood, but back then I hadn't known what they'd meant or where they'd lead. So much had changed in such a short span of time. I was better off now, knowing what I was and what I could do, but that didn't detract from the fondness I felt for this place. The Smiths had been kind to me, and I would never forget that.

For the next ten minutes, I scoured the room, sifting through every closet and drawer for something that might have belonged to

Jacob. The cleanup crew had done a suitably spectacular job of covering all magical trails, which meant finding a potential object was going to be harder than finding a very specific needle in a stack of needles.

I crawled over to the bed and looked underneath. Nothing but solitary boots and loafers that I'd left behind, a couple of shoeboxes, and a flurry of dust bunnies. Undeterred, I wriggled under the slats and hauled myself to the far side of the bed, with the windowsill just visible above me. My hands grasped in the darkness, searching for anything unusual. Delving into a pile of fluff and torn-up paper, my fingertips settled on a curious shape tucked between the wall and the edge of the carpet.

I'm going to need a gallon of Purell after this.

Digging the object out of its disgusting crevice, I struggled back out into the main body of the room and opened my palm to see what treasure I'd collected. A Native American beaded bracelet sat in the center of my hand. I'd never owned anything like it, and nobody else had used this room before me—it had been a study until they'd taken me in. The bracelet had to be Jacob's. Evidently, the cleanup crew had missed it, considering where it had fallen.

I wonder where you got it from, Jake? I didn't know anything about Jacob's real parents, and he didn't seem to know anything either. "Morales" was the name the foster home had given him. His true surname was lost, known only by the people who had abandoned him as a kid.

It reminded me of my own family. There were so many questions I still wanted to ask, and so many answers I didn't have. Isadora was the key to my past, and perhaps the key to my future, too—she knew everything I needed to know, about my mother and father, the Merlin family as a whole, and, most importantly, about Katherine Shipton and her involvement in the murders that had left me an orphan.

Let's hope this bracelet leads me to both of you, before dear Aunt Katie has the chance to strike again.

"Harley! Dinner's ready!"

I pocketed the bracelet and headed out of the room, pausing to take one last look at the only place that had seemed like a sanctuary to me. Before the coven, anyway. It no longer held the same power that it once had. I was older now… wiser, perhaps. I might've spent some happy times in this room, but I would never be a Smith. The history of the Merlins and the Shiptons beckoned, the two melting pots from which I'd been made.

Right now, I was in a race against time to put the puzzle pieces together and stop Katherine from slotting the children into her grand plan.

EIGHT

Harley

The storm blew in with a vengeance, gale-force winds raging across the city. As a torrent of rain lashed down from all angles, soaking through my clothes in a matter of seconds while I waited for Dicky to pick me up, I got the call from the Rag Team that the evening patrol was off. Nobody would be stupid enough to wander around in this kind of weather, not even Katherine's minions. They'd be holed up somewhere instead.

I was kind of glad, now that I had the bracelet Jacob had accidentally left behind. If we could get a tracer spell going, at least we could find Jacob and Isadora and tick one thing off our seemingly endless list of things to do.

Dicky drove me back to the Fleet Science Center, though nobody else was around at this time of night. A few security guards manned the foyer. I wasn't too worried; they were undercover magicals, on the coven's private roster. They nodded to me as I headed through the back way, into the coven itself. Kid City was seriously eerie at night. The playgrounds and jungle gyms just felt weird without the actual kids playing on them.

Once inside, I made a beeline for the banquet hall, hoping I'd find a couple members of the Rag Team there. We'd made a tentative plan to meet in Astrid's room at nine o'clock, but nobody had replied to the group chat yet, and I wasn't in a waiting mood. We'd blown off the evening meeting with Stella and Channing, too, since none of us had anything to report and the storm had cancelled any investigative plans. The bracelet was burning a hole in my pocket.

I paused on the threshold, my gaze settling on two figures at the farthest side of the right-hand table. Wade and Stella looked like they were in the middle of some deep conversation, Stella toying with a strand of her dark hair. *Very cozy.* They sipped coffee, a ripple of laughter slipping from Stella's lips every couple of minutes. *Oh, come on, he's not* that *funny. He's got the stand-up routine of a kindergartener.* Another laugh erupted, echoing down the hall toward me. *Seriously, you're embarrassing yourself.*

A sudden stab of jealousy pierced my chest, taking me by surprise. *Well... that's new.*

Shrugging it off, and outright refusing to be the kind of girl who fawns over some dude because he's chatting with another girl, I readjusted myself and strode down the aisle toward them. They fell silent as soon as I approached, which left me a little suspicious about what they'd been talking about.

"Hey, can I have a word?" I asked bluntly, staring Wade straight in the eyes.

He shrugged. "Sure. What's up?"

"I need to talk to you in private." I flashed a faintly apologetic look at Stella, who seemed taken aback by my abrupt interruption.

To be honest, I was a little embarrassed by my behavior, cutting in on their conversation like that. But this was important information that couldn't wait until he was done flirting.

"Yeah, okay... Do you mean now?" Wade asked.

"No, I mean in about a year or two. Maybe three, if you're more comfortable with that—of course I mean now," I replied, giving Stella a "can you believe this guy" kind of look.

He pushed his coffee cup away and got up. "Thanks for the talk, Stella. It's always nice to get to know LA Coven people a bit better. I guess the cover doesn't always do the book justice."

She smiled at him, revealing perfect teeth. "Anytime. I know Channing isn't all that eager to make friends, but I'm a bit more chilled out than he is."

Yeah, I bet you are. I quickly shoved away the fresh stab of jealousy that weaseled its way into my mind, to stop it from twisting any more of my generally sane thoughts into stupid ones. Green really wasn't my color. And besides, Stella was only trying to be nice. It wasn't easy to be the fresh meat in a new place, no matter how tough you were. I knew that better than anyone.

"Come on," I said, heading for the opposite door. Wade followed after me, the two of us striding side by side down the main corridor beyond the banquet hall. I had no plan past this. Yeah, I needed to tell Wade about the bracelet and the potential tracer spell, but I'd made it sound way too urgent. I could've let him finish his coffee.

Panicking a bit, I shoved him through the nearest door on the left-hand side of the corridor. He staggered backward through it, regaining his balance in the center of a dingy, super-narrow plant nursery. Shelves were stacked right up to the ceiling on both sides, taking up every inch of wall space. Each plank was filled to the brim with cases and trays and pots of fragrant herbs and flowers, all of them recoiling as a hint of light glanced in from the hallway. I guessed they had to be light sensitive, if they were tucked away in a place like this.

Seeing the glint of Wade's eyes in the gloom, I realized it might have been a little rash to pick the first door I came to. The shiver of nervous excitement coming off him wasn't exactly helping matters, either. Clearly, he thought I had some ulterior motive in shoving him in here, with all these dimmed, atmospheric lights. But I couldn't back out now. I'd made my weirdly romantic bed, and now I had to lie in it and hope he didn't get the wrong idea.

"So, what's this urgent matter that can't wait?" he asked, leaning awkwardly against a shelf. He stood sharply a second later as a barbed plant, similar to a Venus flytrap, lunged for his right butt-cheek.

So smooth, Wade Crowley... so smooth.

I stifled a laugh. "I need help with something, and since we're not on patrol tonight, I figured you could use a distraction."

"You want to be a little more specific? I was having a good chat with Stella, and I want to know if this was worth abandoning her for." He eyed the barbed plant warily. "She's not so bad, you know. Way cooler than Channing. If she had her way, I think she might actually join in with the rest of us, but he's not so open and she sort of has to stick with him."

"They come as a pair?"

He shrugged. "Something like that."

"Well, actually, this is definitely worth abandoning the new girl for," I said, struggling to keep the sour tone out of my voice. He'd only rib me for it later. "I found something of Jacob's at the Smiths' place, and I need you to help me put a tracer spell on it—the same one we used to weed out Finch."

"Why just me?"

Oh, I dunno, to get you away from Stella Chan? Touché, Crowley.

"I don't want to go after them with a huge team, in case we spook them, and they take off," I replied, barely missing a beat. It was half true. "Plus, I'm still worried about this mole. If the spy finds out about Jacob and Isadora's whereabouts, we're totally screwed. The last thing we want Katherine getting her greedy mitts on is Portal Opener powers. I know I had to tell the rest of the Rag Team about Alton's orders, but not everyone needs to know that I'm *actually* in the middle of tracking them. Does that make sense?"

He paused for a moment. "You don't trust the Rag Team?"

"I do! Of course I do. But we don't know who else might be listening, through some magical or non-magical, but equally nosy, method. I'd rather stick with just you, for now," I said. "Plus, Garrett's still a bit rogue for my liking. It's annoying that I can't sense what he's feeling. I can let him in on some of our secrets, but I don't have to let him in on all of them, right?"

"I guess that makes sense," he replied with a shrug. "But how come you're trusting me with this? How can you be sure Katherine hasn't gotten to me?"

I grinned. "Because I can read you like a book."

"Only when I let you."

"Yeah, keep telling yourself that." I plucked the bracelet out of my jeans pocket and held it out for him to see. "Anyway, I thought it'd be better if we just kept this between you and me for now. Alton, too. I'll have to tell him what we're doing, since we'll be using a forbidden spell again."

A flurry of intense excitement rushed through me, feeding off Wade's sudden flood of emotion. "Cool, then count me in. When were you thinking of doing the spell?"

"Tomorrow, maybe?"

He shook his head, flashing a wide grin. "Since we're not doing anything right now, and nobody's expecting us to patrol in this kind of weather, why don't we do the spell tonight? We can follow wherever it leads in total secrecy, because nobody would be stupid enough to head out in a storm."

"Except us?"

"Exactly... except us." He paused, jittering with anticipation. "So, what do you think?"

"I think we need to get everything together and get this done," I replied, his excitement melding with my own. I couldn't wait to speak to Isadora again. "Speaking of which, is everything still in the Luis Paoletti Room?"

He frowned. "I'm not sure. We'll need to check it out."

"Please tell me we've still got some of Quetzi's venom left over, because there's no way I'm asking Tobe to risk his life again," I said, remembering the near miss that had almost ended in a dead Beast Master. Quetzi had been moments away from sinking his fangs into Tobe's wing when I'd begged him to stop and give us the venom of his own free will. In the end, he'd given it up reluctantly, but I didn't feel like chancing it again, no matter how important this was.

"There was plenty of it left after last time. If it's anywhere, it'll be in the Luis Paoletti Room with everything else."

"Then we should probably start there and figure out what else we're going to need." A flicker of anxiety wormed its way into my head. "Ah man, I just thought… this isn't going to be as easy as it was last time. We can't just go to Preceptor Gracelyn and ask for wolfsbane, and we can't get Santana to help crush the jasper and diamonds into powder."

Wade rubbed the back of his neck. "Let's just see what we've got, and then figure the rest out from there. I might have a way around those things, if it comes to that."

"You do? What?"

"Patience, Merlin, patience." He moved past me to reach the door, the narrow width of the room bringing us a little too close together. I tried to step back against the nearest shelf to give him space, but another of the vicious plants reared up, preparing to launch itself at my shirt. Stumbling forward to get away from the savage beastie, I wound up pressed against him, bracing my palms against his chest to keep from toppling over.

Man, I'd forgotten how great you smell, Crowley.

I looked up into his eyes. "You know, you could've just let me leave first."

"Yeah, but where would the fun be in that? You robbed me of my coffee date. Call this payback." He squeezed the rest of the way past me and let himself out the nursery door, leaving it open for me to follow. I fought a smile. *Asshole.*

Ten minutes later, we stood outside the double doors of the Luis Paoletti Room. Wade put his hands on both doorknobs and murmured the spell that opened them, his rings glowing white as Chaos worked through him. A soft click echoed down the hallway, and the doors swung wide. Beyond them lay a familiar room, the walls covered with shelves, each one loaded with labeled antique boxes. It reminded me a little of the nursery we'd just left, though there were no biting plants here, only whispering Grimoires that had a nasty habit of sucking me in.

I made it my goal to ignore the allure of the boxed Grimoires, up on their forbidden shelf, as we crossed to the far side of the room and pulled down a waxy scroll—the same one we'd used to discover who was letting the gargoyles out of the Bestiary.

"Diamond powder, mercury, wolfsbane root, dried cypress leaves, ground yellow jasper, feathered serpent's venom… yep, this is the one," I said, my eyes continually drawn to the Grimoires. The last time I'd been in this room, I'd almost read one of the spells aloud. Something about a "Dragon's Kiss," if memory served me right. I still had no idea what I might have done if I'd finished reading it out loud, since Garrett had stopped me. *I guess that's one thing I can thank the guy for.*

Wade sifted through a small box that sat beside the scroll on the dusty shelf. With a smile, he untied the label and handed it to me: *Keep out. No, really… keep out. Love, Astrid. P.S. If you ever need to use this stuff again, please be careful. Please. Okay, thanks. Try not to hurt yourselves.*

"Always looking out for us." I chuckled, handing it back. "So, what's the damage?"

He lifted out each item, one at a time. "We've got everything except the dried cypress leaves, the wolfsbane, and the mercury. There's enough powder left, and half a vial of Quetzi's venom, so at least we won't have to go bothering Tobe again."

"Is that stuff easy to get?"

"It is, if you know where to look." He grinned wolfishly and put the box back up on the shelf. "We're not usually supposed to get supplies outside the coven repositories, but it's all available. Plus, it's not like we're trying to get our hands on super rare stuff."

I laughed. "No, ironically that's the stuff we've already got."

"Precisely," he said, a mischievous glint in his deep green eyes. "So, grab your jacket, Merlin—we've got places to be."

NINE

Harley

Wade parked his Jeep in the parking lot of the Maritime Museum and killed the engine. It was still a bit of a walk to the secret entrance of Waterfront Park's magical underworld, but there was nowhere closer to leave the car. Torrential rain hammered the windshield. I wasn't looking forward to getting drenched in ten seconds flat.

"So what, we make a run for it?" I asked.

"Looks like it."

On the count of three, I flung open the Jeep door and slammed it behind me, before tearing off down the street. Rain battered against me as I sprinted down West Ash Street, on the south side of Waterfront Park. The park was empty of the usual parents and toddlers, the playground shining in the downpour. *See, I was right—really freaking creepy.* I half expected a terrifying clown to appear in the shadows of the distant trees, holding up a red balloon and telling me I'd float too. It was definitely the weather for it.

Edging around the unsettling holes of the city's storm drains, I sprinted until I reached the glass refuge by the bus stop. Wade ran up a moment later, his open jacket and shirt soaked through and his hair dripping. It was impossible not to stare at the ripple of lean muscles beneath the drenched fabric. My gaze jolted away as I realized I'd been staring a couple minutes too long, prompting a smirk to tug at his lips.

"I don't mind you looking," he said.

"I wasn't," I shot back. "I was just worried one of your nipples might put my eye out."

A laugh erupted from the back of his throat, and I turned around, leading the way down the staircase toward the supposed public restroom. *"Aperi Portam,"* I muttered, then pushed through the door.

I didn't think I'd ever get over the awe-inspiring gateway between the real world and this hidden underworld, which sat right on top of Waterfront Park, completely secret from the humans. Ahead lay the main "strip," the whole place laid out like a mall, with impressive steel-and-glass cubes on either side, forming the pathway itself. Even though it was dark out, I could still see the fairytale glow of the city in the near distance, visible through the interdimensional windows that lined the far wall of every shop and bar and restaurant. Above us, the storm clouds continued to swell, like rising waves on a turbulent ocean.

"You know, we could've come in through the Maritime entrance," Wade said, as our feet squelched on the smooth, pale gray floor.

I shot him a look. "Now you tell me?"

"I tried to before, but you'd already jumped out of the car."

Ignoring him, I pressed on down the main path, peering into the shop windows and admiring the beautiful displays. Most of the stores were closed for the day, but the bars and cafés were just getting into full swing. We passed Moll Dyer's, my eyes drawn to the pretty gold cursive letters that ran across the lintel. The Rag Team had taken me there during my first week at the coven, and the good memories rushed back as I admired the cute terrace. Passing the

Black Crow, however, my thoughts turned suddenly to Finch—this tracer spell seemed to be giving me a nasty case of déjà vu.

Shrugging it off, I carried on walking, letting Wade take the lead. He appeared to know where we were going. However, halfway down one of the side paths, I almost skidded to a halt as my eyes found the familiar name of Cabot's Esprit Reliquary. I remembered the promise I'd made to myself, to investigate the bracelet on Imogene's forearm. If anyone knew about an object like that, it had to be Cabot.

"What's up?" Wade asked, walking back toward me.

"Nothing, I just need to have a quick look in here," I replied, stepping up to the door. I pushed on the handle, only to find it locked. The lights inside were dim, protection charms glowing faintly in the gloom.

"Looks like they've closed up for the day."

I cast him a withering look while I moved away from the door and continued down the path. "You don't say."

"What did you want from there, anyway?" he asked.

"I just wanted to browse, see what they had. There's a ton of cool things in there." I stopped mid-step. "Where are we going, anyway? This is just a dead-end." I gestured to a set of doors up ahead, an emergency exit sign glowing red above it.

"Haven't you learned anything about magicals?" He kept on walking until he reached the emergency exit. Gripping the bar, he muttered something under his breath. A moment later, the bar gave way, the door opening onto a whole other section of Waterfront Park without setting off any kind of alarm. Puzzled, I followed him through.

There were no interdimensional windows here, only what appeared to be an empty maintenance room with a bunch of coolant pipes and six manhole covers in the ground. Dumpsters lined the back wall, a rotten aroma that made my nose wrinkle drifting off them.

"Dennehy's World of Wonders," Wade announced, pointing to one of the manhole covers.

"Sounds like a bad sideshow."

He grinned. "Nope, but it's the place we need. Come on." He lifted the cover and held it open for me. Trying to ignore the still-wet fabric of his t-shirt, knowing it made me look like a total perv, I squeezed past him and clambered down into the dank space. A ladder led into the pitch-blackness below. Figuring that was where we were supposed to go, I began my descent.

Suddenly, the darkness dissipated. A wide platform sat below me, a bright light guiding me as I jumped off and landed with a thud on solid ground. Waiting for Wade, I walked over to the central balustrade and looked down. Vertigo hit me like a brick. *I shouldn't have done that.* A spiral staircase twisted down the center of an impossibly tall room, bringing to mind the interior of a very weird, inverted lighthouse. Bright orbs in jeweled hues hung in clusters from every available space, each one glowing with rainbow light that cast a shard of color downward, creating a kaleidoscope of illumination. Balconies ran along the edge of every floor, while three or four doorways branched off from each level.

And absolutely everywhere—leaving me pretty freaking overwhelmed—was covered in boxes and cubbies and shelves, filled to bursting with weird and wonderful items.

A moment later, Wade joined me. He looked antsy, and I could feel the concern churning inside him. *Well, well, well, it looks like Mr. Goody Two-Shoes is breaking some rules.*

"We're supposed to find cypress leaves, wolfsbane, and mercury in *here*? Don't you have a grocery store for all this stuff?" I whispered, fearing a salesperson might suddenly pop out from one of the million boxes.

He nodded. "There is one in Waterfront Park, but they scan your

ID when you buy it. It'll show up on the coven logs, and I thought it would be best if nobody knew what we were up to."

"Look at you, being a rebel for once."

He scowled. "Can you not? I feel bad enough about it as it is."

I chuckled and turned back to the immense space. "You realize we have to get this spell done pretty quick, right? I don't have two years to go sifting through all this crap."

He nodded. "Relax, there's a knack to it. I've been here a few times before, to help out a couple of desperate friends."

"You better have that knack, or I'm out of here," I replied. "I'd rather sneak into the repository than look through every box in this place. Jeez, have you seen how far this goes?" I gazed right down to the bottom, feeling a bit sick at the thought of heading down there.

"I do, don't worry." He set off toward the wrought-iron staircase, the whole thing juddering under his weight. *Well, isn't that comforting?*

I followed him down, glancing at as many objects as possible. It was pretty fascinating, once I got over the initial shock of seeing so much stuff piled everywhere. There were rooms and rooms full of it, the whole place crammed to the rafters. How anyone could find anything in here was beyond me, but I figured it was probably a good laugh to spend time in here, uncovering hidden gems.

On the fourth floor down, I paused in front of a small cubbyhole that had been cut into the wall of the shop. A single ring sat on a scarlet cushion inside it. Getting a closer look, I realized the ring resembled a claddagh—a symbolic ring, shaped like two hands holding a heart, with a crown on top. I'd heard about them a while ago and knew they were popular in Irish culture. This one was similar, though the heart was cut from a ruby, and instead of two hands, two arrows had been carved into the silver band.

A small label stood next to it: *The Matchmaker. Point it at the one you love. If sparks fly, give them a try. If they do not, leave them to rot.*

I couldn't help myself—they'd put the energy into making a rhyme and everything. Reaching out for the ring, I slipped it onto my middle finger and admired it in the dancing light of the bazaar. The ruby was beautiful, the facets glinting this way and that.

"Harley, I found us some dried cypress leaves," Wade said, brandishing a clear bag of withered foliage.

I turned in his direction, startled by his voice. Before I could say a word, a mini-explosion erupted from my middle finger, bright red sparks darting out of the ruby. Clamping my other hand over it in a vain attempt to stop the miniature fireworks display, I winced as the tiny sparks singed my palm.

"What was that?" Wade asked.

"Nothing!" Turning around, I tore off the ring and stuffed it back onto its cushion. *I guess that answers that question.*

"Seriously, what was that?" He stepped toward me, undeterred.

"Nothing, honestly." Blushing furiously, I shoved him back down the stairs, praying he hadn't gotten close enough to read the label. "Come on, we don't have any time to waste on silly trinkets. We still have to find wolfsbane and mercury."

As I trailed Wade down to the tenth floor—or negative tenth—of the lighthouse, a figure burst out of a doorway to the right, almost colliding with the two of us. She froze in an expression of panic, hurriedly putting her hands behind her back before Wade or I could see what she was buying. In the seconds that ticked by, a silent understanding passed between the three of us. *If you're out here, we already know you're buying something you shouldn't be. We're in the same boat. If you don't say anything, neither will we.*

"Preceptor Bellmore, what an unexpected pleasure," Wade said, breaking the tension.

"Yes… an unexpected pleasure," she replied stiffly. Her big, peculiar amber eyes glanced over Wade's shoulder, evidently looking for the exit. The tattoos on her neck and face shifted, revealing the nervous clench of her jaw. With her being a Shapeshifter, I couldn't read her emotions, but I didn't need to be an Empath to know she was keeping a secret—and a big one at that. It was written all over her face. *I mean, come on, could you look any guiltier?*

Weirdest of all was that fact that Preceptor Bellmore was normally coolheaded, walking around the coven in her black clothes and heavy leathers, with her chic blond buzzcut and her no-bull attitude. It was almost scary to see her so rattled. I hadn't thought it possible, but something was definitely keeping her up at night. Judging from the bruised bags under Bellmore's eyes, she hadn't slept in days.

"What brings you out here to Dennehy's World of Wonders?" Wade pressed.

She shrugged, regaining a sliver of composure. "Just a personal project. Preceptor Gracelyn was out of a couple of things, so I thought I'd pick them up here instead of waiting around for the order to come in. You know how it is." She looked to Wade, as though he might understand.

"They didn't have what you needed at the store?" Wade replied.

I stared at him. *Playing with fire much? Pot... kettle... black?*

"I needed something to go with the ingredients that the store didn't have. I thought Dennehy's might have it." Her eyes held a warning. If we told, so would she.

I frowned. "Are you okay, Preceptor? I don't mean to be blunt, or rude, but you don't look too peachy."

"I'm a little stressed over the newly implemented charms that Alton wants put all around the coven, but that's all. Nothing I can't handle, don't you worry," she said coolly. "How about you? How are you feeling?"

"The same."

"Anything I can help you with?" she asked, nodding to the bag of greenery that Wade clutched in his hand. It had other leaves aside from cypress—a kind of foliage free-for-all—which I hoped would put her off the scent.

I shook my head. "Just a bit of research into building a basic dreamcatcher. It seems pretty straightforward. Nothing too tricky."

Sloane Bellmore was a preceptor, but that didn't mean we could trust her. I had no way of knowing whether Alton had told the preceptors about finding Jacob and Isadora, and I wasn't about to risk a security breach. Plus, with her being a Shapeshifter, I couldn't read her to try and figure out if she was trustworthy or not. For now, we'd have to accept that we were lying to each other.

"Well, good luck with that. I really ought to be getting back to the coven." She paused, arching an eyebrow. "You two should probably think about doing the same. With the threat of Katherine looming over all of us, Alton is tightening security. I wouldn't be surprised if he puts a curfew in place soon enough."

"Thank you, Preceptor Bellmore," Wade said. "I hope everything goes well with… whatever your personal project is."

Without another word, she hurried up the lighthouse stairs and disappeared into a room at the top. A few minutes later, she reemerged, making her way out of the shop by climbing up through the manhole tunnel, with a small paper bag tucked under one arm.

"Weird," I muttered.

"Very weird."

"Anyway, we should probably get our stuff and go."

Wade nodded. "Give me five minutes, and I'll meet you back upstairs. It'll probably be easier if I grab everything we need."

"Agreed." As he continued down the spiral staircase, I turned around and hurried back up.

Ten minutes later, we were headed up the rickety ladder with a parcel full of wolfsbane root, dried cypress leaves, and a new vial of mercury. Making our way back through the dingy maintenance room, we passed a few shady-looking characters lurking in the shadows of the coolant pipes. There were no words written on any of the manhole covers and no labels to indicate what any of the other places were, but my interest was piqued.

"What's down the other holes?" I asked, as we made our way back through into the main body of Waterfront Park. This time, I let Wade lead us toward the Maritime Museum exit, rather than taking the long way around and risking a second soaking.

"A casino, a couple of dive bars, another shop that sells contraband," he replied. "I wouldn't advise going there again, unless you *really* need something without the preceptors or Alton knowing about it. Which you shouldn't really be doing anyway—neither should I, for that matter, but this is an exceptional set of circumstances. A whatever-means-necessary sort of deal." I could tell he was trying to talk himself out of his guilt. It swirled in his stomach, making him pale.

I flashed him a smile. "Noted."

Exiting the doorway that led straight out into the Maritime Museum's parking lot, we sprinted the last couple yards to Wade's Jeep and hopped in with barely a drenching. I set the box on my lap and pulled my seatbelt across my chest as we pulled out of the parking lot and merged onto the main road.

I turned the heat on full blast and glanced at Wade. "For your nipples."

He laughed shyly. "They thank you for your kind gesture."

"Don't mention it."

In a curious bubble of contentment, with the rain lashing down against the car, we headed for the coven, and the spell that would hopefully lead us to Jacob and Isadora.

Back in the familiarity of the Luis Paoletti Room, Wade and I gathered around one of the small tables with our ingredients spread out across the splintering surface. My heart thundered in my chest as Wade delved into one of the bottom drawers and pulled out his trusty wooden bowl and kitchen scale. When performing this particular spell, everything had to be exact. A single gram off, and the whole thing could explode… quite literally.

"Are you sure the last email you got from Jacob hinted that they were still in California?" Wade asked. "If not, we're in for a hell of a night."

I nodded. "They're definitely somewhere in California. The emails are never detailed, but I can get bits and pieces from them."

"Okay then. You ready?"

"Yep, I'm warmed up and ready to run like hell, or drive like the devil, when that spark goes off."

He smiled. "Me, too."

"Okay, so we need twenty grams of diamond powder and thirteen of the jasper," I said. Silently, he weighed out what remained from last time, before tipping the correct amounts into the wooden bowl using a silver spoon. The sparkling powders merged, white and yellow, creating a sandy mixture at the bottom of the bowl.

"Do you remember why we only use silver spoons for mixing ingredients?" he asked.

I frowned. "Ah, I know this one… something to do with binding agents? They act like binding agents, to avoid bad stuff happening?"

"More or less," he said, chuckling. "Now, how many cypress leaves?"

"Three." Plucking three from the mixed bag, he dropped them into the bowl. They were already dried, needing no help from his Fire power. "And then, five drops of mercury and nine drops of venom."

"Five drops of mercury and nine drops of venom," Wade muttered back to himself.

Using a pipette, he measured the exact ingredients and added them to the mixture. He glanced at the waxy scroll and picked up the silver spoon, using it to stir the ingredients three times counter-clockwise, then five times clockwise. As he made the movements, my memories of the last tracer spell came rushing back. Finch was becoming a frequent fixture in my head these days, and I didn't like it. He refused to speak about his mother, the brainwashing running deep, but unless he could give us some kind of info on her, he was of no use whatsoever. *I just have to break you... make you see what a monster she is. But how?*

"Harley?" Wade's voice broke my distant train of thought.

"Sorry, what's next?"

He pointed to the bracelet. "I'm going to put the bracelet on top of the mixture and then cover it with three spoonfuls of the stuff, moving the spoon from the left. I'll chant the spell once it's covered."

"Okay, I'll be ready."

He took in a breath, before covering the bracelet with the concoction. *"O, filia luna, cum venenum sanguinem, da mihi oculos, sic ego can reperio dominus hoc obiectum,"* he chanted, his rings lighting up red.

As I stared into the bowl, the shimmer of the mixture intensified, spreading out until it enveloped the bracelet entirely. The rest of the ingredients dissolved into a subtle, rusty-red mass, while the bracelet lay below, as clean as it had been when we'd put it in there. Finch's spark had been green, but this one was copper in color. *What does that mean?* I wondered as I braced my legs to sprint.

Without warning, the spark shot up and darted out of the door. I sprinted after it with Wade in hot pursuit, both of us hurtling down the labyrinth of hallways and out of the coven's front entrance. Fortunately, with it being so late and so grim outside, most people had retreated to their bedrooms for the night, leaving the corridors empty and collision-free.

Outside the Fleet Science Center doors, the reddish spark lingered in the air for a moment, as though sniffing out the location of the bracelet's owner. It zipped this way and that, visibly figuring out its next move. I wondered if it had something to do with Jacob's skillset, confusing the spark for a little while as it scented out the pathway that he and Isadora had taken between wormholes. It recovered quickly, zipping away with renewed certainty. However, the brief hesitation gave Wade and me the split second we needed to jump into Daisy, who was waiting on the curb, before we tore after the bright light with a skid of wheels on asphalt.

There was no way of knowing how far away Jacob and Isadora were. All we could do was follow the spark as it guided us away from the coven and into the unknown.

TEN

Santana

Hours had passed since Raffe first turned, and I still couldn't wrap my head around the djinn's full manifestation. I'd joked about it being like Jekyll and Hyde before, but I'd had no idea how close to the truth that was. The djinn shared the same body as Raffe, but I was surprised at how clear its personality was. It was like two distinct people for the price of one. Either that, or I'd been around the *diablo* for so long that I was finding nuances in its character. Whatever the case, keeping up was a chore.

"Are you still here?" the djinn barked, his eyes glowing red. Black smoke puffed from his red-tinged shoulders, his face twisting up in a nasty grimace.

"I'm not going anywhere," I replied for the millionth time. "I'm staying here until Raffe comes back again."

"You'll be in for a long wait, then. What if he never comes back?" The djinn laughed darkly. I didn't like the warning in his voice.

"Shut up," I shot back. "If you even attempt to take over Raffe's body, you'll have me to deal with. You don't scare me, with your smoky wisps and your glowy red eyes. *El Diablo* is part of my culture, you jumped-up gremlin, and I've seen worse than you rolling out of the bars on Día de los Muertos."

The djinn paused. "Where did mousy little Raffe find the balls to charm a girl like you, eh? How'd he snag such a divine specimen? It's not every sexy vixen who'd sit at a man's prison, staring right into the darkest parts of him without flinching."

I cast him a withering look. He stared right back, his red eyes flickering with a rush of blue light.

An explosion of bat-like creatures erupted from the depths of the djinn's body, each one slamming into the side of the box before bursting into violent blasts of black light. I staggered back, a scream slipping from my mouth. If even a single sliver of the djinn's energy got through the glass box, there'd be trouble. Fortunately, it held the demon's fierce power.

My heart might never recover, though, you sly asshole—nobody scares me like that and gets away with it.

"Hmm… maybe you do flinch," the djinn mocked, cackling.

"Yeah, if you hurl a thousand bats at a person, they'll flinch, you arrogant asshat!"

"Temper, temper." His eyes stayed a glowing blue. *If red means angry, does blue mean amused?* I was still figuring him out when another ball of crackling energy hit the sides of the box. A shimmering pulse flared along the edges, pausing at the veiled gaps in the exterior in an attempt to push through. I let out a huge sigh of relief as the cage continued to hold. *Nice try.*

"Can you stop now? Seems like a waste of energy to me."

"You worried about me burning out your main squeeze?" He walked up to the glass and leered through, his eyes shifting back to red. "He thinks he can push me down, squashing me into all the extra bits of himself. Do you know what happens when you have to sit in the dark for weeks on end, waiting for a moment to catch your true breath?"

"No, I don't."

"It makes you angry," he hissed. "And not just angry… furious. Hatred builds up inside your veins like adrenaline, and when you get that sliver of freedom, out it pours! A molten stream of pure loathing." He snapped elongated fangs at me and smashed his hands into the glass. Another silvery shimmer rippled over the edges, attempting to seep into the runes like an elaborate lock-pick. Once again, the cage held.

I glowered at him. "Seriously, you need to stop banging on the glass. What, do you want me to feel sympathy for you? Give me a break. You share *his* body, not the other way around."

The djinn grinned. "I really hope you're still around when I break out of this cage. You've got this strange way of making me feel calm —all I have to do is picture my hands around your throat, squeezing so tight your skin bulges and your eyes pop out, and I instantly relax. So very soothing."

I refused to give this demon the satisfaction of seeing me frightened. Although, to be honest, he was starting to get to me a little bit. I'd never seen any creature, of the human or spirit world, that held as much malice and violence in its heart. Hatred poured out of this demon in waves. I didn't need to be an Empath to feel it. He wanted to do everyone and everything harm—I saw it in the shadows of his shifting eyes.

"My Orishas would kick your ass if you even tried it, pal."

He turned his back and leaned up against the glass. I preferred being able to see his face.

"Have you ever felt the sweet sadness of an Orisha's energy being devoured?" he asked casually, weaving an orb of raw, golden energy between his palms. The smoke billowing off him plumed thicker.

I cleared my throat. "No."

"There is no sensation like it. It's like electricity in your veins, awakening each cell, bringing everything to life in the most astounding way," he said. "And you are brimming with them. I can almost taste them on my tongue." He licked his lips, laughing softly.

He walked into the middle of the cage and gathered the smoke around himself, filling the interior with it. No matter how hard I squinted into the damn thing, I could no longer see him padding around. *Better the devil you can see...* Checking the gaps in the cage wall, I breathed a nervous sigh of relief that not a single wisp of smoke managed to get through. This was all just a game, for the djinn to amuse himself.

He thundered toward the glass and crashed into the wall with all his might. An enormous explosion went off around him. Flames erupted from the sparks, licking toward the ceiling of the box, growing taller and more volatile by the second. I could feel the heat through the barrier.

"Help me..." the djinn begged, pressing its palms to the wall. "Don't let me burn alive."

I stared at the demon, aghast. "This is just some stupid trick. Stop it, now!"

"If I burn, Raffe burns."

Can Raffe survive this? With the fierce heat radiating out, nipping at my skin, I wasn't so sure. Then again, I had major doubts that the djinn would burn its host alive. After all, for the time being, the djinn needed Raffe more than Raffe needed the djinn.

"You're bluffing," I said, folding my arms across my chest.

"Are you willing to take that risk?"

"Stop it, okay? You've had your fun. I'm very impressed. Yadda yadda yadda."

Through the thick smoke, the djinn's face started to melt. *Raffe's* face started to melt. It trickled down from his skull like red wax against a candle, dripping from his jawline onto the floor. Everything started to slide across bone. I jumped away from the cage, screaming at the top of my lungs. The only problem was, nobody would come to my aid—this room was soundproofed. I howled like a banshee as I lunged forward again, beating at the glass until my hands stung from the blistering heat.

"LEAVE HIM ALONE!"

Like time moving backward, the smoke drew itself into the djinn's body, the flames receding, the melted contours of Raffe's face sliding back into place, until all that remained was the demon. He stood there smugly, in one piece.

"No need to get your panties in a twist, my exotic beauty. Haven't you ever heard of an illusion before?" He cackled, clearly enjoying my panicked screams. "You should have seen your face. I shall dine on that for weeks to come, when Raffe shoves me back into the darkness. Soothing *and* amusing—you're quite the package."

"Piss off!" I snapped, struggling to recover a normal heartbeat. *I'm going to need a whole lot of therapy after seeing* that. Getting the image of a sliding face and melting skin out of my head was going to be impossible. I guessed that was the point.

"Raffe can't keep me down for much longer," the djinn went on. "I'm stronger than I used to be, and he's getting weaker by the year. Not that he could get rid of me, even if he wanted to. We've been together since birth, fused at the core. He and I have grown up together. Sweet, really, if you think about it. Aside from all the unfortunate little flare-ups." He flashed me a grin. "That little girl never stole our toy trucks again, though. Hard to pick something up when you don't have hands."

I gaped at him. "You're lying."

"Maybe. Maybe not."

"Why do you want to get out, anyway? I know you say you hate Raffe, but the two of you must have shared a lot. You both probably have some kind of mutual respect for one another, after a lifetime together," I said, in a vain attempt to soften him up. Demons liked to talk about themselves; they were selfish to a fault. I once let an *El*

Cuco talk about himself for so long that the sun came up and chased him away.

He shrugged. "We're so used to each other now that we despise one another. He liked me when we were kids. I let him get away with naughty things. He doesn't like that so much these days. Although, if he let me out for just an hour or two every day, I could get away with some other naughty things… if you catch my drift?" He winked, his red eyes turning blue.

"I don't think so," I replied. "How did you two end up together in the first place? You don't see djinns too often anymore."

"The boy wonder hasn't told you?"

I shook my head. *Keep him talking. Keep him talking until Raffe comes back.*

"Raffe's birth happened on a very special day," the djinn began sarcastically. "His… or, rather, *our* mother was a tremendously powerful woman. A little too powerful for her own good. On the day she gave birth to Raffe, the pain of labor happened to bring on a Purge. I was expelled as a monster, but I lingered in the womb—staying small and secret—until my energy fused with that of the baby. Raffe came out all pink and bawling, with me attached to him on the deepest cellular level." He grinned, evidently proud. "Our mother died, but what else can you expect? It's not easy pushing out a djinn."

I quickly covered my horror at his casual words about Raffe's mom. "You can't leave him, then?"

"A small price to pay for being able to wander around, instead of being shoved in a glass box." He gazed up at the enclosure. "I realize the irony, but at least I get to see some of the world. There are others of my kind who aren't so lucky. They're chased and destroyed, or put in charmed boxes. Raffe and I can't be separated. We're bros." He chuckled to himself.

"What would happen if someone tried to separate you?"

He arched an eyebrow. "You getting some ideas in that pretty little head of yours?"

"No, I'm just interested."

"A separation would kill him. I might survive, but Raffe would die." He seemed to delight over every word, his glowing eyes darkening to jet-black shadows, before flickering blue again. Anything remotely evil thrilled him. *I bet you squat in Raffe all day, every day, thinking up ways of harming people.* I'd already heard a few colorful examples.

"Would you want to hurt him?"

The djinn paused, his eyes glowing a brighter blue as he looked at me. I figured he was getting used to me or something, because I hadn't seen the red in a while. The scarlet of his skin faded, and the smoke dispersed. Raffe was coming back to me.

"Raffe?" I murmured. He nodded slowly, as though it hurt to move. Eager to help him back into the real world, I approached the box and put my hand through the hole by the door. The forcefield surrounding the box allowed people to reach through, but didn't allow anything—spells or smoke or otherwise—to leave. Before I could react, his hand shot out and grasped my wrist, yanking my arm farther through the hole. His skin turned scarlet again in the blink of an eye. My body thudded into the solid glass pane, a shiver of pain snaking up my arm as he twisted my wrist in a way bones weren't meant to go. He cackled maniacally, pulling harder. Raffe was still buried deep—the djinn had tricked me. I knew how strong djinns were. He was going easy on me, taking his time, savoring my fear as we stared at one another through the glass.

He froze, his expression changing at a rapid pace. The red color faded from his skin, the smoke dissipating, the light going out in his eyes. He staggered back, releasing my wrist and gripping his stomach. A moment later, Raffe came back to me. He looked up at me with his midnight eyes while his chest heaved with the exertion of pushing the djinn back.

"You have to be more careful, Santana," he gasped. "We're fused together, but he keeps some of his thoughts hidden from me. There's a dark room in the back of our mind that I can't reach. I'm not allowed in… He's dangerous. Really dangerous. As in, potentially deadly."

He gripped his stomach harder as the red tone reappeared, spreading out over his skin with a flurry of black smoke. When Raffe lifted his head again, I knew the djinn had returned. He hadn't had enough of me yet. I rolled my eyes at him, annoyed by his persistence. Clearly, when Raffe relinquished control, the djinn became even more temperamental, battling for superiority.

"Well, that was unfortunate," the djinn rasped. "I was just starting to have fun. That's the thing about Raffe—he's a perpetual killjoy. He could rule the world if he would just let me have my way for a while. The boy has so much potential because of me. Instead, he keeps me locked up, or turns me loose every couple of months when he needs some added pizazz."

I almost burst out laughing. "Pizazz?"

"Yeah, like rounding up gargoyles. I can't say that wasn't a hoot, but it's frankly offensive that he only lets me out when he needs something." He pouted dramatically. "All he does is use me. But do I ever get a whisper of thanks? No."

I stared at him in disbelief. I hadn't known Raffe could change so quickly, and it terrified me. He hadn't been able to control the djinn, to stop it from taking over his body again. Did that mean he really *was* getting weaker? I hoped not. After all, there was no easy way to separate the two of them, if things started getting out of hand. But, if Raffe didn't manage to find a way to permanently subdue the djinn, I had a feeling he'd end up in a glass box in the Bestiary. It would be the only way to keep him, and others, safe. Right now, this semi-peaceful coexistence was just about the only thing keeping the djinn under control—as long as it remained mutually beneficial in some small way.

Still, I sensed that the djinn was scheming a way out. Given all that time he had to think about things, stuck inside Raffe's head, it was inevitable that he would eventually come up with something. *Oh, Raffe...*

"I'm sure he's grateful for your strength," I said, keeping him sweet. "I know it's gotten us out of a scrape or two."

"You'd think so, but he's never breathed a word of gratitude," the djinn retorted. "He's never even given me a name. Can you believe that? Would you be happy, walking around this earth with no name? It's rude. It makes me feel like an object. A thing." A note of genuine annoyance rose in his strange voice. "A nameless djinn! Whoever heard of such a thing? Even our worst enemies wouldn't leave us nameless, but Raffe refuses to give me one. What does that make him, huh?"

"Is that why you've been acting up lately?" I asked. Raffe had been struggling more than usual, and it felt like I was getting to the root cause. Demons were notoriously proud creatures. The fact that he had no name probably burned him up inside... more than usual.

He scowled at his reflection. "I've asked Raffe for a name. I told him I'd behave more if he'd just give me a name, but he keeps saying that he won't."

"You don't deserve a name," Raffe's voice suddenly cut in.

The djinn growled in the back of his throat. "I do. Everyone deserves a name. You said you'd give me a name when we were kids, but you never did. Old Daddio stopped you every time."

"You can't just torment me because I won't give you what you want," Raffe's voice chimed through.

"Of course I can. In fact, that's my plan—to annoy you until you give in. I'm tired of not having a name. It's embarrassing."

Raffe appeared. "Well, what name do you want?" His tone was reluctant.

"That's not how it works, and you know it," the djinn spat back. "*You* need to name me, you lazy idiot. You can't leave *all* the heavy-lifting to me."

"Then what else are you good for?"

I stepped up to the glass. "Hey, calm down, both of you. Why don't you make a couple of suggestions, Raffe, and see if he likes them?"

"Yeah, do as the nice lady says," the djinn mocked.

"How about… Cyrus?"

"No way."

"Paolo?"

"Really?"

"Harold?"

"Oh, come on, now you're just messing with me." The djinn folded his arms across his chest.

I smiled. "How about Kadar?"

The djinn turned to me. "Kadar?"

"It means 'powerful' in Arabic," I replied.

"I know what it means, smartass. I just didn't expect you to suggest such a name. Or know a lick of Arabic." A grin spread across his face. "I like it. Kadar… Yes, Kadar will do nicely. Thank you, Santana. At least one of you has some compassion."

With that, he disappeared inside Raffe, allowing my adorable sweet-cheeks to return to the surface. He shook out his body, as though attempting to fling every fiber of the djinn out of his muscles.

"Is he gone?" I asked.

"For now," Raffe said. "I think you made him happy. He's content at the moment."

"You can feel that?"

He nodded. "Right now, it's like I've got a cat curled up in my chest, snoozing on a warm window ledge."

"You know, you should have given him a name a long time ago," I chided.

"How come?"

"Don't you know that names have power? If you know the djinn's name, that gives you greater control over it."

"Yeah, I've heard that, but my dad has always worried a name would somehow give the djinn *more* power," Raffe muttered. "I wasn't willing to risk it."

I wondered if Leonidas had an ulterior motive in preventing Raffe from controlling the djinn, but that was a whole can of worms I didn't want to open. "Are you safe to come out?"

"I am. The key is in the bowl over there, if you want to do the honors?"

I hurried over to the bowl and took out the key, before bringing it back and freeing Raffe from his prison. Hours had passed, and a sudden wave of exhaustion crashed into me. If the djinn had taken this kind of a toll on me, what must've poor Raffe ended up feeling every time?

"I'm sorry if I said anything... rude," he said, dipping his head. "I have no control over what the djinn says or does when he's in the box, especially in cases like today. Nothing sets him off like an argument with my father. Now that I think about it, he's probably pissed that my dad kept me from giving him a name all these years."

"Well, you're okay now, and that's all that matters," I assured him. "Oh, and the djinn has a filthy mouth, but I won't hold it against you. I know it wasn't you speaking."

"I think the only thing we agree on is how much we hate Leonidas Levi," he said. "You know, he was supposed to be a father to me, but, to this day, he still blames me for my mom's death. He blames us both—the djinn and me."

"I'm sorry, Raffe." I took his hand in mine and held it tight.

"Maybe he's right. She did die in childbirth, after all."

I shook my head. "That wasn't your fault. Nobody could have seen something like that coming. It was a tragic, terrible coincidence." My voice grew steely. "The only person your father needs to forgive is himself, for not taking care of you the way your mother would have wanted. He let her down, and he let *you* down. He's the only one who should be sorry."

ELEVEN

Harley

Daisy sped along the coastal highway, the Pacific raging to her left. Rain pounded relentlessly at the windshield while the wipers worked overtime. They were practically screeching. *Eek-eek. Eek-eek.* The spark from the tracer spell had taken Wade and me out of San Diego's city limits, toward Carlsbad.

Suddenly, the spark cut to the right, forcing us to swerve and drive inland. The radio dipped in and out of a country music channel, a mournful voice singing through the speakers about lost love and futile hopes.

"Where the hell is this thing going?" Wade muttered, clinging to the door handle for dear life.

"Who knows," I replied. "Texas, Alaska, Timbuktu?"

"Let's hope not."

A short while later, we passed the perimeter of McClellan-Palomar Airport, red lights blinking from the air-traffic control towers. No planes seemed to be taking off in this weather. Speeding along Airport Road, we turned in to the small settlement of Bressi

Ranch, a sleepy little village bordering the airport. I'd never been here before, and it looked kind of creepy in the driving rain.

The spark hovered for a moment at the intersection of Poinsettia Lane before darting across and leading up a dirt track. With no traffic on the road, I shot through a red light and followed it up and over a shrub-covered hill, desperate to keep the rusty light in our line of sight. If we lost it, we'd be screwed.

After five minutes, the spark stopped again, right in front of a solitary house. Whitewashed walls surrounded a quaint house with a Spanish villa feel. A dim glow shone from the front window, though the rest of the building was steeped in darkness.

"This has to be it." I killed the engine, hoping they hadn't heard us approach. If they ran, I was going to be pissed.

We got out and hurried for the porch, both of us soaked to the skin by the time we reached it. *Not again... At this rate, I'm going to need a week to thaw out.*

I knocked on the door, following the disappearing tail of the glimmering spark. A shout of alarm rose up from inside. I guessed the spark had found its mark, singeing poor Jacob the way it had done with Finch.

I knocked again. "Isadora? Jacob? If you're in there, please don't run! It's Harley."

Everything fell silent.

A few moments later, the door creaked open. Jacob stood on the other side, rubbing a burn mark on his forehead. A lopsided, slightly pained grin turned up the corner of his lips. "What was that?" he asked, a streak of soot smearing onto his fingertips.

"Tracer spell," I replied. "It was the only way we could track you down. Anyone would think the two of you were trying to hide from something." I flashed him a grin.

"Are you going to leave us out here in the rain, or will you let us come inside?" Wade chimed in, shaking out the edge of his sodden jacket.

Jacob stepped back. "Sure, come in. I managed to stop Isadora from jumping through a portal—you scared the living daylights out of us."

I shrugged. "Yeah, sorry about that."

"You shouldn't be here," Isadora said, stepping out of the shadows of the small living room. "Why have you come? I told you not to follow us. I told you I needed to keep Jacob and myself safe, which would mean staying away from you for a while."

I looked at her, trying not to feel too disappointed by her dismissive tone. "I know, I know, but things have changed. We need you to come back to the coven."

"No chance." Jacob shook his head vehemently.

"We need your help," I urged.

"It's not safe for us, Harley," Isadora replied. "I told you it wasn't safe. What were you thinking, using a tracer spell to track us down? Anyone might have followed it. Speaking of which, anyone might have followed *you*. Did you make sure nobody was on your tail?"

I pushed down the bristle of irritation that stemmed from both my aunt and me. The two of us had our reasons for feeling annoyed, but it wasn't going to help anyone. I had my orders. They needed to come back with us.

"Nobody followed us," Wade assured her. "I kept an eye on the rearview the entire way, and we made sure to put the tracer spell together in total secrecy. The rest of our group knows that Alton wants you back at the coven, but only Harley and I took part in tracking you. No one else knows we've come here. They're still twiddling their thumbs over how to find you."

"How *did* you find us?" Jacob asked.

"You left a bracelet back at the Smiths' house. I found it under the bed," I replied. I'd been wondering if he'd left it there on purpose, for me to discover. *Guess not.*

He bit his lip. "Sorry, Isadora."

"Don't worry, it's not your fault," she said. "Accidents happen."

I looked to my aunt for some sense that she was happy to see me. All I got were stony, sky-blue eyes and an ashen expression. Anxiety twirled around her in barbed coils. I felt the sting of every single one, the sensation setting my own nerves on edge.

Wade broke the tense beat of silence. "Alton will make sure you're kept hidden. He'll make your presence at the coven a need-to-know kind of deal. He doesn't want Katherine getting her hands on you any more than we do."

"You realize the danger you're putting us in by even standing here right now, don't you?" Isadora sighed and sat down on the armrest of the nearby sofa.

"There are people who need your help," I replied. "*Kids* who need your help."

Jacob stiffened. "You still haven't found them?"

"Nope. I know it'll come as a shocker, but Katherine seems to want them kept out of the way, somewhere only she knows about," I said sarcastically. "Our leads are pretty much dry. Marjorie is the only one that got away, but even she's managing to evade us."

"I know you'll think me cruel for saying it, Harley, but a handful of lives isn't important in the grand scheme of things," Isadora said. "If Katherine captures us, there's a lot more at stake."

I shook my head. "You don't understand. Those children are important to Katherine. They *are* the grand scheme of things. We don't know how Katherine is going to use them, but she targeted them for some reason—an important, unknown reason. That alone should be enough to get you to come back and help us."

"I don't see how we can help."

"Jacob is a Sensate. He can help us pick up the trail again, in a way the rest of us can't. And you—your portal powers can be used to create an escape route, if the worst happens at the coven. Alton needs you both." Tension gripped my muscles in a vise. "Come on, Isadora! We can't let Katherine destroy the lives of these kids. We can't let her use them. If we don't lift a finger to save them, we seal their fate. We might as well fire the shot ourselves!"

In front of me, Jacob's fear and anxiety morphed into defiance.

"It could have been you, Jacob," I said, putting on the pressure. "The only reason you're not wherever those kids are now is because you're a Portal Opener, too. If you hadn't been able to jump through a wormhole to freedom, who knows where you'd be. I know I'm partially responsible for them finding you in the first place, but I'm trying to make amends for that."

"Maybe… maybe we could go back for a little bit?" Jacob said, turning to Isadora. "If what Wade says is right, then no one would even know we were at the coven. We could even ask for certain things beforehand, to make sure we stay under the radar."

Isadora heaved out a sharp breath. "I know you want to help, Jacob. I can understand your reasoning. I feel the same way." She paused, looking at me sadly. "But we can't risk it. If we go back, you'll never be free. The coven will use you as a commodity for the rest of your life. Say yes now, and they will forever pressure you into doing their bidding. This time it's the kids. Next time, they'll find something else to guilt you into helping them. They'll use Harley against you, they'll use me against you, they'll use anything they can to get you to do what they want. Believe me, I know how these places work. I spent enough time as a pawn in one."

"No offense, but nobody is going to use anyone against me, or me against anyone," I said firmly.

She smiled. "I know you wouldn't allow it deliberately, but you may not even know they're doing it. People can be very devious when they want something, and you can't always be around to protect Jacob. You have other duties and responsibilities now. I'm able to protect him in a way you logistically can't at the moment."

"Still... I'd try."

"I know you would."

I wondered what she meant about being a pawn, but this wasn't the time to ask. Jacob's emotions fluctuated rapidly, revealing the heartbreaking truth—he was just a confused teenager who had no idea what to do. Having been through the wringer of foster families myself, just like him, I knew that all he wanted to do was please the people around him. That fear of rejection never went away. All of this was bigger than him, yet he stood in the middle of it, trying to figure out which side to take.

"This is my choice, Isadora," he said quietly. *Atta boy.*

"And I can understand the temptation," Isadora replied gently. "But here's a bit of tough love for you: the reason I've stayed alive and undetected for so long is because I've kept my number of contacts low. I've kept myself to myself. The more people you know, and the more people you let in, the greater the risk of betrayal. There are so few people you can trust in this world as it is, but put a power like ours into the mix and that number dwindles away to almost zero."

"Then come with us," I urged. "Protect him at the coven."

Isadora sighed. "I stand by what I've said. If we go there, we'll be beholden to Alton and the Mage Council. I'm not going to put Jacob through that, and I'm not going to put myself through that."

"Please, Isadora."

"Don't ask me for something I can't give, Harley." Sadness glistened in her eyes.

"We need you."

As she opened her mouth to speak, the front door burst open

behind us. A slew of rain and icy wind whistled in, bringing a shadow with it. I barely had time to move out of the way as a figure barreled into me, knocking me to the side. A bolt of fire surged forward, hitting Isadora. She fell to the ground with a heavy thump as the assailant whirled around to deal with the rest of us.

I gasped in shock. Preceptor Bellmore stood in front of us, gathering balls of flickering flames in her palms.

What the hell? Is Bellmore one of Katherine's goons? All I could say for sure was that the trackers had become the tracked.

"Preceptor Bellmore, stop!" Wade shouted, gathering fire into his own palms.

As a paltry flare whizzed past Wade's shoulder, missing him by at least ten inches, a sudden thought struck me: this couldn't be Preceptor Bellmore. This attacker's powers were different than those of the preceptor of Charms and Hexes, and clearly weaker—I'd seen her in action before.

Wade retaliated quickly, an orb of whirling red energy zipping toward the agent. The fireball struck her full in the arm, halting a second attempt in its tracks. As the smoke swirled upward and the figure yelped in pain, the guise faded for a second. Dark clothes appeared underneath, leading down to a somewhat masculine hand. It was hard to tell if it actually belonged to a man or a woman, but there was something bulkier about it that instantly rang alarm bells.

Jacob scrambled to forge a portal, but the poor guy's hands were shaking and the ripple of terror that flowed off him was overwhelming. It almost threatened to stifle my own survival instincts as I ducked out of the way of a renewed attack.

"Jacob Morales," the disguised agent purred, in Preceptor Bellmore's familiar voice. "We've been looking for you. You're wasting yourself here, boy, all cooped up in this shoebox. You belong with Katherine, just like your parents before you."

Jacob froze. "My… my parents?"

"There's a lot the coven isn't telling you, kid," the agent replied. "Your friends here have been lying to you. Your mother and father were some of Katherine's most trusted soldiers. You have to continue their legacy."

What legacy? I had no idea who Jacob's real parents were, but I hadn't expected they'd be connected to Katherine.

The spark of Jacob's magic died in his hands, the agent's words throwing him off. I could feel the doubt inside him, mingling with confusion and panic. If we wanted to get out of here in one piece, we couldn't rely on his portal-making.

I focused on the imposter, whoever he or she was, and cast a mental lasso through my Telekinesis. It wrapped around the agent's throat, their cheeks reddening as I tightened the noose. With a forceful twist of my hand, I sent the imposter flying against the far wall. It gave us the window of opportunity we needed. They would be on their feet again in a minute.

"Snap out of it!" I barked at Jacob, then lunged forward to grab him by the shoulders. I shook him hard and saw the lucidity flickering back into his eyes. He looked up at me with an expression of bemusement, as though he no longer knew what was going on around him. "We need you! Jacob, make a portal!"

He shook his head, the last glimpse of terror fading away. "Sorry…" He lifted his hands, and a ferocious fork of green-tinged light shot out of his palms, tearing a hole in the fabric of reality. A savage wind howled from the gap in time and space, the portal swirling open before us.

"Let's go!" I roared.

Wade scooped Isadora into his arms, and we hurtled through the portal. It snapped shut behind us. I hit the ground on the other side with a hefty thump, my face colliding with ticklish blades of grass and churned-up mud. I spluttered as I hurried to my feet, trying not to fall on my ass. The others picked themselves off the ground around me, spitting out grass and dirt.

We'd landed on the green expanse of Balboa Park, right in front of the spot where the interdimensional pocket was built. After all of Isadora's complaints, the choice had been taken away from her. She was coming to the San Diego Coven whether she liked it or not. I only wished it could have been on better terms.

TWELVE

Harley

We ran for cover, settling for Wade's Jeep. Only when I saw his car did I remember mine. My sweet Daisy was left behind, outside that solitary house in Bressi Ranch. I was going to retrieve her at some point, though I wondered if she'd still be in one piece. After only just getting Daisy back, it would break my heart all over again to find her a wreck. We'd also left behind a pissed off agent of Katherine's.

Right now, however, I had other things to worry about.

"I should've been able to open that portal," Jacob muttered, as Wade lay Isadora down on the back seat. "I can't believe I messed up like that, after everything Isadora has taught me. I should've been able to focus." Disappointment poured off him, finding its way into my veins.

"Hey, you did your best. We all mess up," I replied, patting him on the back. "It's not easy to make your powers work in high-pressure situations. It could've been a lot worse—you could've made the portal and not been able to control it."

He glanced at me. "She taught me how to make portals in high-pressure situations. She taught me how to control Chaos and make it work for me. She's spent weeks teaching me all of that, and I still screwed up when it mattered."

"Don't be so hard on yourself," Wade said. "It happens. Take Harley, for example. She's good, but she still glitches. She almost killed an entire room of people because she wavered."

I shot him a look. "Thanks for sharing."

"It's the truth. Self-control and determination are key when dealing with Chaos. All the theory in the world, or the practice, won't prepare you for casting spells in the midst of true danger," Wade replied, then raised an eyebrow at Jacob and Isadora. "I doubt Isadora here was literally chasing you around and trying to kill you when she trained you to open portals." He sighed. "What I'm trying to say is, everyone has to keep practicing. Nobody's perfect. Besides, we got away, and that's all that matters. So just forget about it and move on—that's the only way to learn."

Jacob sat back in the front seat of the Jeep. Wade had a point, but I'd get him back for making me the center of his little lesson. *I didn't nearly kill a room full of people. I dropped a chandelier, that's all. But something tells me I'm never going to live that down.*

I turned in my seat as Isadora stirred. Wade joined her in the back seat, reaching over to help her sit up as she came to with a slow blink of her blue eyes. A smudge of soot streaked her chest, a black mark reaching all the way up to her jaw. The fireball had hit her square in the ribs, knocking her out in one harsh blast. She grimaced as she gripped Wade's arm, forcing her aching body into a sitting position.

"Where are we?" she asked.

"Wade's Jeep," I replied. "More specifically, we're parked outside the San Diego Coven."

A trickle of sweat meandered down the side of her face. "I won't go inside, Harley. I know you want me to, and there are very few things I would not do for you, but I can't set foot inside that place. Not right now."

"Alton will keep you both safe," I promised.

She smiled. "I believe he would try," she said solemnly. "The trouble is, he can't protect us from Katherine and her army of agents. He doesn't even know who the spy is, amongst members of his own coven. Someone followed you tonight, and if what you told us is true—that nobody saw you create the tracer spell and you told no one of your plans to find us—then Katherine is having you watched more closely than you think. The coven has been compromised."

"We'll sneak you in," I replied, struggling to hide the note of desperation in my voice. "We'll sneak you in and we won't tell anyone that you're there."

"Until Katherine's spy has been outed, I can't stay. We aren't even sure if there is only the one."

I stared at her and willed her to change her mind. There was so much I wanted to know, and if she disappeared again, I had no idea when I might see her again. The coven had definitely been compromised, but that didn't mean she couldn't stay. I knew we could always hide Jacob and Isadora in the Bestiary, under Tobe's care. It was more secure than anywhere else in the coven. Either that, or we could give them a secret room, similar to the one that Alton had spoken with me in. We were working on fixing the problem, but that didn't mean we couldn't protect them in the meantime, within the coven. And anyway, soon enough, the spy would be found, and everything would be secure again.

You're not naïve, Merlin. You don't really believe that. They're like dirty little weeds—remove one, another one takes its place.

"We don't know if the Shapeshifter that attacked us tonight is different than the spy who's been feeding information to Katherine," I said reluctantly. "There still might only be one, working from within the SDC. That's something we need to figure out, and fast. We'd be able to get it done quicker if you helped us, Isadora."

A tight chuckle rasped from her throat. "I've made my choice, Harley. Nothing can make me change my mind."

"But how can you continue to train me if you're not with me?" Jacob asked. "Tonight proved that I've got a long way to go, and I can't figure this stuff out without you. You told me yourself, this skill is so rare that there are virtually no textbooks on it. It's not like I can teach myself."

"I can't teach you, Jacob," she replied bluntly. "Not if you stay here and join the coven. I can't train you, and I can't protect you."

Jacob sank down in his seat and turned his gaze out toward the pummeling raindrops beyond Isadora's head, where they rattled against the back window. He looked completely torn. Either he stayed here and floundered over his powers, or he followed Isadora wherever she wanted to go. He'd clearly formed a familial attachment to her, but the coven offered something he'd never experienced before… a true family. A group of people who would rally around him and accept him. As one person, Isadora could never offer him that.

"What did the Shapeshifter mean about my parents?" he asked unexpectedly. "Why did they say that my parents were on Katherine's side?"

Isadora fidgeted, a vein ticking in her temple. My stomach tightened. I felt her dread for what she was about to say. "There's something I didn't tell you, Jake." She hesitated. "I know who your parents were. With abilities like ours, the lineage is fairly limited."

Jacob's jaw dropped so fast. "You hid that from me?" I felt the stab of betrayal as if it were my own. Emotions like that, so raw and visceral, were hard to block out.

"I didn't want to tell you about them, in case you were captured. I feared they would try to use it to persuade you into joining them. I suppose I hoped that, if you ever discovered the truth, you might think they were lying, and you wouldn't listen to them," she explained. "Family is a potent thing. Sometimes, you'll do anything and believe anything to feel close to them, even though they're long gone. And on the wrong side of Chaos."

I had a feeling she was talking to me, too. After all, I would've gone to the ends of the earth to find out more about my parents, even if she hadn't come along to fill in some of the gaps. Turning to Jacob, I could already feel a flurry of inner turmoil gathering.

He frowned. "Shouldn't you have left that up to me?"

"I couldn't, Jacob."

"Who are they?"

"Elan and Zara Sowanoke," Isadora replied after a stilted pause.

"And they worked for Katherine Shipton? *The* Katherine Shipton? The one who sent those twins to try and kill the Smiths?"

Isadora nodded. "Unfortunately, yes. They worked for Katherine at the height of her power," she said. I could tell she was tiptoeing around the subject. "In fact, Katherine was the one who encouraged them to be a couple. Elan was a Portal Opener and Zara was a Sensate. She probably figured that the two of them would create a powerful child."

Of course she did. That sounds about immoral enough for her.

"Great, so you're telling me I'm only alive because of that evil bitch?" Jacob muttered.

"No, I'm saying that something good came out of her wickedness."

He shook his head. "How can you say that?"

"Because it's true," she shot back. "You have to understand that Katherine was, and is, a ridiculously charming woman. She can influence minds without a person even realizing it. Honestly, she's a master of brainwashing. She puts Charles Manson to shame."

"Charles who?"

"Never mind... What I'm saying is, she targeted your parents and she made them feel like part of something important," Isadora explained. "That's how she gets people to do what she wants. If they disobey, or they refuse to budge, she finds a way to bend them to her will. She's spent years researching the most forbidden spells in the world. With them, she uses whatever dark and terrible means she can, until people break and give her what she wants."

The more I heard about Katherine's past exploits, the more I loathed her. There didn't seem to be any line she wouldn't cross. It terrified me, too. What lengths would she go to this time, to succeed in her future plans of total evil?

Jacob dropped his gaze. "Did she brainwash my mom and dad?"

"I think it's highly likely. They had something she wanted."

"But you can't say for certain?"

Isadora touched Jacob's shoulder. "No, Jacob, I can't."

"What happened to them? Are they still working for her?" I heard the underlying question in his words: *Why did they leave me?*

"Katherine wanted your father to open a portal to the realm where the Children of Chaos exist in their raw forms," she said. "He opened the portal, as instructed, and she sent him to see what's out there. He never came back. Before and after your father went missing, your mother was responsible for mapping out the locations of rogue magicals so Katherine could monitor them and collect them as she saw fit. However, something about your father's disappearance snapped your mom out of her trance—not by much, but just enough."

Poor bastard. I wonder what happened to him. It was hard not to think about. He must have gone somewhere and gotten himself trapped. Either that, or something hadn't allowed him to return. I wasn't sure which was creepier. My thoughts lingered on Jacob's mom, too. Just like with my dad, Katherine's actions had awakened a primal desire to protect at all costs.

Jacob looked up. "What do you mean?"

"You had recently been born, and I guess it awakened a protective streak in your mother," she replied. "As Katherine became more crazed, her thirst for power got out of hand, and your mother got scared that something terrible might happen to you. She was so worried about your safety that she snuck away in the dead of night and gave you up for adoption. After that, she ran away from Katherine and the cult. I guess she hoped she could come back for you once everything blew over and the Mage Councils banded together to get rid of Katherine."

But she never did. I'm so sorry, Jacob. I knew what that felt like. He'd probably waited and hoped his real parents would one day return and save him from the uncertainty of the foster system, the same way I'd done.

He shook his head. "How can you possibly know all of this?"

"Because I was the one who rescued her... at least for a while," she said. I gaped at her in disbelief. All the skeletons were coming out of the closet. "You see, it's a little-known-fact that Portal Makers can sense the portals other Portal Makers have created. They have a funny bonfire scent, and they leave a silvery trail in the air. Once you can spot them, you can travel through them. Elan left her with a very rare object called an Ephemera—a one-shot gemstone filled with the specific ability of a magical. As far as I know, only a few exist, though they destruct after use. It can only be used by the person it's gifted to, and your mom used it to escape. I'll show you how to follow these trails one day, though you can only focus on the trail once your skills have advanced."

"You *rescued* her?"

Isadora nodded. "I traveled through her portal and found her hiding out in a shack in the Mojave Desert. We moved around as often as we could. I harbored her in every safe house that I knew about, but... I couldn't protect her, in the end."

A still silence settled across the Jeep. Wade remained quiet, taking everything in. Meanwhile, I wanted to ask the question on everyone's lips, but it wasn't my place. That had to come from Jacob, if he wanted to know. I could understand his reluctance—coming from the kind of past that we'd come from, sometimes it was harder to learn the truth. All our lives, we put these people on a pedestal. It took one truth to knock it all down. Already, I could see he was struggling with what he'd learned.

"What... what happened?" Jacob murmured.

"Katherine's agents found Zara while I was away," she replied. "They tried to get her to go back to Katherine. She wouldn't go with them, and she fought back tooth and nail. The facts aren't entirely clear, even now, but an explosion destroyed the safe house. Your mother was inside when it happened. It killed her *and* Katherine's agents." She took a shaky breath, and I could almost see the memories glistening in her eyes. "I'm sorry, Jacob. But please know that she loved you. She put you up for adoption in order to save your life."

Jacob cleared his throat. "So, Katherine is looking for a replacement? She wants a Sensate and a Portal Maker, and I fit the bill. Two for the price of one, huh? She knows I'm their son, right? That's why she set this whole thing up, as a way to reach me?"

"I believe so."

He sighed wearily. "I don't get it. Why would they have worked for a nutjob like Katherine, knowing what she was? I know you say she might have brainwashed them, but what made them join in the first place?"

"Even good people can fall for cults, Jacob. Lonely people, who don't feel like they belong anywhere—they can find comfort in such groups, because it doesn't feel like a cult when you're in the middle of it. They can make a person feel found again." Isadora smiled. "Your mother had a hard childhood, and even harder teenage years. She told me a few stories, now and then, but I could never get everything out of her. In a way, I didn't have to. Just hearing her speak... you could tell she'd been badly wounded."

My heart broke for Zara Sowanoke, and for the boy she'd had to leave behind. If she'd put herself through all of that, then one thing was clear: she'd loved Jacob more than anything. She'd wanted to keep him safe. It just hadn't worked out the way she might have hoped.

For a long time, nobody said anything. The rain pattered on the windows, reminding me of uncomfortable RV trips with old foster families. Tears brimmed in Jacob's eyes. I watched him fight against them, a muscle twitching in his jaw. I thought about reaching over and touching his arm, to let him know it was okay to cry. Instead, I sat back and let him deal with it however he wanted. That was the only way he'd get through this and process the tarnished memory of parents he'd never met.

"I think I'd like to stay and train with you for another month, Isadora," he said. "I keep thinking about how I messed up back there, and what might've happened if I hadn't been able to get my stuff together. Without my portal ability, I'm pretty defenseless against anything that Katherine might throw at me. Yeah, I have some Air elemental powers, but they're weak as hell. If I'm going to escape sticky situations like that one at the hideaway, I need to know more. Otherwise, I'm a liability and I may as well have none of this power."

"I think that's very wise," Isadora replied.

"And after the month is up?" I asked.

He shrugged. "Once I feel more confident about my portal skills, I'll come back here. I'll make the pledge and stay at the coven... even if that means leaving you behind." He glanced at Isadora with sad eyes. I knew those words couldn't have come easily to him.

"I can't make any promises about my future plans," Isadora said, her tone understanding. "Until Katherine's spies have been dealt with, the coven is off limits to me. If, by some miracle, they are discovered, I may reconsider." Her eyes found mine, the two of us sharing a private moment.

"Can you stay for a while now?" I asked tentatively.

Her shoulders sagged. "We must go before that Shapeshifter decides to come after us again. I'm sorry, Harley."

"I only need half an hour," I pressed. "There's so much I want to ask you about my parents."

"I promise I'll send you a full explanation of everything as soon as I can. I know it won't be the same as hearing it from me directly, but I hope it will be enough." She drew in a ragged breath. "The truth is, you might not want to hear what I have to say. It's dark, and dark secrets are often better left unspoken. But I won't take that choice from you... It just might take you a while to understand."

She turned to Jacob before I could respond. "We need to leave."

Wait, what? What secret could be so dark or bad that I wouldn't want to hear it? Hadn't I already heard enough bad things about my dad and my mom? What else could there possibly be?

Unless this wasn't just about my family. Was it about me? A grip of anxiety seized my chest.

Jacob nodded. "Do you want me to make the portal?"

"No, I'll handle that." Shuffling along the back seat, she opened the Jeep door and got out. Jacob followed suit, the two of them walking out into the driving rain.

Wade and I leapt out after them, though I knew I couldn't change their minds about staying. I needed to know what she had to tell me, but with spies in our midst, Isadora was right: they were safer away from the coven.

Alton was not going to like this, though. *Well, if he wants this job done, he can get off his ass and do it himself. I'm not chasing them through wormholes, all across the country.*

"See you later?" Jacob said, stepping forward shyly.

"You bet," I replied, pulling him in for a hug.

Isadora came up to me next. "I promise I'll explain everything. Take care of yourself, okay?"

"I will," I said, my heart still anxious. We held each other for a moment, before I pulled away and dusted myself off. I'd see her again, I comforted myself. I would.

With the goodbyes over with, Isadora opened up a portal in the middle of Balboa Park, and the two of them jumped through. It snapped shut with a rush of cold air, leaving Wade and me alone in the rain. I was past caring about the water soaking through my clothes. In fact, it felt kind of nice, after all that.

"So, what are we going to tell Alton?" I asked with a sigh, as we turned and made our way back to the Fleet Science Center.

"The truth," he replied.

"You think he'll be pissed?" I murmured.

Wade shrugged. "I think he'll be as thrilled as he'll be disappointed. I mean, this way, he knows Jacob is coming back. It's just a matter of when."

"Yeah, I guess." To be honest, I probably felt most disheartened by Jacob's decision to leave. Without his help, we'd have to track down the missing kids on our own, fumbling blindly through dried-up leads. Then there were these spies to consider. If one of them was a Shapeshifter, which I was pretty sure they were, then the mole could look like absolutely anyone. They'd already tried Preceptor Bellmore on for size. Speaking of which, I wondered if the real Preceptor Bellmore was okay. I guessed we'd find out soon enough.

The situation reminded me of Finch and the way he'd morphed into Tobe, setting him up for planting the charms under the Bestiary boxes. They'd almost thrown the Beast Master in Purgatory for something he didn't do. What if these spies wanted to set up someone else? I doubted they'd try Preceptor Bellmore again. A flashbulb went off in my mind. *They know who has Shapeshifter abilities in the coven. They picked Bellmore on purpose.*

We knew from Garrett that the Shapeshifters of the SDC had their own private group, keeping their secret between themselves. With the spy being a Shapeshifter, too, I guessed that narrowed down our list of suspects. I didn't like to think of any of them being traitors, but one of them had to be. If they'd been outsiders, there was no way they'd be able to get in and out of the coven undetected. No, this was definitely another inside job.

Images of Garrett and O'Halloran popped into my head. *If it's one of you, I swear to God I'll kick your ass.* My mind refused to believe it could be one of them. Honestly, the pool of candidates was pretty big. There were at least thirty Shapeshifters within the coven, and it could be any one of them.

Yeah, but what about that big old man hand? I'd seen a masculine hand in the flicker of the Shapeshifter's fading disguise, but that didn't mean we could rule out the women. We didn't all have dainty little fingers. My hands, for example, looked like they belonged to a friggin' lumberjack.

No, right now, every Shapeshifter was a suspect.

No exceptions.

Not even those I called friends.

THIRTEEN

Santana

My eyes itched like there were grains of sand caught beneath my lids. I wanted to tear them out and hurl them across the room or pour one of the coffee urns straight into my eye sockets. It was taking too long for the caffeine to get into my system properly. Besides, the coven brew was garbage. It might as well have been colored water for all the good it was doing.

"Earth to Santana!" Harley's voice conked me right on the head. I looked up from my mug and found her staring down at me.

"Huh? What? Did you say something?"

She frowned. "I've been calling you for, like, five minutes."

"Sorry… I must've drifted off somewhere."

I'd stayed up with Raffe and the djinn until four that morning, keeping them both company. A weird situation. Like, intensely weird. The djinn had proven himself to be an interesting change of pace, about a million miles away from the Raffe that got my heart racing. Knowing that he had the djinn inside him, twenty-four-seven, three-sixty-five, was crazy to wrap my head around, even now. Fighting that rude son of a bitch had to be hard for Raffe to keep up with, too.

"Alton wants us in his office," Harley continued.

"Why?"

She shrugged. "No idea. He's just called us all into a meeting—GI Joe and Jane, too."

"Still not warming to them?" I chuckled.

"Hell's going to freeze over first."

I scraped my chair back and followed her out into the hallway, cradling my coffee mug like a damn lifeline. I hadn't seen Raffe this morning, but I figured he'd be sleeping off last night's events. Dealing with the djinn had to leave a monster of a hangover.

The coven was eerily silent as we wandered through the hallways, tracing a familiar route toward the ominous black double doors of Alton's office. I liked Alton and everything, but his office gave me the creeps—always made me feel like I was in some kind of trouble. The brass lion heads that served as knockers seemed to roar as we passed straight through, the doors creaking when they swung wide. The spacious office beyond looked like a bomb had hit it. Papers and books were strewn all over the place, everything jumbled in a trail of hurried activity. However, the red roses still bloomed in their crystal vases, dotted about the place on decorative wall shelves.

Alton, Alton, Alton, what's been going on here? Someone's been doing some late-night rummaging.

Alton paced the back of the room. The others were already here. I noticed that two sides had formed in the office itself, with the LA newcomers standing on the right, while the Rag Team sat in chairs on the left. Garrett sat somewhere in the middle, which gave me a satisfying flush of irony. It faded a moment later. With all the chairs taken up on the left, it meant Harley and I would have to break ranks and sit on the right with the LA robots. Glancing at Harley, I could tell she'd rather stand in the hallway than stand with the newbies. *I guess we never really get over high school, do we?*

"Santana, Harley, glad you could join us," Alton said stiffly. Someone else needed their coffee this morning. He looked the way I felt.

"Sorry, it was my fault. I only just heard this little gathering was going on," I replied. "Plus, coffee beckoned."

Raffe leaned over the armrest and offered me a shy smile. I grinned back. *Adorable bastard.* He looked exhausted, his body slumped in the high-backed armchair, his eyes bloodshot and ringed with red. Dealing with the djinn definitely took its toll. I almost felt bad for having laughed at some of the rude things that the djinn had said. That devil had *zero* filter.

"Well, you're here now." Alton perked up a little, doing a subtle jig to get his energy going. "And I'm pleased to announce that we have some good news."

"We do?" Garrett arched a suspicious eyebrow.

The rest of the Rag Team turned in unison to look at Stella and Channing. We hadn't patrolled last night, and we hadn't gathered in Astrid's room to talk about strategy. *We* had nothing to announce. I knew my and Raffe's reasons, but everyone else's excuses in the group texts had been lazy at best. Tatyana and Dylan had mentioned something about looking over books on the Children of Chaos, which meant they'd spent the evening in a veritable flirt-fest. Astrid had shared her evening in Smartie's loving embrace. Garrett had spent his time stuffing his face in the banquet hall with the rest of his blockhead pals and hadn't bothered to give a reason for not doing anything else. And Harley and Wade had said something about checking Waterfront Park for a magical object that Harley was curious about. BS, if ever I'd heard it.

Then again, my excuse had been just as bad. I'd told them that I had a stomachache, and that Raffe was in a bad mood after seeing his dad. Everyone but Harley would have understood the subtext in the last bit. Part of me wanted to tell her what was going on with Raffe, but that was his secret to tell.

Alton nodded. "Yes, Stella and Channing did some digging last night, and they've managed to pick up a trail for Marjorie Phillips."

Channing smirked with glee, satisfaction oozing out of him, and even Stella looked a little smug. *You wouldn't even have a lead if it weren't for Astrid and her crazy-smart genius, so wipe those looks off your faces.* We'd done the legwork, and they were snatching up the prize.

"Has she been spotted somewhere?" Tatyana asked, her voice cool and calm. A freaking ice goddess amongst women. My emotions were far less easy to smother.

"She was seen on the outskirts of the city," Alton continued. "I want you to go after her as soon as we're finished here. Harley, Wade, Santana, Raffe, Channing, and Stella—you will go out in the field and check her last known location. See if you can pick up on anything else that can take us to her. Tatyana and Dylan, I need you to follow up on another lead that Astrid gave me this morning—a shifty sighting of magical behavior not far from La Jolla."

I shot a pointed look at the Californian cyborgs. *Anything you do, Astrid can do better... and single-handed. See how you like those manzanas.*

"What about me?" Garrett asked.

"I was getting to you," Alton replied sharply. "You will join Astrid in the command center—our eye in the sky, if you will. You'll observe the live cameras and watch for any online chatter. The others will have earpieces. It will be your job to guide them through any tricky situations so they can catch Marjorie." He turned his attention back to the field team. "As soon as you have her, I need you to bring her back to the coven without delay. She'll be safe here, but Katherine's agents may be watching you, and they may attempt to intercept Marjorie on your way back."

Astrid was perched on the armrest of Garrett's chair. She shuffled closer, her leg brushing his and a shy smile appearing on her face. *Oh, you've got to be kidding me, chica!* There was definitely some coziness going on that I hadn't seen before. To my surprise, he seemed to welcome it, throwing her a devil-may-care expression. I knew that look from firsthand experience. *You treat her badly, Garrett Kyteler, you'll have me to deal with. If you like your huevos where they are, do* not *break her sweet friggin' heart.*

"Any further questions?" Alton asked, not seeming to notice that he'd become Astrid and Garrett's matchmaker.

A rumble of assent made its way around the group.

"Good, then you're dismissed. Tell Astrid and Garrett as soon as you reach the location. I'll be popping in and out to check up on things," Alton continued. "Good luck, all of you. Let's bring back at least one of these magical kids, safe and sound."

The group got up and headed for the door. Naturally, I gravitated toward Raffe, though he didn't seem too talkative this morning. All through the hallway, he kept casting me hesitant glances, before dropping his gaze to the marble floor, over and over again. I knew there couldn't be anything *that* interesting on the ground. Making it to the foyer of the Fleet Science Center with the looks still darting my way, I reached the end of my rope.

"What's up with you? Something you wanna say to me?" I asked bluntly.

He blushed, making me wish I'd reined in my sharp tongue. "I wanted to know if you were okay—after last night, I mean," he whispered. "I was going to come find you this morning, but Wade dragged me to Alton's office before I could."

I frowned. "Why wouldn't I be okay? You're the one I'm worried about."

"I guess I was wondering if your opinion of me might've changed. You haven't met the djinn before, and he's... well, he's different."

I stopped walking and looked him dead in the eye. "Of course my opinion of you hasn't changed. Are you kidding? If anything, I admire you even more than I did before. I can't even begin to imagine the kind of strength it takes to keep that demon at bay."

Raffe smiled, his cheeks reddening again. "Are you sure you're not completely freaked out?"

"No way. It takes more than a smutty-mouthed demon to frighten me," I replied. "Anyway, we had a pretty good conversation, once he'd calmed down. I named him, remember? There's power in that."

"Maybe there is, but the djinn is way more dangerous than you give him credit for. He can't be trusted, under any circumstances," Raffe said, urgency in his voice. "If he managed to overcome me, and ran free with my body, the djinn could kill everyone in the coven, and he'd laugh like a hyena while he was at it. He takes pleasure in pain. It's who he is."

Across the foyer, Harley cast us a curious look. I noticed that Raffe kept his voice down whenever he spoke about the djinn in Harley's presence. It saddened me to see him hide like that. None of us had judged Harley for her past. She wouldn't judge Raffe for his.

"You know, you can't keep distancing yourself from other people, just because you're afraid of what they'll think," I said pointedly. "Everyone has a dark side. Yours just happens to be a little more... vocal than others'."

"That's a cute way of putting it," he replied dryly.

"You need to give Harley a chance to see the real you, the two sides that make up who you are. Let her decide for herself. She's our colleague and friend." I glanced at Harley. "Plus, she's got some idea that something's going on with you. I imagine she's having a tricky time reading two sets of emotions at once. Honestly, it's probably a dead giveaway."

He sighed. "But the djinn isn't really a part of me... Well, he is and he isn't. He's not part of who *I* am, as a person. He just happens to inhabit the same body."

"I hate to say it, but you wouldn't be who you are without Kadar, whether you want to admit it or not," I said. "He *is* a part of who you are. And I like every part of you."

Raffe broke into a grin. "You do?"

"Hell yeah."

I didn't want to toot my own horn, but Raffe looked pretty smitten at my declaration of adoration. That could only be a good thing, in taking our simmering flirtations to the next level. I liked him, and he liked me. The ball was firmly in his court now. *I'll make the first move, but I'm not doing all the legwork. Get your ass in gear, Raffe, and sweep me off my feet!*

"Hey! Raffe! Santana! You coming or what?" Wade shouted, his voice echoing across the foyer.

"Coming!" I yelled back.

"Good, then keep up with the group!"

Raffe and I exchanged a look, the two of us chuckling all the way out the door.

FOURTEEN

Harley

With a clear sky overhead, yesterday's storm having puffed itself into oblivion, we pulled up in a dingy back alley in the darkest depths of Mount Hope. Wade had taken me back to collect my beloved Daisy earlier in the morning, but we used his Jeep for this mission. Daisy couldn't possibly fit all of us, plus the gear.

Any good feeling I might've had on finding my Daisy intact faded away in an instant. I knew this area. Before the Smiths took me in, I lived a few blocks away from here. I guessed I was one of the lucky ones—I'd managed to get out. But a lot of kids like me didn't get the chance. Those years had been a steep learning curve, but there was something about these streets that still called to me. They were part of who I was. It was a dangerous neighborhood in San Diego's southeast. Even with magical powers, this place put me on my guard.

Mount No-Hope, more like.

"You think the Jeep will be safe here?" Wade asked.

I shot him a look. "I think we'll be lucky if it has four wheels when we get back." Evidently, Wade had never set foot in a place like this before.

"Right... okay." With a subtle glow of his ten rings, he forged a bubble around the Jeep that made it disappear. I eyed it suspiciously; it seemed to work like the one that kept a certain spot frozen in a time-dilation bubble.

"Did you just make it vanish?"

He shook his head. "I put it in a reality pocket, so it's in a slightly different dimensional space than the one we're standing in. It's technically here with us, but it's also not, at the same time. Kind of like the coven."

"All you had to say was 'vanishing bubble.' That's all you had to say."

"Once you two have finished bickering," Channing cut in, "why don't we get down to business? We're here to canvass for any sign of Marjorie Phillips. From her last sighting, we know she's around here somewhere. Now, we need to make sure we keep a low profile. Magic is a last resort. We don't want to have to get the cleanup crews involved because of some messy mistake, do you understand?"

I felt like a soldier standing before the drill sergeant, being reprimanded after a bad mission. He clearly meant that we'd make a mistake somewhere along the line. In his eyes, we were a liability. Anyone outside the LA Coven was. His superiority complex was great at riling me up.

Well, joke's on you, pal, because I know this place and you don't. I hoped it might give me the upper hand.

"Aye, aye, Captain," Santana said sourly, lifting her hand in mock salute.

Channing glared at her. "Good, then let's move out."

We set off down the alleyway and came out on the corner of a pretty ragged-looking street. Down the road, perched on the stoop of a corner store, was a cluster of musclebound dudes, dripping in jewelry and clothes that didn't fit. It wasn't unusual to see guys like that sitting out in the middle of the day. They were waiting for pick-ups and drop-offs. That was their job.

All around Mount Hope, the streets were riddled with drug gangs and violence. Every single guy and girl in that place had a weapon on them, but they weren't inherently bad people. They were out there surviving in a way that nobody could understand, unless you came from the same place. Most of them only used their weapons in self-defense, though drive-bys and gang shootings were par for the course. I'd seen it happen. One night, I'd witnessed a bunch of kids running for their lives as bullets sprayed from the windows of an SUV. There were good people, too—people who wanted to get out, people who wanted the best for their families, and people who avoided those who ran the neighborhood, the gangs and pimps and drug-runners. As with all places, the bad and good existed in a delicate balance, but this area of San Diego had played a big part in who I was now. I'd learned a lot.

"Do not approach anyone who looks shifty," Channing warned. "No confrontation unless absolutely necessary."

"Everyone looks shifty," Wade muttered, gaining another hard look from me. *Ah, Wade Crowley and his upper-class, magical privilege.* Sometimes, his naïveté shocked me.

However, he wasn't the only one who appeared to be unsettled by his surroundings. I could feel wariness spiking off all of them in sharp waves that ran cold in the pit of my stomach, like swallowing minty-fresh chewing gum. Aside from me, the only person who didn't seem fazed was Santana, whose calm demeanor kept me from sinking into the others' fear. I clung to her serenity like it was a life raft. In this neighborhood, I needed to keep my wits about me.

"How are you so calm?" Wade asked, as I maneuvered the group out of the way of the stoop boys. They were loud and rude, but their bark was worse than their bite. They were the kind who'd wave guns around to intimidate, but wouldn't have the balls to pull the trigger, since it was broad daylight on a main street.

"I lived here a few years ago," I replied.

He stared at me, aghast. "You *lived* here?"

"Yep, so I suggest you listen up," I said, casting a pointed look at Channing. "I know my way around this neighborhood. I can keep us out of trouble."

"The mark was spotted going into a dilapidated house on Raven Street. Do you know where that is?" Channing asked.

I nodded. "This way."

We walked along the northern edge of the cemetery, with the graves of fallen veterans on our right. Moving along Market Street at a quick pace, a group of rangy-looking teenagers turned the corner and started coming in our direction. I recognized the gang colors, and hurriedly ushered the rest of the group down Quail Street. If we wanted to avoid confrontation, we needed to avoid the gangs in this area. They didn't appreciate strangers, especially ones who looked so out of place.

Cutting right at the end, I led the guys toward the street we were looking for—Raven Street. An apt name, considering the tangible gloom that settled over the houses. Pink-walled houses and rusty fences greeted us, with twisted trees in the front yards. Sofas and various other junk items were thrown wherever, while a couple of palms swayed in the cool breeze that blew through the neighborhood.

"Let's go door-to-door, see what people know," Channing instructed, taking out a police ID.

I shook my head. "Nope, no IDs. Not here. Not if you want anyone to actually talk to you."

"What do you mean?"

"They won't speak to us if we look like we're from the police or the FBI, or any of those places," I explained. "We just need to ask like normal folks—pretend we're looking for a friend, or a cousin, or someone's daughter. Say that Marjorie has gone missing and we're worried something might have happened to her. Say we want to find her before she gets into any trouble. That's the only way you'll get these people to talk."

He seemed a bit put out that I had more knowledge about the area than he did. "Fine, no IDs," he said, after a pause.

"Excellent," I replied, trying to keep the note of victory out of my voice. "Let's split up and go in pairs. Meet back here in an hour?"

Channing shook his head. "One of us will be with you at all times. Stella, you go with Wade and Harley. I'll go with Raffe and Santana. No arguments."

You just had to have the last word, didn't you?

"Works for me," Stella chimed in, flashing a quick smile at Wade. I realized a second too late that I was giving her the evil eye. Both of us turned away, somewhat embarrassed. Not that I had any reason to be. I was just looking out for a friend. *Sure... super convincing, Harley.*

We separated into our trios, and my group took one side of the street while the others took the opposite row of homes. I led the way, guiding Wade and Stella around snapping dogs and *Keep Out* signs. Most of the pups in this area looked and sounded fierce, but few really were. Plus, I'd always had a soft spot for pit bulls. They had a bad rep, but I thought they were sweet, and fiercely loyal. The Taylors, whom I'd lived with before the Smiths, owned a gray pittie called Barker. I'd loved him more than any human, preferring him to the family. Things didn't end well with them, thanks to their son's roving eye and wandering hands. Hardly my fault that he was carted off to the emergency room. In the end, the only thing I was sorry for, after leaving the Taylors behind, was not seeing Barker again.

As we went from door-to-door with no luck, I thought about the conversation I'd had last night with Alton. Like we'd expected, he'd been thrilled and disappointed in equal measure. He wanted Jacob and Isadora within the confines of the coven, but he'd sort of come around to their reasoning for staying away. I guess it excited him even more to know that he might be receiving a fully-fledged, in-control Portal Opener, even if he had to wait for it. *Delayed gratification at its finest.*

The Shapeshifter had proven to be a slightly more troubling topic of conversation. We'd told Alton everything about the individual, and about the person they'd impersonated. I mentioned seeing a hand that didn't belong to Preceptor Bellmore, though that didn't really give us any more information. It simply took Preceptor Bellmore out of the line of fire. After returning the previous evening, we'd been informed that the real Bellmore was just fine, and had been working late in her office when the attack happened.

What had surprised me most of all was Alton's confession that they'd already been monitoring the Shapeshifters in the coven, ever since the Finch incident. I couldn't get my head around it, even now. If they'd been watching the Shapeshifters, then who attacked us? Alton hadn't given us any answers. Truthfully, he didn't seem to know. With the storm, he'd told us there'd been a few glitches in the cameras and the transmissions coming from most of the tracer beacons. He hadn't thought anything of it, at the time, but he'd since realized that it had been used to the spy's advantage. We'd been well and truly played.

We'd all come away from the conversation with the understanding that the Shapeshifters would have to be monitored even more closely, from now on. I presumed that was why he'd put Garrett on surveillance duty with Astrid, keeping him under the coven's roof instead of out in the field.

Yeah, but it can't be Garrett. Surely not. He didn't know anything about Finch, and I bet all these minions must know about each other. They can't be working rogue. Garrett had seemed genuinely hurt after discovering the truth of Finch's betrayal, and I couldn't fathom it being him. Still, we couldn't rule anyone out at this point... aside from Preceptor Bellmore. Those hands might not have been one-hundred-percent masculine, but they definitely hadn't been the preceptor's.

Leaving those thoughts behind, I moved my focus back to the task at hand. We reached the fourth house along our side of the road. An elderly woman opened her door, and she seemed wary of us—and understandably so, given the neighborhood.

"Sorry to bother you, but I was wondering if you'd seen this girl anywhere?" I asked, showing her a photo. "She's my baby sister and we're worried she might be in some trouble. Anything you can do to help us would be amazing."

Her expression softened. "Sorry, I haven't seen a girl like that around here. Nobody smart lives on these streets anymore. It's all thugs and junkies." She paused. "I hope you find her. This place can make folks disappear like *that*." She snapped her fingers for effect. "It's like the Bermuda Triangle."

"Well, thank you for your help," I replied. "I hope we find her, too. If you hear anything, here's my number." I handed her my card, which she took with shaky fingers. There was still a way to go before we reached the top end of the street, and I was starting to wonder *how* Marjorie was hiding so well.

As we went through another handful of houses, I noticed that Stella had been oddly silent since we'd parted with the other three. There were no flirty looks, no giggles, no toying with her hair. She seemed to have drifted off into a world of her own. However, as soon as we crossed the road to reconvene with the others, it all changed. We'd canvassed about half of the buildings on the street with no luck. It seemed all of us were considering a change of strategy.

"Any luck?" Channing asked.

"Not from the residents, though the company isn't too shabby," Stella replied, smiling in Wade's direction. My body bristled with annoyance. She'd been quiet for ages, and now this?

Channing seemed surprised. "So nobody has seen her?"

"No, they haven't. Have they, Wade?" Stella addressed only him. *Well... seems like I might as well not be here.*

Wade shook his head, and I felt a jolt of joy from him at Stella's attention. "No, there haven't been any sightings so far."

"Not for lack of trying though, right?" She nudged him in the arm. I stared in disbelief. Santana seemed to be stunned, too, though Raffe stayed very... well, Raffe. A mixture of churning emotions that I couldn't read properly.

"Then we need to keep at it," Channing said brusquely. A flicker of disappointment crossed Stella's face, forcing a flashbulb of understanding to go off in my head. Stella was using Wade to see if Channing had feelings for her—to see if she could make him jealous.

I concentrated on Channing's emotions to see what I could discover, but there didn't appear to be a scrap of jealousy in him—only a simmering sense of protectiveness toward Stella, the kind you'd find from a brother or a close friend.

Oof, that's going to sting.

Wade, on the other hand, seemed absolutely delighted. He grinned and nudged Stella back, prompting her to chuckle. I could feel my retinas detaching just by looking at them. He had no idea that he was part of a setup, and he was *loving* it.

A big part of me wanted to expose Stella there and then, but I kept the knowledge to myself. *Girl code and all that.* However, I was *so* looking forward to dumping a bucket of cold water over Wade when we got back to the coven. He couldn't have been more flattered if he'd tried. Heck, his cheeks were pink. Another part of me felt a little salty at the happiness he was showing with Stella. With me, it was almost always business-mode Wade, all the time, with a few sprinkled exceptions here and there. Why couldn't he laugh like that around me, or nudge me in the arm, or—

My stomach twisted into knots. *Oh boy, I am in BIG trouble...*

My reactions weren't the reactions of a sane, indifferent young woman. These were the jealous reactions of someone who was catching feelings for a certain Wade Crowley. The serious kind. The butterflies-in-the-stomach, head-over-heels, tongue-tied, stupid kind. The kind I tended to avoid at all costs. An expletive sat on my tongue, begging to be muttered under my breath.

"Come on, let's go," I said quietly, keeping my feelings firmly to myself.

"Are you okay?" Wade asked as we walked.

I nodded. "Yeah, sure. I mean, I'm fine. Why wouldn't I be? Just tired after yesterday. Running around after people will do that to you." My words came out all flustered and jumbled. *Jeez, Harley, get it together.*

"Did you not get much sleep?"

I shrugged. "Not really. Lots on my mind." *Yeah, like you.*

"Do you want to talk about it?"

"Now?"

"No, I meant when we get back to the coven. We can talk or something—grab a coffee and chat through what's on your mind."

I stared at him weirdly. "Yeah... maybe... if there's not a whole load of other things going on, which there probably will be. Might be a raincheck situation, for when I've got even more mental garbage to spew at you." *Very smooth, Harley. Oh, yeah, let's talk about what's on my mind—how about, I think I have feelings for you and I don't know what to do about it? What would you suggest, Wade?*

He chuckled. "Nice mental image."

"Yeah... sorry for that visual poetry."

He glanced at me with a curious look. "Harley Merlin apologizing? I might have to send you for a psych evaluation when we get back."

"Very funny." I nudged him in the arm, feeling like a middle-schooler again. *Maybe I do need a psych evaluation, or some shock therapy. Maybe that'll get you out of my head, Crowley. If not, a lobotomy might be a good plan.*

"I mean it, though. If you need to talk, I'm here."

"Thanks." My cheeks were burning furiously, forcing me to look away so he wouldn't see.

We moved on up the road, asking the same questions and showing the same picture to anyone who'd listen. Near the top end of the street, there was a small apartment block, with a fire escape snaking down the outer wall. A figure caught my eye, just visible from the sidewalk. A girl was coming down the wrought-iron steps, clutching a plump trash bag in her hand.

Marjorie.

"There!" I hissed, not wanting to alert her.

I waved to the others across the road and pointed toward the apartments. They scuttled over, keeping their distance from the fire escape's line of sight. Slowly, we approached. She was almost at the bottom of the fire escape when she saw us. Her eyes widened in fear. Flinging the trash bag over the railing, she took off at a sprint, racing back upstairs toward the roof. I took off after her, with the others following. Channing, Wade, and Stella hurried up the escape behind me, while Santana and Raffe went around the side of the building, to stop her if she tried to make a break for it through the front door.

Marjorie wasn't stupid. She'd evaded the Ryder twins, and she'd kept a low profile for longer than anyone her age ought to have been able to. It was clear this girl had some serious skills. As much as I admired her for them, we needed to catch her. This wasn't a Jacob and Isadora case—there were no benefits to her staying out here on her own. Nevertheless, I understood her fear.

I tore up the side of the fire escape, my boots pounding on the rickety metal. Reaching the top, I vaulted over the low wall of the roof and spotted her halfway across it. I sprinted after her, my legs pumping to cut her off. Clawing breath into my lungs, I forged a Telekinetic lasso and hurled it at her. She glanced over her shoulder, grimacing from my mental grip, then threw her arm back and sent a violent gust of air toward me. The blast knocked me off my feet, severing the Telekinetic connection.

I jumped up with barely a pause and hurtled after her again. She fired blast after blast of violent air in my direction, the sudden whorls and gusts shaking the palm trees in the front yards of the houses opposite. Above us, the sky darkened, her powers drawing on the energy all around her. In her terror, she seemed to be changing the weather.

Reaching the far edge of the wall, Marjorie didn't miss a beat as she roused a cushion of air to carry her safely across to the next building. I charged on, with Wade at my side, the two of us leaping onto the next building. The gap was small enough that Wade could make it without the need for magic, though I had to grasp the front of his shirt to stop him from toppling backward. Once he was steady, we sprinted after Marjorie with everything we had.

Wade hurled a fireball at Marjorie's feet. *So much for keeping a low profile.* Behind us, Channing and Stella were struggling to keep up. They didn't have enough momentum to cross the gap between buildings, both of them forced to go back and take a run up.

Undeterred, I powered over the next gap and the next, until I realized that Wade was no longer beside me. The gaps between buildings had spread too wide. It was just me and Marjorie now, seeing how far our Air abilities could take us. All around me, the wind howled and snapped, attempting to push me back. I fought Air with Air, creating tiny tornados that spiraled upward before disappearing into the sky.

Marjorie turned at the end of the street, with no more buildings to leap onto. Instead, she jumped the immense distance onto a building on the next street. I hurried after, determined not to lose sight of her. The diamond of my Esprit sputtered for a minute, the air cushion beneath me disappearing instantly. I plummeted toward the ground, with nothing to break my fall.

Filled with panic, I flung out a lasso of Telekinesis and wrapped it around a utility pole, using it to gain upward momentum and bounce back toward the rooftops. Somehow, it worked, my Air ability rushing to meet me, as it pushed me the last few feet onto the opposite roof with a roar of wind.

I didn't stop for breath, or to think about what might have happened. I kept sprinting, my legs burning, until I closed the distance between myself and Marjorie. She fumbled on the edge of the outer wall, teetering awkwardly. I could see she was tired. Using her moment of hesitation to my advantage, I lunged for her, the two of us toppling over the side. I forged a cushion of air beneath us, and we landed with a soft bounce a few feet above the ground. As it dissipated, we collapsed in a heap, the two of us gasping for breath.

Even then, she tried to fight me. She attempted to release a sharp gust of Air, but I was too close and held her too tight for it to work.

"Marjorie, stop!" I urged. "Just stop. We're not here to hurt you."

"Let go of me!" she snapped, wriggling like a ferret in my arms.

"Quit it!" I gripped her tighter, worried she might get away again. I didn't have much juice left in the tank.

The others came hurtling around the corner. Santana darted ahead and ducked down beside us, seizing Marjorie's arms and slapping a set of Atomic Cuffs on her wrists. Mine were in my back pocket, and I couldn't put them on her without loosening my grip. As soon as she was restrained, I sprawled out on the ground, my chest heaving.

"Nice catch, Merlin," Channing commended me. He sounded

genuinely impressed. Beside him, Stella dropped her gaze to hide an impulsive expression of hurt. I figured that maybe Channing had never spoken to her like that, just like Wade had never spoken to me the way he had done with her. *What are these guys doing to us, Stella? We're strong, fierce, formidable women... reduced to this by a couple of dudes.* We both needed a stern talking-to, or a kick in the ass.

"What now?" I wheezed, getting to my feet with Santana's help.

"We need to take this young lady back to the coven and have a long and serious talk about what happened," Wade replied.

Looking down at Marjorie's scowl, I winced. In all honesty, I would've made the same face.

FIFTEEN

Santana

I sat down in front of the terrified teenager, in the safety of Alton's office. It was just me and her. I had been elected to speak with her alone, since she showed a clear unease around authority figures, which canceled Alton out, and all of us piling into the room would have made her just as uncomfortable, which canceled the rest of the team out. Apparently, I had a better bedside manner than the others. I wasn't about to argue.

"All right, chica, well, I just want to start by saying you can calm the hell down. I know we look like them, but we aren't the bad guys," I said. She'd just been chased across a dozen rooftops by a bunch of strangers she'd never met. Given her last encounter with folks like us, I'd be crapping myself, too. Marjorie was shaking like a leaf, her eyes bulging out of her head, frog-style.

She pulled the sleeves of her sweater over her hands, fidgeting. "Why did you chase me if you're not the bad guys?"

"Ah... I can see how that might've given you the wrong idea," I replied. "We were chasing you because we want to keep you safe.

Seems a little counterproductive, considering we nearly ran you off a bunch of rooftops, but our hearts were in the right place."

She looked at me curiously, as though she wasn't quite sure what to make of me. "Nobody can keep me safe. There are bad people after me."

"Nope, those bastard Ryder twins are long gone. That girl who tackled you to the ground like you were heading for a touchdown? She put one of the twins, Emily, in prison. The other… well, he wasn't so lucky. He's dead. You don't have to worry about them anymore."

"Emily? No, there wasn't a girl when they came to visit me; they were two men—kind of old. They said they were from Social Services, but they weren't."

"This is going to get really confusing, so bear with me and just tell me to shut my mouth if it gets to be too much. Those two men were actually two magicals called Emmett and Emily Ryder. They were Shapeshifters. They could disguise themselves as anyone. That's why they looked like two older men, and not what they really were—which was two evil sons of bitches."

A hint of a smile tugged at her lips. "You're not what I expected from the coven."

"You know about the coven, then. What were you expecting? Capes and pointy hats? Maybe a broom and a black cat?"

She giggled nervously. "Something like that. People keep saying the word 'magical' to me, like it's supposed to make sense. I don't really understand anything that's going on."

"No, I don't imagine you do." I sighed. "Right, so if that's the case, let's start at the beginning. Why did you run away from us back there? Also, Raffe took care of your trash, so you don't have to worry about littering."

"Raffe?"

"Yeah, I'm not sure how close a look you got, but he's the tall, lithe dude with the caramel skin and the beautiful eyes. Handsome devil."

She chuckled again. "I think I know who you mean. Are you and him… together?"

"Working on it, but that's not important right now," I replied. "Now, for the second time, why did you run?" I kept my tone light and hopefully funny. In all my years on this earth, I'd found that humor was the best way to get through to almost anyone. Not that I'd fancy trying to crack a joke in the presence of Katherine Shipton. She'd probably get one of her minions to blow my head off before I got to the punchline, and what's a joke without a punchline?

"The first time or the second time?" Marjorie asked.

"Let's go with both."

"Those two men—sorry, those twins—they pretended they were from Social Services and asked if they could speak to me in private. They took me into one of the other rooms and told me they worked for a special group. I think it might have been a cult of some kind. They wanted me to join them. I said, 'No way,' and they got pretty pissed. They said they'd be in touch again, since I wasn't complying." She paused, her eyes filling with tears. "I didn't even say goodbye to the Hamms. I just took off. I was so scared. I didn't want those dudes to come back and hurt them because of me. They must be so worried… Are they okay? Can I call them?"

I shook my head slowly. "Not right now. We have to wait for this situation to be resolved before you can get in touch with them again. It's for their own safety. Although, I *can* tell you that they're doing just fine. They're sad, but we made up a pretty damn good excuse to keep them from worrying too much."

I didn't have the heart to tell her that they didn't even know who she was anymore. No kid wanted to hear that, especially not one who was already being bombarded with all this new information about herself and the world she thought she knew—but clearly didn't.

A weight appeared to lift off her shoulders. "They're all I've thought about."

"I'm sorry, Marjorie. Do you want to keep going? I can get some food in here or something, and we can have a little break. I know it's a lot. Believe me, if I were you, my head would be exploding. There'd be gunk all over that back wall. Alton's books would be *ruined*."

She laughed, wiping her eyes with her sleeves. "You're funny."

"Why, thank you, *mi changuita*."

"Alton's the big guy, right? The one you introduced as the… director, was it?"

"That's the one."

She paused for a moment before speaking again. "I kept seeing this car waiting outside the school, and I knew I had to leave before they snatched me. I took a few things and I ran for it. I hid from them wherever I could. I figured Mount Hope would be the last place they'd come looking."

"Yeah, that's the last place *anyone* would want to go looking for you."

"Then, when you came, I thought you were working for them. I didn't know you were a different group of… magicals." The word stuck in her throat. It took some getting used to, even after a lifetime of knowing you were different. I was lucky; I'd known what I was from birth. Being a Santeria was an honor in my town, readily accepted and even revered. It wasn't like that everywhere else. People feared what we could do.

And if I didn't know what I was, and crazy stuff started happening—fireballs shooting out of my hands and things moving when I got angry or whatever—I'd be totally freaked out.

"Did the twins tell you why they wanted you to join their group?" I asked.

She nodded. "They came after me because of what I can do. They told me they were trying to recruit the *really* special kids, kids with abilities that hardly anyone else has. I didn't totally understand what that meant, but I'm starting to."

"Why, what can you do?"

"You won't believe me," she said sheepishly.

"Try me."

She took a nervous breath. "I can, sort of, see into the future. Just bits and pieces, here and there. It happens when I touch people or objects—I get glimpses into potential outcomes. It's how I knew the twins were bad news. They slipped this card into my backpack, and I didn't find it for a while. As soon as I touched it, I pictured them stalking toward the school. It's what made me run." She paused, biting on the edge of her sweater sleeve. "They're not complete visions. Like, I can't see the way someone's whole life might turn out, or what's going to happen to someone tomorrow. I just get waves of it. It's like a film is playing but a bunch of scenes are missing. A sloppy trailer. Does that make sense?"

I whistled. "Looks like you're a Clairvoyant, Miss Phillips. Congratulations. It's a super rare ability." I'd read about it, but I'd never seen someone with the skill in real life. The textbooks described it as a temperamental ability; it could take years and years for a Clairvoyant to be able to harness their powers properly. I guessed that was what Marjorie was experiencing.

"Is that good?"

"I'd say so." I flashed her a grin. "Would you mind testing it out on me? I know it's a lot to ask, and you're probably exhausted after today, but I'd be interested to see what you can do. Is that cool?"

She tilted her head to the side. "I guess I can try. It doesn't work as well when my head's all over the place, but I'll do my best."

"That's the spirit."

"Hold out your hand," she instructed.

I put my palm flat on the table and let her cover it with hers. Her bright green eyes closed, her breath slowing. Glancing at her, I saw no movement at all. It was eerie.

"You'll have to choose between Darkness and Light... but there's a chance you might lose both," Marjorie said, her eyes flying open. Her irises had turned black, melding with the pupil in an unsettling way. As she took a few deep breaths, her green irises came back, everything returning to normal.

I nodded. "Dark and Light, huh? I think I know what that's about." *Raffe. He's Dark and Light combined. I don't want to lose him.*

"That's cool. A lot of the time people don't have a clue and they get all weird. It's why I stopped telling people what I could see—it didn't help them, and they didn't believe me most of the time. They just thought I was a nutjob."

"It's a very powerful skill, Marjorie, and you're in the right place to learn more about it," I said. "Do you think you could try it out on a few more people? You got stuck with me because we thought it'd be better if we didn't swarm you. The other guys are nice, I promise. Would you be okay if they came in?"

She smiled shyly. "Yeah, if they're anything like you, I think it'll be fine."

"You flatter me."

I grinned at her and got up from my seat, opening the massive doors of Alton's office to let them in. They filed in like awkward schoolkids, taking up different chairs around the room. The only ones who were missing were Garrett, who was in a meeting with Alton and the steroid twins, and Tatyana and Dylan, who were still out on their mission in La Jolla.

"She's a Clairvoyant," I said cheerfully. "And she's going to try her abilities out on you. I told her she could, so play nice. She's got some interesting things to say." I shot a pointed look at Raffe, who instantly squirmed in his seat. *Ah, I do love to tease you, mi amor.*

"You first," Marjorie murmured, gesturing at Harley. "There's something different about you."

Harley frowned. "There is?"

"I can kind of feel stuff coming off you," she said.

"Then sure, I'll go next," Harley replied, with a wary smile. "And sorry for tackling you to the ground like that. Desperate times called for desperate measures."

Marjorie smiled. "It's okay, Santana explained everything. I'm sorry for running."

"Don't be. I'd have done the same thing in your situation," Harley said.

"Can you hold out your hand for me?"

Harley obeyed, putting out her hand for Marjorie to hold. The girl's eyes closed again, the whole room getting weirdly still. Everyone leaned forward in their seats, waiting for the verdict. I'd seen it happen once already, but when she spoke, shattering the silence, it still made me jump out of my skin.

"I see rivers of blood… I can't tell where they're coming from… It's pouring, but… it doesn't make any sense," she said, her eyes returning to normal. "I'm sorry. It's like I was telling Santana: the omens aren't always clear. Sometimes, I get a lot to go on. Other times, I just get little fragments—it varies from person to person."

"Well, at least it wasn't anything terrifying," Harley joked. Beyond the amused tone, I could see real fear in her eyes. Rivers of blood could *only* be a bad thing.

Marjorie shrank back into her chair. "I'm sorry… I wish I could tell you more."

"Astrid, do you want to go next?" I suggested, wanting to break the tension in the room.

"Absolutely!" she chirped.

"Now, Astrid is a little different. She's human. Does that make things clearer or less clear?"

Marjorie frowned. "I don't know. Clearer, maybe? Up until now, I didn't know if I was using my abilities on humans or magicals, so I'm not really sure."

"No worries. I guess we'll find out in a couple of seconds," I said.

Astrid held out her hand before Marjorie asked, an excited smile on her face. Marjorie grasped the outstretched hand and held it for a few moments. Without warning, tears began to trickle down her face, her body shaking.

Her eyes flew open. "I'm so sorry, I'm so sorry, I'm so sorry," she whispered.

"Are you okay?" I asked.

She shook her head. "I can't say it."

"Go on, I can handle it," Astrid said encouragingly.

Marjorie closed her eyes. "You're going to die soon. I… I, uh, saw you on the ground. There was blood and… a blinding light around you, but it was no good. I'm so sorry… the life had gone out in your eyes."

Astrid shrugged it off like a pro. "Not to worry. I've died three times already. Did someone come and bring me back to life? That always tends to happen." A ripple of nervous laughter made its way around the room.

Marjorie grasped for Astrid's hand again, as though desperate for good news. When she drew away, however, we could all tell that she'd seen something that none of us wanted to hear.

She shook her head with agonizing slowness. "No… nobody's there. Your heart has stopped and you're completely cold. That blinding light has gone, and you're still on the ground. You're dead."

"Is it possible that you're not seeing the whole thing?" I asked urgently.

She nodded. "Yeah, completely. I never see the whole picture. Someone might run over to you five minutes after what I saw and resurrect you. If that's happened before, then maybe it happens again, and I just didn't see it." She sounded so heartbreakingly hopeful. I shared in it. There was no way that we'd let Astrid die for good —no way.

"I'm never out for too long," Astrid replied with forced cheer. She sounded more worried than she wanted to let on, which unsettled me. Then again, surely Alton would bring her back again, if that image came to pass. I tried to offer her a look of encouragement, but she wouldn't hold anyone's gaze.

"Do your visions *always* come true?" Wade asked.

"No, not always. They're suggestions of what might happen. Loads of variables can change the outcome. I could look at Astrid again tomorrow and see something completely different."

Raffe frowned. "So it's not an exact science?"

"No, it's pretty hit and miss."

Maybe Marjorie just didn't see all of it. Maybe if she looked again, she'd see Alton bringing Astrid back. I had to cling to that hope.

"That's something the coven can help with," Harley said. "They'll help you to hone your skills so you can see things more clearly. It's like anything, I imagine; you just need practice."

Marjorie nodded. "That's what Santana was saying."

Harley cast me a congratulatory glance that I was only too happy to accept. It looked like Marjorie and I were developing ourselves a nice friendship. I'd never had sisters, but I figured this was the closest thing to a little sister I was going to get. She was cool. I liked her. More than that, I knew she'd fit into the mechanics of the coven like a perfect cog. And we were lucky to have her.

"What do you know about these other kids?" Wade asked, sliding a folder over the desk toward Marjorie. She took a glance at the names and abilities listed beside the children.

Her brow furrowed. "They might be like me. The twins said that they were specifically looking to recruit 'particularly gifted' kids. They didn't say I was a Clairvoyant, but they said I was one of the rare creatures that they were looking for—someone with a special power. To be honest, they made it sound like they wanted exotic animals for their private zoo."

"Sounds about right," I said.

"Yeah, clearly there's a method to Katherine's madness," Harley conceded. "Sounds to me like she's rounding up the children with super rare abilities, like Clairvoyants, Morphs, Herculeans, Sensates, and Portal Openers. Micah had Earth and Telekinesis abilities, but who knows what else he's capable of? We might have only just scratched the surface, but Katherine may know something about them that we don't. Take that Devereaux girl—she appeared to have some kind of Telepath quality. That's why she ran."

Wade grimaced. "That's what I was thinking."

"Yeah, but the twins killed her," I chimed in. "I saw the limbs when I went to get her file from Krieger."

Marjorie gasped, clamping her hand down over her mouth. I guessed she realized it could've been her. Poor thing. She looked horrified. Clearly, we were scaring her with our chat. She knew some aspects about Katherine Shipton—before handing the interview over to me, Alton had made sure she knew what we were dealing with, and who had snatched the rest of the kids—but being in the know didn't make it any less terrifying.

"It might have been an accident. They'd never have purposefully killed someone as powerful as that," Harley replied.

She had a point. "Katherine is probably pissed about losing that one."

"Why is she doing this to us?" Marjorie whispered. This couldn't possibly be easy for her. It wasn't for us, either, but she was the one with the target on her back.

"Hey, don't worry about a thing. We've got you covered, and we're not going to let anything happen to you," I promised. "Sorry about all of this. You must be exhausted. Do you want to go to your room, settle in a bit?"

Marjorie nodded.

"Okay, no problem. You'll have twenty-four-hour security while you're here with us, so you've got nothing to worry about. I'll also give you this so you can call me for help if you feel threatened, or any kind of emergency comes up." I handed her an ancient Aztec coin with markings etched across the surface. I'd charmed it so that it connected directly to my Orishas. As soon as Marjorie called for me, I'd know about it. It would be like fireworks going off in my head.

She took it gratefully in her trembling hands. "Thank you, Santana."

"Not a problem, *mi changuita.* Like I said, we're all here to keep you safe."

Having two magical guards at all times and an emergency charm with her was the only way that Marjorie could stay at the SDC, given that Katherine still had her spies in our midst. Alton was trying to keep her presence here quiet, but news always leaked out in places like this. Our plan was to be better prepared this time, in case anyone came after her again. With the guards and the charm, we'd have a better shot at catching whoever was working for Katherine, without having to deal with the bloody aftermath of another Cranston and Devereaux scenario.

As the two Security Magicals came in to take Marjorie to her room, I wondered what abilities these other kids might have, beyond the ones we'd seen and written down. We still had Louella's limbs in the coven mortuary. There was only one problem… A Reading couldn't be done on dead people.

SIXTEEN

Santana

The following evening, I lay back on Astrid's bed and covered my face with a pillow. Music played from Smartie's speakers —a slow ballad that was making me sleepy. Exhaustion was already creeping in, after a full day spent following leads that went nowhere.

Marjorie had touched a few of the belongings from the rest of the missing kids and done her best to piece together where they might be, but every location we'd visited had been a dead end. Either the kids had been moved, or it had been an old vision of where they'd been. Nobody nearby knew anything about them, nor had they caught a glimpse of them. All these false steps were starting to annoy me.

"This is hopeless," I muttered into the pillow.

I knew I was being a defeatist, which wasn't like me at all, but exhaustion had a way of wrecking my positivity. There were still a bunch of leads for us to follow, and we were set to try again tomorrow. After all, Marjorie had told us that her visions changed, shifting like the colors in a kaleidoscope. One day, they showed one thing, another day they might show something else. We were hoping for the something else; otherwise, we were right back at square one.

"No, it's not," Astrid replied sternly. Tatyana, Astrid, and I had retreated to the comfort of Astrid's room. There was something about the way she'd decorated it that felt welcoming, with Christmas lights covering one entire wall and crystals clinking soothingly overhead. Harley and Wade were off making moon eyes at each other, Dylan was in his room, cramming for a college exam, GI Joe and Jane had gone for dinner in the banquet hall, and Raffe had gone to speak with Tobe about reinforcing his Hyde box. According to Raffe, he was worried about its integrity. *Super comforting, considering I spent a whole night beside it, thinking it was safe.*

"It is annoying, though," Tatyana conceded. "We keep thinking we're getting somewhere, that we have this upper hand, and then it vanishes again. Having a Clairvoyant should have made this easy, but she lacks the strength to be of considerable use."

I pulled the pillow away from my face and sat up. "Hey, she's trying her best."

"I'm not saying she's not, but I don't think I'm wrong in assuming that we all thought this would be the key to solving our problem. If she were stronger, and more in control of her powers, it might have made a difference. As it stands, we just have visions that lead us nowhere," Tatyana replied bluntly.

I hated to admit that she was right. Tatyana was one of my best friends, and I adored the bones of her, but sometimes she lived up to her reputation as an ice queen. Every time Marjorie strained to use her powers, seeking to delve deeper, it left her weak and worn out. The trouble was, we'd all been given the gift of time with *our* powers. Marjorie didn't have that luxury, not if she wanted to please everyone around her. It riled me up to think of the pressure she was under. *For heaven's sake, she's only been at the coven a day! Give her a friggin' break.* I didn't say it out loud because it wasn't Tatyana I was annoyed with. It was Alton. For the director of a coven, he wasn't being particularly patient with the newbie.

"She must be so confused," Astrid said. "I bet all she wants to do is go home to the Hamms and forget any of this ever happened."

"Yeah, which is what the Hamms have done," I replied wryly. "I'm not looking forward to the day I have to tell her that."

Tatyana smiled. "You two seem to have a nice connection. It'll be good for her to have someone like you. She looks up to you already, I can tell. I just hope your foul mouth doesn't rub off on her."

"My language is perfectly clean, thank you very damn much," I shot back, laughing. "Anyway, I can't help being fiery. It comes with the territory if you're a Catemaco."

"Speaking of which, how're you feeling about the Family Gathering next week?" Astrid asked, looking up from her book. She'd been delving into the realm of rare abilities to see what we might be up against. There were some insane ones that had fallen into extinction, as far as the history books were concerned: Flyers, Amphibians, Regens, Electros, Time Jumpers. A mad bunch of awesome powers that had been cut off somewhere down the bloodlines.

I exhaled and flopped back onto the bed. "I'm looking forward to it about as much as I would look forward to jumping into a baboon cage slathered in peanut butter."

"That good, eh?" Tatyana chuckled.

I flipped over and crawled to the end of the bed. "You're looking forward to it?"

"Yes and no. I guess I'm a bit nervous about seeing my parents again. I anticipate the usual barrage of Vasilis charm," she said sardonically. "However, *this* time I'll have something good to tell them. It won't all be doom and gloom and disappointment."

"Oh?"

"I've been thinking about it for a couple of days, but I'm planning to talk to them about the Merlins and Katherine Shipton." She set down her phone and looked up at me, her legs dangling off the end of the bed. "It makes sense, right? They know their history, I'm sure they do, and they might have even been around during some of those events."

I frowned. "Weren't they in Moscow?"

She shook her head excitedly. "No, not back then. Twenty years ago, they were still in New York, working their way through the ranks of the NY Coven. It was a few years later that they took their positions as directors of the Moscow Coven—because, you know, they don't do anything without each other. Like they're joined at the hip or something." She rolled her eyes, making me laugh.

I grabbed the pillow and chucked it at her head. "Hey, that's romantic!"

"Not when it's your parents."

"If Raffe gets off his ass and tells me he likes me, that might be us one day." I grinned at the thought. My encounter with the djinn hadn't done anything to put me off. We all had our flaws. His just happened to be a smoky demon that took over his body every now and again, giving him improved strength and stamina. *There might even be a couple of benefits to that…*

"Believe me, you don't want to be anything like my parents," Tatyana said.

I laughed. "I think it's a good idea to speak to them about the Merlins and the Shiptons. They might have some useful insider knowledge that we've missed, or that *certain people* don't want to tell us."

"Hey, those *people* might end up your father-in-law one day, from the way you're going on about Raffe," Tatyana teased.

"See, that's the one thing that could put me off Raffe… but if he can cope with my family, I can cope with his."

"We'll find out next week, won't we?"

I grimaced. "Ugh, don't remind me. I haven't even thought about how I'm going to navigate that minefield," I said. "My parents will sweep in with their nosy questions and their high expectations and their constant hassling. 'When are you getting married? When are you coming home? When will you find a good man and take your place at the head of the Catemaco Coven?' The usual stuff. It's always a broken-record kind of thing. It never sinks in that I'm not interested, that I don't want to bow to that kind of pressure."

"So, you're thrilled about it, then?" Tatyana joked, throwing the pillow back up onto the bed.

"I think I'm the same as you," I admitted. "I'm half dreading it, half looking forward to it. At the end of the day, they're my family, and I love them right down to their overbearing core. I'm just not too eager to be married off, you know? I like to keep my romantic options semi-open."

"Raffe will be glad to hear that."

I glanced at Astrid, who hadn't said much as Tatyana and I had babbled on. She held Smartie close to her chest as it played a sweet song, her gaze somewhere off in the distance. All she needed was raindrops on the window and she'd have been a still from a romcom. I nudged Tatyana and pointed to our friend.

"Since we're talking about romantic options... what's going on with you, Astrid? Any options you want to tell us about, hmm?" I asked.

Tatyana nodded. "A certain Garrett Kyteler, perhaps?"

Her cheeks flushed pink as she turned to look at us, evidently remembering that we were still in the room. She put Smartie back down on her desk and fidgeted uncomfortably. I might as well have shone a flashlight in her face and demanded she tell me everything, she was so on edge. Up until that moment, I hadn't been positive that there was much going on between her and Garrett, but now I was sure. This looked like the face of an entirely smitten young woman.

She shrugged. "I… I like him."

I shrieked. "You do?"

"I really do," she whispered, looking anywhere but at me. "I know he gives off this rude, abrasive vibe, and he's a major sufferer of foot-in-mouth syndrome, but he's fun to be around. He's funny, and he's intelligent, and he… well, he seems to like me back. I'm not one-hundred-percent sure, but I really do think the feeling might be mutual."

"How could he possibly resist? You're a dreamboat!" Tatyana cried excitedly.

"Recently, he's been giving me all these subtle signals—a joke here, a touch there, a thoughtful moment now and again. Plus, he's responsive whenever I attempt to flash a little signal in his direction. I'm not the greatest flirter of all time, but I think I do okay. He laughs quite a lot, which I think is a good thing?"

"Of course it is," I assured her.

Astrid looked up sheepishly. "I know this must be awkward for you, Santana."

"Pfft, what are you talking about? Garrett and I dated a million years ago. All of that is way in the past now," I replied, meaning every word. "It was when I first came to the coven, and I think it was more out of loneliness than anything else. Besides, it all went sideways pretty quickly."

"I don't think I've ever asked you *why* it went sideways," Astrid said. She looked worried, visibly bracing for bad news.

I shrugged. "We just weren't meant to be. We didn't work out. I think we were too different," I replied, not wanting to delve too deep into it. I didn't care about Garrett in that way anymore, but the scar of our bitter breakup still had its place in my heart. He'd hurt me and betrayed me, his eye constantly roving, and it had taken me a long time to forgive him for that.

"Are you sure that's all there was to it?" Astrid pressed nervously.

"It doesn't matter how we ended, because everybody changes. What matters is, we didn't work out. I'm sure he's a good guy now."

"Do you think it's a good idea to pursue this?"

I smiled at her. "I think you should follow your heart, *mi querida*. I only have one word of advice, and that would be to look after yourself. Keep a guard around your heart, because he might end up breaking it. He might not, but it's always a good idea to protect yourself."

"A few weeks ago, I'd have agreed with you. In fact, I probably would have stayed away completely," Astrid said. "But recently... I don't know what's happened to him. Garrett seems to have changed a lot since he and Wade patched things up. It's like a weight was lifted off his shoulders, or something. I can't explain it. I'm not saying there's a major friendship rebirth afoot, but they have a better idea of where they stand with each other. It seems to be having a pretty wonderful effect on Garrett."

"That's great, Astrid. It really is." I meant it from the bottom of my heart. I wanted her to find someone awesome. She deserved an ace guy who adored the ground she walked on. There wasn't a smarter, funnier, wiser woman alive than Astrid Hepler, and she was worthy of the best of the best. I didn't think Garrett fit that description, but that wasn't up to me. If she liked him, then more power to her.

The lingering sting of betrayal clouded my judgment where Garrett Kyteler was concerned. A bit of patching up couldn't change someone's nature. Garrett had always been an ass, and I was willing to bet my life on the fact that he would continue to be an ass... in some form or another. The only difference was, if Astrid opened her heart to him and he crushed it, he would have me to deal with. I would rain down on him with the fury of a thousand *tormentas* and wear his balls as earrings.

"Anyway, enough about me," Astrid urged. "I'm not the only one in this room with a fledgling romance. Tatyana, have you got anything exciting to tell us?"

"Yes, the tea must be spilled," I encouraged, grinning like a loon.

She sighed and rolled her eyes, but I could tell she was looking forward to telling us about Dylan. "Things have… progressed a little bit, I suppose. He's extremely hard to read. Sometimes, I think he's really into me, and the next I think he'd prefer to be with his college friends. That is the problem with American men—they aren't very open with their feelings."

"And Russian men are?" I flashed her a knowing grin.

"No, I suppose you're right about that," she said with a giggle. "Well, I say he isn't showing signs of interest, but he did take me on a date the other night."

Astrid grinned. "He did?"

"First of all, he picks me up from the coven with a bouquet of flowers in his hand and takes me on this surprise journey through San Diego. I have no idea where we're going, but I decide to enjoy the not-knowing part of it," she continued. "We drive up the coast and park beside this tiny church that overlooks the ocean, and it has the most beautiful cemetery I've ever seen attached to it."

A cemetery didn't exactly sound like an ideal date spot to me, but Tatyana looked almost smitten.

"We walk through this pretty little gate and sit beneath the shade of some trees at the far side of the cemetery," she continued. "There are spirits all around, gentle ones, who are content to wander in such a beautiful spot. They tell me that the bad ones come out at night, never in the day. I realize, as I'm walking, that he's arranged a picnic in the cemetery for us, with a blanket and a basket full of my favorite foods—soft cheese, fresh bread, blueberries, truffles. He's thought of everything. We sat there and we talked for hours, before he drove me home. No kissing, no fumbling, just one of those perfect dates where all you do is talk and get to know each other."

"And you think he's not interested?" I gasped. "The man is clearly head over heels in love with you. No man puts on a picnic unless he loves you. And he set it all up in a cemetery, knowing you'd be at home there with all the ghoulies floating around. I imagine he had an idea or two about *his* ghoulies, too, even if he didn't make any moves on you." I flashed her a wink.

"You're awful, Santana." She chuckled, flashing a coy smile. "I don't know. See, he was lovely and charming at the picnic itself, but then as soon as we got back here, he went back to being odd again. All the confidence kind of drained away, and he got all shifty and weird. I think we might be going on another semi-date this week, so I may be able to figure him out better this time."

"He's just shy, that's my guess," I said.

"But then why was he cool at the cemetery, but weird here? I don't get him."

"I think you should definitely see how the next date goes," Astrid chimed in. "The more you get to know him, the more he'll loosen up around the coven. It's probably this place that makes him nervous, not you."

"Maybe you're right," she mused. "Anyway, why haven't you and Raffe been on any dates? You're into him, right?"

"I'm *definitely* into him."

"And he's into you, right?"

I shrugged. "It's been bugging me for a while, but I really don't know. I like to think I know myself and that I can turn on the charm. But with him… I've got no idea if he's just easily flustered and kind of blushy as a person, or if he's, as you say, into me. I want him to like me the way I like him, but we don't always get what we want. Which sucks, by the way." I buried my face in the duvet cover. "If you think Dylan is hard to read, try reading Raffe. That boy, quite literally, blows hot and cold."

"Trouble with djinn djimminy djinn djimminy djinn djinn djaroo?" Astrid asked.

I chuckled. "Surprisingly not. In this scenario, Raffe's the one I'm having trouble with. The djinn is pretty freaking blunt. He says it like it is."

"You sound like you admire it."

"Him. Like I admire *him*," I replied. I'd come to know the djinn well enough not to consider him anything less than a person in his own right. "No, I just wish Raffe could be a little more forward sometimes, you know? Well, as long as he's being forward with the things I want to hear."

Tatyana smiled. "I have a solution to all your romantic problems, my dear."

"You do?"

"Harley."

"Hey, I know she's cute and everything, but ladies don't exactly sugar my coconuts, if you catch my drift?"

Tatyana burst out laughing. "No! I mean, why don't you talk to Harley about Raffe? Being an Empath, she'll be able to tell you what he's feeling without anyone else knowing about it. Raffe included."

As if summoned by the mere mention of sugared coconuts, Harley thundered past the half-open door of Astrid's bedroom. Striding at breakneck speed, she seemed to be headed somewhere important. I thought about going after her, but, considering her pace, I decided against it. She looked determined and kind of angry, and if she was angry at something, I didn't want to get in the way of that freight train.

Alas, my romantic woes would have to wait.

SEVENTEEN

Harley

I strode through the hallways like a woman possessed, overwhelmed with the need to get a couple of things off my chest. I'd spent the last few hours stewing in my room after a fruitless day of scouring San Diego for the kids, and I couldn't take the silence anymore. The girls were in Astrid's room, but I didn't want to bother them with my silly problems, not when there were so many things on all of our plates. I wasn't exactly a chatterbox when it came to personal issues. As such, there was only one man—well, man-beast—who was up to the task.

"Harley, what a nice surprise," Tobe growled warmly, as I plonked myself down on one of the glass boxes and let out an enormous sigh. "Or, not so nice, by the sounds of it. Bad day?"

I nodded. "You could say that. Bad month, if I'm being totally honest."

"Do you need someone to talk to?"

"Would you mind?"

He stopped what he was doing and sat down on the box next to mine. "Not at all. What seems to be the problem?" he asked. "Is it the missing children?"

"See, it should be," I replied sharply. "Those kids *should* be all I can think about, but my mind keeps wandering off to these weird places. I can't get my head to think straight; it keeps getting filled up with a bunch of useless fluff."

"I doubt there is such a thing as useless fluff, but could you be more specific? I cannot advise on something as vague as… well, fluff."

I held my head in my hands. "The Family Gathering. I didn't realize it was such a huge deal. I thought it was some casual thing that you could go to if you wanted to. Alton's already said he's expecting me to be there, but what's the point in me going?" I rambled. "It's not like I have anyone to bring along. I'll just be wandering around by myself, putting on a smile to keep the coven happy."

This wasn't like me at all, to get so bogged down in a mire of self-pity. That was the trouble—this was one scenario that I couldn't shrug off. I'd spent the last few hours trying to snap the hell out of it, to no avail. Everyone else had families that were coming to the Gathering. They might have been complaining about them, but they'd all have someone there at the party.

"I mean, it's not like I can invite the Smiths, is it? They're human, so that's a no-go, even though they're just about the only family that I have," I went on. "Well, the only family that aren't in hiding, and still seem to want me around."

"Slow down there, Harley, or you'll end up having an aneurysm," Tobe said.

"See, this is why you should *never* get attached to anyone or anything," I spat. "All they do is leave… or get themselves killed."

"We are not talking about the Smiths anymore, are we?" Tobe asked.

I cast him a look of pure mental exhaustion. "I don't know what's up with me, man. I knew Isadora wasn't going to be here to stay. I knew it the moment we met and she explained who she was. I'm such a freaking idiot."

Not to mention this whole Wade thing. This was why it was a terrible idea to get attached to people—it never ended well. I was better off forgetting I liked him. At least it would stop me from acting like a complete goof around him. *Yeah, good one. As if you can just switch it off and on like that. It would be freaking useful if you could, but you can't. Wade Crowley is stuck in your brain and there's no getting him out. Ugh.*

Tobe ruffled his white-and-gold feathers, the sound oddly calming. "It sounds to me like you're experiencing a crisis of identity, Harley. Through no fault of your own, I might add," he said. "You've spent your entire life building walls to keep people out, and being reunited with someone you could call family has torn a hole in those walls. You wanted to let Isadora in; it is only natural. However, the only way to let her in was to lower your defenses. Now, you must decide—were those fortifications hiding who you really are, or were they the very fabric of who you really are?"

"Are you sure you don't write fortune cookies in your spare time?" I teased.

He smiled. "I do not, though perhaps I should. Being the Beast Master doesn't pay as well as you might think."

I chuckled. "It's just hard, you know? I've learned nothing else from my aunt. She keeps making these promises to tell me more about the family history, but I get nothing. Off she zips into some tear in the fabric of time and space, and I'm left twiddling my damn thumbs. I've been waiting for nineteen years, Tobe. I've got zero patience left."

"It's hard to wait, but it shall be worth it all the more when you finally get the whole truth," Tobe said. "Also, you must understand that there may be things that you don't want to hear. We know your father may have been under a spell when he killed all those people, which came as some relief to you, yes?"

I nodded.

"But what if Isadora has other secrets that may not be so easily swallowed? What if, by waiting, she is protecting you from a truth you may not be ready to hear?"

"That's not her choice to make."

He chuckled, rumbling like a purring cat. "That's her job as your aunt. You may feel as if she has abandoned you again, and you'd be well within your rights to endure such emotions, but she loves you. You are all she has left in this world, just as she is all you have. I think there's more to her reluctance than meets the eye."

"Still… it's really freaking frustrating."

He nudged me in the arm. "So I gather."

"And I've still got absolutely no idea what to do about this stupid Gathering. Do I go stag? Do I put on a show? Do I suck it up and go through with it, same as always?"

"Self-pity does not suit you, Harley. You're stronger than that. After all, nobody likes a wallower. Believe me, I have one in the Bestiary."

I laughed. "What does a wallower look like?"

"You, if you don't stop."

"Okay, okay, no more wallowing." Absently, I kicked my feet against the front of the glass, scaring the life out of an armadillo-looking critter in the box below. "I'll go to the damn party and I'll smile and schmooze with the best of them. See, this is why I came to you—I knew you'd talk me around."

"It seems I am quite the 'agony aunt' of late."

I frowned. "You are?"

"Yes, Santana was in here a while ago, voicing similar concerns about her identity," Tobe said. "I wouldn't ordinarily share the words of another, but the two of you appear to be dealing with the same sorts of problems. She doesn't believe she is destined for the life her family wishes her to have. At least, in some small way, it's a benefit that you don't have to bend to the will of those dearest to you."

"Great, make me feel guilty, why don't you?" I muttered, throwing him a wry smile.

"I'm merely saying that the two of you are rather alike. You come from exceptional legacies, yet both of you are so very different than what has come before," he explained. "I would guess that, ironically, it's the reason that you get along so well. You are a similar sort of creature. Take the Bestiary, for example. Both of you are more fascinated by it than afraid of it. That cannot be said of all people. I have seen grown men and women sprint out of this room as if I had set a boogeyman loose."

I couldn't entirely wrap my head around what he was saying, but some of it rang true. Santana and I did have a lot of similarities, as well as differences. Although, it did make me wonder, for the gazillionth time in my life, how everything might have turned out if I'd had my mom and dad around. Would they have had similarly high expectations of me? Would they have tried to coerce me into a marriage I didn't want? It was hard to imagine a different picture than the reality, even now.

"I guess you're right," I said. *You're a wise old beast; I'm not going to argue.* "So, what do you know about my other aunt? About Katherine? I know she used to frequent the Bestiary, with her connection to the gargoyles and all."

"I believe she held a respect for me, but we did not talk as you and I are doing. We would exchange pleasantries, and I would always ask if she needed anything, but she was forever content to sit and chat with her gargoyles," he replied. "She was a brilliant woman, really. Had she been valued in her own right, perhaps she would not have ended up the way she has. You see, she was always living in the shadow of your mother. Like a starved plant, that lack of spotlight made her gnarled and twisted, sapping her of compassion and righteousness."

Tobe, my man, you're a freaking poet.

"Do you know why my mom and Katherine might have fallen out?" I glanced across at Quetzi's glass box, the Aztec snake slithering in the fog. He paused against the pane, as though listening to what we were saying.

Tobe pinched his fluffy brows together, his whiskers twitching. "I don't quite know the cause, but I remember the day things started to fall apart. Katherine stormed into the Bestiary one afternoon, in a violent fit of rage. I had to hold her back and physically remove her from the premises, because her magic was becoming a hazard. Boxes were shaking, the beasts were going wild, and my defense charms were threatening to explode."

I nodded along. "Do you think it might have had something to do with my dad?"

"The course of true love never does run smooth, and rejection can be wounding when the love is one-sided," he replied. "I imagine such a vehement reaction stemmed from the sisters' competition for Hiram's affections, and Katherine's subsequent loss. I believe that was why she stormed into the Bestiary that day, because Hiram had cast her aside for Hester. She held a fearsome grudge, that much is clear. If she really did use Sál Vinna on your father, then we can be certain that she is quite insane. No person would use that unless they were entirely unhinged. Although, I hear a broken heart can often tip even the sanest of individuals over into insanity."

"Someone else seems to be holding a bit of a grudge," I said, gesturing at Quetzi. Every time Katherine's name was mentioned, he hissed and ruffled his feathers.

Tobe frowned at the serpent. "Hmm… how curious. I don't know why Quetzi would be acting that way."

"Maybe Katherine gets his snaky senses tingling."

"There is power in a name. Perhaps you're right—he may sense the evil in what we're discussing."

"Well, he might have to hiss a few more times, because I've got another question to ask you regarding little Miss Shipton," I said nervously. "Do you know anything about the process of becoming a Child of Chaos? Like, is it even possible? You've been around a long time; have you ever heard of that happening?"

He looked genuinely shocked. "The Children of Chaos would never allow a magical to join them. They have existed for all of time. They cannot be *created,* just as magicals are born and not made. If that is her plan, Harley, then she shall find herself sorely disappointed. She would barely be able to set foot inside their realm before they destroyed her for her insolence." He paused briefly. "Unless…"

"Unless?"

"There have been some rumors, over the centuries, that a Child of Chaos can be replaced. Nobody knows how, exactly, and it has never been written anywhere. These are mere stories, passed on by word of mouth. If Katherine has deciphered a way to achieve this, then… perhaps she knows something that nobody else does."

I sat in silence for a moment, gathering my thoughts. Before I did anything else, I needed to go to the New York Coven and find out the truth about my father. Isadora had told me that he was under the spell of Sál Vinna, but Tobe's previous words had thrown me off—what if she was trying to protect me from the truth there, too? Morbid as it sounded, I needed to see for myself if there was any evidence of the Icelandic love spell on my dad when he died. If Isadora wasn't going to spell it all out for me, I had to get the pieces together myself.

I'd been thinking a lot about my parents' Grimoire, too. They'd written that Grimoire together—an unusual notion in its own right

—and I was desperate to see what powerful spells it contained. I figured there might even be something useful within its pages, like a journal entry or something, that could shed light on what had happened between them and Katherine. My motivations for reading it were a bit more selfish than that, though. Honestly, I thought it might make me feel closer to them in some way.

But the more I learned about the Merlins and the Shiptons, the better I could prepare for what was to come. Armed with a crap-ton of intel, we'd have the means to take Katherine down.

Now, how to get to New York? I already had clearance to travel through the liquid-like mirrors in the Assembly Hall, since Alton hadn't revoked my free pass. Although, he'd definitely want me to tell him I was going through them before I actually did.

Yeah... not going to happen, Alton.

Just then, my phone rang. The tone echoed through the Bestiary, startling me out of my skin. I looked at the caller ID and saw that it was Wade. My heart beat harder at the sight of his name, my mouth going dry.

"Are you going to answer that?" Tobe asked, with a knowing smile.

"Yeah… uh, I just… never mind." I pressed the call button and lifted the phone to my ear. "Wade?"

"Are you busy?" *Blunt as ever.*

"I'm… uh… kind of busy, yeah. Although, you know, I can make some time… or something… if that's why you're calling?" I replied, stumbling over my words. What the heck had this boy done to me? Seriously, it wasn't cool. I'd never bumbled in my entire life, and now I couldn't stop.

"So, are you free, or aren't you?"

"Uh… actually, there was something I wanted to… you know, if you're not doing anything… there was a—well, it was more of an idea, really." My heart was hammering like crazy, a cold sweat trickling down my neck. This was starting to get downright embarrassing. I could barely mutter one coherent sentence to the guy. On the other end of the line, I imagined him rolling his eyes or wondering what the heck was going on. The vision of his face made me smile. Even when those deep green eyes were looking at me in total despair, they were hard to look away from.

"Is there something wrong with your connection?"

I reddened, not knowing what to say. Tobe and Wade had both thrown my mind for a loop, for very different reasons. Since hearing about Sál Vinna from Isadora, I'd believed it as fact. Tobe had reduced it back down to mere speculation. I couldn't let anyone else come to New York with me, if there was even the slightest chance of discovering that I was wrong about everything. Especially not Wade. What if my dad wasn't under the spell at all? What if he'd committed those terrible crimes of his own volition? I couldn't even bring myself to think about that outcome. It made me sick to my stomach.

"Yeah, I think there must be," I said quietly. "I've got some stuff I need to do. I'll call you later, or something—if that works for you."

"Yeah, fine. If you do find yourself without anything to do, send me a text and I'll let you know where I am. We've got a massive stack of folders to look through, and there are plenty with your name on them if you have nothing better going on."

"I have to look into something first," I murmured. "I don't know how long it's going to take."

"What thing?"

"Some books on the Children of Chaos. I keep thinking I've missed something." The lie tripped easily off my tongue—the smoothest sentences I'd spoken throughout the entirety of our conversation.

He sighed. "Fine, just call me when you're done."

The phone clicked, leaving me in an awkward silence. I'd made the right decision in not inviting him along. Judging by the sound of it, everyone else had enough on their plates with trying to find a new lead on these missing kids, and I didn't want to distract them from that. Marjorie's visions had proven temperamental at best, leading us on a wild goose chase around San Diego. Poor girl. I knew she was desperate to help us, and she was trying her best.

Tobe nudged me out of my reverie. "Penny for your thoughts."

"Thanks for the talk, Tobe. Sorry, I've got to go."

I hopped down from the box and hurried out of the Bestiary. Nope, nobody was coming with me this time; I had to do this alone. *This is between me and my dad.*

Hiram Merlin, do not *let me down.*

EIGHTEEN

Santana

Still lounging on Astrid's bed, I had a sudden change of heart. Harley had looked stressed out, striding past the door like that. Not a normal kind of stressed out, but something a bit more troubling. If she was having a hard time, it was my job to cheer her up.

Don't worry, hermana, I'm coming for you.

"Where are you going?" Astrid asked. "We were just getting to the juicy part."

"Astrid, I love you dearly, and I'm insanely happy that you're getting your flirt on, but having Garrett brush your hand while you were both reaching for the salt isn't so juicy. Come back to me when there's a smooch." I winked at her and darted for the door.

"Hey, who are you abandoning us for?" Tatyana called after me.

I ducked back into the room. "Harley just went by. I want to check on her, make sure she's doing okay. Things have been a bit crazy since she got here, and I don't think the Family Gathering is helping."

Tatyana grimaced. "I'd forgotten about that. Do you think Alton might make an exception for the Smiths? The cleanup guys could always wipe their memories afterward."

"I doubt it. With this mystery spy in the coven, and everything else that's going on with the kids and Katherine, I'm guessing Alton doesn't want to add any more complications to the mix… even if it would be kind of nice for Harley."

"That sucks," Astrid muttered.

"Yeah, here we are, complaining about our families…" I sighed, feeling like crap. "Ah man, she must have heard us talking from the hallway."

"Do you want us to come with you?" Tatyana asked.

I shook my head. "Nah, it's probably best if we don't crowd her. You know how much she hates talking about stuff. She's like a tortoise. One mention of something personal and in she goes, back into her shell. If it's just me, I might be able to coax some truth out of her," I replied, waggling my eyebrows. "Anyway, if we need some Amazonian backup, and a few drinks at Waterfront Park, I'll send you both a text. That cool?"

"Sounds good to me," Astrid replied.

"Oh, and don't think you're off the hook about the Family Gathering, Ms. Hepler. I want to hear all of your family woes later, *entiendes*? There have *got* to be some skeletons in your closet."

She flushed. "I've got nothing to tell!"

"Sure you haven't." I flashed her a mischievous grin and hurried out into the hallway, leaving them to discuss the juicy details of Astrid's hand-brush.

Reaching the magnolia trees in the circular courtyard below the living quarters, I realized I had no idea where Harley had gone. I racked my brain for places she might be, in a state like that. An idea sprang into my mind—the banquet hall. Whenever I felt like crap about something, and Tobe was too busy doing his actual job, the banquet hall became my sanctuary, my confessional, my therapy, all rolled up into one. There was *nothing* that the Coven's caramel apple pie couldn't fix.

Coming to a halt outside the doors to the banquet hall, I peered in to find it eerily empty. Channing and Stella were pretty much the only people inside, and they didn't seem to be enjoying each other's company. Stella was pushing tomato pasta around her plate, her head resting on her hand, while Channing wolfed down a stack of pretzel sliders that was almost as tall as him. Not a single word passed between them. *Daydreaming about Crowley, are we, Stella?* I liked the girl, for the most part, but she was barking up the wrong tree if she thought she could nab Wade for herself. The cringeworthy display of flirtation she'd put on during our search for Marjorie was still seared into my brain.

Hate to burst your bubble, mi fresa, but Crowley isn't for you.

I ducked back out into the hallway before they could see me. This required a rethink.

Figuring I'd eventually cross paths with her, even if it was back up in the living quarters once she'd blown off steam, I started my evening stroll around the coven. Along the way, I stopped at all the places I knew she liked to go. The courtyard with the dragon fountain, the Luis Paoletti Room, the library. I couldn't find her anywhere.

Well, this is freaking hopeless, I thought, coming almost full circle. I'd tried calling, but it kept going straight through to voicemail, and she hadn't texted me back yet. Having ended up on the opposite side of the building, I walked toward the main doors of the Assembly Hall and pushed them open with an almighty heave. Pushing both at once gave me a childish cheap thrill; it made me feel like a warrior princess striding into her great hall after a victorious battle. Plus, the Hall was the quickest way through to the other side.

I froze. Up ahead, standing in front of the travel mirrors, was the very person I'd been looking for. Harley stood on the raised platform, staring into the liquid-like pools of the event horizon. The scalloped bronze edging of the mirrors glinted in the low light of the chandeliers. Everything had been put back in its place since Harley's pledge incident. Looking around, nobody would ever have known that anything had happened here—apart from the poor bastards who nearly got crushed to death by a falling lampshade, that is. *My little Harley, already making a legacy for herself, like all the Merlins before her.*

Letting the doors swing slowly shut behind me, both of them whispering across the marble floor, I edged toward Harley. She seemed transfixed by the swirling matter that made up the mirrors. Either that, or she was contemplating what the hell she was going to do next. Frankly, I was wondering the same thing.

"Going somewhere?" I asked, once I was close enough.

She whirled around, her eyes wide in fear as she clutched her chest. "SANTANA! You nearly gave me a heart attack!"

"I didn't want you jumping through before you told me where you were off to," I replied. "Having a little evening jaunt? Going to read Finch a bedtime story?"

"No."

"Does Alton know where you're going?"

Her cheeks flushed. "I've already got clearance to use the mirrors. He doesn't need to know."

"You had clearance to use the mirrors when you went to Purgatory. Does he know you're using them for something else?"

"He doesn't need to, I already told you."

"*Mi cuate,* come on! This is ridiculous," I said, aware of the hard edge to my tone. "I hate to say it, but you shouldn't be going anywhere on your own. None of us should. I know it sucks, but it's not safe for you to go rogue like this. You heard Finch—Katherine is coming for you. If you just wander off on your own, who's to say she won't snatch you the moment you set foot outside this building? At least tell someone what you're doing before you do it, okay?"

I realized I was being a little hard on her, but she'd scared me. She was one of us now, and the thought of her just disappearing into the night sent a shudder of fear up my spine. Katherine might have been keeping to the periphery of her master plan, but she was a very real threat. Just because she hadn't ridden in on the back of a nuclear warhead or rolled through the front doors in a tank didn't mean she wasn't a danger. The woman was clearly patient, coiled up like a snake, ready to strike the moment we crept too close.

I sighed. "Where are you going, anyway? Can you at least tell me that?"

"The New York Coven."

"To get intel on your dad?"

She nodded slowly. "Yeah, that and the Grimoire. I need to be a hundred-percent sure that my dad was under Sál Vinna when he killed those people. I don't know why, but I've been having doubts. Part of me thinks Isadora might have been trying to protect me from the truth when she led us to that love spell." She paused for breath. "It makes sense, right?"

I shrugged. "I think you'll have to find out for yourself."

"So, you understand why I can't tell Alton what I'm doing."

"Now that you've told me it's about your dad… I'd probably do the same thing in your position," I replied reluctantly.

"People keep saying we've got a lot in common." She flashed me a nervous smile. She might've had her Empath powers, but I, too, could read her like a book right now. Clearly, she'd gotten it into her head that she could nip out to New York for a quick snoop around and get back before anyone noticed. *Bold, but stupid.* One false move, one minor delay, and she'd have had the coven in a panic, especially Alton.

"I like to think that's true, but there's one thing I would've done that you didn't," I said.

"What's that?"

"I'd have freaking told someone what I was up to. We're your crew now! You can trust us."

She heaved out a sigh. "I just didn't want to bother anyone during the investigation. There's so much going on, and—"

"Hold up, let me stop you there, before my BS meter blows a fuse," I interjected. "What's really going on here, huh? I know you've only been here less than two months, but I like to think I've got an idea what you're like. You'd have at least whispered something to Wade about this, and since he isn't here trying to stop you, I'm guessing he doesn't know either. Why are you hiding this from us?"

"I'm not 'hiding' anything," she shot back, seeming genuinely wounded.

"Then what's the deal? *Cuate*, you can tell me anything. I won't judge—I don't know how to," I promised. "Well, unless it's Stella trying to flirt with Wade. Then, I *have* to judge. For a girl who looks as bomb as that, and goes out on covert missions for a living, you'd think she'd have mastered the art of subtlety. I was dying of cringe."

Harley laughed. "You saw that, huh?"

"I think the space station saw it."

"Can I let you in on a little secret?"

I leaned in. "Please do."

"From what I could feel coming off her, it was all for show. She's totally in love with Channing, and she's trying to make him jealous by flirting—and I use that word generously—with Wade."

"Oh God. I was kind of irritated with her before, on your behalf, but now I just feel sad," I said. "Poor Stella. Nobody should put themselves through that kind of humiliation for a guy. Nobody. Especially for one who's not even interested."

"Right?"

I cast a conspiratorial glance in Harley's direction. "So, nice subterfuge there, trying to put me off the scent with a little Stella-related tidbit as a diversion. Not going to work, *hermana*. What's the deal? Why the secrecy?"

Harley scuffed her boot against the edge of the mirror. "Honestly... it's because of what I said before. I'm terrified I might be wrong about my father's innocence. I figured, if I found something in New York that, in the end, proved his guilt beyond a reasonable doubt, I didn't want any of you knowing about it—at least not yet. I mean, that would crush me, man. I'd need to figure out how to deal with that disappointment before I could breathe a word of it to any of you. Not because I don't trust you, but because I... I don't know. I'd want to be able to process that on my own first, if that makes any sense at all?"

"Makes perfect sense to me." I folded my arms across my chest, realizing I was in danger of striking up one of my mom's poses. "But there's no use worrying about it until you can find out for sure. I guess, in a way, he's both innocent and guilty. Think of it as a Schrödinger's Dad kind of situation."

She smiled. "Comforting." Like the famous experiment, where the cat in the steel box was both dead and alive in the minds of observers, her dad was both innocent and guilty. Until she opened the proverbial box, that was.

"I try. Anyway, what I'm trying to say is, you can deal with the outcome when it arrives, but not a moment sooner. Otherwise, it'll drive you nuts. You'll end up doing something stupid, like, I don't know, venturing off without telling anyone and jumping through to New York even though there's a terrifying über-witch out for your blood."

Harley lifted her hands in surrender. "Okay, okay, I'm sorry."

"Glad to hear it, but you're still not going through that mirror without me, so there's that."

"At least you're entertaining," she teased. "Plus, you're fearless. Seriously, I don't think you're scared of anything. It's one of the coolest things about you. Someone could say, 'Hey, Santana, you wanna help me hunt a bunch of sixty-foot spiders that are gobbling up San Diego?' and you wouldn't even bat an eye. You'd have a word with your Orishas, and *boom,* it'd be game over for the creepy-crawly suckers."

I smiled at her. "Of course I get scared. To be honest with you, I'm scared most of the time. I just choose to let that fear ignite my fire, you know? Get my engines roaring, my fuel burning, my marshmallows toasting." I paused, grinning. "It's like anything—you've got to use the energy that something gives you, instead of fighting against it."

Without warning, my mind drifted back to my encounter with the djinn. That fiery demon was scary as all hell, but there was something intoxicating about him, too. I hated to admit it, but being around the djinn had given me one heck of a thrill. It was exciting, almost, to get that close to the weird manifestation of Raffe's dark side. The power, the strength, the raw energy that had crackled from his reddened skin... I shivered just thinking about it. *Not that I'd want it to come out when it's not in that glass box. I'll take Jekyll over Hyde any day of the week.*

"You're a wise old soul, aren't you?" Harley chuckled.

"Runs in the family," I replied, the two of us exchanging a knowing look. "I'll provide the magical muscle while you're at the New York Coven. You won't even know I'm there. It'll be like you did this on your own."

"Thanks for that," she said.

I frowned, a wave of solemnity washing over me. "Seriously, though, I'm here for you. Whatever you need, any time of day or night. I'm your backup, for every magical, emotional, or physical need... well, maybe not every physical need. Look, what I'm saying is, we're pals, and that comes with the perk of always having someone around for you. You've got me for life, Harley. I'm not going to up and leave you, I promise. I hate to get all Woody and Buzz on you, but you've got a friend in me."

She laughed so hard that her cheeks turned red. "You can be the Woody to my Buzz any day, Santana."

"Glad you got it the right way around."

She wiped the tears from her eyes. "Seriously, I'm so happy to have you guys in my life. I never expected to have friends like you. I don't exactly make them very easily."

"Gee, I wonder why that is?" I tapped my chin.

"Hey, I'm working on my people skills, and that's all thanks to you and the others."

"Well then, let's go work some more on these people skills in New York, before Alton comes in here and finds us. What do you say?"

Without another word, she turned and stepped through the mirror. I had permission to use them, too, and my girl needed some backup.

Right, well, I guess that answers that question.

NINETEEN

Harley

Stepping through to the other side of the mirror, I stood for a moment and gaped at the sight before me. A towering hall of granite and chrome arched over us, with a painted frieze above us that would've put the Sistine Chapel to shame. It depicted witches and warlocks in the midst of a great battle, sparks and twists of color flashing, while a horde of shadowy monsters charged toward the powerful magicals. There was no scene of victory, presumably to remind us that the fight against evil was always ongoing. *Nice. Really gives the place that warm and cozy feeling.*

Santana whistled. "Well, this is intense."

"Tell me about it," I replied. "I feel like we've wandered onto a horror movie set. All we need is a bunch of vampires and zombies to complete the mood."

"You know, the undead get an unfair rap. They're actually not that bad; they can just be a bit of a nuisance sometimes. Banging on family doors and stuff. Plus, the gravediggers don't like it much—means twice as much work for them."

I stared at her. "You've seen the undead?"

"They can get a bit frisky around Día de los Muertos. Happens every year, though it's our job to make sure they stay six feet under. People think they want their dead loved ones back, but they'd run a mile if they actually saw the rotting corpse of their *abuelos* and *abuelas* crawling out of a grave. It's not pretty, but they don't mean any harm. They just get a little bit excited. It's a national holiday for them. They can't help it."

A stern figure with a sweep of black hair, gelled to within an inch of its life, stormed across the hall toward us. His eyes were a weird shade of gray, almost too light, and his thin, angular physique gave the impression of a hawk or a vulture. Either way, I sensed we were the prey.

"Excuse me," he barked, in a strange, transatlantic accent. "Might I ask who you are? No arrivals are scheduled for today."

My neck had somehow already started sweating. "I'm… Harley Merlin. And this is my associate, Santana Catemaco. We're here to gather some information on Hiram Merlin and Katherine Shipton, on behalf of the San Diego Coven." It was a risky move using my real name, but I figured the New York Coven knew about me by now. The only trouble was, I had a feeling he *definitely* wouldn't let me near my mom and dad's Grimoire.

He whipped out his phone and scanned it for a moment. "No, no record of your arrival. No record of intel requests. Are you sure you're supposed to be here?" He eyed us both curiously.

"Director Waterhouse sent us," Santana replied, without missing a beat. "We can't leave empty-handed, or he'll have our heads on a silver platter."

I nodded. "I guess we presumed he'd have sent word ahead that we were coming."

The man sighed. "Well, there's no record of it here. Someone must have screwed up. I'm supposed to be clocking out shortly, but I suppose I can stay and guide you in whatever you require." His hand shot out with such violence that Santana and I staggered back. "The name's James Salinger. Preceptor of International Cultures... and cleaning up other people's messes, apparently. Now, you said something about Katherine Shipton? Popular name at the moment. Can't turn a corner without hearing *someone* muttering 'Shipton' under their breath. I'm not particularly surprised that you of all people, Miss Merlin, would be sent to investigate the matter, given your...unfortunate...connections to the issue."

"We're trying to gather as much information as possible," I replied, putting my hand into Salinger's. He grasped it with intense force, his grip as stiff as his demeanor.

Santana nodded, avoiding his handshake altogether. "Better the devil you know, right?"

"Better the devil indeed, Ms. Catemaco," Salinger muttered.

"We're interested in learning more about Hiram Merlin, too," I reiterated.

Salinger pulled a face. "Well, there's another devil right there. When he swanned in here like an overstuffed peacock, thinking himself the big 'I am,' I knew he'd come to no good. And I was right." He paused, seeming to remember that Hiram's daughter was literally standing right in front of him. "No offense."

Maybe if you sounded a little more genuine, I might believe you.

"None taken," I replied coolly. This guy was already starting to grind my gears. I tried to give him the benefit of the doubt—maybe he'd had a bad day—but that didn't give him the right to start jamming insults down my throat about my dad. It was going to be a challenge to try and keep my cool around him, if he kept on like this. The thought of gathering information was just about the only thing that maintained my sense of calm.

"Pride comes before a fall, and that man had it in spades. That's all I'm saying."

I frowned, feeling offended on my dad's behalf. "I take it you didn't like him very much?"

"Hard to like someone who used to look at everyone as though they were bugs under his shoe, Miss Merlin. Very hard indeed." A weird smile crossed his face. "Not to mention the murders. Naturally, that's the main reason he's not liked around here."

"What about Hester? Did you know her well?" I couldn't help myself. If he was going to keep insulting my dad, I at least wanted information.

"She was a bit of a goody two-shoes, though she knew how to keep your father on his toes, which seemed to thrill him. I doubt he'd ever met anyone who'd told him no in his entire life. He chased after her like a dog after a bone. Hester was a favorite around here—'universally adored' is a fitting term. Tragic, really, what happened to her. I might not have liked her much, but that doesn't mean I wasn't saddened by her death. Not that I didn't see it coming. Hiram was a black hole who sucked the life out of everyone around him and dragged them all into his pathetic nonsense. He'd have been a great man if he'd put his efforts into the right places."

"Should we get going? We're on a bit of a tight schedule," I said, through gritted teeth. One more insincere word out of him, and I'd shut him up myself.

"I suppose so, now that you're here," he said. "This way, if you please." He whirled around and stalked toward the main corridor. He walked fast, leaving Santana and me to sprint after him. Santana shot me a sympathetic look, but I was still wrestling with the desire to use my Telekinesis and make snooty Salinger trip over his own feet.

We walked through gothic hallways draped in tapestries, with a thousand doors branching off. Lamplight flickered in silver sconces, casting shadows across the black marble floor. They were definitely going for a Transylvanian vibe, which seemed pretty fitting considering the witches and warlocks who lived here. Occasionally, through medieval-style arrow slits and stained-glass windows, I caught a glimpse of the city beyond. It seemed the New York Coven inhabited a similar interdimensional bubble as the San Diego Coven, though this one had been built within the sprawling grounds of Central Park.

Heading down a spiral staircase that plunged us deeper into the belly of the coven, we stopped at the lowest floor and moved along a bleak corridor. There were no windows here, only an endless array of curved doorways that reminded me of a monastery, or a medieval castle.

"Here we are," Salinger said, pausing outside one of the doorways. "We don't bring people here much, since it's easier to forget that *those* miscreants belonged to our renowned coven. Anyway, this is where you'll find everything you need to know on the Merlins and the Shiptons. Most of the files concerning them were never copied to the electronic database, so you might have to do a bit of sifting. If you're that eager for the information, I'm sure you won't mind." That eerie smile tugged at his lips again, unsettling me. There was something dark and strange about Salinger that left a bitter taste in my mouth.

Santana and I exchanged a glance, neither of us impressed. He pulled out a gigantic set of keys from his gray suit and slotted one into the lock.

He led us into a medium-sized room filled to the brim with labeled boxes. It was a fairly plain storage room, which was a little disappointing. I'd been expecting the antithesis of a trophy room, where details on all the bad guys were kept. *Not that my dad's a bad guy. We don't know that yet.*

We followed him down one of the aisles formed by metal bookshelves and stopped in front of a shelf at the back.

Salinger sneered. "Merlins and Shiptons, side by side until the bitter end. Even in the Dewey decimal system. You'll find all that you need here—mortuary records, family trees, details that were generally kept out of the magical public spectrum. I must ask that you don't actually take anything out of here, but feel free to make all the notes you like and take some pictures. I can make some copies, if I must."

"Thanks," I said tersely. I didn't like his tone.

"I'll leave you to have a look and come back in ten minutes or so. As I said before, I should really have clocked out by now, but there are a couple of things that I still need to attend to. I'll be back shortly. And, again, don't take anything out of this room, and please leave everything as you found it." With that, he turned on his heel and strode back out of the storeroom, leaving us to it.

"I'm going to punch him, I swear," I muttered, after making sure he'd really left.

Santana whistled. "Definitely not a fan of your parents. I doubt he could have been less sympathetic if he'd tried."

I let out a heavy sigh. "Should we start looking?"

She nodded, reaching for the first box labeled "Shipton." I went for the box beside it, labeled with my family name. Taking them down, we sat cross-legged on the floor and sifted through the contents. A few moments later, Santana took out a folded length of cream vellum that had been scrawled on with curling black ink.

I eyed it curiously. "What's that?"

"Shipton family tree," Santana replied. "There's not much to go on, by the looks of it. Katherine is on here, but there's no mention of her being a Shapeshifter. No mention of any of her ancestors being a Shapeshifter, either. It's just names, no abilities at all."

I grimaced. "Well, that's annoying."

"Yeah, Finch isn't on here either."

"Poor bastard can't catch a break when it comes to family," I said. "You know, I wonder what he'd have been like if he'd actually had a family to take care of him. Like, a real family, not just Mrs. Anker."

"With Katherine as his mom, I doubt it would ever have turned out good for him."

"I know what you mean, but Katherine can't have always been like that, either. Something has to happen in a person's life for them to turn into a monster. Nobody is born evil. At least, I don't think so."

"Maybe she's one of the exceptions."

"I guess." I thought back to what Tobe had said in the Bestiary, about heartbreak tipping someone over into insanity. I doubted that could be the entire story of what had turned her evil, but it might have been the catalyst. The final straw.

"I've got one here, too," I said, finding the Merlin family tree and pulling it out of the box. It was the same as the Shiptons—just names, no abilities. One stark truth jumped out at me. "They're all dead." On my dad's side, there were no grandparents, no great-grandparents, no cousins, no aunts, no uncles. All of them were deceased, aside from Isadora.

Okay... that's super weird. I'd expected a long-lost second cousin or something.

"All of them?"

I nodded.

"Weird. It's the same with the Shiptons."

Eager for more information, I reached for the mortuary photos. As I brought them out of the box, I could barely look at them. My father lay cold on a slab, his face drained of color and oddly bruised. Black, inky patches peppered his pale skin. I gripped the photos and tried to feel for any flicker of emotion coming from them. A faint whiff of love and grief drifted off, like the last notes of a sad song, but those feelings could well have been mine. I wanted to reach through the picture and touch him, as macabre as that sounded. He didn't look like my dad, and yet he looked exactly like him. A horrible, changeling version of the man in my dreams.

Tears brimmed in my eyes, a sob catching in my throat. The emotional trail was too cold for me to be able to pick up anything useful. Besides, by the time my dad died, I supposed nobody shed a tear for him. Everyone had thought he was a murderous psychopath. Isadora and Hester were the only ones who might have cared, and the latter had died a long time before this. At least she'd never had to watch him get executed. *Small mercies.*

"Any sign of tampering?" Santana asked. "We're looking for a rune on his neck and a small puncture wound, kind of like vamp fangs. Those are the telltale features of the Sál Vinna spell. Astrid sent me a picture." She got out her phone and showed me an image of a previous victim of the Icelandic love spell. The poor woman had a small rune inked into the side of her neck, with two tiny holes beside it. It really did look like Dracula had sucked on her jugular.

I looked over the mortuary images again, trying to find one of Hiram's upper half. I peered at one of the pictures that focused in on his neck and head. Sure enough, a tiny rune had been inked below his earlobe quite far back, almost in the shadow of his hairline. Two small puncture wounds sat beside it. Comparing it with the coroner's report, it said that my father had a small tattoo behind his ear, though it was written down as an emblem of Katherine's cult. *She was already starting all of this back then? Jeez, she's really serving her revenge cold.*

Tears bubbled over as I realized what it meant. It had taken a moment for the facts to sink in. My father *was* under the grip of the Icelandic curse when he did all those terrible things—the things they'd listed with great relish in some of the other folders. He'd been under that curse until he died. *He was innocent... He didn't want to kill anyone. She made him do it.* Then what was the hard truth that Isadora was keeping from me? If this wasn't it… what was it?

"Is it there?" Santana asked quietly. I could sense her anxiety.

Slowly, I nodded. "It's here."

She scooted over to me and wrapped her arms around me. "I'm so glad."

"Me, too," I whispered, burying my face in her shoulder.

TWENTY

Harley

"Sorry to interrupt." Salinger's voice cut through our silent moment, cold and unfeeling. "I must say, your conversation was rather intriguing. I couldn't help but hear from the hallway. If I'm not mistaken, I heard someone mention a very specific Icelandic love curse—very dangerous, very illicit, very illegal. I hope you're not planning to execute such a spell? Not that either of you would be capable. These sorts of curses are not for the beginner."

Santana bristled at my side. "Actually, if you must know, we just discovered that Hiram Merlin was under a spell called Sál Vinna when he died," she explained, as I wiped my eyes. I didn't want this asshole to see me cry. "It's a powerful love spell that binds a person to another person's will. They can't fight against it. We believe Katherine Shipton put him under it, and that's why he ended up doing the things he did."

Salinger snorted. "You think I don't know what Sál Vinna is? I'm the preceptor of International Cultures. It's my job to know about this sort of thing," he said curtly. "That spell hasn't been used in centuries. It's forbidden, as I said. To use it would mean one individual going to extraordinary lengths, not to mention the fact that they'd have to find the spell in the first place. It's been tucked away at a secure facility in Reykjavik for generations."

I shook my head. "Katherine used it, and we have proof. If you know about it, then you know about the rune and the puncture wounds, right?"

"Naturally."

"Then look at this." I shoved the picture at him.

He looked over it for a moment, his black eyebrows pinching together in a sour frown. "Impossible."

"Perhaps you should call Reykjavik, see if that spell has been tampered with."

He shot me a cold stare. "If you would excuse me for a moment. Stay exactly where you are."

He stalked out of the room and closed the door behind him. I looked at Santana, the two of us equally irritated by the arrogant, cold preceptor. Turning back to the boxes, worried that Salinger was listening in again, I distracted my angry brain by compiling a stack of documents that I wanted copied from the Merlin files, while Santana set to work on the Shipton files.

"I'm going to smack his smug smirk off his face," I muttered.

She flashed me a grin. "Not if I get there first. Ignore him. It's this place—New York seems to go to everyone's heads."

Fifteen minutes later, Salinger returned. He looked pissed, a dark cloud hovering over his head as he strode back into the room. I knew as soon as I saw him that he was about to confirm exactly what I'd told him, but I wanted to savor the moment of knowing that I was right. He was going to have to apologize in some capacity.

"Well?" I prompted.

"The spell is gone," he replied evenly. "Nobody knows how it was taken, but it is gone from the vault. Other spells have been taken, as well. I am having a list of the missing items sent over. I find it rather remarkable that you would know of such a curse, however. How did you come by this information?"

"An inkling that Alton had," I said. "He wanted us to check it out. He's got this theory that Hiram might have learned to live with the effect of the spell, because he didn't kill me when he could have. Instead, he tried to raise me and keep me out of Katherine's reach. As you can see, it worked. I'm living proof."

"You're very full of yourself, aren't you?" His gaze was stony. "A Merlin trait."

"Now that I know my dad isn't a murdering psychopath, I'll take that as a compliment. I prefer to call it self-assurance."

"Call it what you want, it's an unpleasant attribute. Don't think we haven't heard about you here in New York, Miss Merlin. We know how powerful you are, but that doesn't grant you immediate superiority. Respect has to be earned—it doesn't come from a name."

Seriously... don't test me. If he wasn't one of the only people who might be able to help us, I'd have let fly with my emotions by now. And then some.

I shrugged, suppressing my anger. "Well, I plan to bring respect back to the Merlin name. You say you're familiar with this spell, right?"

"Yes."

"So, can someone live through it? Can someone fight against it?"

He paused for a moment. "If it's done properly, then no. Hiram was extremely powerful, but that doesn't make him almighty."

"Well, he did it," I said stubbornly, losing my cool for a moment.

Salinger tapped the side of his temple. "There is a logical possibility."

"There is?"

"Maybe it's because you lived that he was able to resist the spell's true power," he mused, his expression changing to one of personal intrigue. "You see, I'm not sure how much you *actually* understand about it, but this curse requires great sacrifice to perform the spell. Specifically, it requires the lives and the blood of all those who are closely related to the spell's target. With that in mind, it stands to reason that your presence prevented the completion of the curse. His blood ran, and still runs, in your veins. Without it being harvested by Katherine, there would have been no way for her to finish the job. In this instance, he may have been able to muster the strength to fight it, although he would never have been able to do so forever. Even unfinished, it would have worn away at him eventually."

I glanced at Santana. That made a lot of sense. *I* was the reason my father could resist the pull of the curse. *I* was the reason he hadn't killed me. Had I saved myself from the effects of Sál Vinna, without even realizing it? *Maybe, if there wasn't one other Merlin still breathing. A Merlin that Salinger doesn't know about.*

Isadora, I mouthed to Santana. She nodded, while Salinger looked over the image once more. Isadora had never been found, though presumed dead. If Katherine hadn't been able to kill Isadora, then my aunt was the one who'd rendered the spell incomplete. Her survival must have given Hiram the slight relief he needed to learn to live with the spell's grip on his mind. Although, I realized it must've eaten him up inside, to keep battling against a force like that. Salinger had said as much.

Oberon? Santana mouthed to me. Immediately, I understood the connection. Ever since Oberon Marx had taken over Tatyana's body and tried to kill us all in the name of Katherine, it had been clear he'd been under the same spell. Katherine would have had to kill all of Oberon Marx's family to make it happen. *Maybe he was the test run, before she tried it out on my dad.*

"Might I suggest we leave this room and take our conversation to the Flying Dutchman?" Salinger said, unexpectedly. "We are supposed to make guests feel welcome, and there is much I should like to speak with you both about. I have been remiss, I suppose. You will forgive me—your arrival was unprecedented."

"The Flying Dutchman?" I asked.

"The New York Coven's bar."

Santana nodded effusively. "Yes, that sounds perfect!"

"I can see to your copies first," he said stiffly.

"Great." I forced a smile onto my face as we followed him out of the archives.

We sat around a table in the far corner of the bar, which reminded me of an old-timey smoking room, with dark mahogany furniture and dark green wallpaper printed with black fleur-de-lis. A few other patrons sat around, sipping tankards of ale and glasses of wine, with a few grizzled gentlemen partaking in crystal tumblers of amber whiskey. The ice cubes clinked as they lifted the drinks to their lips and set them down again.

Salinger was four drinks in. He'd tried to refuse and stick to water, clearly wanting to grill us on what we knew and what we thought about all of this, but Santana had been plying him with whiskey sours and tequila chasers since the moment he sat down, evidently hoping he'd loosen up a bit. She'd claimed it was part of her Mexican culture, guilting him into accepting the drinks or risking insulting her. Being a preceptor of International Cultures, he clearly knew not to cross a fierce Latina, especially not one who wanted to ply him with booze.

However, the plan had worked a little too well, and now we were struggling to shut him up.

"You know, I always thought Hester and Hiram were a handsome couple, and both were good friends of mine for a while, but we had ourselves a falling out." Salinger pulled me out of my thoughts. He twisted his features into a comical face as he downed a chaser that Santana had pushed into his hand. "Always the way, when a bro finds himself a… girlfriend. Suddenly, they don't have time for you anymore, and it's 'Hester this' and 'Hester that.' And then things start to get ugly, as they always do, and Hester's running through the hallways in tears. That was Hiram's problem: he toyed with too many women's hearts—Katherine's included. Me being a doting friend, I went to Hiram to try and talk some sense into him, but he thought he was this rock star amongst men. He thought he could keep doing what he was doing, have all the cake and eat it too. Saving none for the rest of us, I might add."

I stared at him, not wanting to believe that my dad was this arrogant lothario. It didn't match up with the Hiram I'd seen in my dreams. Plus, part of me was desperate to believe that he and my mother had been head over heels in love, and that he'd only had eyes for her. The same part that had waited at the front door of the orphanage, convinced that my parents were coming back for me.

Isn't that every kid's dream, to have the perfect parents?

His eyes were starry. "Mind you, Hester was no better. She was an obnoxious overachiever, if you ask me. She didn't mind stepping on a toe or two, if it meant advancing through the coven. Oh, I had my feet squashed many a time by her, just to gain a brownie point or two," he went on, slurring slightly. "You hear about these twins who can't do anything without each other—they finish each other's sentences and are totally inseparable? Well, Katherine and Hester weren't like that."

"They weren't?" I asked, coaxing him.

"My word, no. You see, Katherine had been eyed for a position on the board of this coven. She was far more gifted that Hester, though not as vocal about it. As soon as Hester heard about it, she scooted her way around Katherine's back and snatched it for herself. You should have seen the argument! I thought they were going to blow the roof off this place. There were sparks, literal sparks, flying everywhere. I nearly lost an eyebrow trying to get away from it. You know, I asked them both out, and they both rejected me for Hiram. Can you believe that? And then you ask why I hated him so much! Murders aside… well, not murders, I suppose, if he had that curse on him. Poor bastard. What a way to go. She was always a jealous one, that Katherine. But *what* a peach!"

I narrowed my eyes. "Are you saying Hester goaded Katherine into doing what she did? Killing her like that?"

"No, certainly not! They might have had their differences, but Hester didn't deserve to suffer and die like that at all. None of Katherine's victims did. I'm just saying there was no love between the two of them. They were always sniping and bickering, wandering around these halls with a black cloud above them. We'd always whisper if they were coming and get out of their way." He cackled and knocked back another half-glass of whiskey sour. Any more and he'd be on the floor. "How strange… I brought you here to question *you,* and here I am, telling you all of this. How absolutely hilarious!"

I sat in silence, letting the information sink in. Yes, it was coming from a man who was very tipsy, but people always tended to speak the blunt truth when they were drunk. Plus, I could sense honesty coming from him. A swirl of mixed emotions churned in my stomach. It was hard to feel proud of my parents, after hearing all of that, but like Salinger had said, nobody was perfect. They'd had fears and flaws and worries of their own. Somehow, despite the bad image Salinger conveyed, it made them seem more real to me. It made them seem like people I could have understood, instead of a perfect fiction in my head. *I love you regardless...*

"It says here that the Shiptons are all dead, too. Did Katherine do that?" Santana asked, brandishing the family tree from the folders we'd made. He'd copied them for us before we'd come here.

Salinger nodded. "Killed them in the midst of a violent rampage. Can't imagine it had much to do with that spell, though. She probably just did it for the"—he hiccupped violently—"and giggles."

"You're probably right," I muttered bitterly.

"You know, I'm so glad we decided to do this. I rarely have the chance to let my hair down," he said, chuckling. "I'm not normally allowed in here. I've got a rap sheet for all the silly stuff I got up to when I was a youth."

"You understand that reparations will have to be made in the near future, to clear Hiram's name of any wrongdoing?" I hoped he wasn't too incapacitated to understand.

Salinger wore a puzzled look. "You're quite right, Miss Merlin. Reparations will *have* to be made. Although, before such a thing can proceed, we'll need absolute proof that what you've discovered is true. The coroner seems to think that rune is just a tattoo—we all did. You'll need to convince the New York Mage Council, and then the Supreme Court of the United Covens of America. I don't envy you!"

He was right, although the news wasn't particularly heartening. "But if we could somehow get a confession from someone who was around when it happened..." I said, not even sure where I was going with that thought.

"A confession would be good, though you'd have to get it from Katherine herself, or one of her little minions. And good luck trying that! Until then, dear old Hiram will have to wallow a while longer in the quagmire of his apparent guilt. A confession may be a *long* time coming. Poor bastard. He doesn't deserve the bad reputation if he was under a spell. Hell, I've done some ridiculous things in the name of love, and nobody put a curse on me." He giggled into his drink.

"Since we've got zero leads in that direction, looks like we've still got a lot of work to do before we can clear Hiram's name," I muttered, fixing my gaze on Santana.

"Yeah, a hell of a lot of work," Santana said. "Seems pretty unfair, if you ask me."

"Life is unfair, my dear," Salinger replied. "Believe me, I'd be the first to champion Hiram's innocence, and I'll offer this new information to the board. However, I know what the old shrews are like. They won't accept it unless they've got the goods to back it up. They'd be crucified if they suddenly overturned their verdict. I mean, they killed the guy, for goodness' sake—they executed him, even though he maintained his innocence throughout the trial. Think about how that'll make them look. My word, they'll be eager to cover it up instead of going about singing his innocence."

Fear gripped my chest in a vise. Unless we could find considerable evidence to back up what we'd found, nobody would lift a finger to announce Hiram's innocence—or lack of culpability, at the very least. It would make them all look *really* bad.

"Well then, if you're all done here, why don't I get us some more drinks?" He grinned like an idiot. I would've felt bad for putting him in this state if he hadn't been such a stuck-up asshat when we first arrived. Plus, this was *all* Santana's doing.

"That'd be great, but there's one other thing," I said.

He arched an eyebrow. "Oh? Do tell."

"I was wondering if you could grant us access to Hiram and Hester's Grimoire."

Salinger sighed. "Ah, I'd forgotten about that. Despite it all, those two lovebirds were made for each other. He drove her crazy, and she was way out of his league, but they adored each other like you wouldn't believe. I think she was the only woman who ever stopped his eye from roving, even if he floundered from time to time. Impulses and whatnot. I don't believe in that sort of thing, myself. I'm a loyal sort of chap. When I'm with a gal, I'm *with* a gal. Like superglue! No separating us. Still, I know not everyone can believe in love the way I do."

Just what we need, Salinger waxing romantic. I'll never get him to focus!

"Can we see it?" I pressed.

"You know, I'd love to let you have a look at it, so you could see their unconventional love in action. It's a powerful thing—you can feel it radiating off the pages," he said wistfully. "However, that's beyond my control. It's stored in the Special Collections reading room, but you'll have to file an application and prepare for an interview and jump through about a million hoops before anyone will let you within ten feet of that book." He paused, a smirk spreading across his face. "Do you know, I shouldn't have even told you that. That's the trouble with alcohol: it slithers in and turns your brain to jelly. Brain, arms, legs, everything! Ah well, you won't tell anyone I said anything, will you?"

I smiled sweetly. "No, of course not. Like you say… alcohol, eh?"

"Exactly!"

So, the Grimoire was in Special Collections. We had the location, but that didn't give us any feasible way of getting in there to have a look at it. *Magical bureaucracy, the great big thorn in my side.* Even so, I wasn't about to let something as insignificant as red tape stop us from seeing the Grimoire. I needed to touch it, to use my Empathy to sense my parents' emotions. My soul ached to feel close to them, even just for a moment.

"Could you show us where the Special Collections room is, on our way out?"

He pondered my request for a moment. "I don't see why not. Let's have a guided tour! You're new here, and this place is nothing if not impressive. Although, personally, the gothic touch is not to my taste. I like a warmer color palette."

"A guided tour sounds like a great idea." I smiled sweetly. "Should we head upstairs then?"

"Yes indeedy. If you'd all form an orderly line and follow me, we can get out of this hellhole with time to spare. Oh, I wish I had a flag, so I could wave it and you'd know where I was," he said, giggling as he turned around and left the bar.

"So, what's the plan?" Santana whispered, while we followed.

"Can you create a diversion while I duck into the Special Collections reading room? I only need a couple of minutes," I begged, unashamed of the pleading note in my voice. "I need this. I can't leave without at least touching it."

She smiled. "It's important to you, huh?"

"Very important."

"Then how can I refuse?" she said. "I'll create the best damn diversion the magical East Coast has ever seen. Although, we'll have to make sure that we don't get caught, obviously."

I grinned at her. "Obviously."

TWENTY-ONE

Santana

Giddy from all the drinks I'd plied him with, Salinger took us on the promised tour of the New York Coven. He was well and truly out of it, chattering on like nobody's business.

"Now, here on my left you'll find the repositories. I don't like to go in there much, since I don't have that big of a need for spells and the like. Books and essays are more my speed. I don't think there's anything in the world that you can't find in a book. All of this is extraneous," Salinger explained, his words slurring a hell of a lot. He was swaying, too. I'd had to reach out a couple of times on the spiral staircase to stop him from keeling over. How the guy had managed to get so tipsy in such a short span of time was beyond me. Then again, I had been giving him double measures and chasers to go with them. *Oops.*

As we walked along, Harley and I kept exchanging glances. We'd agreed to come up with a diversion so Harley could get a shot at checking out her parents' Grimoire. How hard could that be with a wayward audience like this?

"Are we close to Special Collections?" Harley asked. Meanwhile, I was wondering where everyone else was. We hadn't passed too many people on our guided tour, which led me to believe we were in a fusty wing of the coven that nobody liked to visit. Good for us, though.

Salinger waved a hand down the corridor. "Two doors up, but you simply *must* come in here and take a look at the Global Library. I bet you've never seen anything like it, not if you've come from the San Diego Coven, anyway. That place is a dump compared to New York. We've got every book of global mythology you could ever hope to find, all under this one roof." He chuckled to himself. "There are artifacts and ancient Esprits from bygone eras. There are so many wondrous things behind these doors."

This was the moment to start diverting. *Come on, Santana, let's show this ninny what the San Diego bunch are really made of.* Reaching within myself, I urged my Orishas to come to my aid. I turned my back to Salinger for a moment—not that he was looking. The guy was fixated on his beloved books.

The Orishas rose up inside me, that familiar cold-and-hot feeling pulsing through my veins, like putting icy hands in front of a fierce fire. My palms burned blue, and I knew my eyes would be doing the same. They whispered all around me, the spirits asking what I wanted of them. Focusing on their multitude of voices, I mentally explained what I needed them to do for me. My Orishas could cast identical images of people, but the facsimiles couldn't speak or hold a solid form. *Not that that's going to matter, with Captain Chatterbox over there. He'll be glad nobody's interrupting his pompous ass.*

Two whorls of blue light twisted up from my palms and landed close behind Salinger with a puff of azure sparks. A trickle of sweat dripped down my spine. This was going to take a lot out of me, but it would be worth it to keep the boozehound busy. He'd already stepped into the Global Library, gaping into the room beyond with his back to us. *Perfect.*

The forms took shape, imitating Harley and me. I nodded to my friend, urging her to hide behind something. She darted into the shadow of a suit of armor, while I stepped into one of the creepy alcoves that lined the hallway.

"Well, don't dither in the corridor, come on in! I have a world of merry wonders to show you, ladies. You'll certainly appreciate what this place has to offer," Salinger said, beckoning for the imitations to follow him. He paused in front of the door and murmured, *"Da nobis accessum,"* before disappearing inside. The imitations did as they were told, my Orishas controlling them as they dutifully followed. A mental link existed between me and the spirits in charge of the facsimiles, so I'd know what they were up to while we were busy.

Not wanting to waste a moment, in case Salinger suddenly got hit with a dose of clarity, Harley and I hurried along the hallway to the room marked "Special Collections." It didn't look any different than the other doorways, but the energy within felt instantly more powerful. The items inside here were valuable, I could tell.

Harley turned to me. "Did you hear what he said?"

I nodded. *"Da nobis accessum."*

She put her hands on the doorknob and repeated the words. Something clicked, the door opening wide. Not wasting a moment, Harley ducked into the room. I lingered a second longer on the threshold, looking up and down the corridor to make sure there was nobody else around. Satisfied that we were alone, I followed Harley inside.

"Orishas, warn me if someone is coming," I whispered.

We will stand sentinel for you, Santana, they replied, their voices echoing in my head. There was something kind of soothing about the way they spoke to me in unison.

Crossing the threshold, I felt a strange throb of Chaos energy, letting me know there were some magical defenses in place. Considering no alarms had gone off yet, I figured these measures were there to stop anyone from taking items from inside the Special Collections vault—like a tag being put on certain books in a city library to stop them from being taken out, only *way* more powerful.

The Special Collections reading room had definitely been done up by the same person who'd designed the rest of the New York Coven. Thin windows of jeweled stained glass showed glimpses of Central Park, while a cavernous ceiling of dark gray granite curved to an apex above us. A gothic chandelier of bronze and silver cast its light downward. One long table stretched the entire way up the room, with the bookshelves and stacks tucked away to the sides. Halfway down, a staircase led up to a second floor, which held even more shelves of intense leather-bound tomes alongside a handful of desks with emerald-green reading lamps.

"You know, I'm starting to wonder about this place. This whole Coven would be enough to turn anyone a bit batty, old Katie Shipton included," I muttered. The room was, thankfully, empty. "I'd say it encourages a sort of murder-and-mayhem vibe, don't you think?"

"I was just thinking that," Harley replied, as she moved across to the first stack of books. The room wasn't particularly big, but we didn't have a lot of time to scan through everything. Even to a drunk guy who liked the sound of his own voice, the imitations would start to look a little off soon enough.

"Should we get started?"

Harley nodded. "Let's take a side each. We'll cover more ground that way."

"Aye, aye, Captain."

I moved over to the opposite side of the room and started to search. By the time I reached the end of the right-hand wall of books, it became clear that Hester and Hiram's Grimoire wasn't in here. The shelves were labeled weirdly by content, with related Grimoires intermingled with ordinary tomes. The Merlins' book didn't seem to be anywhere. We had no idea what sort of content it contained, which made things a little trickier.

Harley seemed to have come to the same conclusion. I could hear her muttering angrily under her breath as she ran her fingertip along every dusty spine. Magic brimmed from the Grimoires, setting my remaining Orishas on edge. These weren't dangerous ones, from what I could sense, but they were still majorly powerful.

Drawn by the staircase to the smaller second floor, I walked up the black-iron steps until I reached the platform above. This part of the Special Collections room was more of a study than anything else, a place for peace and quiet. The heavy stone walls seemed to deaden any sound coming in, rejecting even the slightest whisper of noise. *Creepy, creepy, and even more creepy.*

"It's not here!" Harley's muffled voice barked from below. I leaned over the balcony of the weird study-cum-platform to look at her.

"No luck?"

She glanced up at me and shook her head. "It's not on any of these shelves. They've got a few Grimoires, but none of them belong to my parents. Do you think they might have locked it away somewhere else? They thought my dad was a murderer, so it makes sense that they'd want to keep it away from snooping eyes. Although, we don't know what's in it, so maybe not." She grunted. "But then, why would Salinger have said it was in here?"

"If Salinger said it was in here, then it has to be. I don't see why he'd lie about it. Plus, he mumbled something about it again after his third whiskey sour," I replied. "I'll keep looking up here. Shout if you find anything."

I wandered to the back of the enclosed platform. Two bookshelves jutted out at the far side. Curious, I skirted around them, only to find a glass display case behind each stack. The one on the right-hand side was empty, but the one on the left… I approached it cautiously; a weird vibe was emanating from inside. A closed book rested on a golden stand, but there was no card or description. The cover was bound in a beautiful, cream leather, embellished with swirling vines of silver and gold. A glittering jewel had been embedded in each corner of the front cover—sapphire, ruby, emerald, and diamond, to represent each of the elements. In the very center, a white pearl and a black pearl, side by side.

"Harley!" I hissed, hurrying back over to the balustrade. "Harley! I think I found it!"

She darted across the room below and pounded up the stairs, following me back to the glass display case. It didn't seem to be locked with any kind of magical prevention system, though I presumed that would be triggered if we tried to take anything out of the Special Collections room. That's what I'd felt on my way in—the defense mechanism to prevent theft. Everything in here had to stay in here. And besides, there'd be no point in putting a magical lock on something like this. It wasn't finished, by all accounts, and Grimoire spells couldn't be used unless they'd been finished by the creators. This was, for all intents and purposes, a really pretty book with no actual purpose.

"Oh my God, this is it," she gasped. "I can feel their energy pouring out. This is it. This is my parents' Grimoire. The black pearl and the white pearl—that's Hester and Hiram. Light and Dark, two sides of the same coin."

I smiled. "Nice catch, right? There's always something hidden behind bookcases in creepy places like this."

"But how do we get into it?"

"I was thinking about phasing through the glass to try and grab it, but those spells are way too advanced. I'd give myself a cardiac arrest just trying it, even with the Orishas protecting me," I replied reluctantly. "Plus, they're kind of split at the moment, with half of them watching our fake counterparts."

She exhaled. "What if we just smashed the glass and took it?"

"I think we'd have half the coven in here before we even reached the stairs."

"I'm not coming this far only to fail now."

I peered at the padlock that held the glass door closed. It wasn't charmed or engraved with runes. It appeared to be a simple, run-of-the-mill padlock. "How controlled is your Telekinesis these days?"

Harley frowned. "Pretty good. Why?"

"How would you feel about picking the lock with your powers?"

"Won't that set off the alarms?"

I shook my head. "I don't think so. The padlock doesn't seem to be charmed at all."

"I'll give it a try," Harley said, after a moment's pause. The poor girl was desperate. I could see it in her eyes. To be honest, after all this hassle, I was getting a little too eager for my own good, as well.

A sliver of shimmering air snaked out of Harley's palms, the pearl on her Esprit glowing bright as she fed the thin stream of Telekinesis into the padlock. Her brow furrowed with the strain of fiddling with the finicky lock pins inside. In the silence of the second floor, I could almost hear them moving.

"Well, this is infuriating," she muttered.

"I'm guessing this isn't hairpin easy?"

She shook her head. "Nope, this is next-level lockpicking. Don't get me wrong, I've broken a lock or two in my time, but this is ridiculous."

"You've picked a lock or two?"

She smiled. "Sometimes, a girl's gotta do what a girl's gotta do. Mainly foster parents confiscating my stuff, but there've been a few secret trips to the principal's office to change a few grades, too."

I kept quiet as she continued, her face contorted in a mask of pure determination.

"Can you say something?" Harley asked. Her voice startled me.

"You're freaking me out, standing there watching over me like a ghost."

"Sure... uh... you know, it's one of my goals in life to create a Grimoire someday. Most of my ancestors forged one—be rude not to keep in line with *some* Catemaco traditions. That one I'm down with. The arranged marriage, not so much."

Harley laughed tightly, straining with the lock. "Where do you even buy the kind of blank journal you need to start one? Do they, like, sell them at a magical store?"

"In a way," I replied. "There are magical bookbinders out there who specialize in Grimoires. They make the special paper and bindings to accommodate powerful Chaos energy, judging the levels of protection needed based on the magical who's making it. You can't just grab a notepad from any old stationery store and jot down your spells and charms. Well, you could, but they wouldn't work the way a Grimoire does. It's not just normal paper. There's an artistry to the work, which is why all the Grimoire covers are so intricately designed. The bookbinders work with the creators to forge the right book for their needs, matching it perfectly."

"All that work for one book?"

I nodded. "Yeah, I think you're right about the white pearl and the black pearl having something to do with your mom and dad being of Light and Dark. The intertwining vines of silver and gold probably represent their unity and love," I said, pointing to the symbolic details. "This star up here likely has something to do with your mom, as Hester means 'star' in Persian. And this triskelion down here, that's an ancient druid symbol that has been linked to the Merlin mythos for centuries. So, that's probably your dad." I gestured to an image of three connected swirls, curving out like the coiled legs of a starfish.

"How do you know so much about Grimoires?"

"Like I say, they've been in the family for generations. Call it a professional interest."

Just then, something clicked inside the lock, the heavy part sagging as the top came loose.

"I did it!" Harley whooped, covering her mouth quickly in case the sound alerted anyone.

Eagerly, she tugged open the glass door and reached inside. I stepped back, giving her a moment alone with the Grimoire. She ran her hand across the cream leather, over every indented embellishment and jeweled detail, before opening the cover to reveal the first page. I could only imagine how it felt to hold something like that—something so special and intimately crafted.

"'With you, I am never in darkness. With you, there will always be a guiding light. With you, I fear no shadows. With you, I am whole.'" Harley's voice caught in her throat as she read the dedication aloud. "'With you, the night becomes a gift. With you, I will always find balance. With you, I do not need to hide. With you, I am whole.'"

"They dedicated the Grimoire to each other," I whispered.

Harley nodded. "Their love... I can feel it, rolling off the pages. It's... it's almost too overwhelming. I can feel them in here. They're in every word. All the love and power and time they poured into it... I can feel every little bit." Her breathing became ragged, her eyes blinking rapidly. "The intensity... it's... I can't put it into words. Every part of who they were... it's all—" She stumbled before she could finish, gripping the book as she swayed to the side. Her knees were shaking, her whole body drenched in sweat.

My hands shot out to grab her around the shoulders and set her upright. "Hey, take it easy. If it's too much, put the book back."

She shook her head. "I'm fine. I want to keep looking. We're running out of time here." Her gaze fixed on me with a fierce defiance. "I haven't come all this way just to put the book back, not until I've seen more."

"I get it, believe me, but I don't want to have to carry you out of here."

"Let me try again," she insisted. "I'll be fine."

I let go of her as she started to flip through the book, settling on an index of spells. She ran her finger down the list, her mouth moving as she read each one. Halfway down, she froze.

"What is it?" I asked, feeling nervous.

"There's a section dedicated to the Children of Chaos," she replied, turning to the corresponding page. The sweat poured off her, her cheeks a worrying shade of red, like she'd fallen into a fever of some kind. As she scanned the pages, I made out a blur of colored ink and haphazard illustrations, before Harley settled on the right one. At the very top, someone had sketched an inky image—a wispy rendering of shadow and darkness, hooded and winged, holding a scythe in one hand. *Erebus, the Child of Darkness. No one else would give me shivers like this... aside from my mom.*

I peered over Harley's shoulder and tried to read the words beneath the sketch. My eyes drifted across the first few lines, which spouted the usual mythos: "From Chaos came forth Erebus..." I was about to read on when I became aware of Harley murmuring the spell under her breath. The whites and irises of her eyes had turned a worrying shade of black, her body fixed in a trance-like state.

"Whoa there, Harley," I said, shaking her by the shoulders. "Hey! Harley! Snap out of it!"

A black mist pooled off the page, dripping down in wispy tendrils and swirling around us. My Orishas shuddered in the air beside me, freaking out at this sudden appearance of powerful magic. *Stop her... Erebus must not be summoned... Stop her or we shall be forced to,* they whispered, their voices echoing in my head.

I lunged for the Grimoire and tried to wrestle it out of her hands.

Harley's head whipped around to face me, a pulse of intense Telekinesis surging from her hands. I barely had time to think as she hurled me down the length of the second-floor platform, my back hitting the balcony with a jolt of agonizing pain.

Gathering the Orishas to me, I scrambled to my feet and sprinted back to where Harley stood. A circle of icy wind whipped up around her, creating a dark tornado of near-impenetrable black fog, with her at its center.

What the—what's it doing to her? This shouldn't be happening!

I'd never seen anyone respond that way to a Grimoire before. A few people passed out if the magic inside was particularly strong, but this was something else. And it was getting way out of hand. In a few moments, Harley would lose control completely. My Orishas could sense it.

Forced into survival mode, I thought back to what my mother had taught me about my Santeria heritage and the magic that came with it.

This is going to come at a high price, but there's no other way.

I called to my Orishas and felt the steady pulse of their strength within me. Using the raw core of their energy, I raised my hands and gathered a swirling vortex of blue-and-black light between my palms. As I pushed the orb of intense energy forward, the midnight-blue tendrils snaked through the air, wrapping around the cover of the Merlins' Grimoire.

Unable to pull the book free, the slithering fronds sank beneath Harley's flesh. I could feel each one venturing inside her veins, tugging at the sinew of her muscles to try and break the link between her and the book. I gripped tighter to the essence of my power as the inky tendrils reached her brain. With another push of energy from me, the dark magic pulsed inside her, freezing every spark of electricity that jumped between synapses.

As if an electromagnetic wave had gone off, Harley slumped to the floor with a thud. The Grimoire tumbled down beside her, and the tornado of black fog disappeared with a snap of ice-cold wind. I let go of the black tendrils as soon as she collapsed, the raw, Orisha-fueled magic zapping straight back into my body. It hit me in a bitter rush of frosty sparks, each one biting into my skin. Still, I wasn't worried about me. I'd never used this spell before, and I had no idea whether I'd held it for too long. *Please... please say I haven't killed her.*

Harley's eyes popped open, her lungs gasping for air as though she'd been on the brink of drowning. She struggled to sit up, looking around at the Grimoire and the open display case. Her face had drained of color, the feverish red of her cheeks dissipating.

"What happened?" she asked, turning to me.

"The Grimoire happened." I walked back over to where she sat. I put the book back in the display case, fixing the lock into place. *We've had quite enough of you for one evening.* I felt relieved to see it back behind glass—and a little bit sick, although I knew that had nothing to do with the Grimoire.

Someone is coming, my Orishas whispered.

"Just what we need," I muttered.

Harley frowned. "What?"

"Someone's coming. Can you stand?"

She nodded, getting to her feet. "I think so."

"Good, then let's get the hell out of here before they throw us in Purgatory."

With her leaning on me for support, we hurried out of the Special Collections reading room. Salinger was just coming from the Global Library ahead, still chattering on about something or other. I couldn't quite hear what he was saying, but it didn't matter. Our imitations walked obediently after him. With a flick of my wrist, and a word to the Orishas, the facsimiles vanished into thin air, the spirits rushing back to join me as we darted down the hallway. As he turned and saw the empty space behind him, he glanced about in confusion. An embarrassed look drifted across his features. *Been talking so long you've lost your captive audience? Sorry, Salinger. You're going to wake up with a lot of regret tomorrow.*

We rushed toward the mirrors, my stomach churning with every step we took. Cold sweat drenched my body, and nausea gripped my insides. *Well, this isn't good... but I knew the price would be high. At least it was worth it.*

What troubled me more than the sickening feeling in my stomach, however, was the fact that Harley had been able to read the spell aloud and make it work. The Grimoire was unfinished. She shouldn't have been able to do that. And yet, the evidence was overwhelming—I'd *seen* it happen. Something had allowed her to bridge the gap. *Her bloodline, maybe? Crazy-strong Shipton and Merlin power lurking inside her?* Whatever it was, she had almost completed the spell of her own accord… and that was a terrifying thought.

Even with the Suppressor in place, she was too powerful for her own good.

She was becoming a danger to herself, and everyone around her. I only hoped that Shipton blood didn't run too deep.

TWENTY-TWO

Harley

Stepping back through the mirror, into the Assembly Hall of the SDC, my body felt electric. If someone had told me I'd just shot-gunned a six-pack of energy drink, I would've believed them. My nerves were wired, and I was pretty sure I could hear colors. There was definitely *something* buzzing in my ears. A rush of blood, zinging through my veins at a million miles an hour.

Santana, on the other hand, looked like she was recovering from a heavy night after a six-pack of something else. Her face had a green tint, and a waxy sheen coated her skin. As we came to a halt on the Hall podium, her breath heaved from her chest, her hand shaky around my waist. She'd been helping me along after what had happened in the Special Collections room, but now I felt like I was the one who should be helping her.

"Are you okay?" I asked, breaking away.

She nodded. "A bit tired, but that's all. That took a lot out of me."

"What happened back there?"

"You wouldn't stop reading some spell in your parents' Grimoire. It had something to do with Erebus," she replied. "You went into this weird trance and wouldn't snap out of it, so I had to break the link. It wasn't easy. I feel like someone just drove into me with an eighteen-wheeler."

I made a face, feeling guilty. "I'm sorry for dragging you along to try and find it. We should've just taken the copies and come back here."

"Hey, I'm all for rule-breaking when it counts, *mi compa*," she replied with a grin. "If we're going to go running into the fire head-first, we can't go around feeling sorry for ourselves when we get burned. Although, if I'd known you were going to go all *Exorcist* on me, I might've tried to persuade you that looking for the Grimoire wasn't such a good idea. You kind of… disappeared for a minute there. And you might have cracked a vertebra or two." She rubbed her spine for dramatic effect, making me feel even guiltier.

"I threw you, didn't I?"

"That's putting it mildly." She laughed, showing there were no hard feelings. I was grateful for that. I'd only just started to make friends here; I didn't want to lose any due to my volatile reactions to Grimoires.

I shook my head. "I'm so sorry. I should've known something bad was going to happen."

"What do you mean? You couldn't have known you were going to go ape after touching it."

I flashed her a sheepish look. "Well, actually, it's happened before."

She gaped at me. "Are you kidding?"

"Afraid not," I said. "It was a while back, but I was looking through one of the Dark Grimoires with Garrett, and I completely clocked out. I started reading it out loud, and he had to stop me before I did something terrible. I don't know if it has something to do with my affinity for Darkness, or if it's something else, but the Grimoires seem to have this weird effect on me. Still, it was even more intense this time. Last time, Garrett could break me out of it, but my parents' one gripped me and wouldn't let go."

"You should have told me that."

"I know. I'm sorry. I wasn't even thinking about it."

She shrugged. "Well, no harm done. I imagine reading a Grimoire that was created by someone you're related to is different than reading a normal one. It is always going to be more intense," she replied casually. "Although, I've been wondering how you managed to read the spell and make it work. Your parents' Grimoire was never finished, which means you shouldn't have been able to. It's been bugging me."

I frowned. "You think it has something to do with me being their kid?"

"I think it has something to do with your bloodline—there's something about it that let you read that spell without it being finished. That's my theory, anyway. Maybe it's like a safeguard, a way of continuing the Grimoire, even if the creator dies. Or creators, in this case. I'll ask my mom about it at the Gathering. She's an expert on these things. If anyone knows why you can do what you just did, it'll be her."

"That'd be great." The more I could learn about that Grimoire, and my link to it, the better. My mind had been racing ever since we left the Special Collections room and my memories had started to drift back, piece by piece. Touching my parents' Grimoire for the first time had been an otherworldly experience. Even now, I struggled to put it into words, or think about it clearly. It was like the full force of my powers had called out to the book and tried to push past the Dempsey Suppressor in order to reach the content within, recognizing something in it.

I didn't dare mention it aloud, for fear of worrying Santana, but I was starting to wonder if using one of my parents' Grimoire spells might be the key to breaking the Dempsey Suppressor. If I could perform one of them, maybe it would be powerful enough to push me to my absolute limits, shattering the Suppressor in the process. I wasn't an idiot; I knew that performing a spell like that would be incredibly dangerous, but if it could set my powers free, then maybe it was worth the huge risk.

"Don't you go sneaking around again, okay?" Santana chided. "If you want to do something *loco* like that again, you come to one of us and you tell us. Nine times out of ten, we'll come along for the ride, and we'll make sure you don't cause yourself a whole bunch of trouble. Wade might not be game for the rule-breaking stuff, but you've always got me or Tatyana to provide some hefty backup. Astrid, too, if she's in the right mood. There's a rebellious streak in that girl that is a glorious thing when it comes out."

"Okay, no more sneaking," I promised. "I've done things on my own for so long that I'm not used to having people I can call on for help."

She smiled. "I know, *mi cuate*. That's why I'm here to keep telling you."

I chuckled, glancing at Santana. She continued to surprise me. Out of everyone in the SDC, she was the most interesting person I'd come across. With the Catemaco legacy at her disposal, she could've easily breezed through magical life, and yet she'd chosen a harder path. She'd come here to carve her own way in this world. I admired that—I admired defiance in people. Plus, she was much more powerful than she'd previously let on. I couldn't remember much of what had happened when the spell got out of hand, but I knew she'd done something immense. I could feel the after-effects of it still pulsing through me.

I'm lucky to have someone like you by my side, Santana. The voice of reason for when I go over the line. Glad you came with me.

"Well then, now I owe you a favor," I said. "It's the least I can do after all the crap I've put you through."

"Honestly, I'm just glad we're both in one piece. No favors needed."

"Come on, there's got to be some way I can make up for the almost-cracked vertebrae. Name it!" I flashed her a grin.

"Seriously, we're cool. I'm not in the habit of taking favors. It's not the way we do things where I come from. We just help where we need to, and don't ask for anything in return."

I pulled a sad face. "Please let me make it up to you, Santana. I feel like a prize twonk for dragging you into this."

"Twonk?" She chuckled.

"Yeah, a twonk. Now let me do something for you. There's got to be *something* you want. Laundry? Chocolates? Cleaning?"

She paused for a moment. "Now that you mention it… no, never mind. It's not important."

"No! Go on, tell me what you were going to say. There's no favor too big."

She eyed me cautiously. "I do have a *tiny* idea in mind."

"Do tell."

"I'm a pretty patient girl, but this impasse with Raffe is driving me nutty," she replied shyly. "I wouldn't mind knowing how he really feels about me, if you'd be happy working your Empath wizardry on him. An experiment of sorts."

I burst out laughing. "I'm in! It would be my pleasure."

"Do you mean it?"

"One-hundred percent," I replied. "To be honest, I thought you were going to ask me to do your laundry. This is so much better. What did you have in mind? A slinky red dress—see if his eyes pop out? Or an accidental smooch with GI Joe, see if steam starts coming out of Raffe's ears?"

Santana grinned. "Always glad to see you're on my wavelength, Harley Merlin, though I was thinking swimsuits."

I frowned. "Now I'm confused."

"Did Wade not show you the pool when he gave you the guided tour of this place?" A smirk tugged at her lips.

"No... Wade Crowley did *not* tell me there was a pool. Sly bastard!"

"Come on, I've got a spare suit you can borrow. We can see if Tatyana and Astrid want to come with us," she said, smiling. "Although, it might be a bit counterproductive if Tatyana comes along. I love her with all my heart, but you can practically hear the jaws hitting the floor whenever she goes to the pool."

As luck would have it, when we knocked on Tatyana's door, both Astrid and Tatyana answered with face masks and fluffy bathrobes on. "Not tonight, I'm afraid. I'm cleansing away the free radicals and plumping my skin with a cocktail of peptides," Tatyana explained, half-sarcastically. "My mom is worried about me getting wrinkles in the American heat, so she sent an entire crate of sheet masks from Korea. Useful, yet slightly insulting. I think that encapsulates my mother perfectly."

Astrid nodded eagerly. "If you thought magic was confusing, you should check out the ingredients in one of these things. There's stuff in this that I've never even heard of! Did you know you could put bee venom on your face?"

I chuckled. "You know what, I didn't."

"Well, you can!"

"And that's why we're going to have to decline." Tatyana sighed apologetically. "If any of these products touch pool water, I fear I may spontaneously combust. Did you want to borrow a suit, Harley? I've got a whole rack you can choose from."

"Mind if I borrow one, too?" Santana asked. "Yours are way better than mine."

"Of course."

Twenty minutes later, I walked out of Tatyana's room in a sultry black two-piece. It hugged me in all the right places, but it had so many ties and cut-outs in it that it'd taken me fifteen of those twenty minutes to get in the damn thing. She'd given me a bathrobe, too, for the road. I wrapped it around me as we walked down the hall.

Santana had borrowed a stunning, deep red bikini that looked insanely good against the olive tone of her skin, like she'd just walked out of the cover of *Sports Illustrated*. To be honest, all of this borrowing and lending of clothes was a little new and strange to me, considering I'd never really had any close female friends before. I had no idea how to react. *Might as well get used to it. Tatyana's closet is all* Devil Wears Prada. *She offered, and I love it.*

With towels under our arms, we set off to find Raffe's room. Santana was wearing a robe over her bikini, too, just for the sake of wandering around the coven. In the living quarters, it was pretty much anything goes, and nobody would've batted an eyelid if we'd been strutting our stuff, but there was a cunning plan afoot. A plan that required mystique and subtlety.

A few minutes later, we arrived outside his room. Santana shot me a conspiratorial look before loosening the belt of her robe and knocking on the door. Raffe answered shortly afterward, rubbing his eyes and flattening his hair down. Clearly, he'd been napping, and boy was he about to get the surprise of his life. I stifled a laugh as he gaped at Santana, his eyes bulging out of his head as he noticed the red bikini, visible beneath the open lapels of the robe. I didn't need my Empath abilities for this one.

"Sorry, did we wake you?" Santana asked innocently.

"It is… kind of late," he stammered.

"We were just heading down to the pool for an evening swim and wondered if you wanted to come with?"

He gulped audibly. "It's a bit cold, isn't it?"

"The pool is *inside*, Raffe. It doesn't matter if it's cold." She chuckled, making a subtle show of closing her robe again. "Come on, why don't you join us? Harley's never been to the pool before. I figured it'd be nice if a group of us went."

His eyes flashed red for a moment. "I'm supposed to be meeting Alton in half an hour."

Santana sighed. "Oh well… maybe next time, then?"

Reaching toward the edges of his emotions, I struggled to make any sense of them. Raffe was always a bit of a puzzle to me, his emotions all jumbled and confusing. There were threads of disappointment and a burst of something that made me blush suddenly—that had appeared when his eyes had flashed red. He was totally smitten with Santana, I could feel that, but a dark undercurrent of anger and bitterness rippled beneath, combining with peaks of admiration and complete shock.

Raffe looked to me with a hint of pleading in his eyes. "I'm sorry, both of you. Tonight's just not a good night for me." He knew I was reading him, and he knew that I knew. A desperation flowed toward me, hinting at his desire to put an end to the conversation as quickly as possible—out of sheer embarrassment for the mix of emotions that swirled within him. Some were totally unmentionable, but they didn't seem to fit Raffe's character. He'd never have let his feelings stray so intensely to the saucy side of things, not when he clearly admired her for more than her physique. *You dark horse, Raffe.*

"Like I said, maybe another time?" Santana replied coyly.

"Yeah, sure, of course. Another time."

"Good luck with Alton. Shout if you need us for anything," she said.

He nodded so hard I thought his head might fall off. "Absolutely. Sorry again. I've got to go—I've got some… uh… things to get in order before I go to Alton's office."

"Goodnight, Raffe."

"Goodnight, Santana… and Harley. Goodnight, Harley."

"'Night, Raffe," I replied, feeling a little sorry for him. His emotions were all over the place. *It's like there's two of you—a good you and a bad you. A split personality kind of gig.* Not for the first time, I wondered what was going on inside him. Nobody seemed to want to tell me, and I was all out of guesses.

Laughing, we turned around and headed for the pool.

"I'll let you know what I felt when we get there," I told her. "That might be more private than the hallway."

"Okay, okay." Santana's cheeks were pink, and her smile was wide. I had a feeling she already knew the outcome.

Heading through the courtyard of magnolia trees, we ambled north, through the usual network of halls and corridors. I was expecting a long walk, but five minutes later, we arrived outside a large set of golden double doors. A pair of mermaid tails took the place of ordinary handles while two large statues of Poseidon flanked the entrance. Santana heaved one of the doors open, and we both ducked through.

I gasped at the sight beyond. The pool was set within a huge room of white marble pillars and archways that reminded me of ancient Roman baths. Above, a twinkling star-scape glittered, though I didn't recognize the constellations as ours. Soft lighting cast a flattering glow on everything and everyone, making the swimmers look like bronzed gods as they cut through the water. Cloistered walkways bordered the deep blue pool. A few magicals sat on the edges, dangling their feet in the water.

A doorway led out onto a balcony that overlooked Balboa Park, the shimmer of the interdimensional bubble glowing overhead. On the deck, four hot tubs bubbled away. A group of young women, about the same age as Santana and me, were giggling away in one of them, their raucous laughter drifting in.

Why didn't Wade show me this place? As he popped into my thoughts, I found myself looking forward to telling him about my visit to the New York Coven. He wouldn't approve of me sneaking through the mirror, but he didn't have to know all the details. I'd *definitely* have to keep the whole almost-cast-a-dark-spell-and-summoned-a-god thing out of my story. Santana and I had decided to keep it to ourselves for now, until she'd spoken to her mom about why it might have happened. I'd tell Wade as soon as I found out more about it, so I'd have some good news to take the edge off the potentially chaotic thing I'd almost done.

Either way, I just hoped he'd be happy for me, and for what we'd found there. My dad hadn't killed those people—he'd been forced into it. It wouldn't bring the families of those he killed any comfort, but it brought *me* a whole lot.

"So?" Santana asked, as we took off our robes and slipped into the shallow end of the pool. The tepid water enveloped my body like silk, loosening up the tight muscles and easing a few recently acquired aches and pains.

"He likes you," I replied. "There were a couple of weird things going on, but he likes you. He's definitely interested in you in *every* possible way, but you didn't need my Empathy to tell you that. Raffe couldn't have been more obvious if he'd tried. I thought he was going to lose an eyeball."

She giggled, resting her arms on the ledge of the pool as she kicked out her legs. "I thought so, but suspecting something isn't the same as knowing for sure. I needed you for that extra bit of confirmation."

"So, you're happy?" I could already feel the joy brimming from her, but it felt polite to ask.

She grinned from ear to ear. "Ecstatic."

"Although… you know how I mentioned those weird things?"

"Yeah."

"Well, it felt like he was trying to suppress his feelings for you. Like he was trying to fight to keep them hidden," I replied. "Obviously, that was pretty hard for him to do, considering… well, you, standing in front of him in a bikini. He was battling it like a trooper, though."

She frowned. "That's just him, I guess. He doesn't like to give too much away, and he must've known I'd asked you to Empath for me."

"Maybe you're right, but what's the dual personality about? I don't get it. Every time I feel his emotions, it's all mixed up and jumbled, like there's more than one mind vying for the top spot."

Santana gave an exasperated sigh. "I wish I could tell you, but Raffe will have to do it in his own words. It's not my secret to share, and I can't break his trust. I promised I wouldn't." She offered me an apologetic glance. "The thing is, Raffe has trouble opening up sometimes. He worries about how people might react to him."

"I can understand that," I murmured, dipping my head below the water.

All my life, that had been my constant worry—how will this family react to me, how will these classmates react to me, how will these strangers react to me? Even now, it lingered, like a gnawing ache in the pit of my stomach. Maybe that was why I was so interested in clearing my dad's name. If people realized that he wasn't a monster, they might see that I wasn't one, either.

"Speaking of hidden feelings," Santana said as I resurfaced, "there's something I've been meaning to tell you about Wade."

My heart jolted into my mouth. "Oh?"

"You know the pledge, when Wade led you into the hall?"

I nodded.

"It's tradition for a family member, or a loved one, to do the honors—to lead the pledger into their new life, so to speak," she explained, with a knowing smile. "Because the Smiths couldn't attend, and given your family history, Wade stepped in to do that for you. I'm guessing he didn't tell you the significance of the act?"

I stared at her. "Um, no… he didn't."

"So shines a good deed in a weary world," she replied.

I frowned. "Did you just quote Willy Wonka at me?"

"If the quote fits, you must… I don't know, accept it?" She chuckled to herself.

I paused, her words still sinking in. "So… he really did that?"

"Oh yes, he really did that."

"It's not like Wade to do something without getting credit for it."

Santana grinned. "Must mean he *really* likes you. It was a cool thing for him to do."

I stared at the pool's surface for a long time, contemplating what had happened. All that time, and he hadn't mentioned it to me. I'd nagged at him that day, when he was just trying to do a nice thing for me. My heart pounded in my chest at the notion of his good deed. He hadn't wanted me to go up there alone, looking like the sad foster kid who had nobody to cheer her on. *Wade Crowley, you're just full of surprises.*

TWENTY-THREE

Harley

Feeling loose and relaxed after an hour in the pool, I got out and left Santana to do a few more laps. With my robe on, I headed back out into the hallways of the coven and walked toward the living quarters. The pool was nice, but I needed a hot shower. Plus, I was going to need an hour to get out of this damn swimsuit. *If I don't strangle myself with it, I'll chalk it up as a win.*

I hurried along the cold marble, wishing I'd worn flip-flops or something, almost sprinting around the magnolia trees in my rush to get back to my room. I didn't see the figure striding in the opposite direction until we collided. As I stumbled back, strong hands stopped me from falling to the floor, my robe flying open in the process. *Don't let it be Alton, don't let it be Alton, please don't let it be Alton.* Frantically grasping at the belt, I pulled the robe closed and looked up into the disgruntled face of Wade Crowley. Despite his gruff expression, a wave of shock and desire hit me in a torrent of emotion, mingling with an undercurrent of annoyance. His eyes were fixed on my robe, his Adam's apple moving in a subtle swallow.

"Wade! I nearly jumped out of my skin," I said, scrambling to cover my embarrassment. "What are you doing lurking in the hallways so late at night?"

"Looking for you," he replied curtly, tearing his eyes away from my robe. He knew that I knew what he was feeling after seeing me half naked, and jumped to try and cover it with a stern demeanor. Maybe he'd seen something he liked.

"I've been at the pool. Santana showed it to me, since *someone* didn't bother putting it on the guided tour." I forced a tight smile onto my face. "I was doing all kinds of neat new tricks with my Water abilities—a few twisting pillars, firing droplets really fast, making watery hands to pull Santana under. I wasn't trying to drown her or anything, although I might've almost drowned a couple of teenagers who got in the way of my tidal wave. Still, it was cool to get a grasp on my powers."

Why the hell was I rambling on like a freaking monkey up a tree? *Get a grip, Merlin! We're supposed to be channeling super-cool "single-ladies" vibes, remember?* Easier said than done when standing in front of Wade with nothing on but a bikini and a robe. These newly awakened feelings were going to be nothing but trouble, I could tell.

"Are you done?" he said.

I frowned. "At the pool? Well, obviously, otherwise I wouldn't be—"

"I've been looking for you all evening, and you've been ignoring my texts," he snapped, the desire dissipating. "We've still got missing kids to find, in case you'd forgotten? You might've given up after the failed day we've had, but while you've been off gallivanting at the pool, some of us have carried on with the grunt work. The kids aren't going to find themselves, Harley. Frankly, I'm starting to wonder just how much you care about this task we've been given."

My eyes narrowed. "I haven't been shirking, if that's what you're getting at. I spent an hour at the pool—one *measly* little hour, after a whole day of working on the case. Come on, man, we all need a break sometime. Otherwise our heads will fry."

He took a deep breath. "We don't have time to mess around."

"So, you've found some new leads, have you?" I couldn't keep the bitterness out of my voice. Who did he think he was, storming through the halls with a face like thunder, then more or less accusing me of being lazy? He was being a total drama queen about it. Yes, I'd been gone a while, but I hadn't been twiddling my thumbs. He didn't know about New York, that was true, but just because I hadn't been around, it didn't mean I didn't care about the missing kids. I cared deeply. It was just that I cared about clearing my dad's name, too.

If you're frustrated with the case, fine, but don't you dare take it out on me.

"What's that supposed to mean?" Wade asked.

"Nothing. It's a question. *Have* you found any new leads? Judging by the way you're stomping through these halls like you've got crocodiles snapping at your ass, it would suggest you've found *something* worth telling. I'm just waiting for you to spit it out."

He folded his arms across his chest. "Actually, Marjorie is making some decent headway with finding Micah Cranston. We gave her an object that was brought back from the Cranstons' as evidence, and she's using it to read his future." He paused, intense frustration twisting his features. "Although, we keep hitting a ton of dead ends as to where he could be. The images aren't clear enough, and we don't recognize any of the locations she's seen."

"How long have you been working her?" The poor girl had to be exhausted.

"A couple of hours."

"Tell me you've let her go to bed."

"Of course we have," he shot back. "That's why I came to find you, to see if you had any thoughts about it."

"Can't we use a tracer spell on Micah's object?" I asked, trying to keep my tone level.

"Nope, there's some kind of block on his physical signature. We tried putting a tracer together, but it sputtered out the moment the spell was cast. Katherine is stonewalling us when it comes to the kids," he replied. "Alton has no idea how she's drawing enough energy to keep them hidden like that, even from a tracer spell, but she's doing it. Glad to see you're at least asking the right questions."

"Listen, I know I haven't been around, but I *have* been asking the right questions this evening," I replied, a little chastened. "Right this minute, there's a huge folder in my room with a bunch of stuff about Katherine Shipton and the Merlins in it. I haven't been wasting my time, okay? I thought we could try a different angle."

The air between us went very still. "What do you mean, Harley?"

"I was going to tell you this tomorrow, but... well, I visited the New York Coven tonight," I replied firmly. I wasn't about to let him make me feel bad about the progress Santana and I had made on the personal matter of my dad's innocence. It might not have had much to do with the missing kids, but I was certain the Grimoire spells could help me break the Suppressor. If I could get this thing out of me, I knew I'd be able to do more to find those kids.

"What?" His face remained exasperatingly blank, but I could feel his confusion.

"Santana and I went to the New York Coven to find out more information about Katherine, Hiram, and Hester. We got a load of copies from the archives, and... yeah, we got a lot of good stuff. There was information about Katherine's former associates and old hideouts she'd used in the past. We even found out that she'd broken into a spell repository to retrieve rare spells. The guy there, Salinger, said he'd send a list of other missing spells. It might help us out."

I'd almost told him about the Grimoire. *Nope, I'm keeping that little nugget to myself. Seeing steam come out of Wade's ears isn't exactly on my agenda for this evening.* He'd rat me out, for sure.

"You went to the New York Coven?" Disbelief still poured off him.

"*Yes,* Wade. Don't give me that look. It was worth it. I found this photo of my dad from the… from the mortuary. On his neck, there was this tiny rune and two puncture marks. It fits with the description of the Sál Vinna curse." A sad smile spread across my face. "He didn't kill those people of his own volition. Katherine forced him into doing it. She put that vicious spell on him and *made* him do those horrible things."

He shook his head slowly. "I can't believe you went to New York without me." There was an undeniable note of disappointment in his voice. I could feel it, too, the cold tendrils slithering under my skin.

Anger spiked through my chest—*my* anger. "No congratulations? No 'glad to hear your dad's not a murdering psychopath'? Is that all I get—disappointment?"

His face changed, a flicker of panic in his eyes. "No, no, of course not. I'm really happy your dad was truly innocent in all of those things. Sorry, I should've led with that."

"Yeah, you should've."

"Does that mean they're going to clear his name?" Agitation churned in my stomach, feeding from him. Clearly, he wanted to get something else off his chest. *Well, you're going to have to listen first. Show some friggin' compassion.*

I tilted my head from side to side. "Yes and no. The guy who took us around the place—James Salinger—he said we'd need to get a confession from Katherine or one of her accomplices if my dad's ever going to get his name cleared," I explained. "If they just went out and announced his innocence, it'd make the coven look bad. After all, it would mean they executed an innocent man. So, we need a solid admission of guilt, otherwise they'll just sweep it under the rug." The system was corrupt, and it made my blood boil. My dad was innocent. I wasn't going to let them sweep anything under the rug.

Wade nodded. "With a confession, they won't be able to ignore the truth."

"Exactly."

"We'll catch her someday soon, and when we do, we'll bring her to justice," Wade assured me. "We'll make her pay for every single crime she's committed, including using Sál Vinna on your dad. *Especially* for that."

A flurry of warmth and affection enveloped me like a hug, all of it coming from him. *Just when I'm about to hate you, Wade Crowley, you know exactly what to say to get me all hot and bothered again.* I couldn't help but feel touched by how dedicated he was to proving my dad's innocence. The strength of conviction in his voice was enough to make my heart beat a little faster.

"I've got another couple of bones to pick with her when the time comes," I continued, holding back sudden tears. "See, Salinger also found some info on how Katherine fueled the spell in the first place. She murdered my entire family on my dad's side. That's the price required for Sál Vinna—the whole line of the spell victim's family has to be killed, or it won't work fully."

"Is that how Hiram was able to fight it, because Katherine didn't get everyone?"

I nodded. "She missed Isadora and me, and something stopped her killing Finch. I'm guessing she got desperate and did the curse anyway, hoping ninety-eight percent of my family tree would be enough, which gave my dad enough leeway to keep it from overwhelming him."

"I'm sorry, Harley." He touched my hand, for the briefest second. A shiver of unspoken feelings shot up my arm and into my heart—a mixture of his and mine.

"Oberon Marx was the test run," I went on, battling with my emotions. "At least, that's what Santana and I think."

"Do you think Katherine snatched all these kids to fuel a different kind of spell—a similarly dark and powerful one?" Wade mused aloud. "Thanks to Marjorie, we know they're all incredibly skilled, beyond anything we'd previously thought. Each one seems to have a rare power, combined with the usual Elemental abilities. It's like they're a new breed, almost."

"Must be something in the San Diego water," I joked. "But what kind of spell would involve Clairvoyants and Portal Makers and Herculeans, and who knows what else?"

"A damn terrifying one," he said. "If Katherine is aiming to become a Child of Chaos, like Finch and the Ryder twins claimed, it would take a lot of juice to pull off. One would need a tremendous amount of power to kill or replace a Child of Chaos, I'd imagine."

A curse word danced on the tip of my tongue, begging to be let loose.

"Alton and I have been researching the subject in a little more depth," Wade continued. "Alton reached out to the United Covens of America and acquired their consent to look through their secret archives. We got through a chunk of it earlier. It seems that, in ancient times, magicals actually used to *summon* the Children of Chaos, individually, to speak with them and make requests. Apparently, they didn't keep their distance from us mere mortals back then —they were a bit more involved."

I frowned. "Why do I feel like I know where you're going with this?"

"Our theory is that Katherine might be trying to summon a Child of Chaos so she can bargain with them and become one herself," he said. "It's only a theory, but if she wants to become one, she'll have to come face-to-face with one at some point. It's the *how* that still doesn't make any sense. Even Alton is stumped. A magical can't just take up a spot in the primordial pantheon, no matter how hard she might try and bargain. So, there has to be more to it that we don't know yet."

I nodded. "I imagine there's a bucketload of stuff we don't know about it. That's probably the point."

"Now, if you'd come to find me and let me come with you to the New York Coven, I might've been able to ask this Salinger guy more about Katherine's spell-work," he said, that note of disappointment coming back. "Did he seem to know a lot about her?"

"Yeah, a decent amount," I replied, realizing he was probably right. He could've helped out. Still, it was too late to change anything now. No use crying over spilled spells.

Wade shrugged, and I felt waves of hurt roll off him. "I can ask him next time, but I'm sure I could've gotten something good out of him if I'd gone with you tonight."

I frowned. "We *did* get something good out of him. Why are you so upset that I didn't take you with me? Santana had my back, and we got some decent information. I don't understand the problem here."

"I'm not 'upset,' I'm just…"

"Don't you dare say 'disappointed,' Wade."

He shrugged. "But I guess I am, maybe. A little bit."

"I thought you'd give me a slap on the wrist or something, but I didn't think you'd be so bothered," I said, confused. "I mean, I figured you'd rather stay here and work with Stella anyway. She's way more exciting to be around, judging by your reactions to her." I shot him a pointed look, reminding him that I could sense his emotions around her.

Wade turned suddenly serious, taking me by surprise. "I'm not interested in Stella." His deep green eyes fixed on mine, and a wave of desire sent my nerves into overdrive. My heart thundered in my chest, pounding like a stampede of wildebeest. *Is that... my desire, or his?* It felt like both.

I opened my mouth to speak, but he beat me to the punch.

He cleared his throat. "There's one other thing I wanted to say to you, Harley."

"What did you want to say?" My eyes went wide with anticipation. *Is this it? Is this where he admits he likes me? Is this the start of Merlin and Crowley? Sheesh, that sounds like a bad law firm. Still, I'm all for it.*

"Your hair is dripping all over the place. You should probably get upstairs and get changed before someone slips and cracks their head open."

Wow... way to pop my thirsty little balloon. You, Wade Crowley, are a colossal asshat.

"Didn't realize you'd been promoted to head of custodial services," I muttered, blushing furiously. Snatching my towel from under my arm, I bent over and mopped up the puddle of pool water from the slick marble. I didn't care that my stupid robe had come undone again. I just wanted to clean the mess up and get out of there before I could suffer any more blows to my ego.

"Happy now?" I asked, standing up. His eyes snapped straight to my black swimsuit, with all its complex cut-outs and slinky gaps and strings. A rush of unrestrained emotions barreled into me, filled with an intense longing. Well, a couple of those boys back there at the pool did whistle and call me a snack. I yelled a couple of curse words at them. *But looks like they aren't the only ones who appreciate Tatyana's ridiculous swimwear on me.* The sight of his bugged-out eyes amused me.

Wade coughed loudly, finding a spot on the ceiling to look at. "I need to get back to... um... Alton asked me to gather some... um... yeah, I need to get back to the investigation. There are a couple of potential places that Marjorie saw in her visions, and I promised

Alton I'd go over them before the morning. Correlate them with a map of California, you know, that kind of thing."

I smiled. "Happy hunting. I should probably get to my room before I get thrown out of here for indecent exposure."

"I… goodnight, Harley." He dipped his head in a quirky half-bow and skirted past me, hurrying off down the hallway beyond.

As I made my way up to the living quarters, with a huge smile on my face, I thought back to what Wade had said about summoning the Children of Chaos. I'd deliberately kept the whole debacle with the Grimoire from Wade, since it had involved breaking the rules and he'd definitely have given me more than a slap on the wrist for it. Plus, I was gripped with a crippling fear that the Mage Council might somehow find out about what I could do and lock me away for their own purposes. Isadora had mentioned something about being a pawn. What if they did that with me? Or, what if they locked me away because I was too dangerous?

I trusted Wade, but I had no way of knowing whether the information about me might somehow get leaked. They might not even be able to keep my secret, given the implications. If I could do something *that* dangerous, they might have to tell someone—for my own sake as well as everyone else's. The thought left me jangling with terror.

However, as I walked, I vowed to submit a formal request to view the book again so I could read more on the sections about the Children of Chaos. Especially Erebus.

I'd have to come up with a way of viewing the Grimoire without getting utterly consumed by it every time I touched its pages. I wondered if removing the Dempsey Suppressor might give me the strength I needed to overcome the power of the Grimoire and control it, rather than be controlled by it.

A previous thought flashed like a firework in my head. I felt surer of it now. *If I can get rid of the Suppressor and harness my full strength, maybe I'll be able to find a clear way to get to these kids.* My Empath abilities had seen things in the past, using photographs as a medium—they'd seen and felt Marjorie's fear, after she'd run from the Ryder twins. If I was stronger, maybe I could follow that scent to wherever Katherine was hiding these children. It might be enough to break through her barriers. It was just the Suppressor that was holding me back.

There was only one man who could help me.

I hurried to my room and threw some clothes on. I twisted my wet, red hair into a bun, then darted straight back out. It was late, but I needed to see Dr. Krieger immediately, to discuss the surgery again. With all these dead ends and false steps, we'd reached an impasse in our investigation. Right now, he was my only hope... Scratch that, *our* only hope.

TWENTY-FOUR

Harley

I arrived at the infirmary ten minutes later, cold water dripping down my neck from my hastily tied bun. Krieger had been sick for days now, but I figured he had to be well enough to talk about the surgery. He hadn't been sent to the hospital or been quarantined or anything—at least, not that I knew of. There hadn't been a lot of news on him at all, the whole situation being kept on the down-low. With everything else going on, and the coven in turmoil, I guessed Alton hadn't wanted to make a fuss about it.

Walking into the triage room, I glanced around for a nurse, but there was nobody around. Puzzled, I pressed on to the long-term injuries wing, knowing there had to be someone in there who could help me find Krieger. The infirmary was staffed twenty-four-seven, at least in this part.

I pushed open the heavy double doors and froze on the threshold. The space beyond was eerily empty and quiet, the beds vacant and neatly made. I let the doors fall closed behind me and made my way through to the ward at the far end. It was our equivalent of an ICU, and I'd been here a couple of times before. After the gargoyle incident, this place had been teeming with victims of the attack, myself included. Still, hospitals freaked me out.

Slipping into the smaller room, I peered through the dimly lit gloom. There were no harsh strip lights here, only the soft glow of bedside lamps, illuminating the empty beds. A scuff of bare feet on linoleum made me pause. Someone stood in the middle of the room, their shadow barely visible.

A shiver of fear ran up my spine as a zombie-like groan wheezed through the air toward me. I flipped the light switch, and the main lights blinked into life.

Krieger stood in the central aisle. He gazed at the walls and the beds, but nothing seemed to register. It was as though he couldn't quite focus on his surroundings and didn't know how he'd managed to get there in the first place.

What the...

"Dr. Krieger, are you okay?" I asked. My eyes darted toward the mottled, warped skin of his bare arms. He was wearing a hospital gown, though the back had mercifully been tied shut. I couldn't tear my gaze away from his arms. The flesh had been severely burned, raw patches glistening in the cold light. By the looks of it, he'd tugged away his bandages, exposing the tender wounds beneath.

He turned around with a weird, fixed smile on his face. "Everything is just fine," he replied, in his Germanic lilt. I was instantly reminded of clowns at kids' birthday parties, with their fake smiles and too-bright voices.

I approached him slowly. "Are you sure, Doc? You don't look too good." I glanced at his arms again. "What happened to you?"

"Nonsense, I am perfectly well," he said cheerfully.

"I'm going to go and get someone. Don't go anywhere, okay? I think your meds might be messing with you." Something was clearly off about him, and I wasn't about to wrangle him back to whichever room he'd come from. Not on my own.

I turned to leave, only to hear the rustling shift of his body as he lunged toward me and wrapped his clammy hand across my forehead. His fingers and thumb dug into both my temples. Every cell in my body screamed to break free, but my limbs wouldn't listen. It was like a blockade had been put up between my muscles and my mind, stopping them from communicating. I couldn't move at all, everything frozen in one position.

"What do you plan to do about Katherine Shipton?" he asked, in an icy voice that didn't seem to belong to Krieger at all.

"We plan to find the powerful children and stop her from using them in her attempt to become a Child of Chaos," I replied, the words tumbling out of my mouth unbidden. He might as well have cracked my skull wide open with a can opener and scooped out the intel he wanted.

"Stop!" a female voice shouted. Someone burst into the room through a door at the far end of the ICU. With my body half twisted, I couldn't see who it was. A moment later, I heard boots pounding on the linoleum, Preceptor Bellmore's face coming into view shortly after. It didn't feel like Krieger had any intention of stopping or letting me go.

Preceptor Bellmore scanned the room, settling on a pitcher of water that stood by one of the beds. Her Esprit glowed as a twisting pillar of liquid rose out of the glass jug, mixed with a healthy dose of ice cubes, and swirled toward Krieger. It careened in a tumbling orb into the side of his face, splashing down with a spray of ice-cold water that hit me in the back of the head. I wanted to cry out in shock at the freezing cold pellets biting into my skin, but Krieger had yet to relinquish his hold on me.

As Preceptor Bellmore brought another orb of icy water down over his head, soaking him completely, his hand loosened on my forehead. Regaining my senses, I ducked away from him and staggered forward, clawing breath into my lungs. He blinked rapidly and stared at his palms as though they belonged to someone else. Slowly, he raised his gaze to me, a bemused look glinting in his eyes.

"Are you kidding me, Krieger? I was gone for *five* minutes!" Bellmore chided. "You promised me you could stay awake for five damn minutes, if I left you alone. I guess it's my fault for believing you, huh?"

Krieger dropped his gaze, looking ashamed. "I thought I had control. I was reading a rather interesting book to help with the magical detector project—I was right in the middle of a fascinating chapter, and then… well, I suppose I ended up here. I don't remember leaving my bed. I don't know how this could have happened." He glanced at me again. "Oh, Harley, please accept my humblest apologies. I hope I didn't scare you too much. I was not in control of my faculties."

I shook my head, blinking in confusion. A few seconds ago, I was sure he'd done something to me, but now… I couldn't remember anything from the last couple of minutes. There was a slight throbbing in my temples, but that was it. *Did I hit my head?* I had a couple of hazy memories of walking into the ICU and seeing him in the central aisle, but after that—well, that was anyone's guess. *And hey, why is the back of my shirt soaking wet?*

"What did you do?" I asked. "I can't remember anything. You were standing right there, looking at something, and then… I don't know what happened. I can't focus on it. Did you throw water at me?"

Preceptor Bellmore shook her head. "The water was my doing. I had to stop Dr. Krieger from digging into your memories, and cold water seems to be the only thing to snap him out of it. Well, short of smacking him on the back of the head with a blunt object and knocking him clean out," she replied, with a wry smile. "You forgetting everything that happened is exactly how the curse works."

Now that's freaking creepy.

"Not to be rude, but can one of you tell me what the heck is going on? I'm coming up empty here."

"Someone in the coven, likely one of Katherine's spies, managed to break into my office while I was sleeping and put a mind-control curse on me," Krieger explained. "It's the kind of spell that's used to create spies out of normally loyal insiders—the perfect cover. You see, I didn't know it had been put on me until Bellmore found me wandering the halls one evening. The cursed individual is unaware that they've been cursed."

Bellmore nodded. "Whenever he goes to sleep, the curse is activated, and he sleepwalks. That's what he was doing when I found him. The curse makes him seek out people of interest—people the curser has told him to reach out to, from a list whispered when the spell was first put in place. He then places his hand on their forehead, the way he just did with you, which immobilizes them. After the person is frozen, the spell sinks into their mind and forces them to tell him the truthful answer to any question he might have."

"I am then able to erase the memory of the incident, thus gaining all their secrets without them even knowing they have been spilled," Krieger added reluctantly. "Now, given that the whole thing involves many complex spells, all mixed together in the body of one curse, it is incredibly taxing on my person. Indeed, it would've taken an exceptionally skilled magical to conjure a curse like that and set it loose within me. Few possess the stamina for spell-work of that magnitude."

I know of one. I'm just not going to think about it. Nope.

I frowned at Krieger. "Wait… does that mean you've been trying not to sleep all this time?"

"Yes, exactly. I've been trying my hardest to stay awake."

"But that's *days,* Dr. Krieger!"

"Yes, indeed it is."

Bellmore smiled tightly. "I've been babysitting him, so to speak, to stop him from falling asleep. When it hasn't quite worked, I've also been here to subdue him every time he's fallen under the spell."

"Does that mean you've been awake for days, too?"

She nodded. *Well, that explains the massive dark circles under your eyes. I could pack for six months with bags like those.* I wasn't being unkind; she just looked completely exhausted. I'd thought the same thing back at Dennehy's, though now it made a lot more sense.

"Can't you restrain him?"

Bellmore shook her head. "We've tried everything, believe me. Staying awake for days on end is the last resort in a long line of ideas. Whenever I tied him down, he simply broke out with his magic. You see the burns on his arms?"

"Yeah."

"Krieger is a Fire Elemental. He kept burning the restraints off, to the point where I've gone through four pairs of Atomic Cuffs, all melted now." She sighed, sitting down on the edge of the nearest bed.

"Wait, what? He can burn through Atomic Cuffs?"

She nodded. "There's something in that curse that allows him to do it. It's insanely powerful—terrifyingly so." She glanced at Krieger with sad eyes. "I've been trying my damnedest to break the curse, but nothing has worked so far. You'd think the lack of sleep would kill him, but this spell is keeping him strong, no matter what. I, on the other hand, can only do so much in a state like this. Even with eight hours of sleep, I haven't been able to do a single thing to break it."

I looked at the two weary souls, wondering how they'd been left on their own like this. "What does Alton think about all of this?"

Now, I understood why he'd been keeping Krieger's illness on the down-low, since no one else in the coven knew about this weird turn of events. Not a single soul had mentioned insomnia, or their foreheads being grabbed, or a crazy-strong curse that nobody could break. This was clearly need-to-know, and I'd just walked in at the wrong time. Still, I was pretty peeved at Alton for keeping a secret like this, though all my mind could say to that was, *hypocrite*. Right now, I was the reigning queen of secrets.

A stilted silence settled between us.

"Let me guess, Alton doesn't want the rest of the coven to know, so he's leaving you to figure it out?" I asked.

Bellmore shrugged. "He knows I'm capable, and I can understand his reluctance to disclose this. If word of it got out, there'd be mass panic. Nobody would know who's been compromised, and everyone would become a suspect. Dangerous things happen when people start to become suspicious of one another, especially when some decide to take matters into their own hands. Folks like me would be first on the kill-list."

"Shapeshifters would be the first targets, huh?"

"Precisely. Alton doesn't want any more paranoia about spies leaking into the coven. Warning everyone to be extra vigilant is all he's willing to do, at this point. He's confident we can find the spy in our midst, and so am I. The trouble is, we need more time, and that time is running out."

"All of this is why you were acting so weird at Dennehy's, right?" I asked. "You wanted to keep Krieger's condition a secret?"

Bellmore nodded. "I wasn't exactly expecting to see people from the coven there. In fact, that's why I went to Dennehy's in the first place, so I wouldn't run into anyone. Bad timing on both our parts, I guess." She glanced at me curiously. "I know why I was there, but why were you?"

"We were looking into something for Alton."

She glanced at me with suspicious eyes, prompting me to change the subject, pronto.

"Have you had any luck tracing the curse back to the culprit?" I asked.

"None." She propped her head up with her knuckles. "Nobody

else in the coven has shown any signs of being cursed, so it's not like there's a specific trail or a pattern to follow."

Krieger cleared his throat. "Anyway, what's brought you to the infirmary? You don't appear injured, aside from two very minor contusions on either side of your forehead. My fault, I fear, though they will fade within the hour."

I almost felt guilty mentioning it. "I wanted to come and talk to you again about removing the Dempsey Suppressor. We're struggling to come up with any leads on these kids, and I'm convinced that if I just had my full strength, I could do more to trace them."

Krieger sighed. "I worried that might be the case."

"So… you can't do anything?"

"I am deeply sorry, Harley, but it seems rather unlikely that I'll be able to help with the Suppressor's removal right now. I'm extremely sleep-deprived, for one, which is not conducive to surgical procedures. And two, Preceptor Belmore is concerned that I may have been permanently compromised. I would not want Katherine knowing more about you than she already does, should the curse ever overtake me and force me to share my intel with its creator."

I realized that Alton was probably going to have to hire a new physician, if the curse couldn't be lifted. Krieger had been compromised. And yet, the thought of having to go through all the Suppressor stuff again, with a new physician, worried me. I had hopes for Krieger.

I shuddered at the thought. "How would they do that, if they wanted to?"

"They can summon me at any time and have me recite whatever I've learned. I would not even know that I had done it," he explained.

"I can see why they chose you," I muttered, feeling on edge. For us, Krieger was an especially dangerous choice for a spy, since he had access to everyone in the coven and knew all of their abilities, thanks to the Readings. *Including mine...*

Krieger nodded slowly. "Yes, it would appear that whoever did this chose very carefully. I know a great deal, and I have access to everyone's records. I know their strengths and weaknesses, and what talents they possess. I have been utterly compromised. It is my deepest shame."

"Hey, you didn't do this to yourself," I replied sharply. "This isn't your fault."

"No, but I failed to be more vigilant."

Bellmore sighed. "Dr. Krieger, this isn't on you. Yes, you've been compromised, but you're taking pretty hefty steps to fight it. You get points for that." She turned to me, her amber eyes narrowing slightly. "Now, we're going to need your assurance that you won't breathe a word of this to anyone. I hardly think I need to tell you why."

"I'll keep my mouth shut about Krieger's curse," I promised. "The coven is crazy enough right now without adding to everyone's panic."

"We're grateful for that," she said quietly.

"No problem." I didn't want to mention it out loud, but this whole thing made me feel really uneasy, to know that anyone in the coven could be controlled or impersonated. We'd been worried enough about a spy who might be able to Shapeshift. If that person could Shapeshift *and* had the means to control minds, we were royally screwed. I hated getting downhearted about things, but what else could I do when faced with such a crap-storm of insane hurdles?

"Are you okay?" Bellmore asked.

"Yeah, I was just thinking about something that happened while we were out investigating," I said, keeping it vague. "I don't know if Alton mentioned it, but someone attacked us while we were working, and they were impersonating you. We knew it wasn't you because they were weaker, and their mask slipped for a second, but it's kind of concerning that they used you like that... whoever they were."

She turned her gaze away for a moment. "Alton told me about it, yes," she replied, after a pause. "I'm just glad that you knew me well enough to recognize that it wasn't me. I might be a Shapeshifter, but I'd like to think that doesn't immediately make me guilty of every crime."

"You must get that a lot, huh?"

A tight laugh rippled from her throat. "It's all too easy for people to suspect or condemn those who are different, simply because they possess a power that others don't. We don't choose to be this way; we are born with the abilities we have. And yet, people judge us and fear us because of something we have no control over."

I reddened, looking away. *I'm sorry, Sloane... I'm sorry that I'm guilty of that very thing, where Shapeshifters are involved.*

Just because I couldn't read someone didn't mean they were inherently bad. I'd come to this realization a long time ago, but I'd let my fear and suspicions cloud my judgment, regressing me to former thoughts that weren't valid in any way. Looking back at Bellmore, I vowed to do better. The spy was a Shapeshifter, we knew that much, but that didn't mean *all* the Shapeshifters were spies.

TWENTY-FIVE

Santana

I'd hoped a couple of hours in the coven pool might make me feel better, the soothing water washing away the sick feeling that had been nagging me since coming back from New York. Unfortunately, my body seemed to have other ideas. With my stomach still churning, and my skin drenched in a sheen of cold sweat, I dressed in comfy clothes and padded along my curve of the living quarters to find Raffe.

If he likes me in a slinky bikini, then he can damn well like me in sweats and a t-shirt, looking like death warmed over.

My last few peaceful laps of the pool, without Harley spraying pillars of water at me or creating tidal waves, had proven pretty useful in getting the mental juices flowing. The Children of Chaos had already been playing on my mind, ever since our little trip through the mirror, but I kept fixating on one particular point: Erebus, the Child of Darkness. *A nice, non-threatening title if ever I've heard one.* I'd seen him mentioned in the spell that Harley had been reading. Plus, the creeping, unsettling black fog whipping around her had been a damn good indicator of who was involved in the spell.

A memory came back to me, floating through my mind on a wave of tranquility. There'd been a book in Astrid's room—one of the texts we'd been reading through during our gossip sessions. At the bottom of one page, there'd been a footnote in an embossed text box. It had mentioned djinns and how they were directly connected to Erebus. According to that book, a djinn's powers were fueled by Erebus's energy, and so these demons could be called upon to help perform the incantation that would summon him. It could be done in other ways, but using a djinn as a sort of gateway appeared to be the easiest method. It was only after a peaceful swim that the pieces started to make sense, coming together in my mind.

It had given me an idea. As friggin' terrifying as Kadar was, I figured he might have insight into how a magical could become a Child of Chaos, like Katherine wanted to. It didn't sit too easy with me that I'd have to get Raffe to let the demon loose for a bit so I could speak to him one-on-one, but right now we were clutching at a whole bunch of nothing where Katherine and the kids were concerned. That psycho-bitch would stop at nothing to get what she wanted, which meant we'd have to do the same.

Fire with fire, and all that jazz. Although, if this ruins my dating plans, I swear I'll come down on you like El Niño, Shipton.

I knocked on Raffe's door, hoping he was in. He'd mentioned something about a meeting with Alton, but it was almost eleven. I doubted Alton would have kept him so late. A shuffling echoed beyond the door. He answered a moment later, looking even sleepier than before.

"Santana?" He frowned at me. "Is everything okay?"

I nodded. "Are you busy?"

"I was about to go to bed, but I can stay up for a bit if you need something."

"I was wondering if I could ask a favor," I said tentatively. "Only trouble is, I don't think you're going to like it."

"Oh?" He sounded wary.

"Can I come in?"

He stepped back and ushered me into the room. He'd never invited me in before. I glanced around the place, admiring the black-and-white photos on the wall. They were mostly landscapes, with the occasional portrait mixed in—a group of kids sitting in a circle, an old lady on a porch stoop, a soldier kneeling in the middle of a vast desert. Raffe had never struck me as the kind of guy who liked photography, but these were amazing. I walked over to one and touched it—a landscape of a boating lake, with a single vessel out on the water.

"Are these yours?"

He nodded shyly. "I used to like taking pictures. Not so much anymore."

"How come?"

He shrugged. "Other stuff got in the way, I guess." He sat down on the edge of the bed. "How was your swim?"

"Really nice," I replied, with a smirk. "Harley didn't even know the pool existed."

"Are you sure you're okay? You don't look too good."

I pulled a face. "Just what a girl wants to hear."

"No, I mean... you always look beautiful, and you still look beautiful now, it's just... uh... you seem a little pale. Did you swallow pool water? I know it's clean and everything, but you can never be too careful."

I smiled, my heart swelling at Raffe calling me beautiful. "I'm fine, honestly. I think I'm just worn out after everything that's been going on. I'm guessing you're the same, with all this napping you've been doing."

"The djinn is being louder than usual," he admitted. "It's draining, but I'm doing okay. Weirdly, he gets more volatile whenever… never mind. I'm fine, just sleepy." His cheeks flushed pink, his gaze dropping for a second. *So, Kadar gets feistier whenever I'm around, eh? I suppose I should be flattered, but not if he's sapping Raffe to do it.*

"I won't keep you too long," I promised.

Sitting down at his desk, I launched into conversation, quickly filling him in on what Harley and I had been up to earlier. I left out the bit about the Grimoire, making up a white lie about another book on the Children of Chaos. After all, I'd promised Harley I wouldn't say anything about it. She was scared about what might happen if it got out. If the Mage Council caught one whiff of it, she'd be toast. Frankly, I was scared for her, too. I'd witnessed it with my own eyes. They'd lock her up and throw away the key if they found out what she was capable of. Levi already loathed her for her power, even with the Suppressor keeping things on an even keel.

"Anyway, there was this passage about Erebus and his relationship with djinns," I explained. "I was hoping you might let me talk to Kadar about Erebus, see what I can get out of him. If he's got some info on whatever Katherine is up to, we need to know about it. I hate to ask you to let him loose, but we're desperate."

Raffe sighed. "I've always known that djinns shared ties with Erebus, and I thought the same thing as you. I've already tried to talk to Kadar about it, but he just mocked me the whole time. He flat-out refused to say anything useful and told me to deal with whatever Katherine had in mind. He's not bothered if she gets the power she wants. I guess he thinks it won't affect him."

It surprised me to hear that they'd already talked about it. For some reason, I hadn't thought they spoke to each other that often, even though they shared the same body. Raffe seemed to hate Kadar, and Kadar wasn't exactly Raffe's biggest fan. Then again, I supposed it made sense that they'd chat from time to time. It probably made their life sentence go a bit faster.

"I don't want to press the issue if you're too tired, but would you mind if I tried anyway?" I asked. "Kadar might be more willing to speak to me. I can't explain it, but he doesn't seem to mind me that much. I guess he's grown to like me, just like you have." I flashed him a cheeky grin.

He smiled back, chuckling to himself. "That's true about Kadar, but I wouldn't say you grew on me, Santana," he said. "I liked you from the moment I met you. You have this energy about you that I've never seen or felt before. I'm not good at showing affection. I never have been. It's probably a family trait. But you make me want to show my feelings more. I'm still learning when it comes to this." He gestured to the space between us.

My pulse quickened. For the first time in my life, I'd been rendered speechless. And by Raffe, of all people—the man of so few words, silencing me in the space of a few moments. There was a delicious irony in that, though my mind wasn't functioning well enough to appreciate it. All I could do was sit and gape at Raffe like a moron.

"Do you want to go to the cage and try this out?" he prompted, grinning.

I struggled to find something to say. "Try what out?"

He laughed. "Coercing Kadar into talking."

"Oh… yeah, of course. Right. That." I smacked my forehead. *One-nil to Raffe, you sneaky, surprising, handsome bastard.* "Yeah, we should go before it gets too late. If you're already tired, I don't want to keep you up until four in the morning again—talking, that is. Talking to Kadar."

"Fortunately, I haven't had a recent conversation with my father, so we should be fine on that front," he replied, a pleased smirk tugging at the corners of his kissable lips. "I'll be able to control him better this time, since my anger isn't feeding him. He feeds off other things, but I'm pretty sure I can control those feelings for a couple of hours." His gaze met mine, my heart damn near stopping at the sight of the irreverent glint within them. *Raffe Levi, are you being saucy with me? Now this I can get used to... once I can think straight again.*

We left the living quarters and headed through the hallways of the coven, until we reached the hidden door that led to Raffe's glass box of emotion. It still felt eerie to wander through the narrow corridor toward the main room, every sound deadened thanks to the soundproofing.

"Are you sure you're okay to do this?" I asked nervously, the sight of the "cage" making me feel guilty. Giving Kadar the reins put a lot of pressure on Raffe, in every way possible.

"If it gets us the answers we need, it'll be worth it." He cast me a reassuring smile. "He'll listen to you. I know he will. And if he doesn't, he gets shoved back down. That's how this works." I wasn't sure he was talking to me anymore. It seemed to be a warning for Kadar.

Raffe walked over to the glass box and unlocked the padlock with the key. He left it in the bowl on the table to the side of the room, before retreating behind the clear façade. I followed him, the padlock slotting into place automatically behind him as he entered. He smiled at me through the glass as I stepped back and waited for the magic to happen.

"My spicy señorita. I was wondering when you might get bored of dear old Raffey and beg to have me back," Kadar purred. I hadn't even noticed the transition. A few wisps of black smoke wafted up from his shoulders, his skin darkening to that strange, deep red before my very eyes. "Admit it, I'm a lot more fun, aren't I?" His eyes flashed crimson as he pressed himself to the glass, doing a less-than-enticing dance against it.

"Is that supposed to be impressive?"

He grinned. "I've got plenty I could impress you with, Santana. I've never felt more alive, thanks to the name you gave me. It'd be rude of me not to offer you something in return, and I have *just* the thing in mind. Although, you'll need to let me out first. I'm aching to get my hands on you. I've been picturing the terror on your face as I put my hands around your throat—you won't know if I want to kiss or kill you until the very last moment. What a tasty thought." He licked his lips, a throaty cackle rippling from his mouth.

"Not going to happen, Kadar," I replied. "There's no way you're getting out of there."

"Don't you think about me? Let's not lie to each other. I know you do. Raffe isn't here; you can tell me anything," he whispered.

"I think about how glad I am you're stuck behind a glass wall."

His eyes flashed blue. "Fine, be coy. I am a patient demon. I will win you over, and when I do, I will sink my teeth into your flesh and bathe in your blood, until we are one entity. Your soul will bind to mine, and nothing will separate us."

"You should read a Hallmark card if you want some flirting ideas," I retorted. "Telling a girl you want to bathe in her blood isn't exactly romantic."

"But you aren't just any old girl, Santana. Your energy is intoxicating. I want to lap it all up until there's nothing left. It's all I can think about, all hours of the day. It feeds me. It makes me want to thrive. It makes me want to devour you in one bite."

I rolled my eyes at him. "I'm not here to hear about all the nasty things you want to do to me, Kadar."

"Have you come to bargain?"

"I suppose."

He leered at me through the glass. "Name your terms, and I'll name mine."

The thought of entering into a bargain with a djinn didn't sit well with me. Making deals with the devil was a notoriously bad thing to do, but desperation didn't give me many other options. If I wanted more information on Erebus, I needed to offer something in return.

Knowing Kadar, I wasn't going to like his suggestion. *No flesh-biting or blood-bathing, Diablo.*

"I want to know more about your connection to Erebus," I said confidently. He could probably smell my fear.

He laughed coldly. "Such a tiny, insignificant question. I suppose I can answer anything you want to know about that, as long as you're willing to answer a few of my questions afterward. A fair exchange, I'd say. Believe me, I could be asking for more. My sweet girl, I *want* to, but I figured we'd start small. Next time you come begging for me, we'll move on to bigger and better things."

Questions? Could be worse. I felt a little wary about what those questions might be, but he was right—he could've asked for a lot more. This seemed like an even exchange. That was the problem; it seemed a little *too* fair.

I shrugged. "Fine, I'll answer some of your questions if I'm satisfied with the answers you give me."

"I only give satisfaction, Santana. Care to find out more?"

I narrowed my eyes at him. "Let's just stick with the questions, shall we? Now, tell me about your connection to Erebus."

He paced the floor of his cage, his eyes turning red again. "I can go one better, even if you won't indulge me. If you like, I can channel the inner knowledge that all djinns gain from Erebus and relay the answers back to you. Think of me as your spiritual mediator." He appeared to be disappointed by my lack of enthusiasm for his advances, and yet there was a weird softness to his tone that intrigued and terrified me in equal measure. It was as though he genuinely wanted to do me a favor, to keep me happy.

"That would be very kind, Kadar."

His eyes glittered like sapphires, shifting from red back to blue. I'd pleased him, somehow.

"My first question is, what is the process for becoming a Child of Chaos?"

He fell silent for a moment. "The act is nearly impossible," he said, his voice returning with a thousand whispering echoes. It sounded similar to the way my voice changed when my Orishas spoke through me. *Creepy.*

"Nearly?"

"That's what I said, didn't I?" he shot back, with a sly grin.

I clung to the word. "Has anyone in the history of magicals ever attempted to become a Child of Chaos?"

He slipped back into his brief trance. "It would appear that they have, and foolishly so."

"Who?" My heart gripped in my chest. I was getting somewhere.

"That is not a question that we care to answer. We do not speak names—names are much too powerful," he replied. "Ask something else."

I frowned, trying to reword it. "Are there any records of this attempt here on Earth?"

"Clever girl," he purred. "Erebus and the other Children of Chaos have a particular interest in a Clairvoyant called the Librarian. They are keeping a watchful eye on her. This bookworm has kept track of all the magical spells ever created and attempted. I may not be able to reveal any names to you, but if you can find the Librarian, you may find the rest of your answers yourself."

I stared at him, overwhelmed with gratitude. If anyone knew what was required to become a Child of Chaos, it had to be this Librarian... wherever she might be. However, the fact that someone else had attempted this insane act filled me with dread. They might not have succeeded, but that didn't mean Katherine wouldn't. *Nearly* impossible didn't mean impossible.

"Where is the Librarian?" I asked.

Kadar shook his head. "No."

"What do you mean? Don't you know?"

"I mean no. You've drained my knowledge repository dry. Even if

I wanted to say more, I won't," he replied. "If you want more detailed answers, you'll have to talk to Erebus himself." He erupted into cold, brutal laughter. Clearly, the thought of me calling on Erebus himself to get more answers was hilarious to a demon like Kadar. I, on the other hand, thought it might be the right idea. *I'm clearly going loco if that's what we've come to. Less fighting fire with fire, more fighting crazy with crazy.* Then again, it might be mad enough to work.

I thought about Harley's reaction to the Grimoire and wondered if she really had almost summoned something terrible. Had Erebus been about to come on through to the mortal realm? Or was it something else? I couldn't be entirely sure, but it sparked an idea in my head. A safer, less-charged way to call upon the Children of Chaos. There had to be a way to do it without risking Harley's life, and the lives of everyone around her. It couldn't always be smoke tornadoes and fire and brimstone; otherwise, nobody would have bothered in the past.

"What are you thinking, my exotic flower?" he growled, pressing himself to the glass again.

I flashed him a smile. "I'm thinking I want Raffe back now."

He waggled his red finger at me. "I don't think so, *chica*. You've got your end of the bargain to hold up. You wouldn't go against a deal made with a demon, would you? You know what happens to people who cross creatures like me, right?"

Growing up in Catemaco, I knew all too well the kinds of things that could happen to a person who broke a deal with a devil. We were taught about evil spirits from a young age and how to protect ourselves against them. The first rule was never to get involved with a demon, but it was too late for that one. The only way to send a demon away was to fulfill your end of the bargain, or to get a bunch of powerful Santerias to send them packing for you. Since I didn't have the latter with me, and there was no way of sending the djinn packing without killing Raffe, I'd have to settle for plan A.

"Fine, ask your questions," I replied.

He rubbed his hands together in delight. "You must answer truthfully. I'll know if you're lying, and you don't want to lie to me."

"I swear to tell the truth, the whole truth, and nothing but the truth." I held my hand to my heart and scowled at him.

"Then tell me, do you have feelings for Raffe?"

"That's easy—of course I do."

"A little too easy, perhaps," he mused. "How about this: do you find this darker side of him attractive, as well? If that wasn't clear, I'm asking if you find me attractive, too?"

I paused. I couldn't lie. My throat constricted as I forced the word out. "Yes."

Kadar smirked. "That's all I wanted to know."

He disappeared a moment later, his red skin fading in a flurry of smoke and his eyes shifting back to the midnight gray that I adored. He'd gotten what he wanted, and now he was giving the reins back to Raffe. *Why did you make me say that? You smug pendejo!*

"Santana?" Raffe murmured.

"Is it you?"

He nodded. "It's me."

I grabbed the key from the side and rushed toward the glass box, letting him out of his cage. He strode out and scooped me into his arms, swinging me around before bringing me back into a tight embrace. I wrapped my arms around him, my fingertips toying with the back of his soft, black hair. Gripping him tighter, I buried my face in his neck, inhaling the fresh, clean scent of him. A touch of something sweet and burnt lingered underneath, like spun sugar at a town fair. My Orishas chattered with nervous excitement, bubbling happily inside me. They liked the feel and scent of him as much as I did.

He pulled away slightly, his hands moving to cup my face. My heart stopped beating as he leaned in, time slowing around us. His gaze lingered on my lips, my own fixed on his handsome face, anticipating the deliciousness of his next move. A gasp slipped from my throat as his lips grazed mine, the touch of his mouth searing my skin. I pulled him closer, kissing him back with every fiber of my being. It was everything I'd been hoping for and more.

With surprising strength that made me giggle against his lips, he lifted me up and carried me over to the table, where he set me on the edge. He gazed down at me for a moment, pushing a strand of hair behind my ear. I stared back, my heart thundering in my chest. He smiled and tilted my chin up, before leaning down to meet my eager kiss. Every nerve ending in my body was ablaze, my skin flushed and hot, my breath coming in short, sharp gasps. The slightest pressure of his lips on mine felt like the world had stopped spinning, and the stars were somehow aligning. I couldn't get enough—every sense was amplified tenfold, intensifying everything.

Somehow, I had a feeling we had Kadar to thank for this.

TWENTY-SIX

Santana

In a haze of complete happiness and full-body tingles, I wandered back to the living quarters. Humming to myself, I couldn't wipe the smile away from my face. Every time I replayed the kiss in my head, I wanted to do it all over again. I could still feel the graze of his lips on mine. *Really, Santana—humming? You've never hummed a tune in your damn life, you sap.* Still, the tune wouldn't stop. I was too damn happy to make it stop.

Letting myself into my room, I flopped down on the bed and pulled a pillow to my chest. I grinned like an idiot as I gazed up at the ceiling. Those kinds of kisses only happened in cheesy romcoms, usually in the rain. Rain would've been nice.

I jolted upright. A spark of electricity shivered through my nerves, but not the good kind that had been there moments before. The Orishas started to whisper around me, their voices getting louder and louder in a cacophony of panic. It felt like a thousand alarm bells ringing at once in my brain.

The magical charm I'd given Marjorie… it was going off.

"Take me to her," I urged the Orishas. I jumped off the bed and hurried for the door. My palms shone a bright blue, my eyes burning with the light of the spirits as the wispy forms of the Orishas danced around my field of vision. They shot off down the hallway, and I followed, sprinting with every scrap of energy I had left. *No way, Shipton. You are* not *ruining tonight for me!*

I leapt down the stairs two at a time and powered along the corridor toward the Aquarium, keeping an eye out for anything moving in the shadows around me. It was almost one in the morning. Clearly, the spy had waited until they thought everyone was in bed and used that peace and quiet to strike at Marjorie in the dark. Fury surged through my veins. Whoever this punk was, I wanted to strangle them for all the hell they were putting us through.

I followed the Orishas past the banquet hall, the path looping back around and leading me toward the Aquarium instead. They seemed to be tracing the scent of wherever the charm had been. I only hoped I wasn't too late.

Rounding the corner that led up to the Aquarium doors, I skidded to a halt as a figure jumped out of the darkness. My heart leapt into my throat, fearing it might be the spy. I'd been two seconds from slamming straight into them. However, as I calmed my racing pulse and steadied myself, I saw there was nothing to worry about. Catching my breath, I grasped Marjorie by the shoulders. She'd evidently crept out of the shadows at the sound of my footsteps approaching, though my presence had done nothing to shake the panicked expression in her wide eyes. Her whole body was trembling, her lips bitten raw with nerves.

"Hey, hey, hey, it's okay. I'm here now," I murmured, pulling her into a hug. She gripped onto me for dear life as I moved her back into the shadows. If someone was watching her, I didn't want them to see us standing in the hallway. *I'm not making this easy for you, you bastards. You want her, you're going to have to go through me and my Orishas.*

"I was so scared," she whispered, her tears drenching my t-shirt.

"What happened?" I pulled away, looking her dead in the eyes.

"Someone knocked out my security guards," she replied, her voice shaking. "They got the one outside my door first, then they took out the one in the chair at the foot of my bed. They tried to come for me next, but I managed to get away. The security guard... well, the guard held her back so I could run. I don't know what happened to him. Oh God... do you think he might be—"

"Wait, *her*?" I cut her off. There was no time to worry about the guards now.

Marjorie nodded. "Yeah, the one who—"

A fireball whizzed past my face, hitting Marjorie square in the shoulder and knocking her back. She sprawled across the floor, her face contorted in a grimace of pain. Smoke smoldered from the hole in her gray hoodie, but the damage didn't look too severe. Knowing she was in a lot more trouble than a simple burn, I whirled around to face the assailant. *Right, you've really pissed me off now.*

Going into attack mode, every cell pumped up with the energy the Orishas fed into me, I scanned the darkness beyond. A figure stepped out.

"*You,*" I growled.

Stella Chan stood in front of me, a half-smile on her lips. Before she could take another step, the Orishas swept toward her, launching a barrage of fierce energy in her direction. The blue-tinged sparks singed Stella's skin, prompting her to duck and dive to avoid them.

Using them as a screen, I charged at Stella and knocked her to the floor. With savage fury, I clocked her in the jaw with a neat right-hook and wrapped my hands around her throat, squeezing hard.

Meanwhile, the Orishas continued their onslaught of fiery rage. If I could just get her to slip into unconsciousness, I'd be able to restrain her properly and call for help. *Stop wriggling!* Her dark eyes met mine as she pressed her palms flat to the ground, a tremor of an earthquake rumbling underneath. She rolled out of the way as a tree shot up, slamming hard into my ribs.

I gritted my teeth, a sharp punch of pain searing through my right side. Ignoring it, I scrabbled to my feet and tackled her to the floor once again. We both went down hard, her fingertips clawing to get hold of Marjorie, who was struggling to sit up. The Orishas swirled around Stella's wrists, trapping them behind her back, while the others darted in and out of her skin in an attempt to freeze her in place. After my ill-advised spell in New York, I wasn't as strong as I could've been. Every pulse of the Orishas sapped me of what little energy I had left.

Hang back, I urged them. *Please, hang back for a moment. I've got this.*

The Orishas did as I'd asked, except the ones who swirled around Stella's wrists. I straddled her back and shoved her face into the cold marble, pressing my knee between her shoulder blades. My breath came short and fast, my lungs burning with the strain of trying to keep her under control. Thanks to the LA Coven's bootcamps, she was in crazy good shape and was way stronger than me.

Without warning, she twisted out from under me and kicked me halfway across the corridor, her boot cracking into my sternum and knocking the air out of my struggling lungs. A second rumble followed, though I managed to dive out of the way of another tree as it shot out of the ground. Jumping back up, I wrestled with the branches of the tree as they curled toward me, the twigs snapping at my face like bullwhips.

Up the hallway, Marjorie stood on shaky legs, trying to harness the power of her Air Elemental abilities. A gust of icy wind blew open the doors of the Aquarium up ahead, the surging squall whistling toward Stella. It knocked her off her feet as she tried to grasp at Marjorie, who fumbled to create a second gust of wind. That gave Stella the window of opportunity she needed. I lunged forward to stop her from reaching Marjorie, missing her by half a foot. Stella's hand locked around Marjorie's wrist.

Marjorie's eyes turned black, her Clairvoyant powers taking over at Stella's touch. She began to judder violently, her knees giving way as she crashed into the ground. Stella tried to haul her back up onto her feet, but she wouldn't budge. Somehow, the Clairvoyance was keeping her frozen to the floor.

"What's going on?" Dylan sprinted around the corner, with Tatyana in tow.

Her icy blue eyes fixed on Stella. "We heard a loud crash."

"It's Stella—the spy is Stella! She's trying to take Marjorie," I shouted, holding my side as another spike of pain shot through me. The Orishas were flitting around me, worried about my wellbeing. I didn't have the strength to send them after Stella again. The cost of every blast was becoming too much for me to handle.

Tatyana's eyes glowed white as she drew on the spirits around her, using their powers to supercharge her own. Meanwhile, Dylan took off, barreling toward Stella and severing the link between her and Marjorie. Stella flew back against the wall as Dylan scooped Marjorie into his arms and set her down a short distance away. Recovering quickly, and evidently seeing that she was fighting a losing battle, Stella shot two huge fireballs at Tatyana and me and used our evasive reflexes to make her getaway.

"Dylan, go after her!" I yelled, unable to run. "Call for backup!"

He nodded and took off down the hallway at breakneck speed, his phone to his ear, before disappearing into the shadows. In the near distance, fireballs sizzled as they found a target, and Dylan shouted at Stella to stop. Given his Herculean abilities, I hoped he'd be able to catch up to her. If he couldn't, we were well and truly screwed. Stella had a lot of intel on us.

I knew we shouldn't have trusted her! What the hell was Alton thinking, even letting her come here in the first place? If we made it out of this without a whole heap of collateral damage, I had a couple of bones to pick with the director. He would end up feeling the sharp end of my wrath before dawn rose.

"Are you okay?" Tatyana asked, her eyes returning to normal.

I nodded. "I'm fine, just go and help Marjorie."

"Are you sure? You look like you might keel over at any moment."

"Marjorie needs more help than me," I urged. Taking a second to drag air into my exhausted lungs, I staggered over to where Dylan had set Marjorie down. She was curled in a ball at the foot of a bronze dragon, tears streaming down her face. Raw flesh showed through the hole in her sweater, where Stella's fireball had singed her.

"Is she gone?" Marjorie whimpered.

I sank down next to her. "We're trying to catch her. Tatyana, can you do something about this?" I gestured to the burn on Marjorie's shoulder.

"I can help it heal," she replied, kneeling beside Marjorie and placing her hands over the wound. A white light shone beneath her palms, her eyes turning the same shade. I sat back against the dragon, feeling hideous after such a huge expense of magic. Sweat covered every inch of my skin. Every muscle hung on my bones like so many lead weights, a dull throb squeezing at my ribs, my eyelids heavy as all hell. I'd never felt so tired in my life.

"I'm grateful for the intervention and everything," I muttered, forcing myself to stay awake, "but where did you and Dylan come from? It's one o'clock in the morning. Shouldn't you have been in your rooms?"

She glanced at me for a moment, with her eerie white eyes. "We were in one of the empty classrooms."

"And what, pray tell, were you doing in there? A little late-night studying?" A weary grin tugged at the corners of my lips. I wanted to laugh, but I was worried my ribcage might implode.

Tatyana gave the ghost of a smile.

"Ah, a little lesson in human biology, eh?"

She chuckled, saying nothing as she returned to the task at hand.

"What happened back there, *mi changuita*?" I cast a tired glance at Marjorie. "You went all black-eyed on us. Did you see something?"

Marjorie nodded. "I think I saw Micah when I touched Stella. I recognized him from all the pictures and objects that I've touched of his, and I guess he must've been on my mind when Stella grabbed me," she replied nervously. "He's all I've been focusing on all day, so I knew it was him right away."

I sat up a little taller. "You saw Micah Cranston?"

"Yeah."

"Holy crapbags, do you know what that means?" I gaped at her. "It means Stella is one-hundred-percent involved in the missing kids… and, therefore, Katherine friggin' Shipton. I knew there was something up with the GI twins. I just knew it!" Channing wasn't off my radar, either. If Stella was involved, it was likely that Channing was, too.

Tatyana sat back on her haunches. "Did you see anything else, or was it just Micah?"

"I saw an old abandoned factory. There was some rusty paintwork on the side—the name of a place. Hoffman something."

"Hoffman Millwork?" I pressed. I typed the name into my phone's Google search, with some snippets of information coming up. It was an old company that dealt in wood and metalwork, though I'd never heard of it.

Her eyes widened. "Yeah, that was it. Hoffman Millwork. I don't know if that's where he's being kept, or if that *was* where he was being kept, but he was definitely there at some point. A big old factory—nothing inside, just a bunch of junk and machinery."

"This is the lead we've been looking for, you absolute *hermosa*!" I went to hug her, then remembered she was in the middle of being fixed by Tatyana. "This is the kind of good news we need. We should tell the rest of the Rag Team, right now."

Tatyana nodded. "Marjorie, you should be well enough to stand. I have done what I can with the burn, and it shouldn't scar, but there will be some tenderness for a couple of days."

"I'm okay to walk, just a bit shaken up," she replied.

We helped Marjorie to her feet and let her lean on us as we headed down the hallway. Well, Tatyana bore most of the weight, while I fought to catch my breath. Marjorie's knees were still trembling. I felt sorry for her, but there was no time to waste; we were eager to inform the others of our glorious Micah update. After so many days of nothing, this would boost morale and get us all going again.

Quarter of the way to Alton's office, Tatyana's phone rang. She held the cellphone to her ear and nodded along, making a few noises as she listened to the speaker on the other end.

She hung up and turned to me. "Dylan lost sight of Stella, but he's already told Alton about what happened. The others are being brought in as we speak. We're going to come up with a game plan to decide on our next move, and the coven has been put on lockdown until further notice."

I was about to reply when something caught my eye. About twenty yards ahead, our hallway crossed another, and Stella walked right through it. The lights were brighter in the junction, and I had no doubt that my eyes weren't deceiving me.

Practically shoving Marjorie into Tatyana's arms, I sprinted the length of the corridor and leapt onto Stella, sending us both careening to the ground. *Déjà vu.* She screamed in surprise, struggling to break free of my grip, but I wasn't about to let her get loose again. My Orishas twisted around Stella's wrists, restraining her with very little fuss from Stella herself.

"What the hell, Santana!" she snapped. "What do you think you're doing? Let go of me, now!" A tremor of fear shivered through her voice, taking me by surprise.

"The only place you're going is a dark cell, for a very long time!" I shot back. "Don't play games with me. We know you're working for Katherine. We know you're involved in stealing the kids. We know you're a spy, Stella."

She stopped writhing. "What?"

Oh, nice try. Am I going to get waterworks next?

"You heard me."

"Are you kidding? Get off me!" she barked. "I'm not involved with Katherine in any way—have you gone crazy? Seriously, what the hell?"

Puzzled, I glanced down at her neck and realized she had none of the bruises from before. There were no singes on her from where the Orishas had burned her skin. I sat back slowly, keeping the Orisha-driven restraints on her wrists. All I could do was sit and stare at her as a horrifying possibility dawned.

What if there was more than one Shapeshifter working for Katherine? *Well, wouldn't that be the freaking cherry on top of the damn crazy cake.* It could well have been the same one who attacked Harley and Wade at Isadora's hideout, but what if it wasn't? The uncertainty made me nervous. Shapeshifters made the perfect spies; there was no way of knowing how many Katherine might have at her disposal.

"Come on, we're going to see Alton," I said, helping Stella to her feet. I kept a firm hand on her as we walked to the director's office. If this *was* a super elaborate trick to get me to look elsewhere for the spy, I wasn't going to be the one ending up with egg on my face. Until I could be completely sure that Stella was innocent, there was no way I was relinquishing my grasp on her.

If it turned out she was clean… I would owe her an apology for this.

TWENTY-SEVEN

Harley

Everyone assembled in Alton's office, a tense atmosphere bristling within. The only ones who weren't present were Raffe and Wade. The latter had gone to check with the Fleet Science Center security guards, to see if they'd seen anyone matching Stella's description. And the former was apparently coming down with some sort of flu. At least, that's what Santana had told me. She and Tatyana had quickly brought me up to speed on everything that had happened, which explained why Stella was sitting in one of the high-backed armchairs with two loops of swirling Orishas around her wrists.

Seriously, what else can go wrong tonight? Better not answer that.

After so many days of nothing, everything seemed to be hitting us at once. Although, nobody else knew about Krieger's particular situation. I'd vowed to keep that to myself, and I wasn't about to break that confidence.

"Hang on, if Dylan was chasing Stella and lost her, then how come Stella is here?" I asked.

"We think we might be dealing with another Shapeshifter," Santana replied, with a roll of her eyes. I frowned at her. She might have been trying to put on a show of strength for the others, but I could feel the underlying current of exhaustion and concern running beneath her fierce exterior. She shot me a telling look that pleaded with me not to say anything. *Relax, your secret is safe with me.* I'd ask her about it later, once we were alone. Clearly, something was up.

Stella pulled a sour face. "I can't believe you actually thought it was me. As if I'd attack Marjorie like that!" she said. "Why would I have gone to such effort to find and protect these missing kids if I was in on it the whole time? Can someone explain that to me?"

Alton paced the floor at the back of the office. "I really am sorry for the inconvenience, Stella, but we have to make absolutely sure that it couldn't have been you. There are several healing spells you might have used, and laying the blame on a Shapeshifter is always a very convenient excuse for anything." He paused, offering an apologetic look. "I really am sorry, but we can't take any chances right now. Everyone is a suspect, as much as I hate to admit it."

"It's because I'm new here, isn't it? You all claim you aren't prejudiced against us, but I can see it in your eyes: none of you trust us. And you know what, I bet you all *wish* it was me or Channing so you wouldn't have to find out that one of your colleagues is lying to you. Well, tough luck, because it's definitely one of your people."

Part of me felt bad for Stella. There was no clear way of knowing that it wasn't her, since the "other Stella" had vanished into thin air. If I'd been around at the time, I could've used my Empath abilities to figure out whether it was her or not. Unfortunately, I'd gone back to my room after the infirmary visit and was half asleep when I got the call that something was up. If the spy really was a Shapeshifter, I wouldn't have been able to feel their emotions. If it had been Stella, then I'd have known right away that she was the real deal.

"Can't you get the Clairvoyant to touch me? She'll be able to see it wasn't me," Stella complained.

"I can try," Marjorie said. "She'll feel different than the impostor, if she's telling the truth."

Santana stood in her way. "Hold on a minute. This girl has just been through hell and back, and every vision she gets drains her of energy. Not to mention the fact that she's been at her Clairvoyance all day and is probably exhausted. So, how about, before we start touching people, we hear what Stella has to say about where she was and what she was up to? Let's compile a little evidence before we start sapping injured victims, okay?"

Channing got up from his seat and squared up to Santana, who looked about ready to take anyone down, regardless of the fact that she was a little green around the gills. The two of them glowered at one another for what seemed like an hour, before Channing finally spoke.

"If you must know, Stella was with me," he said curtly. "We were working late on the missing kids case, since the rest of you seem to clock out at five on the dot. When you accosted her in the hallway, she was on her way back from the Bestiary. We've been there all evening. Whoever this impostor was, it wasn't Stella."

That seemed a little convenient. All of us were looking at him with suspicious eyes, wondering if he was in on this attack, too. It was unlikely that, if Stella was involved, Channing wasn't. They'd come here together, after all.

Stella turned and gazed at Channing, a flurry of affection drifting off her. His protectiveness warmed her heart, making her fall even deeper for him. It almost pained me to sense that there was nothing romantic behind his actions—he had no such warmth brimming inside him. His emotions were stark and logical. He cared about her, and he wanted to clear her name, but his feelings didn't match hers. They didn't come from that same intense place of adoration. *Ugh, poor girl. Accused of being a spy and dealing with unrequited love, all at the same time.* Tonight wasn't going well for anyone.

"Smartie's cameras have also confirmed her location at the time of the attack," Astrid added.

"So, *not* Stella then?" I said, my voice breaking the unnerving silence that had fallen on the group. Even Alton didn't seem to know what to say. Meanwhile, Santana and Channing were still scowling at each other. In any other situation, their war of wills might've been funny. Now, it just seemed to perpetuate the divide between us.

Alton sighed loudly, running a hand through his dark waves. "I didn't want to do this, but I'm going to have to implement a new rule on the Shapeshifters amongst us. From now on, they will all be required to wear body cams. I'd already suggested this kind of approach to Preceptors Bellmore and O'Halloran. They agreed it was necessary." He offered a sorrowful look to Garrett. "I'm about to make the call now. As of tomorrow morning, it will be mandatory for every Shapeshifter to wear a body cam at all times."

"That's insane!" Garrett leapt out of his seat and stormed across the room, slamming his hands down on Alton's desk. "This isn't some sort of nanny state, where you can control us all like that. Do you even understand the precedent you're setting? We have a hard enough time as it is!" He shook his head in a rage. "There have to be at least thirty of us here at the coven. You're exposing every single one of us by doing this. You get that, don't you? I just want to make sure you haven't lost your damn mind."

"I understand your anger, but—"

"No, Alton, you don't," he shot back. "You've got no right to do this to us. For all you know, the Shapeshifter might not even be from the coven! Has that little thought even entered your mind, huh? It could be some magical pretending to be someone we know, or it could be someone just hiding in the shadows, waiting for all these opportunities to Shift into others. You're playing into their hands and punishing *us* for it. It's disgusting! I thought you were better than this."

All of those possibilities sent a shudder of doubt through my body, making me feel even more uneasy. Each one was viable. It could even be all three—someone in the coven, someone out of the coven, and someone hiding in the shadows. I suddenly understood why Alton had told me to be vigilant about any unusual behavior. I'd thought he was being overcautious, but now I realized we couldn't be cautious enough. We were in a whole lot of danger, standing on the brink of being completely compromised. Leonidas would have a field day over this. This was the excuse he'd been looking for, times about a million.

"Garrett, I know you're upset, but you will not speak to me like that, do you understand?" Alton said firmly. "It's nothing personal, I can assure you. I would have preferred to do this a different way, but necessity has forced my hand. This is a precaution we have to take. If you have nothing to hide, then there's nothing for you to worry about."

Astrid shook her head. "Technology should never be used to take away freedom. I agree with Garrett—this is an extreme and downright ridiculous measure. You're risking their safety by taking away their anonymity. Revealing their Shapeshifting is *their* choice, not yours. You're making a mistake."

Alton seemed wounded by the side she'd chosen to take. Evidently, after everything he'd done for her, with all the resurrections, he was surprised by her words. Astrid rarely criticized him, and never this harshly. Astrid was his right-hand woman, but it felt like she was shifting her allegiance because of a crush. Garrett seemed to be the instigation for this rare outburst. The sting of it found its way to me, a subtle heartbreak sitting in my chest cavity.

I could understand her aversion to the body cams, but I also understood the necessity of putting the Shapeshifters under surveillance. The discomfort of some might help save the lives of many others—that was a move worth making, as uncomfortable as it felt.

"Astrid, you're more pragmatic than this," he replied, his tone softer. "Surely, you can understand why this measure *has* to be implemented? This decision has been made for the safety of the coven as a whole, and to ease paranoid minds. I will ensure the Shapeshifters are protected, if that makes it better?"

"Not really," she said coolly.

"Nevertheless, it's happening. We are fresh out of options."

Glancing at Alton, I realized he didn't have as good a handle on things as he made it seem on the surface. He was as terrified and confused as the rest of us. Plus, with Krieger's curse, and the fact that he hadn't told anyone about that, he seemed to be flying by the seat of his pants. He felt weirdly lost, like he was close to just handing the reins to someone else. *Don't you dare, Alton Waterhouse. Don't you dare.*

An awkward silence stretched between the group. Nobody wanted to break it. To my surprise, it was Marjorie who finally spoke, her small voice finding its way through the stillness.

"I do have some good news," she said. "At least, Santana told me it was good news."

Santana turned to her encouragingly. "Yes, of course—I almost forgot! Tell everyone what you saw."

"When the Shapeshifter grabbed my wrist, I got a vision," she continued. "I saw Micah standing in an abandoned factory. The Hoffman Millwork factory. It didn't look like it had been used in a long time, but that was where Micah maybe was… or is… it's kind of hard to tell. I never know where in the timeline these things have happened or will happen."

I grinned at the shy girl. "That's awesome news. That's exactly the kind of lead we've been looking for."

Santana beamed proudly. "That's what I told her. My little *changuita* is a genius."

"Changuita?" Channing asked sourly.

"My little monkey, not that you'd understand a pet name if it smacked you in the face. Which, incidentally, is what I'd like to—"

"How about we all get to work on this new lead, huh?" I interjected, before she could say something she might regret. I adored Santana, but her fieriness was going to get her into trouble one of these days. "I'll call Wade and let him know what's happening."

Alton raised his hand. "You should all go and get some rest. Start with this lead bright and early in the morning. There's no use chasing these ghosts if you're all dead on your feet. You're all dismissed." He looked at me. "And don't worry about Wade. I'll talk to him myself."

With that, we broke off in our own factions and headed back to the living quarters. Alton was right: we needed clear heads if we were going to track down the kids. Spending the whole night downing coffee and struggling to stay awake wasn't going to do anyone any favors. Plus, I was getting more and more worried about Santana. She'd been fading all through the meeting, even when she'd squared up to Channing. Something was wrong with her, but I doubted she'd tell me what it was, even if I tried to force it out of her. *Who knows, maybe she's just tired.*

I got halfway up the stairs back to my room, when I realized my stomach was growling. I'd barely eaten all day and, right now, a little two a.m. snack was sounding pretty damn delicious. Saying goodnight to the others, I hurried through the silent hallways until I reached the banquet hall. There was always food available, with snacks set up on a table in the corner, alongside urns of hot tea and coffee and various fruit juices in a myriad of gaudy colors. Slipping through the doors, I froze. There was already someone in the banquet hall.

I ducked down behind one of the tables and strained my ears to listen in. If the spy was in here, I wanted to know about it.

"Thank you for what you did back there," a female voice said. *Stella.*

"I was doing my duty, protecting a fellow colleague," Channing replied. His voice was unmistakable. "You already had an alibi. I was merely informing them of the circumstances."

"I know, but you didn't have to defend me like that," she went on. "Channing, I know that now isn't a good time, but there's something I've been wanting to tell you for a long time. And when you spoke up for me like that, it got me thinking it's now or never. The truth is... I'm in love with you."

A stiff pause followed, my whole body cringing for Stella. I already knew his reply before he even said it. If I could have crawled to the door without being seen, I would have. This wasn't the kind of thing I wanted to be eavesdropping on.

"Stella, I'm flattered," he began, "but I don't think of you like that. You're like a sister to me. I care about you, and you're beautiful, too —don't go thinking you're not—but when it comes to romance... I'm sorry, Stella. I'd rather be honest now and spare you from wasting your time on something that just isn't going to happen. You know?"

"Of course," Stella replied, her tone tight. "No, thank you for being honest. I appreciate it. And, honestly, things will always be cool between us. Like, don't think this will change our working relationship, because it won't. It's all good, honestly. Honestly, it's fine. I just wanted to get it off my chest. Now that I have, it's all honestly cool."

Jeez, say "honestly" one more time and he might believe you.

"I'm glad to hear that," Channing said. "I don't want anything to change between us."

"No, absolutely. It's all good."

"Okay, well, I'm going to bed. You want me to walk you back to your room, or are you still eating?"

"I'm going to finish this. I'll be fine on my own."

"You sure?"

"Positive."

"Okay, well, goodnight."

"Goodnight, Channing."

I listened to the pad of his footsteps across the hall floor, before he exited the double doors and headed into the hallway beyond. Waiting a couple of minutes, to make sure he'd really gone and wasn't about to run back and confess his love after all, I crawled on my belly toward the doors. Halfway there, I stopped. A small, sniffling sound echoed from the other side of the banquet hall. Stella was crying.

Ah man, what am I supposed to do now?

I couldn't leave her here in tears. That would just be sad. Still, I couldn't let her know I'd been listening in, either. Coming up with a cunning plan to crawl outside and then re-enter, making a show of just happening upon her, I continued my slow wriggle across the floor. I'd just reached the doors when my boot squeaked on the polished marble, giving the game away.

"Is someone there?" Stella's panicked voice asked.

I grimaced. "Yep… only me." I didn't want her thinking the spy had come back to take her identity again. With red cheeks, I jumped up and flashed an awkward smile. *Stupid stomach, why couldn't you have just waited until morning?*

She frowned at me and wiped her eyes. "I take it you heard everything?"

"I did." *No point lying now.*

"You're going to go back to the others and have a good laugh about it, aren't you?"

I approached her slowly. "No, of course not. This might come as a shock, but nobody here delights in other people's misery. To be honest, I was going to come back in and check on how you were doing."

"You were?"

"Yep. Then my boots ratted me out."

She smiled sadly. "You know, you're lucky to have found someone who reciprocates your feelings. I guess you realized I was flirting with Wade to make Channing jealous, huh?"

"I noticed it a little bit, yeah."

"It didn't make a difference," she said. "When I was flirting with Wade, he'd always look over to you to see if you were watching *him*. I guess he feels like he needs to make you jealous, too. Stupid, really, when the two of you so obviously like one another."

My heart beat faster. I mean, it was possible that Wade liked me back, but what was I supposed to do about that? "Even if he does have feelings for me, it's not like he'd ever admit it."

"Then you should tell him how you feel," Stella whispered. "You shouldn't keep your feelings hidden, not when the outcome could be so good."

I shrugged uncomfortably. "What if the outcome isn't good?"

"At least you'd know the truth." She wiped away the last of her tears. "It might not look like it, but I'm happier now that I know where I stand. It wasn't the answer I was hoping for, but at least I'm not hanging everything on a hope. I suggest you do the same. A few tears are better than months of uncertainty, believe me."

I smiled at her. "I guess."

"You know, even though this place is a little flawed in its operations, the people here aren't so bad. I think you're all growing on me." She chuckled.

"We might be the scrappy little underdogs, but I bet we stand out because every single person inside this building shares the same mission."

"What's that?"

"The protection of innocents—magical or otherwise." I smiled at her and nodded toward the door. "Come on, let me get some chow and then we'll get some rest. We've got a long day ahead of us."

TWENTY-EIGHT

Harley

Based on the information from Marjorie's vision, surveillance was set up around the old warehouse, on the edge of what was now the Tijuana River Mouth State Marine Conservation Area. With the beautifully crafted fake ID cards at our disposal, the coven had little trouble implementing our members into the security team who patrolled the area. Despite not knowing where in Micah's timeline the vision sat, Marjorie felt confident that he was eventually going to be moved there. She claimed that, after learning more about her skills, she had developed a feeling about visions that gave her some indication as to when they might happen or had happened. For Micah, she sensed it was going to occur sometime in the near future, so we had to be ready for that possibility.

We suspected that the reason behind the children being brought there was because Katherine and her associates—more her associates, since she didn't seem fond of doing the dirty work herself—had been moving the magical kids around, to reduce the likelihood of being caught or tracked by any of our people. The supposed robberies all across the magical nation were keeping everyone else busy; they only had to fox the San Diego Coven and its boosted security entourage.

All we could do now was wait.

Naturally, I wasn't particularly good at that. Patience had never been one of my virtues, and with the Family Gathering happening the next day, I was way more antsy than normal. I'd tried swimming; I'd tried running; I'd tried reading; I'd tried practicing my Telekinesis and Elemental powers in the coven training rooms, but nothing could tire out my anxious streak. To be honest, I wasn't even sure it was anxiety. It felt like something else—deeper and far more confusing. A deep-seated sensation of being unsettled.

Maybe the problem was that I didn't have any real roots. My whole life had been a series of uprootings, being handed from one family to the next. Sure, I'd learned a bunch from every single place I'd been to, but all kids like me had ever wanted was… well, for someone to truly want us. We wanted someone to claim us as family.

So, the whole idea of the Family Gathering seemed difficult to me, since I had no parents, and my closest surviving family were two aunts. One was in the wind, protecting her protege and unable to contact me safely, while the other was a raging psychopath with a god complex, who wanted to find me and gut me like a fish.

You've always been on your own, Harley. So chin up and get through it. Oddly enough, the notion cheered me up and gave me a sudden idea. In honor of the Family Gathering, I figured I'd give my half-brother a visit. There were more similarities between us than either of us probably wanted to admit, considering our fairly lonely paths in this world. He'd been carted off to Ms. Anker, and he'd been manipulated a lot more than I had. I felt it was time I shared a little more of my sisterly wisdom, in hopes that it reached some sane part of his mind.

I'd made more copies of the files that Salinger had given us, regarding Hiram and Hester—the ones that proved Hiram was under the influence of Katherine's curse. He needed to see them.

Plus, I supposed I should see at least *one* of my family members in the leadup to the event. Purgatory wasn't exactly a nice place to visit, but Finch might experience a bit of gratitude after weeks without seeing a single soul.

Gathering a folder full of documents, I headed to the Assembly Hall shortly after noon, when I knew most people would be at the banquet hall, stuffing their faces full of lunch. I felt a little guilty about slipping through without Alton's permission again, but he'd granted me access and had yet to revoke it. And I felt even *more* guilty for hiding a pretty massive secret from him. Still, I figured I ought to use it as much as possible before he noticed, although I had a feeling he knew where I'd gone. Alton kept a tight lid on these things. But until he confronted me about it himself, I was going to keep at it.

Arriving in the familiar reception hall of Purgatory, I scanned the surrounding area for a friendly face. Not easy to do in a magical supermax prison. As I walked toward two prison guards who were deep in conversation, my eyes lifted to the impressive architecture. Almost like an elaborate honeycomb, every passage and floor forged from clear glass, the corridors crisscrossed above my head. Cell doors lined both sides of each hallway, reaching up to a vertiginous ceiling that seemed impossibly high. I could see people moving about inside a few layers of the stark, gray cells, each person ticking down the time until death or release. Whichever came first.

"Excuse me, I was wondering if you could help me?" I asked, reaching the two officers. They were dressed in the same black Kevlar uniforms that Officer Mallenberg had worn, the first time I'd visited this place. Two electroshock batons graced each of their hips, and their faces were grizzled and broad. I could only imagine the kinds of people they'd dealt with in this prison and the things they'd seen those people do.

The first man frowned. "Visitor?"

I nodded. "I spoke to Officer Mallenberg last time. Is he around?"

"Gone on lunch. Who're you visiting?" the second guy answered, his voice as gruff as his face.

"Finch Shipton." I'd thought about going to see Emily Ryder while I was here, but there didn't seem to be any point. The prison's interrogation team hadn't been able to get anything out of her, and I doubted my skills were better than theirs.

"Do you want to take her, Timpson?" the first man asked.

The second nodded. "Sure, I've got nothing else to do. The name's Officer Arrowsmith."

"Nice to meet you. I'm Harley Merlin."

He arched an eyebrow. "Merlin, huh? Not seen one of your ilk in here in a long time. Don't you be getting yourself locked up in one of these here cells. It'd be a travesty."

"I won't." *Thanks pal... I think.*

"Follow me, Miss," he said, turning around and leading me down a familiar path.

Even though I knew where he was taking me, Purgatory took some getting used to. It was a labyrinth of hallways and cells, all lit with severe white neon bulbs that cast a clinical light against the cement-gray walls. Having honed my skills a bit since last time, I was better prepared for the barrage of dark emotions that slammed into me—violent rage, bubbling resentment, desperate panic, solemn resignation, penetrating sadness, and that reminiscent hint of curiosity as I passed the prisoners. I paid them no attention, figuring it was best to keep my gaze fixed on Arrowsmith's shoulders. His emotions were easy—boredom and a flicker of bitterness.

I noted the usual runes engraved across every frame of the cells as well as the crackle of the modified cuffs the prisoners wore. Part of me wondered what awful things these people had done to get in here. Nobody came to Purgatory for misdemeanors.

As we reached solitary confinement, the overwhelming pulse of the prisoners' emotions eased up, the agony and despair much easier to control. The prisoners' emotions were far louder than those of the SDC assemblies, and the rage inside them was nearly impossible to drown out. It permeated everything, ricocheting off every wall. Thankfully, there were fewer inmates here, where the bars gave way to solid steel doors with hatches built into the center.

Ah, good old number 230.

"Here you go," Arrowsmith said, unlocking the latch and opening it. He hadn't even bothered to let Finch know I was there, though I could see him lounging on the bed at the back of the room.

"Thanks, Officer."

"No problem." He turned and pointed to a glass box of a room nearby. "I'll be over there at the guard station. Press the panic button if he gets too fresh for you."

As Arrowsmith retreated, I knocked on the side of the steel door to alert Finch. He sat up in surprise, a scowl scrunching up his face as soon as he saw me through the hatch. Dropping the book he'd been reading on the bed, he stalked over and leaned against the door. He was so close I could smell the standard-issue medicinal soap on his skin.

He leered at me. "The redhead returns."

I frowned at him, scrutinizing him closely. He looked slightly different. His sky-blue eyes were filled with the same venom I'd seen before, burning with a blood-chilling hatred of me, but strands of rich, dark auburn were starting to show through his platinum hair. Clearly, they hadn't allowed him whatever dye he'd been using. It had grown longer, too, revealing unexpected curls. *He's a total mix of my dad and his mom. Weird.*

"Says you," I retorted. "Looking a little more copper these days, Finch."

He flicked his wrist absently. "Red is my mother's color. I've got nothing to be ashamed of. You, on the other hand..."

"Come on, I know you're happy to see me," I half-taunted. "It's got to be pretty damn boring, sitting in a cell all day with nothing to do. Don't you get cable in this place? I thought that was the main perk of prison." My strange desire to send him into a rage disturbed me somewhat. Like poking a sleeping bear. I couldn't help myself. It was too easy. I was practically licking my lips at the prospect of him seeing the files. *He's going to be so mad.*

"I've been expanding my mind with books from the library, if you must know," he replied, with that eerie grin of his. "Now, what brings you to my cell door, Little Sis?" He spat the last two words as though he hated the taste of them in his mouth.

"Nice to see we're on the same wavelength, Bro. Since the Family Gathering is tomorrow, I thought I'd bring you a gift," I continued, anticipation throbbing in my veins. "Here, I thought you might like to have a look at these. I must be psychic, bringing you some decent reading material."

He stared down at the flap in his door, where things could be passed through. Ducking down, I slid the folder to him. He picked it up and flicked through it, his eyes darting left to right as he read the words. A curious hesitation passed across his face as he paused on the image of our father on a mortuary slab. I'd circled the rune on Hiram's neck and detailed the reason for its existence above. He quickly moved on to the next page, reading the notes I'd made on Sál Vinna.

A moment later, he scoffed. "Is this supposed to impress me, Harley? Did you think this would warm my ice-cold heart to daddykins?" A bitter laugh rolled from his throat. "All this proves is that our father was weak and disobedient to my mother's greatness. Being consumed by a curse doesn't make him a good person. I'm sure you've been telling everyone that he's innocent. I can picture your gleeful little face when you found this out. Well, I've got news for you: this doesn't clear him of his part in those murders. He killed men and women. He still did it, even if the curse forced his hand. He's as innocent as I am."

His words chilled me. I felt the sting of them deep in my soul. The dark curse had made him do it, but those people were still dead. *Harley, your father was a good man.* Without the curse, he would never have done those things. Without the curse, he would have tried to stop Katherine. I was certain of it. In that way, I could reconcile his part in the murders and still call him innocent.

"Well, I've got news for you too, Finch," I shot back, struggling to keep the anger out of my voice. "Do you know how that kind of spell is fueled? I'm guessing you don't, since you haven't gotten to the last pages yet."

He frowned. "There's nothing you can say to make me change my mind about our father. He was a pathetic specimen, not fit to lick my mother's boots."

"Katherine fueled that spell by killing everyone else in our family line," I continued, undeterred. "She killed the Merlins because she had to, in order to make the curse work, but she killed the Shiptons because she *wanted* to. They weren't part of the curse, but she did it anyway."

Finch's gaze shot up to meet mine. "No... you're lying." His voice caught in his throat. "My mother told me that there was a terrible accident. *Hester* released a deadly sickness curse that killed them all at a family reunion. The Merlins and the Shiptons. My mother said so."

I gaped at him in shock. Was that what Katherine had told him? Had she made him think she was innocent of *that*?

I shook my head slowly. "Nope, Katherine lied to you, just as she lied about getting you out of here. I don't see any locks being picked or any wrecking balls coming through the wall, do you? She doesn't care about you, Finch. You were a pawn, and your moves on the board are finished. She's still playing, but you're out of the game. She doesn't give a damn about you. She'd happily let you rot here for the rest of your life—to her, it's just another family member ticked off the list."

"*You* are the liar."

"Think about it for a moment, Finch. I know you want her to love you; I know you want to be wanted by her, but it's never going to happen. You need to wake up," I snapped. "Look at the Ryder twins. Where did their loyalty get them, huh? Emily is rotting in this place, and Emmett is worm food. Does Katherine care? No, of course she doesn't. She's got plenty of others to take their place. Every single one of you is expendable to her. It doesn't matter if you're tied by blood or blind devotion. You're all the same to her."

Finch's eyes flashed with rage. "You don't know what you're talking about. You don't know the promises she's made to me! You don't know anything about us. You might share our blood, Harley, but you don't know a damn thing about me and my mother!"

"What promises? To break you out of here? I've already told you, she's not coming." *That's right, poke the bear some more. Get him to pour his soul out.*

"No, you pathetic halfwit! She *is* coming for me, not only because I'm her son but because of the promises she made," he spat. "She promised she would fix my mind and give me my sanity back. She swore she would take away the torment in my head—the schizophrenic part of me that has ruined my life, for all these years. She *will* keep that promise because she caused this. She *made* me this way. She hexed our father, and I was born under the curse of that hex. It damaged my mind. It damaged me... and she has vowed to repair it."

I frowned. "There was no hex, Finch. She's lying about that, too. I hate to admit it, but my father and your mother created you because they slept together—because they wanted to, for whatever reason. Too many tequilas, a moment of weakness, a shoulder to cry on; I can think of a thousand scenarios that led them there, but none of them involved coercion. You were conceived before she'd used Sál Vinna on him. Going by the timeline of events, you couldn't have been born after."

"It was another hex." He didn't seem sure.

"She told you that?"

He slammed his fists into the door. "She said it was a hex to protect me from a far larger curse. She didn't specify after that. You don't ask my mother prying questions. Nobody does, not even me."

A shocking realization catapulted into my brain. I couldn't believe I hadn't thought of it before. Finch was part Merlin, too. For Sál Vinna to work, she should have killed Finch. But she didn't. Perhaps she *couldn't*. Despite her monstrous tendencies, maybe she hadn't had it in her to kill her own son.

I wondered why Katherine had told him he was hexed in the first place. Was that what all of this was—a way of punishing him for making her weak? Had she used the ruse as a way of manipulating him? A way of getting payback for her missed opportunity? Or a way to keep her son tied to her? Honestly, right now, I had no idea which one seemed more plausible. The only thing I knew for sure was that all this talk of a hex was a load of garbage. She'd clearly told him she'd get him out if he got caught, but the removal of the supposed "hex" was evidently part of the deal too, to get him to do her bidding.

Unless Finch isn't my half-brother. What if Katherine had lied about that too, as a last-ditch attempt to get my father back? That kind of deceit was child's play compared to what she'd done since, but I didn't have the heart to investigate. Finch had done some bad things, but he'd been molded that way. Who was I to pull the rug completely out from under him, regardless of his dark streak?

"You need to accept that part of yourself, Finch. I've seen your medical records—there wasn't anything weird in your blood. There weren't any magical markers to suggest a hex." I'd looked through his folder after he was brought here. We'd found it among Adley's things. "If I was a betting kind of girl, I'd say it wasn't caused by a hex at all, or any other outside influence. You are the way you are because… well, you are. No hexes, no being born under a bad sign, or a blood moon. You're just you." I offered a smile, though I didn't know why. "You can't blame anything or anyone, not even yourself. You've got to learn to live with your demons, quiet them down until they become easier to handle. Thinking someone can 'fix' you will only make it worse."

"You don't know what you're talking about," he said coldly, his voice carrying an edge of sadness. "And you certainly don't know what you're up against."

"I know all about Katherine's aspirations to become a Child of Chaos. You told us most of that yourself, and we filled in the gaps. It wasn't hard," I replied. "We know what she's trying to do, and we're on to her. There's no way she's completing this mission. No way in hell."

He smirked. "She's already close to completing the first of the five rituals. When she rises, she'll only let the worthy yield Chaos, and she will take it from those who have been gifted unjustly—from people like *you*."

I grinned at him, feeling victory flow through my veins. "Oh Finch, what will your mother say?"

"You were… bluffing?"

"Hurts, doesn't it, to be lied to?" I could see it in his face, the shocked realization that I'd pretended to know more than I did. Unintentionally, he'd revealed new information. Helpful information that *could* help us defeat Katherine.

"You little bitch," he hissed, grabbing the files on Hiram and hurling them through the hatch. "When the time comes, you *will* have your powers stripped bare from your bones, and you'll feel every agonizing tear as they're taken from you. My mother will make it fair—you don't deserve what you've been given."

I shrugged. "But the world *is* unfair, Finch. It always has been, and it always will be. You and I know that better than anyone," I said. "The thing is, you will always have a choice in how you react to that unfairness. I'm a forgiving kind of gal. The offer still stands. Side with your sister over your mother and leave the world as it is. Fight to protect—don't fight to destroy."

With a smile on my face, I closed the hatch, leaving Finch quietly seething. I gestured to Officer Arrowsmith to lock up, before heading out of Purgatory. Walking through the halls behind Arrowsmith, I felt beyond pleased with everything I'd learned about Katherine's plan. Now, we had the knowledge of her future steps within our reach.

Plus, who doesn't enjoy a little family bonding every now and again?

TWENTY-NINE

Harley

"Hey, how come we don't know anything about Astrid's family?" I asked. The Rag Team had gathered in the Aquarium while we waited for our families to arrive. Well, while everyone else waited for their families to arrive. We were all smartly dressed in our official SDC uniforms, and my breast pocket was adorned with six gems—white for Air, blue for Water, green for Earth, red for Fire, dark gray for Telekinesis, and purple for Empathy. It felt weird, wearing my abilities on my chest like that, but I was kind of digging the outfit. I wondered what Shapeshifters did in this situation. I doubted they wore that particular ability as a badge of honor, as unfair as that seemed.

Wade shrugged. "She doesn't mention them much. In fact… I don't think she's ever mentioned them. Does anyone know anything about them?"

"They've got to be human, right?" Dylan replied.

"I heard it was a powerful couple high up in the US government, who put her into Alton's care so she wouldn't be a kidnap risk," Santana said. "They wanted to hide her away here for extra security."

"Where'd you hear that from?" Wade asked, an eyebrow raised.

"The usual grapevine of juicy gossip. No idea if it's true or not."

"Mysterious. I like it," Tatyana replied.

Nervous energy hummed throughout the room, everyone's emotions going haywire with the prospect of seeing their loved ones again. Dylan was the only one who didn't seem too worked up, but then, he was in the same boat as me. We'd both vowed to stick close to each other throughout the event, making our own version of going stag. If we had to be on our own, we were going to do it together. Besides, it riled Wade up to see us chatting secretively about it. I still got a little thrill out of it, even after Stella's sage words of advice.

There was another reason for everyone's anxiety. After returning from Purgatory, I'd filled the Rag Team in on the new slices of information Finch had unwittingly given me. Aside from the Family Gathering, it was all anyone could talk about. They were struggling to wrap their heads around Katherine's intentions, though I'd stopped doubting her evil a long time ago. She was capable of anything, if it meant getting what she wanted.

"I don't want to go around in circles, but there's something that's been bugging me. How would Katherine even figure out who can and can't use magic?" Dylan asked, evidently trying to change the subject.

Wade shook his head. "It's not the *how* that worries me so much. It's the why," he said. "It all sounds insane, if you ask me. Why would a person go to such lengths just to decide who gets to wield Chaos and who doesn't? It's complete madness."

Nope, sounds about right for dear old Aunt Shipton. Probably not crazy enough, to be honest. Somehow, to me, it almost made sense, given what we'd learned about Katherine so far. She wasn't one to pull her punches. Plus, she'd been upstaged by her twin sister for most of her life and so, in her eyes, had been treated unfairly, considering the strength of her own powers. So, I guessed she wanted to even the scales on a universal level. Make up for all those lost years of being made to feel inferior. It was one hell of a way to get her own back. *Yeah, she's clearly dealing with some issues. I doubt even Freud could figure this one out.*

"I didn't want to say anything, but I get the feeling there's more to it than meets the eye, even with this new knowledge," I said quietly. "Honestly, it sounds to me like Katherine has an even grander vision in mind for herself, and for this leveling. We just don't know about it yet. We probably won't until it smacks us in the face."

Santana sighed. "I agree, which is why we have to cut her off before she even makes that first leap toward becoming a Child of Chaos. It has something to do with this Librarian, I know it does."

The others nodded, confusing me. Clearly, I was out of the loop on a couple of things.

"Librarian?" I asked.

"Well, thanks to Finch, we know that there are five rituals involved in becoming a Child of Chaos," she replied. "I discovered earlier that there's this woman called the Librarian—a Clairvoyant—who might have some answers about those rituals and what they entail. The information I got was all pretty vague, but with that stuff and Finch's revelation, we've actually got something meaty to work from."

"Where'd you get the info?"

She shot a look at Raffe. "Uh… Raffe helped. He knows some folks who know some folks. Some friends of his dad." She glanced at Wade, who gave a small nod. *More secrets?* It felt like all of us were hiding something from each other, and it made me uneasy. Even though my secret probably topped everyone else's.

"Well, it feels good to have some leads," I conceded, with a smile.

"We should probably head to the party before people start to wonder where we are," Wade suggested. "We can go over this new information tomorrow. For tonight, why don't we try to enjoy ourselves? It doesn't happen very often. Not lately, anyway."

I flashed him a grin. "Got your dancing shoes on, Crowley?"

"I don't dance."

"We'll see about that." I chuckled, taking his arm and leading him to the door. I paused at the threshold. "Wait, isn't Astrid coming? I thought she'd be here by now."

Santana shook her head. "She said she'd meet us there." A smile turned up the corners of her lips. "I think she and Garrett were having a little pre-Gathering party of their own."

"The scandal!" I flashed a grin. "Come on, let's see what all the fuss is about. I can't wait to mingle with a bunch of folks I don't know and shock them with my surname. If only the Council gave points for the number of people you can freak out in an evening."

Wade frowned. "Don't mention points. I'll be surprised if we don't lose the ones we managed to gain by the end of the year. Leonidas and his merry men will crucify us if we don't get these kids back."

"Hey, think of it this way: if Katherine kills us all, we won't have to worry about the points system ever again," I said.

"Silver linings, eh?" Santana chimed in.

With that, we left the Aquarium and headed toward the Main Assembly Hall. A huge crowd of people had amassed in the time we'd been away, and the rumble of their chatter hit us in a wave as we pushed through the double doors. Their emotions were twice as loud to me, bombarding me head-on. I paused for a second to gather my Empath powers, forcing them to dull the sensations to a background throb of mixed emotion. *Nicely done, Merlin. Looks like you're getting the hang of this, Suppressor or no Suppressor.*

"Dios mio, did someone crank up the heating?" Santana whispered, mopping her brow with the back of her sleeve. "I'm roasting in here. Does it feel hot to you? Are you hot?"

I glanced at her. "It is pretty toasty. Probably all the people. You okay? Do you want to go back outside and grab some fresh air?" I was hoping she'd say yes so I wouldn't have to speak to anyone, but she shook her head.

"No, I'll be fine. I just need about three gallons of water and I'll be okay. I'm sweating buckets."

"These uniforms aren't exactly helping," I conceded. "They look cool, for sure, but the fabric isn't exactly breathable. I feel like I put on a plastic suit."

"You're damn right. Ugh, I'm already drenched," she muttered. "I'm going to be absolutely rancid by the end of the night."

I laughed. "Lucky Raffe."

Raffe flushed red. "I'd like her even if she was a puddle of goop on the floor."

"I might be if I don't find some freaking air conditioning," she replied, planting a tender kiss on his cheek.

The expressions on my friends' faces changed as the families started to move to their own sections of the room. They were looking for familiar folks in the crowd, meerkatting over my head to see if they could find their parents. A swell of mixed emotions flowed through me—the nerves and excitement of my friends, combined with my own envy. I wished there was a friendly face in the crowd for me.

Santana was the first to abandon ship, hurtling through the crowd toward a buxom, middle-aged Latina with graying hair that lay in a braid, all the way down her back. She was waving frantically. Wade disappeared through the throng without so much as a "see you later." Part of me felt disappointed; I'd have liked to have been introduced to Wade's family. Although, maybe it was a little soon. I hadn't even told the guy I liked him, so I doubted meeting his parents was a good idea. I could imagine how that introduction would go: *"Ah, Mom, Dad, this is Harley Merlin—yes, those Merlins. Yes, the one who killed all those people, although he actually didn't mean to; he was under a curse at the time. She doesn't have any psychopathic tendencies, so you don't have to worry there."*

Tatyana ran off third, dragging Dylan by the arm to meet her parents. Well, so much for our bond of parentless solidarity.

I turned to Raffe, who was the only one still standing with me. He seemed more anxious than anyone. Instead of scouring the room with excitement, he was casually glancing across the heads of the congregation with a mixture of resentment and hesitation. *The Leonidas Effect.*

"You okay there, Raffe?" I asked.

He shrugged. "Not looking forward to seeing my father again, to be honest. I'm going to bet we're at each other's throats within the hour," he said. "These things just feel pointless to me. I see my father every time the Mage Council gets summoned, which seems to be all the time right now. He's always watching me. I hate it. I wish I could just blow this whole thing off."

"Amen to that." I smiled at him. "Your father doesn't seem to trust me at all. I think he wishes I'd never been brought here in the first place. Either that, or he'd have preferred me to be at his coven, where he could keep an eye on me. Same as you, probably?"

Raffe laughed. "My father doesn't trust anyone, so I wouldn't be too worried about that. He'd have us all rounded up and put in one big enclosure if he could. For someone on the Mage Council, he doesn't like magicals that much—he despises their power. I think it scares him, though he'd never admit it to me."

"Yeah, that's super weird."

"At the very least, he'd prefer it if we were all Mediocre. Take you, for example. That much power in young hands freaks him out completely. He'd probably be all for you being permanently stuck with the Suppressor, if it meant holding you back. Obviously, he can't dictate that, since it has nothing to do with him. But he *can* control *me*. He's been scared of me my whole life."

"Why's that?"

Was I finally going to get some answers about Raffe's… issues?

"For one, he blames me for my mother's death," he said sadly. "She died in childbirth with me, and I've got no siblings as a result. They wanted a whole bunch of children, but I screwed up their plans for that."

"I'm so sorry, Raffe. I had no idea." I wanted to reach out and hug him or something, but it didn't feel appropriate. Nevertheless, my heart ached for him. I couldn't even begin to imagine the torment that must have plagued him throughout his life, knowing that. I had some measure of it in my own life, but the revelations had only come to me recently. He'd lived with it since he was a baby. That couldn't have been easy.

He shrugged. "At least that's what my father has always told me. Whether he just wanted to rub salt into the wound, I don't know. He's hard to read."

"Must run in the family," I said, trying to lighten his mood, as I felt a flurry of sadness drift off him. It came to me in a clear ripple, unadulterated by whatever was usually going on inside him. It pleased me, to feel his emotions so definitively. He was opening up to me more as a friend.

Raffe rolled his eyes. "Speak of the devil."

I turned to see Leonidas approaching us, his eyes narrowing once he saw us together.

"Well, well, well, I did not expect this. Although, I suppose you two would make quite the pair," Leonidas said as he stopped in front of us. He didn't sound too happy, and I wasn't entirely sure what he was insinuating.

"What, you think me and Raffe are—no, you've got the wrong end of the stick," I replied, flashing Raffe a wink. "I'm happily single, thank you very much." *Yep, and methinks you're protesting way too much!*

He cleared his throat. "Santana and I are the ones in a romantic... situation."

Leonidas's frown deepened. "What possible interest could a girl from somewhere as powerful as the Catemaco Coven have in my son?"

I half expected Raffe to lunge for his father, but he didn't. Instead, he stayed frozen to the spot, a flood of resignation hitting me as it came off him. The realization prompted a pang of sadness to wrench at my heart. He, too, didn't think he was good enough for Santana. His reaction gave him away. Where he should have been defiant and angry, he was quiet and stoic. *Oh, Raffe, of course you're good enough! Don't listen to that old bastard. What does he know about it?*

"Well, you're wrong," I said bluntly.

Leonidas looked at me in surprise. "Excuse me?"

"You're wrong. She does, and I'll prove it." I searched the crowd for Santana and waved for her to come over. She frowned for a moment, before whispering something to her mother. A moment later, she appeared at my side.

"What's up?" she asked. "*Ay dios mio,* it is boiling over here! Can't they put some fans on or something? I'm melting, I'm melting!" She waved her arms, *Wizard of Oz* style, and collapsed into a fit of giggles. Glancing at her, she looked weirdly woozy on her feet, as if drunk. The dopey smile on her face did nothing to help her case. I hadn't seen her drink anything, but there was no other explanation for the way she was acting.

"We were just discussing your relationship with Raffe. Leonidas here doesn't believe the two of you could be an item, but I beg to differ."

Santana glanced at Raffe in shock, before sidling up to him and toying with his curls. "What *are* we to each other, Raffe? You tell your dear old papi, but you don't tell me? I'd love to know, because I don't have a clue what's going on." She fanned her face furiously. "Jeez, it's hot, though. Is that you, Raffe, making me all hot under the collar?" She clung to his shoulder and giggled uncontrollably.

Leonidas looked on, apparently pretty uncomfortable with the situation and Santana's odd behavior. A sheen of sweat slicked her face, but her lips were a funny shade of blue, as if she were cold instead of boiling hot. A trickle of perspiration made its way down the side of her jaw, before dripping to the floor. *Man, she really must be warm. She looks like she's just hit the gym for an hour.*

"You may have had one too many glasses of champagne, Miss Catemaco," Leonidas said coldly. "Perhaps you should get a drink of water before you embarrass yourself entirely."

"Me? I'm not embarrassed. I feel so good… and so hot. Ugh, so friggin' hot."

"Shall I escort you back to your parents? Perhaps they can keep you under—"

Santana's eyes suddenly turned black, the rapid change silencing Leonidas.

"She's about to Purge!" Raffe shouted. "We need to get her out of here, fast!"

Santana doubled over in pain, clutching her stomach as her face drained of color. Her arms jerked in a way that told me Santana had lost control. Her legs spasmed, her shoulders jolting backward with such force I thought she'd fall. I reached out to grab her, only for an Orisha to pop out from beneath her skin. More followed, all of them swirling around her in a vortex, the spirits buzzing about her in terror.

Feeding my Telekinesis out toward them, I tried to contain them in a wall of shimmering energy, but their fear was overwhelming. It shattered the Telekinetic shield and the magic that Raffe was hurling toward them. They didn't want to be trapped with whatever was coming out of Santana.

"We need help!" I yelled toward Santana's parents. They came running, their own Orishas bursting out of them to help calm Santana's worried spirits. Her mother began to chant something under her breath, releasing a powerful gust of energy that caught the Orishas in an invisible net. They tried to break free, but her mother's magic was too strong.

"EVERYONE OUT!" Leonidas led the frightened crowd out through every available door. Alton was nowhere to be seen, but a few of the preceptors assisted in the evacuation. Pretty soon, there was nobody left in the room but Santana, her parents, me, and the rest of the Rag Team. All except Astrid and Garrett, who still hadn't shown up.

"Everyone prepare to fight this thing," Wade said, breathing hard. "It looks like it's going to be a strong monster. What the hell caused this? It's way too soon for Santana to be having a Purge like this."

My cheeks burned with guilt. This was because of me. She'd stopped me from summoning whatever I'd been about to summon, back in New York, and this was the result. She must have used a more powerful spell than I'd realized.

"Whatever happens, we can't kill it," Raffe chimed in, before I could answer. "It's part of Santana. She would want it to be kept alive."

Her mother nodded. "I agree. Do you have any jars here?"

"I'll get them," I said, sprinting for the door. I didn't stop until I reached the entrance to the Bestiary. Tobe was in the middle of cleaning some of the glass boxes, but he looked up as I screeched to a halt on the marble floor.

"Harley?" he asked, his tone concerned.

"Purge… happening now… Santana… BIG one!" I wheezed, catching my breath. "We need a jar."

He nodded and pulled one out from beneath his golden wings, before chucking it at me. I caught it in one deft swoop. *Seriously, what else does he have in there?*

"There are crowds," I explained. "We need to hurry."

"Get on my back," he instructed. Lowering himself down onto all fours, he folded his wings behind his back.

I frowned at him. "Are you serious?"

"It is the swiftest way of reaching Santana," he replied.

With no time to argue, I hopped up onto his back and looped my arms around his neck. We took off across the Bestiary and out into the hallway. With his paws scraping on the floor, he bounded through the evacuating crowds, who quickly dispersed at the sight of a hulking Beast Master coming at them at full speed. He could really move, covering ground way quicker than I could've. Within a couple of minutes, we were back inside the vaulted space of the Assembly Hall.

The Rag Team, along with Santana's mom and dad, were busy trying to subdue a serpent-like creature with a ruff of feathers and glinting scales. At first glance, I thought Quetzi had somehow escaped, only this beast was smaller. Orishas zipped through the air, spiraling around the serpent to confuse it, while Wade shot fireballs to stop it from escaping. It recoiled as one hit it in the side of its head, giving Dylan the opportunity to slide in and grip it by the tail, holding it fast as it wriggled and writhed, its jaws snapping violently in every direction. It moved like a whiplash, striking without warning.

With the jar still clutched in my hand, I leapt down off Tobe's back and rushed toward the fracas. I put the jar down in front of the serpent, only to have it strike at my chest, the blow sending me hurtling back against the far wall. I put out my arms in an attempt to lessen the impact, my hands smashing against the thick stone with a sickening crunch.

I sagged to the ground, struggling to shake off the pain that ricocheted through my bones. When I lifted my hand up, I gasped. Two of the gemstones on my Esprit had shattered. They were the ones channeling Earth and Air—the two elements I had yet to fully master.

Getting to my feet, I scanned the ground for the missing shards, but they were too small to find.

Great... that's just what I need.

Glancing over at the others, I watched as Wade reached into his pocket and deposited a bunch of the small, green entrapment stones in a circle around the serpent. It reminded me of the first time we'd met. He was still as cocky as he'd been back then, but he'd well and truly won me over. He stopped, dropped, and slapped the ground hard, the way he'd done that first time, his mouth moving as he muttered something. His rings lit up, while the crystals glowed to life, greenish-white beams crisscrossing over the Purge beast. The serpent thrashed against it, looking for a way out of the entrapment net as the glowing ropes flattened the creature to the ground and singed the shimmer of its scales.

Standing up, Wade lifted his hands across the beast, his rings turning that familiar shade of red. He whispered something as the snake writhed and slithered, before it disintegrated in a puff of black smoke that sank down into the glass of the Mason jar. *Major déjà vu.* The net vanished a moment later, leaving Wade to pick up the used stones and the Mason jar to glow red.

I was relieved to see that they'd managed to capture the serpent safely in the jar, though Santana had slumped to the ground in a broken heap. Her body shivered all over, her teeth chattering. I could hear them from where I stood.

At least she's alive, and that beast is in a jar. At least there's that.

My smashed gemstones paled in comparison to her suffering. Still, I could feel their loss moving through my veins. I'd only just started to get used to the Esprit, and now I'd lost half of my channeling power. With Katherine looming large around us all, the timing couldn't have been worse.

THIRTY

Santana

I bolted upright, bright light streaming into my eyes. With my chest heaving and my heart pounding a million miles a minute, I struggled to get my vision to focus. Black spots danced like Orishas in my line of sight. A hand grabbed my shoulders.

"Hey, it's okay, you're safe." Raffe's familiar voice cut through the panic in my head. "Calm down, you're in the infirmary."

As I took a few deep breaths, the anxiety fled from my body. My head felt fuzzy and everything ached, but if Raffe said I was okay then I had to be. *Ugh, what the hell happened? Why do I feel like I've been hit with a freight truck?* Slowly, my vision cleared, revealing Raffe perched on the edge of the bed. He smiled at me, a furrow of concern pinching his brows together.

A nervous chuckle rippled from the back of my throat. "I'm so glad to see you, Raffe. I thought I was losing my mind for a moment," I said. "Seriously, I had this freaking crazy nightmare, right before I woke up just then. I dreamt that I was at the Family Gathering and I Purged right in front of your dad. I think I might have said something to him before it happened, which was embarrassing enough. Dreams are so weird, aren't they?"

Raffe nodded slowly, a strange expression on his face. "They are… but that actually happened, Santana. That's why you're in here. You're in recovery after a pretty nasty Purge."

I gaped at him in horror. "Is everyone okay?"

"Everyone's fine, although my dad probably should've worn his brown pants to the party." He chuckled, but I couldn't bring myself to laugh with him. All I could think about were those poor bastards who'd witnessed me Purge, right in front of everyone. Frankly, I was mortified. It was on par with calling a teacher "Mom" or not noticing you had toilet paper on the bottom of your shoe.

"Oh my God, I can't believe I did that," I said. "I just thought there was something wrong with the heating. I never thought… I've been so absorbed in everything else that's been happening lately, I didn't notice the signs my body was giving me. The sweating, the slurring, the pains. I've been a total idiot. I can't believe I put so many people in danger." I held my head in my hands, wishing I could turn back the clock. I'd done some stupid things in my time, but this topped the lot.

What must you think of me, Raffe? You saw me like that... What am I going to say to your dad the next time I see him? "Yeah, sorry about the whole Purging everywhere thing. It happens, right?" I'm sure that'd go down well.

I looked up as Harley entered, a broad grin on her face. Everyone seemed determined to cheer me up, but I felt like hiding under a rock for the rest of my life. Purging in public wasn't exactly a common thing to do, and I felt like I'd broken rule number one of the coven guidebook. I'd put people in danger. No quantity of smiles or jokes could put me in a better mood. *Nope, you're going to have to deal with Captain Sourpuss for a while.*

"How're you feeling?" Harley asked, taking the chair on the opposite side of the bed.

"Grim."

"Wade just came to tell me that your Purge beast is safely stowed away in the Bestiary," she said brightly. *A little too bright, Merlin. Your acting skills are terrible.* "It's like a smaller, less terrifying version of Quetzi. Like, I wouldn't try to keep it as a pet, but I wouldn't fear for my life if I got in a box with it. Tobe seems pretty smitten, though I guess he gets like that with most of his creatures."

I smiled despite myself. "I'll have to go and visit it sometime, see what kind of monster I've managed to conjure. You know, I thought it'd be something super impressive—I think we all hope we'll be the kind of magical that can churn out a beastie like Tobe. Apparently, I'm not quite there yet."

"Hey, it put up a hell of a fight. You shouldn't be too hard on yourself," she teased.

"It's weird, but I feel kind of attached to it," I said shyly. "Is that meant to happen? I don't want to be around it all the time, don't get me wrong, but I'd like to visit it now and again. Please don't tell me this is what childbirth is like, because I am *so* not ready for that kind of responsibility. Next thing I know, my Purge beast will be all grown up and off to college, and I'll end up in debt for the rest of my life trying to make sure it stays on the straight and narrow."

Harley laughed. "Nice to see you've got your sense of humor back."

"Not really. I'm forcing it."

"I hear that's bad for you."

"Feels like it," I muttered wryly, turning to Raffe. "Seriously, though, are magicals supposed to feel attached to their Purge beasts? That seems really freaking odd to me."

Raffe shrugged. "It happens sometimes. I think it depends on the level of energy it took to Purge it. By the looks of things, you exerted a *lot* trying to get that creature out."

"Yep, that definitely sounds like childbirth to me," I replied. "My mother always likes to tell me, in graphic detail, how bad her labor was with me. This all sounds very familiar."

"Can you remember much about your Purge?" Harley asked.

"Yes and no. To be honest, I thought it was all a dream, and then Raffe kindly told me that it actually happened and I'm now an embarrassment to myself and the coven."

"I didn't say that!" Raffe protested.

I smiled at him. "I know, I'm just ad-libbing a little. Dramatic license and all that."

When I turned back to Harley, my eyes snapped toward the broken jewels of her Esprit. The empty sockets stood out like a sore thumb, the vacant holes dull beside the glittering gemstones that remained. She caught me looking, before hurriedly putting her arms behind her back. I realized it must have been broken in the fight between my stupid Purge baby and everyone who'd tried to stuff it in a jar.

"I did that, didn't I?" I asked. "You don't have to hide it; I can see the stones are broken."

Harley shook her head. "If I had better control of my own powers, I wouldn't have had to worry about it breaking. It's like Nomura says, we shouldn't have to rely on these things. It's just hard not to, when they make everything so much easier."

"Dammit, Harley, I'm so sorry…" I swallowed hard, the guilt almost overwhelming me. Esprits were so personal and not easily repaired, from what I knew.

Harley's expression softened. "Don't feel bad. If it hadn't been for me, you wouldn't have Purged like that. You performed a powerful spell because of me, and this happened. In a way, the Esprit breaking is my own fault."

"Whoa now. Harley Merlin, self-deprecation doesn't suit you. You're tough as old balls, so stop being so damn hard on yourself. What happened in New York isn't your fault. It just so happened that I had to step in to stop something… freaking nasty from coming out of your weird fog tornado," I chided. "Honestly, even without the Esprit, and even with the Suppressor, you're a million times stronger than most magicals. Swear to God, if I hear another self-pitying word come out of your mouth, I'll slap it off."

Harley collapsed in a fit of giggles. "There's motivation for you, if ever I heard it."

"You're damn right."

Raffe cleared his throat. "What the heck went on in New York?"

Harley and I exchanged a glance. "A spell went wrong, and I had to do a little bit of on-the-fly fixing. No biggie, it just brought on the whole Purge thing way sooner than I would've liked," I replied. "I was already tired, so it used up a lot of energy. Still, nobody got hurt. No harm, no foul. All's well that ends well and all that clichéd fluff."

Harley's ringtone cut through the awkward silence that followed. Clearly, Raffe didn't believe what I was telling him, but I could come clean later. The Grimoire debacle was Harley's tale to tell, not mine. I wasn't about to snitch on her.

"Who's calling?" I asked.

"It's Wade," she replied, putting him on speakerphone. "Hi, Wade, I'm in the infirmary with Raffe and Santana."

"Good, that saves me a couple of phone calls," he replied.

"Compassionate as ever," I teased.

A short silence followed. "Sorry… I hope you're feeling better, Santana."

"That's better. You were saying?"

"We've received word from the surveillance crew. They've spotted some suspicious activity around the abandoned factory; a few cars pulled up and parked by the fences for a while, before driving off again. There have been people walking close to the building, too, though surveillance agents have kept their distance so they don't scare these guys off. We think Micah will probably be moved there soon, so we've got to go ASAP."

Harley nodded. "I'll meet you in the foyer in five minutes."

"See you there. And hurry up."

She rolled her eyes. "Will do."

"Punch a few of those nasty little punks for me, will you?" I said, looking up at her with mournful eyes. I wanted to go and help, but I was in no condition to fight a sickly octogenarian, let alone a horde of powerful magicals.

"I'm sorry, Santana. I wish you could come."

"That's right, rub that salt deep," I teased halfheartedly. "You should get going before Wade throws a hissy fit."

She turned to Raffe. "Raffe? You coming?"

"I should stay," he replied.

"Pfft, don't be ridiculous! There's no way you're staying here with feeble old me," I said. "I mean it, Raffe. They might need help from… They might need a bit of your hidden strength, if it turns nasty. Protect the others, okay? Make sure they all get back safe."

"If you're coming or staying, I need to know," Harley urged. "We've got to move now."

He looked at me with uncertain eyes. "Will you be okay on your own?"

"Raffe, I'm not helpless. I've just had an embarrassing experience. My ego is more wounded than anything else. Go on, scoot! Don't make me chase you out of here, because I will. With my hospital gown flapping in the breeze, I swear I will."

"Stay safe, okay?" he murmured, dipping his head to kiss my cheek.

"And you," I replied. "I mean it, make sure everyone comes back safe. Do you hear me?"

"I will," he said, before sprinting out of the room with Harley.

I watched them leave, my heart heavy. *I'm talking to you, too, Kadar. Bring my people back. Bring Raffe back to me. I'm counting on you.*

THIRTY-ONE

Harley

The Jeep sped along the coastal highway, heading for the edge of the Tijuana River Mouth State Marine Conservation Area. *That's one hell of a mouthful—couldn't they have come up with a catchier name?* It was the very spot where Marjorie had pictured Micah, though her visions weren't exactly reliable. However, since the Shapeshifter had grabbed her and put that image in her mind, she had envisioned Micah at this location a couple of times, after touching objects belonging to him. It was almost as though the Shapeshifter vision had opened up more images to her, channeling them through the items we already had. It made her able to focus properly on Micah, feeling him out, expanding her Clairvoyance so she could more reliably confirm his location. The highest probability for where he was going to be was the warehouse, and he was due to arrive there… well, pretty damn soon.

Channing had wanted Marjorie to come with us, so we'd have her by our side if we needed more visions, but Alton had vetoed it completely. I liked to think it was for protective reasons, but I knew there was likely a selfish element to it, too. Marjorie had an impressive power; he couldn't risk the coven losing that.

Astrid had stayed behind with her, to keep her safe from any further attacks. She'd set up a perimeter of cameras and shocking devices with Smartie, alongside a sizeable security detail. Marjorie's initial guards had survived the attack but were recovering in the infirmary. Nowhere was safe with this mole in our midst, but she was better off at the coven than risking being snatched mid-mission. We couldn't afford to give Katherine what she needed. After learning about those five rituals from Finch, I figured that's what she needed the supercharged kids for. How and where and why—those were questions we couldn't answer yet.

Garrett had been permitted to come with us, on the proviso that he wore the camera on his chest. He'd relented, eventually. He didn't want to miss out on something like this. As we'd left the coven, Astrid had watched us from the foyer of the Fleet Science Center. Her fear for all of us had been palpable, though much of it had been directed toward Garrett. I guessed things were really starting to heat up between them, if she was feeling that worried about him.

It was a pretty packed vehicle, with Channing, Stella, Wade, Garrett, Tatyana, Dylan, Raffe, and me all squished into five seats. Somehow, Raffe was in the trunk, peering over the seats, while Tatyana was happily curled up in Dylan's arms. There hadn't been time to take two, with my Daisy's keys still in my bedroom. It would have cost us more time for me to run up and get them, so we'd decided to squish into one. Now, I was starting to regret our decision. My muscles were cramping, and Channing didn't appear to understand the idea of deodorant. With Wade in the driver's seat, I was stuck next to GI Joe.

Still, it gave me an opportunity to observe the behavior between Channing and Stella, after Stella's confession the other night. To my surprise, things didn't seem too awkward between them. The mission was probably a good way of distracting both of their minds, and their emotions were fairly constant. Channing felt tense and focused, while Stella seemed to be nervous and fired up. A good mix for a mission like this. For the first time since they arrived, I was actually pretty happy that they were with us. Right now, we needed all the muscle we could get, and these two were more military-minded than any of the Rag Team.

"Are you sure you should be coming with us, Harley?" Wade said unexpectedly, breaking the tense silence in the Jeep. *Gee, thanks for that—way to call me out in front of everyone.* I had as much right to be here as anyone.

"Why shouldn't I?"

"With your Esprit broken, do you think you'll be okay in the event of a fight? I know Air and Earth aren't your forte, but you might need them. You needed Earth when you took on Emily Ryder. Plus, your powers can be a little on the wild side. I don't want you injuring yourself, or anyone else, because your Esprit is damaged."

I forced a smile onto my face. "Thanks for the vote of confidence."

"I'm just worried, that's all."

"You shouldn't worry so much. It'll be fine, honestly. I have enough control to muddle through." *Did he just say he was worried about me? Wade Crowley is worried about me!* That still didn't mean he liked me like that, but I'd take it. I just wished he hadn't mentioned it in front of a carload of people. Now, everyone was going to think I was some kind of liability. *Well, I've got news for you, ladies and gents—I'm not! Occasional loose cannon, yes. Liability, no.*

A short while later, we pulled up just around the corner from the abandoned factory. With a whispered instruction from Channing, who seemed to have named himself leader of this operation, all of us piled out of the Jeep and headed toward a gap in the fence. The surveillance team had told us where to go, marking the gap out on a map for us. The abandoned factory stood approximately a hundred yards from the outer fence. I could see the rusty machinery within and the peeling paint that Marjorie had mentioned.

"We need to scout out the place," Channing murmured, as we ducked down behind a stack of old metal crates. "See if there's anyone inside yet. Surveillance mentioned cars and suspicious pedestrians, but they haven't seen anyone enter the premises yet. That doesn't mean there aren't guards watching the place on Katherine's behalf. We need to get to them before they can sound any kind of alarm."

Stella nodded. "The surveillance team has dealt with any civilians who might interfere, so we have a clear run at the building. We should stay in a group—there's strength in numbers, if they come at us in force. Divide and conquer likely isn't going to work here."

"So, which entrance do we take?" Wade asked. "There are gaps in the exterior, or we can use the main doors."

"Surveillance noted a staircase on the outside of the building," Channing replied. "We should climb it and observe the interior from above. If we spot anyone, we might be able to use the element of surprise. I doubt they will be watching anything over their heads—not if they're expecting an arrival via the road. A blitz attack may work in our favor."

"Sounds like a plan," Dylan chimed in.

"People rarely look up. It is a peculiar trait in humans and magicals alike," Tatyana agreed.

Garrett shrugged. "I still think divide and conquer is usually the best way to go, but I'm happy to go with everyone else."

Raffe stood at my side, his eyes shifting strangely from their usual dark gray-blue to a deep shade of scarlet. He was almost pulsating, a surge of mixed emotions pouring off him. I tried to block the sensations out, but something inside him was calling out at the top of its lungs. *What* is *that? I really want to know, because this is confusing as all hell.* It didn't feel like the right time to ask the question aloud, but it didn't stop me from thinking about it.

Without another word, we set off across the marshland, covering the distance between the fence and the factory in a matter of minutes. We took a curving route toward the building, ducking behind every crate and box and lump of stone that we passed. It probably looked ridiculous to an outside eye, but we hoped there were none glancing in our direction. This was supposed to be stealth at its finest.

Around the back of the factory, a rickety ladder led up to a hatch in the top floor of the building. Channing went first, his bulky weight causing the metal bolts to strain and groan. Fortunately, the sound wasn't too loud, blending in with the whistle of the sea breeze that whipped up from the ocean beyond. We let him reach the top first, making his way through the hatch, before the next person followed. There were a few hairy moments, where Stella's foot almost slipped, and Dylan almost lost his grip as he tried to get through the hatch, but everyone managed it in the end.

I brought up the rear, clambering up the rusting rungs until I reached the upper floor of the factory. As I glanced back down at the ground, my stomach churned. If anything gave way beneath me, it was a long way down. After seven other people, I was beginning to doubt the structural integrity of this ladder. It creaked and juddered beneath my feet as I took each step upward. *One at a time, Harley. One at a time. Focus on the top rung.* Heights had never been my thing.

A few moments later, I dragged myself through the hatch and dusted myself off. The others were crouched at the edge of a platform, staring down at something below. Edging across the rotting boards below my feet, I crept toward them. My gaze followed theirs as I joined the team, discovering two individuals in the center of the abandoned factory floor below us. They were just standing around, their eyes fixed on one particular spot in the middle of the room.

Glancing down, I wondered where Micah was. I couldn't see him anywhere.

"There aren't any ladders leading down, except that one," Channing muttered, pointing to a ladder nearby. "They'll see us if we try and climb down, and it's too high for us to drop to the ground. I'd hoped these floors might lead down to further floors that we could sneak down. Seems like that's no longer the case. Which of you have Air abilities?"

I shook my head. "I wouldn't want to risk it."

"Leave this to me," Raffe said suddenly. "Take my lead. I'll apprehend them, if you follow as fast as you can. I won't be able to hold them for long without something bad happening, so you'll have to get to them quickly. After that, I suggest you tie them up so we can take them away for interrogation."

"No offense, but I don't think this is a job for you," Channing protested.

Raffe shot him a scarlet stare. "Trust me."

Before Channing could say another word, Raffe leapt through the air, clearing the heady drop down to the ground with ease. He landed effortlessly, a smoldering fog of black smoke billowing from his shoulders. From here, it almost looked like his skin had changed color, moving from a warm olive to a bright, devilish red. He jumped up and tore toward the two individuals—one male, one female. Now, I understood what he meant when he'd said we wouldn't have long. Something had taken over Raffe. I just didn't know what. He barreled into the two guards, knocking them to the ground in one fell swoop.

"Go!" I urged, running for the ladder. Within minutes, we were beside Raffe, launching ourselves at the two cronies with two sets of Atomic Cuffs. His skin began to change color again, shifting from bright red to his ordinary shade of olive. The smoke faded, his eyes returning to their usual blue-gray.

Dylan and Tatyana managed to get the guards under control, fastening their wrists together and binding their mouths with a gag similar to the Atomic Cuffs. They glared furiously at us, but we had them in our grasp.

"Micah!" Wade cried, his gaze fixed on a spot in the corner. The young boy sat on the ground, half hidden by the shadows of an old conveyor belt, a terrified expression on his face. Our presence didn't seem to have made him feel any calmer. Then again, he didn't know all of us.

I rushed toward him, ducking down to get to his level. "Micah? Are you okay? It's Harley—do you remember me?"

He nodded slowly, tears streaming down his face. "Yes."

"Are you hurt?"

He shook his head, prompting more tears to fall. "My cat… my cat is gone. I had my cat, but I don't now."

"Did you have him with you?"

The boy nodded. "He was here. Now he's not."

"We'll look for him soon, okay? I'm sure he'll turn up."

"He's gone," Micah murmured miserably.

"We're going to look for him later, okay?" I had no clue why Micah might have had his cat with him—maybe it was a stuffed animal or something—but he'd been through enough already. The least we could do was come back and look for it, after we'd gotten Micah to safety.

"We can't look for a cat, Harley," Wade barked. "We need to leave here, pronto!"

"I know, that's what I just told him!" I snapped back.

Wade and the others spread out to check that there was nobody else hiding in the warehouse. Feeling bad for Micah, but worried for our safety, I turned back to him.

"Where did you last see the cat?"

He pointed to the shadows up ahead.

Two birds with one stone, right?

I left Micah where he was for a moment, moving behind the conveyor belt to see if I could find anything that resembled a cat, as well as hidden guards or any sign of danger. Discovering a fallen tower of heavy metal boxes, I skirted around them, ducking beneath to see if something had been trapped when the tower collapsed. My stomach sank at the sight of orange fur. Micah's cat, which had clearly once been an actual living thing, was stuck beneath the first box, crushed to death under the weight. I realized the tower must have fallen when Raffe landed, the shockwave toppling them like dominoes.

Reaching underneath, I managed to pull the squashed creature free. I held it carefully and carried it back out into the open. Kids were tough, but I didn't want Micah to get too close. Nobody needed to see this mess of crushed bone and flat organs.

"I found your cat, Micah. I'm sorry, but there's nothing we can do for him," I said, keeping my distance.

Jumping to his feet, Micah sprinted toward me. "Fluffers!" he yelled. "Fluffers, don't go!"

"Holy hell!" I almost screamed as the cat wriggled in my arms, its ears pricking up and its eyes blinking open. Somehow, it seemed to re-inflate, like a grim sketch from a cartoon. Beneath my hand, I could feel its heart beating rapidly, and a soft meow came from its mouth. I wanted to drop it and run, but Micah's presence stopped me. This was his pet. I couldn't just hurl it away, as much as I might have wanted to.

He reached up to me with eager eyes. As freaked out as I was, I could see how much Micah adored the cat. Carefully, I settled the orange tabby into his arms. He held on to the kitty for dear life, and it contentedly purred against Micah's shoulder. *For me it's dogs, for you it's cats. I guess that's cool. That's right, Harley, tell yourself everything's A-Okay when you've just had a cat come back to life in your arms.*

Wade walked up to us, a confused expression on his face. Evidently, he'd just seen what I'd seen. "Micah, can I ask you a question?" he said, crouching low.

Micah nodded. "Yes."

"How many times have you made Fluffers wake up like that?"

Micah counted the number out on his fingers, reaching six before stopping.

"Looks like Fluffers has three more to go," I joked.

Wade ignored me. "You've made Fluffers wake up six times?"

"Yes."

"Oh my God," he murmured.

"What?" I replied.

"Well, either Micah is a Necromancer, like Alton, or this cat is Micah's Familiar. If it's the latter, that's incredible for anyone to do, let alone a five-year-old."

I frowned. "A Familiar?"

"They're extremely rare, but a Familiar is an animal that a magical takes on as a sort of highly gifted pet. They have special abilities of their own, acquired through a series of magic rituals. However, it takes years for a magical to find an animal they can form that kind of bond with—it's a soul bond, so it runs deeper than anything ordinary. That tends to be why only elder magicals have them, because they have spent years discovering their Familiar and helping them gain abilities. It can be any animal." He paused in thought. "If the Familiar dies, it causes incredible pain to the magical owner, as that soul bond is broken. It's supposed to be worse than living through a Purge."

"Then how can this cat be Micah's Familiar?"

"One of the cat's abilities may be Necromancy, though I'm struggling to believe Micah could give Fluffers that gift. Then again, I've seen crazier things recently. It might be that he has some kind of magical power related to animals, which has allowed him to acquire a Familiar so young. I'd have to check a couple of books to see if there's an ability that matches up."

"Occam's Razor."

"Huh?"

I smiled. "A bit of philosophy for you. The simplest solution tends to be the right one."

"You're probably right." He turned to the others. "We need to get moving. Bring those two along—we can drop them off with the surveillance team and get them to bring them back to the coven."

"Good idea," Channing replied, attempting to reassert his authority.

I took Micah's hand as we moved toward the front entrance. A lock dangled from the middle, preventing us from leaving. Undeterred, Dylan grabbed the side of the metal door and hauled it open, using his Herculean abilities to prize it from its hinges.

We were about to step out into the open when a blast of ice-cold air powered through the derelict factory, a rumble like thunder rising to a deafening roar behind us. I whirled around in time to see a portal split the seams of time and space. A red-haired woman emerged. Despite never having met her before, I recognized her face immediately.

Katherine Shipton.

THIRTY-TWO

Harley

I gaped at Katherine. *How the heck did you manage that, you evil bastard?* A moment later, I understood. Trailing behind Katherine, her wrists lashed together with a glowing rope, Isadora stepped out of the portal. She looked miserable, her chin dipped to her chest, a dappled mass of bruises and burns covering the bare skin of her arms and chest.

"No..." I whispered.

Katherine smiled as she spread her arms wide, like a corrupt politician taking to the stage.

"How nice to meet you all," she said.

An incredibly powerful wave of Telekinesis pummeled into us, throwing everyone against the hard wall. My skull smacked against the stone, and I crumpled to the ground. Beside me, Garrett lay still, knocked unconscious by the impact—I hoped he was only unconscious. I shoved him in the shoulder, trying to get him to wake up, but he wouldn't budge. A blinding pain pulsed behind my eyes, searing through my brain. It took every ounce of strength I had to shake it off and stand once more, turning to face Katherine.

I reached out toward her with my Empath abilities, attempting to feel for any kind of emotion. A blockade of nothing met me. I had felt that kind of emotional wall often enough to recognize it. She was definitely a Shapeshifter. *As if you weren't bad enough.*

"Tatyana, Dylan, take Micah and run!" Wade cried, raising his hands toward Katherine. His ten rings glowed as he sent a wave of Fire back toward Katherine. She swept it aside as though it were nothing, an amused expression on her face.

Strength in numbers, Auntie dear.

I lashed bouts of Fire and Telekinesis at her, while Channing and Stella jumped into action. Channing sent a pulsing ripple of Earth energy through the ground. A semicircle of stone shot up around Katherine, blocking her exit from behind. Stella matched it with a swirling vortex of Fire that hurtled toward Katherine, hitting her in the shoulder as she ducked to get out of its way. Wade shot out another wall of searing flames, the blazing fire almost hitting its mark. Katherine was quicker, sending up a Telekinetic shield that blocked the attack.

Raffe began to smolder again, until he was entirely enveloped in a dense mist of black smoke. I stared at him in shock. *I'll never get used to this.* Snapping out of my trance, I sent fireballs after Raffe to help him as he barreled toward Katherine, leaping on her with the force of a lion. She collapsed beneath him, only to throw him back with a renewed thrust of insanely fierce Telekinesis. Raffe sailed through the air, landing on his feet with an impressive skid that dug deep into the ground. Bite marks had appeared on Katherine's shoulders, a trickle of blood meandering down the front of her emerald-green dress.

Tatyana and Dylan raced toward the entrance with Micah in tow, but a whipping lasso from Katherine's palms swept them off their feet. They hit the dirt with an unsettling thud, Fluffers letting out a screeching meow. I retaliated with a lasso of my own Telekinesis, but she merely smiled and pushed it back. Focusing on the exit, she swiped her hand through the air, slamming the metal door back into place, blocking our escape. Dylan jumped to his feet and tore the door away again, but Katherine was one step ahead. She picked Dylan up with her Telekinesis and slammed him into the earth.

"Hide here until we come for you," Tatyana urged, as she ushered Micah through a small gap in the entrance. He grabbed his cat and tucked himself behind the door, keeping out of sight, while Tatyana turned around and wasted no time in calling to the spirit world. Her eyes glowed white as she transitioned into Kolduny mode. Her voice echoed eerily, several glimmering wisps appearing all around her.

The air in the factory went cold, the spirits charging forward at Tatyana's request. Light was practically pouring out of her, her whole body lit up by the ghosts she was channeling. Dylan followed it up with a show of his extraordinary strength, while I tipped the stagnant water from a nearby barrel over her head in an attempt to distract her. With Raffe at his side, the two boys hurtled in Katherine's direction. This time, she wasn't fast enough to stop them. With everything else being thrown at her, she couldn't keep everyone at bay at once.

Dylan landed a blow to her face, her neck snapping to one side, while Raffe began to pummel at her as though she were a punching bag. A second later, they soared backward, carried on a violent wave of Telekinesis. Raffe hit the wall first, the impact barely affecting him. Seeing that Dylan was careening toward the same fate, he jumped up and caught his friend, lowering him safely to the ground.

Meanwhile, I launched every attack I had at her. Torrents of water poured down above her, while fireballs thundered, and my lasso of Telekinesis sought out her throat. She fought back against every single one, undeterred by our greater numbers. Although a few of our hits got through, they didn't seem to bother her in the slightest. She matched us blow for blow, always able to retaliate before we could make a dent in her magical armory.

Why did I get the feeling she was holding back? This wasn't all she had; I knew it wasn't.

As if sensing my thoughts, she upped the ante. Smiling at us all, she gathered a shield about herself. It slithered across her skin, removing every cut and bruise and burn.

"Are you kidding?" I yelped, turning to Wade. "She can heal herself!"

"Then we keep going. We break her down!" he replied, though his expression belied his concern.

A moment later, every Elemental power rained down on our group, while barrage after barrage of Telekinetic attacks hit us with unyielding force. Our bodies and our minds were taking a savage beating. We fought back with everything we had, but it wasn't enough. We couldn't break through. Not even Dylan or Raffe could make it past her onslaught of Telekinetic tidal waves. She *had* been going easy on us, testing out our strengths and weaknesses, making us reveal them to her.

Oh, you're clever. Very clever. If she weren't a colossal, murdering, psychopath bitch, I might have admired her.

Channing darted toward Katherine, using his Earth abilities to shoot up small blockades of stone to protect himself from her powers. She tried to attack him, but he kept ducking down behind the cover he'd created. Soon enough, he found himself standing in front of her. He lifted his hands to strike her down, but she moved like lightning. A blow of ferocious energy—Telekinesis and Fire combined—slammed down on him from above, knocking him to the ground.

She smiled at him, her eyes cold. Keeping her gaze fixed on him, she raised her hands again, gathering a storm of combined elements above his head to execute the finishing blow.

"Stella, NO!" I roared, as she leapt forward with startling speed and knocked Katherine to the side. The blow intended for Channing powered into Stella's shoulder, deflecting the hit from Channing and sending it toward the far wall. It exploded in a burst of stone and metal. Stella stumbled backward, dragging Channing away from danger.

As Katherine got to her feet, shaking off the indignity of being knocked over, Wade sent a ball of fire toward a rotting beam overhead. It went up in flames instantly, a lick of fire spreading across the ceiling. Manipulating the fire he'd created, he brought it down in a thick curtain of searing hot inferno, separating us from Katherine momentarily. I couldn't even see her through the sheet of fire.

Wade kept one hand trained on the fiery divide as he ran toward an unconscious Garrett. He managed to drag him upwards and hurl him over his shoulder with his spare hand, then headed for the exit. The adrenaline must've given him some kind of Herculean strength.

"Dylan, the door!" he shouted.

Dylan ran toward it and tore it away once again. "Should we follow?"

Wade nodded. "Get after Micah. Bring Tatyana." He looked to me. "That goes for you, too."

He darted out of the doorway, with Dylan and Tatyana following after. I was about to make my escape, too, when I spotted a figure moving to the side of the blaze. Isadora huddled in the shadow of the ancient conveyor belt, her glowing wrists giving her away. Katherine was still working her way around the fiery curtain. Isadora was on my side of the blaze, while Katherine remained on the other. I knew this might be the only chance I had to free Isadora. I wasn't about to leave her behind.

I sprinted toward her and reached for her wrists, but she tugged them back. "It's no use, Harley."

"What are you talking about? I have to get you out of here," I urged. "Come on, you need to come with me."

She shook her head. "I can't, Harley. Katherine has cursed me. She has placed a spell upon me that, if broken, will kill me instantly. The moment I run, she will bring the axe down upon my head. I won't get beyond those fences before she breaks the spell. I'd end my life if I thought it would help, but the curse stops me from even attempting it."

"I don't understand," I said, panicked and horrified that my aunt might commit suicide because of Katherine. I couldn't lose Isadora, not now. "How did this happen?"

"After that Shapeshifter found us, they never stopped tracking our location," she replied solemnly. "They found me. I was careless, just for a moment, and they snatched me. Jacob is still safe, though. He's a smart kid."

A stab of guilt pierced my heart. It was a painful truth, to realize that my searching for her was ultimately what had led Katherine to her. If I'd just let her stay hidden, the way she'd wanted, then none of this would have happened. *Maybe not now, but it might have happened one day.* Katherine was determined. She'd have found a way to snatch Isadora, even if I hadn't gone to her that day. I had to convince myself that it was true.

"He's safe?"

Isadora nodded. "They won't find him. He knows how to hide now."

Before I could ask any more questions about Jacob, Katherine stepped through the sheet of fire as though it were nothing but water. Her eyes sought me out, a triumphant smirk tugging at the corners of her lips. She stalked toward me, her emerald dress flowing behind her like it was an extension of her body. It irked me that I'd picked a similar dress for my pledge. We might have been related by blood, but that was where I wanted the similarities between us to end.

"My dear, sweet niece," she purred. "What a treat to finally meet you. I have waited such a long time for this moment. Your selfish mother didn't want me to know you'd even been born, and your oaf of a father was no better. Curious, though, don't you think? I can't imagine why they wanted to keep me from you." A cold laugh bubbled from the back of her throat.

"I have a few ideas," I shot back. "Murdering someone's entire family doesn't tend to get you in the good books. Maybe that's hard for you to understand, since people like you don't have any feelings at all."

She grinned. "Shapeshifters, you mean?"

"You know what I mean, Katherine."

"Auntie, please. We are family, after all."

"Hell will freeze over the day I call you Auntie," I snapped.

"I can arrange for that, if you like? I know a guy." She held out her palm, a perfect crystal of ice forming above her pale skin. It hovered there for a moment, before zipping straight at my heart. It paused just short, the tip of the crystal pressing into my chest. "I could run this through your heart, and you wouldn't even realize you were dying. I could do it right now."

I narrowed my eyes at her. "Then why don't you?"

"Delayed gratification, dear Niece. I want to savor the moment of your death, and watch the light go out in your eyes bit by bit," she replied casually. "I have all the time in the world to end your pathetic existence. Besides, at this moment in time, you're more use to me alive than dead. In the meantime, I've had a little thought. I figured I'd kill every single friend you have, in a myriad of ways. You'll get to enjoy every show that I put on for you so you'll know there's no use in fighting power like mine."

"I'll stop you," I said through gritted teeth. What the heck did she know about me, that she wanted to keep me alive? The Grimoire incident came rattling back into my brain. I guessed that kind of thing would be *just* up Katherine's street.

"Is that a promise?"

"I'll wipe that smirk off your face, one way or another."

She chuckled. "You are a feisty little thing, aren't you? You don't get that from your mother or father. Maybe a little of Auntie Katherine has rubbed off on you, after all," she mused. "You know, there is an alternative to all of this nastiness. You could always—"

"Join your side? I don't freaking think so."

She shrugged. "Doesn't hurt to ask. Maybe I'll ask you again once your first few friends are dead. Grief and loss can be a powerful motivator. Even if it's just a 'cut your losses' kind of deal, I'll still welcome you with open arms."

"Go to hell," I spat.

"I've already been. Weren't you listening?"

Raw power thrummed through my veins, starting as a minor pulse and rising to an all-consuming tremor that tore through my body. It surged with such vehemence that I feared it might tear me apart. Every Elemental ability I possessed had gathered inside me, combining in a destructive mix of dark, burning Chaos. It was like holding slippery eels that had no desire to be captured.

With my broken Esprit and my lack of discipline, the violent energy ricocheted out of my searing flesh and into the ground below us. A sinkhole formed in front of Katherine's feet. She tried to stagger back, but the sinkhole spread out to meet every step she made. I fought to curtail the rapidly expanding edges.

"Just think what I could do for you," Katherine called from the other side of the gaping crevasse.

Her voice and her words tipped me over the edge. *I want nothing from you!* my mind screamed.

As soon as the thought passed through my brain, a brutal swell of combined Chaos ripped through every cell in my body, before thundering into the earth. As I lost control completely, the sinkhole heaved outward in a final push that took us both down into the dark pit below.

THIRTY-THREE

Harley

I scrambled to my feet and raised my fists, using a small spark of Fire to cast a glow in the dark space. Walls of earth rose up on all sides, with the factory somewhat shrunken in the distant gap overhead.

On the opposite side of this makeshift arena, a rustle disturbed me. A shadow grew taller in the gloom as Katherine stood. There were barely thirty feet between us, making an out-an-out firefight a dangerous thing. Anything more than a little spark would burn us both, and trying to use my Water abilities would drown us.

Stuck at the bottom of the black pit with Katherine Shipton, I'd somehow managed to level the playing field. At such close quarters, her advantage of impressive shields and powerful waves of energy was gone. We'd both have to be careful with our powers, to stop the whole sinkhole from toppling in on us. *If she gives a crap about me surviving, that is.* She seemed pretty eager to keep me alive until the bitter end of whatever she was up to, so maybe this wasn't going to be an execution…

Before I could open my mouth to speak, a shivering snake of

Telekinesis swiped me off my feet. I tumbled backward, hitting the dirt with a thud. The spark of Fire sputtered out.

"That's for ruining a perfectly good dress." Katherine's voice echoed from the darkness. "Do you know how hard it is to get Tibetan silk at this time of year? Honestly, couldn't we have had this little fight up there, where there was room to breathe? It might come as a shock to you, since you've no doubt heard of me as this almighty being, but I'm not fond of small, cramped, dirty holes in the ground. I'm not a mole, Harley."

"You hire them, though, don't you?" I shot back, as I dragged myself back up.

"What—small, black, furry creatures who dig tunnels? Can't say I've ever hired one. Besides, dear Niece, Familiars aren't really my cup of tea."

"Stop calling me that!"

Anger pulsed in my veins, fueling the raw energy within me. A blast of Telekinesis shot out of my hands, thudding into the far wall of the sinkhole with an unsettling spatter of rocks and soil.

"Very sad to see so much potential, so poorly trained," she mused, her voice somehow all around me. "If you keep going like that, Harley, you'll bury us both alive. Ooh, unless that's what you're going for? Heroic self-sacrifice? Give the Merlin surname a bit of *oomph* after the negative spin your father put on it? Interesting idea, though it'll never work. I've clawed my way out of deeper holes."

"Why's that? Because you're a life-sucking vampire?"

She laughed, the sound shuddering up my spine. "Oh, my sweet, sweet girl. I'm far worse than that."

A Telekinetic lasso wrapped around my throat without warning, squeezing tight like a python. In the shadowed gloom of the pit, I hadn't felt it approach. It wasn't as though I could read her emotions to try and preempt what she was going to do, and I couldn't see a freaking thing. A few shadows, maybe, but that was about it.

Feeling my eyes bulge out of my head and my cheeks turn hot as the blood strained to find somewhere to go, I sent out desperate tentacles of my own Telekinesis. They slithered across the rubble-strewn ground, before pausing at a decent-sized boulder. I could feel the weight and shape of it under the edges of my magic. My lungs were burning, my throat all but closed up. With one last-ditch surge of power, I picked up the huge boulder and smashed it down on the back of Katherine's head. At least, where I hoped her head might be. A groan signaled that my blow had made impact, while the grip of Telekinesis loosened around my throat.

I dragged oxygen into my lungs, inhaling deep gulps of the stale pit air. "I thought you… wanted to leave me for last?"

A ripple of bright green light illuminated Katherine for a few seconds, before the pit faded to black again. I'd managed to hit her, but it didn't matter. With her ability to self-heal, nothing I did would even make a dent. Still, there was a small satisfaction in knowing I'd whacked her with a hulking great boulder.

A story for the grandkids I'll never have, once she's watched the light go out of my eyes. Man, this is a perfect case of "be careful what you wish for." I'd wanted a family, and boy did I get 'em.

"That was the plan, but I'm open to improvisation, and you're really starting to bug me," she replied. "First you ruined my dress, then you conked me on the head with a rock—not very friendly of you, is it?"

She hurled a refreshed snap of Telekinesis at me, but my own rose to meet it, forcing it away with a bristle of energy that sounded like a thunderclap. White sparks showered off the tendrils, revealing the occasional glimpse of Katherine's manic face in the near distance.

Lassos of Telekinesis whipped through the gap between us, a scuffle of feet kicking rocks and skittering stones as we both ducked and dove away from one another's powers. I thought about giving

Air a try, but after my pledge fumble and the break in my Esprit, I figured it was best not to risk it. That was a surefire way to get us both smothered in twenty feet of soil and concrete, if I didn't end up bringing the entire weight of the factory down on us, too.

"You know this is futile, right?" Katherine announced, as she paused and put up a shield between us.

"What's the matter? Getting tired?"

"No, I'm just way too busy for this kind of nonsense. Bonding with my niece is, naturally, very important to me, but I can't be giving all of my time to these silly games. I'm an independent businesswoman with a very tight deadline to meet. You'll have to take a raincheck." I could hear the satisfied smirk on her face. *You think you're hilarious, don't you?*

"You mean completing those five rituals?"

A sharp intake of breath pierced the dull acoustics. "What did you say?"

"That tight deadline—it wouldn't have anything to do with those five rituals you're looking to complete, would it? Finch told me that's what you need to do to become a Child of Chaos." I waited for a moment, trying to listen for a change in her emotions. "Tell me, Katherine, when you write out that naughty-and-nice list of yours, like a messed-up magical Santa, which one will I go on? I'm dying to know—am I worthy, in your eyes? Do I automatically get a spot, since I'm family? Finch thinks he'll get to keep his powers, so it only seems right that I do, too. I'm half Shipton, remember?"

The atmosphere felt very still, as though all of the air had been drawn out of the sinkhole. In the darkness, I could hear her pacing like a wild animal. My muscles braced for the strike that didn't come, my eyes narrowed at the gloom to try and make out her figure. *Too far?*

"Finch would never breathe a word to you, Harley. Nice try with the subterfuge, but I'm not buying it. He's an obedient son, just like his father was an obedient—and *very* tender—lover. I've got fond memories of Hiram Merlin. We could've been something together. Still, he let me down. Easier to bend people to your will than expect true loyalty."

"No, you don't like a challenge, do you?" I shot back. "I bet you hate it even more when you come in second place. That must have stung, right? To know that he preferred your sister? It can't be all that satisfying when you have to force somebody to love you by binding them with a crazy-ass spell. I mean, come on, you went to some *extreme* lengths, didn't you?"

I knew it was a risky tactic to taunt her like that, but I needed to buy myself a sliver of time. Her angry silence gave me the breather I needed to scour my brain for memories of Nomura's lessons on how to use my powers without my Esprit. I'd complained so much during those sessions, but now I was grateful I'd been forced into them. Nomura was right: we couldn't rely on trinkets to channel our energy into something great. We had to do it regardless. We had to know our own strength and enhance it with the Esprits rather than use them as a crutch.

Funny what being face-to-face with a nutjob will make a girl understand.

Gathering a controlled ball of Fire between my palms, I shot it at Katherine. It hurtled through the air, though I didn't bother to wait and see where it landed. Even if I missed Katherine herself, it would've hit the shelf of rock behind her. That was good enough for me. All I needed to do was distract her while I harnessed the most terrifying power in my arsenal.

With jagged bolts of white light emerging from beneath my hands, I turned them downward, mustering a whorl of ice-cold Air beneath me. It puffed up like a haphazard cushion, lifting me up a short way. Amassing more and more, using my rage to give it strength, I pushed down hard with my hands, feeling the give and resistance of the air pocket as it exploded with sudden violence. I shot upward like a bullet out of a gun, sailing way too high out of the gap above. I landed with a sickening crack on the concrete floor of the factory, knocking the wind clean out of myself as I faceplanted on the ground.

Got to work on that precision, Merlin. Not too shabby, though.

Wasting no time, I slammed my palms down against the hard concrete and sent a rumble of Earth energy through the stone, urging it all the way down into the walls of the sinkhole. I squeezed my eyes shut, my entire body drenched in sweat, my muscles shaking with the effort. I kept my hands pressed to the floor, even when my lungs began to scream, and my nerves began to sear with white-hot electricity beyond my control. A roar exited my throat, mixing with the tremor of the earthquake that would bury Katherine twenty feet under the soil. My howl didn't stop until the sinkhole had crumpled in on itself completely.

As soon as it was done, I rolled over onto my back and panted so hard I thought my chest might burst. The others appeared in the doorway of the factory, gaping at me in shock. Wade sprinted toward me, but I waved him away, picking my broken body up off the floor with shaking legs.

"I came back for you, but you'd—"

"Pit of Hell... dragged me down... don't worry about it," I wheezed.

Isadora stood off to the side, curled up in a fetal position. Evidently, whatever spell Katherine had put on her was affected by whatever state Katherine herself was in. Right now, Isadora was in a lot of pain. Her face was scrunched up, her arms gripping her stomach against the agony.

I hurried toward her and ducked down at her side. "We need to get you out of here," I said, trying to get her up. Wade helped, putting Isadora's arm around his shoulders and hauling her to her feet.

"Whatever spell she's put on you, we can find a way to block it. We can get you out of this."

Isadora winced. "No… you can't. You have to… go. It's too late… for me."

"I'm not leaving you!"

"I know it is… hard, my sweet girl. Let me go. Save yourself. That is all your… father and I ever wanted. *Your* survival. We don't… matter. Only you do."

I shook my head, feeling furious tears gather. "That's bull. You're just as important as I am. Come on, we have to go now!"

A deep tremor thundered beneath my feet. A moment later, Katherine burst out of her stony grave on a powerful wave of Telekinetic power, sending debris flying everywhere as soil exploded upward.

Isadora shoved Wade away from her, her eyes widening in panic. "RUN!" she screamed. I could see her strength fading in front of my eyes. "Harley, RUN!"

Katherine unleashed a bombardment of incredible magic. I'd never seen anything like it before. Spiraling shards of black ice sprayed out like spears, while miniature thunderclouds gathered in the central atrium of the factory. Bolts of lightning shot downward and struck the ground in front of my feet as I tried to make a run for it.

A blockade shot up, forcing my friends back into the factory. They couldn't break through the shield, which sent out machine-gun rounds of tiny, dark gray orbs if anyone got too close. One struck Tatyana in the shoulder, sending her tumbling to the ground with a bloodcurdling scream. Dylan scooped her up in his arms, her body spasming. There was no way out. My actions had made Katherine change her mind about waiting to kill us, that much was clear.

We could fight her until we were blue in the face, and it wouldn't make a scrap of difference. With her self-healing abilities, we'd wear ourselves out long before we managed to capture her. Plus, I doubted Atomic Cuffs would have much effect on her. She had powers I didn't even know existed, a way of combining the Elements to make entirely new forms of natural energy. Lightning, ice, torrents of molten lava.

Garrett had managed to wake up, and Stella was leaning on him. The ricochet from Katherine's blast was evidently taking its toll on her body, her eyes unfocused. Meanwhile, Channing tried to pry a way out between two splintered sheets of metal. Dylan handed Tatyana over to Channing and tore the side of the factory open like a can of beans. The outside world beckoned—so close and yet so far. The same volatile shield faced them. Beyond, a wispy figure poked its head out from behind a stack of crates.

Micah... If he makes it, then maybe this'll be worth something. But we weren't finished yet. I was determined to fight like hell, until there was nothing left of me.

Raffe stepped forward. He stalked past me and headed toward Katherine. I grabbed his arm, prompting him to whirl around and face me. His eyes burned with scarlet flames, wisps of black smoke unfurling from his skin, which was changing color before my very eyes.

"What are you doing?" I hissed, thinking of Santana. If anything happened to Raffe, she'd never forgive me. "Don't be an idiot. We can figure this out. There's strength in numbers, remember?"

Raffe's eyes burned even brighter. "I'm letting my dark side out, for real this time. What you saw before was nothing compared to what I am capable of. I'm giving Kadar the reins."

His face morphed into a twisted mask that was both Raffe and not Raffe, at the same time. The crimson of his skin deepened to a dark maroon, the black smoke billowing out from every inch of his body until it became difficult to see the figure beneath. Below the hairline of his curls, two sharp horns appeared, glinting black in the sunlight that glanced in through the factory's broken roof. Flames danced atop each one.

What the—?

I tugged my hand away from his arm, my fingertips singed by the heat of his flesh. Blisters appeared, though they were the last thing on my mind. Raffe charged toward Katherine before shooting up into the air with inhuman strength. He hurtled back down to earth like a comet, slamming into the ground with all his might. A pulse of delayed explosion jetted through the ground, spreading out like ripples in a pond. Rings of fire followed, expanding outward and knocking down the load-bearing beams of the factory. One hit Katherine square in the stomach, and she stumbled. The shimmering shield around the factory glitched for a moment, before dissipating into the air.

"RUN!" I bellowed, knowing this might be the only chance we had. I didn't want to leave Raffe behind, but the factory was about to cave in on us. I only hoped that whatever had taken over his body was strong enough to protect him from what was going to happen next.

Everyone else turned and sprinted out of the factory, while my eyes sought out Isadora. She lay on the ground by Katherine's feet. How she'd ended up there, I didn't know, but Katherine was performing some kind of weird ritual on her. She held Isadora by the throat, two streams of purple light traveling from Isadora's eyes and into hers. A second later, a portal tore open behind them, the rush of icy air spreading the licking flames of Raffe's retribution.

I lunged forward, wanting to get to my aunt, but a firm hand pulled me back. Wade dragged me toward the exit of the factory as the first beams fell. Looking over my shoulder, I saw Raffe charge again at Katherine, the two of them locked in a fierce and terrifying battle while Isadora sank to her knees.

I struggled against Wade's grip. "We have to go back for them!"

"We can't, Harley," he replied.

"We can't just leave them!" As I spoke, the roof shattered, and the walls began to fold in on themselves. Debris tumbled from the ceiling, slates and beams crashing down. Before I could even react, Wade threw himself on top of me, protecting me with his body as the factory fell in. Through a gap in his hold, I watched Katherine shove Raffe away with a powerful shard of ice, before disappearing through the portal with Isadora in tow. As soon as the portal snapped shut, the rest of the factory gave way. Raffe ran for cover, the maroon shade of his skin fading to his normal olive as he dove out of a fissure in the wall.

A few minutes later, everything stilled to an eerie silence. We lay in the rubble of the old building, the whole thing collapsed around us. We were lucky not to have been hit worse, since it looked like only a few wooden planks had made any impact on my savior.

Wade slowly straightened out with a groan, his eyes gazing into mine. "Are you okay?"

I nodded. "I feel like I should be asking you that. You're the one with a bunch of wooden slats on your back."

"It was worth it," he said quietly.

As I glanced past his shoulder, my eyes widened in a macabre sense of awe. The roof had gone, and there was nothing but blue sky above us, with a chorus of birds chirping in the distance.

THIRTY-FOUR

Santana

"You could've been killed, you stupid, stupid, adorable, beautiful man!" I chided, as Raffe came to the end of his story. "Which one of you thought that'd be a good idea, huh? Because I'm going to soundly kick the ass of whichever one of you is responsible, do you hear me?"

He'd come back from the mission an hour ago and had been filling me in on what had happened ever since. It had taken him some time to warm up to admitting what he'd done in the fight against Katherine, and rightly so—I was horrified. To think that he might not have come back just didn't even bear contemplating. *You both promised me you would, and then you go and do a stupid thing like that? What were you thinking?*

He shrugged. "I'm not sure which one of us took the lead on that."

"Convenient," I retorted, unable to keep the relieved smile off my face. I wanted to be pissed off at them both, but I couldn't be. They were home, they were safe, and I was eternally grateful for that.

He smiled. "It all worked out, though, so you don't have to worry."

"I don't have to worry?" I snorted. "When you go and do crazy things like that, I *definitely* have to worry. It sounds like you went a little deeper than you normally do. That was insanely dangerous, Raffe. I know you meant well, but don't you ever do that to me again, okay?"

"Okay," he conceded, taking my hand. "As for Kadar, he came out in a way I'd never experienced before. It was like there was more of him than there was of me, for the very first time. I didn't entirely lose control, but it felt different than the other times I've let him loose. To be honest, I'm pretty shocked he went back inside afterward. He was so strong, he probably could've overwhelmed me for a bit longer, if he'd wanted to."

I frowned. "You could have fought your way back through, though, right?"

"Yeah, of course. It just would've taken a lot more effort," he replied, though he didn't sound entirely convincing. The thought of Kadar taking over unnerved me. He was intriguing, but he wasn't Raffe. The fact that Raffe was even using Kadar's given name made me feel odd; he'd never done that so frequently before.

I might've named you, Kadar, and I might make your eyes flash blue all sexy-like, but it's never going to be you over him. Team Raffe all the way, Diablo.

"How do you feel after letting him take control like that?"

Raffe shrugged. "Tired, kind of buzzy, a little bit weird."

"I'm not letting you off the hook, by the way. I still think you're both completely stupid for doing that; it's just that you're too cute to stay mad at." I grinned at him, squeezing his hand tighter. It felt good to have him back.

"I think he's trying to impress you by being on his best behavior."

"Well, color me impressed, *mi amor.*"

Raffe's eyes flashed red for a moment as I pulled him toward me with a seductive smile. My arms slipped around his neck, and he leaned across the hospital bed, his lips grazing mine with that same intoxicating passion that we'd shared before. My breath caught in my throat as he wrapped his arm around my waist and flipped me around, so my body was curled up beside his. I sank deeper and deeper into his embrace, reveling in the sensation of his mouth on mine and his tongue gently exploring.

Raffe's kisses didn't match his demeanor. Quiet, shy Raffe was an absolute demon when it came to the old smoocharoos. I could've kissed him for hours and never gotten bored. It was kind of weird, not knowing whether the passion came from Raffe or Kadar, but they were part of each other, so I guessed it didn't matter. It definitely didn't feel like it mattered right then.

The sound of someone clearing their throat by the door, in the most awkward way possible, made us both freeze. I didn't want to turn around. If it was Harley or Tatyana, or even Astrid, they'd have made a quip or whistled or something. This presence felt infinitely more… parental.

Grimacing with hot embarrassment, I relinquished my saucy hold on Raffe's chest and glanced at the door. My mom stood there, looking just as mortified as I felt.

Well, at least we both wish the ground would open up and swallow us all whole, so there's that.

"Might I have a moment in private with my daughter?" my mom asked.

Raffe jumped up as though I'd suddenly sprouted scales. "Yes, of course. Sorry, Mrs. Catemaco. I… well, it wasn't… what I'm trying to say is, I was just—"

"Getting an eyelash out of her eye?" my mom interjected, arching a killer eyebrow.

"Never mind," Raffe muttered. "Sorry about that. I'll catch you in a bit, Santana. Sorry again. Really didn't mean for… never mind. I'll stop. See you soon, okay?"

I smiled. “See you in a bit.”

“He seems… nice,” my mom said, as soon as Raffe had vanished. “A little jumpy, maybe, but he’s cute. Interesting eyes. So, what’s going on with you? I presume that if you’re munching on one another’s faces like that, there’s something more to this than just a fling? I hope you’re not giving away the milk for free, Santana. I brought you up better than that. Be the cow that men want to buy, you understand?”

“Nope, not sure I understood a word of that. I’m a cow now, am I?”

“It’s metaphorical, and you know it. In fact, I was just saying to your father the other day, before you Purged in front of everyone and gave us all a heart attack, that you were looking extremely beautiful. It must be all these talks we’ve been having about you coming home—you’re blossoming, ready to return to Mexico like a desert rose, opening to the first droplets of rain after a drought.”

I rolled my eyes so hard I thought they might fall out. “Where do you get this crap?”

“Watch your mouth, *mi hermosa*. You’re not too old for a smacked backside.”

“You’ve never smacked me in your life. I doubt you’ll start now.”

She narrowed her eyes, meaning business. “I brought the slipper, just in case. Never travel without it.”

“Listen, what you and dad get up to in your spare time is entirely up to you. I don’t ever want to hear about it. You could *not* afford the counseling.”

“You’re evading the subject, Santana. What is he to you, hm? What are his intentions? Is he worthy of you? I know what these Levis are like—a snaky, oily, slippery sort of folk. Raffe doesn’t seem too slimy, but I can only go by what I know of his *papi*. There’s a snooty flamingo of a man.”

I frowned. “Flamingo?”

"All show and no substance. Poses about in lakes on one leg, squawking and making himself look like Mr. Big when he's probably Mr. Small."

"Mom!"

"What? I have a sixth sense for these things. Now, stop stalling. I have to know if he's worthy of you," she said. "You know, you were born under a blood moon, on the shores of Lake Catemaco, bathed in its mystical waters from the moment you took your first breath. When you cried, your little lungs announcing your presence, the wolves howled back, and the eagles spread their wings in reverence. You are wild and graceful and powerful. You are the beating heart of the Catemaco Coven."

I shot her a look. "Do you know how many times you've told me that story?"

"It doesn't make its message any less potent. Your ancestors tinged the moon with red that night, letting their blood flow to show that you were special—that you would bring our family to greatness, like no other before you."

"I bet all the moms say that to their daughters."

"They do not, Santana. Being a smartass doesn't suit you. You were not born to the squeal of braying donkeys, so do not act like one."

I sighed, knowing she wouldn't leave me alone until I revealed every gory detail. "I don't know where things are going with me and Raffe. We're just starting out, getting to know each other better. That's how normal people do this kind of thing, Mom. They date, they talk, they discover things about each other that they like, and then they move on from there. We're still in the honeymoon phase… although, we're barely at that. It dips here and there in the romance stakes, but he's a complex kind of guy."

Obviously, "complex" was putting it mildly, but what was I supposed to say? *Oh, by the way, Mom, he's part demon and I'm kind of digging the fiery bad boy in him, too. What's a woman to do, right? We love a bad'un. All I need to do now is get the demon side to stop talking about peeling off my flesh, and we'll be peachy with a side of keen. Best of both worlds. Bing, bang, boom.*

"That doesn't sound very promising, Santana," my mom replied, deflating my puffed-up pride in Raffe. "You need a man who can challenge you and stand at your side, as an equal. Jumpy and cute probably doesn't cut it. You know what we expect of you. One day soon, you'll marry and you'll take over the Catemaco Coven. That has been your destiny ever since the doves landed on the edge of your basket, woven by the ancient Santeria of old, and cooed a lullaby to soothe you to sleep each night."

"I'll bear it in mind," I said bluntly. "Although… don't you think all of this marriage stuff is a little backwards? Fair enough, it made sense when the coven needed protection, and they needed strong leaders to follow, but everyone's cool doing their own thing. They don't need strong leaders, and they definitely don't need married ones. Why can't I just do it on my own? What difference does it make?"

My mom reeled back as though I'd just told her that her favorite telenovelas weren't real. "That isn't the way we do things. There are expectations. They've been there all your life, so don't act surprised now. You've always known that this day was coming."

"Doesn't mean I have to like it."

She sighed. "No, it doesn't, but that changes nothing."

"Agree to disagree?" I said with forced brightness.

"Santana, this is serious."

"And I'm serious. You can't keep ramming this marriage thing down my throat, because I'm about ready to choke on your damn expectations. Let me come to a decision in my own time, because if you don't, the last thing you'll see of me is a cloud of dust as I run full-pelt in the opposite direction. And you know I'm speedy as all hell."

She shook her head. "I wish you wouldn't use such vulgar language, Santana. It doesn't become you."

"This isn't Regency England, Mom. You've heard me say far worse," I shot back. "Hell, I've heard *you* say far worse when you've had one too many tequilas around the dinner table. Do you remember that time you told grandma to go—"

"Don't you dare say another word," my mom interjected sternly.

I laughed. "Good times, eh?"

"She didn't speak to me for a month after that."

"Maybe you should have asked those doves to coo an apology. I bet that would've worked like a treat."

"This rebellious streak is your father's doing, you know—he spoiled you. I may never forgive him for it."

I grinned at her. "And I'll always thank him for it."

"Speaking of your father, we—"

I covered my ears dramatically. "If it's about that slipper, I don't want to hear it."

"No, it's not, you cheeky devil," she replied, her tone exasperated. "We brought you a gift, to celebrate your first Purge. We were hoping to give it to you once you announced your engagement, but this seemed like as good a time as any. A Santeria's first Purge is a very special thing, and it deserves a reward."

I looked up at her in surprise. "A gift?"

"Ah, that got your attention," she replied with a smile.

Delving into her bag, she pulled out a wrapped parcel and handed it to me. I tore at it like a woman possessed, revealing the beautiful present underneath. It was a blank journal, intended for the writing of a Grimoire. The cover was a burnished, bronze leather with shimmering blue stones embedded in the material. They trailed up the spine and across the front like the wisps of my Orishas, weaving in and out of the embossed shapes of a lake with a full blood moon above it. I was surprised to find a stylized version of Quetzi at the bottom right, representing my Aztec heritage. Still, the whole thing suited me perfectly. I couldn't have designed it better myself.

"Thank you so much!" I gushed, clutching it to my chest.

"You must choose the spells you put in there wisely, for once they're written, they can't be undone," my mom warned.

An idea drifted toward me through the haze of my Purge-weary mind. I remembered what Kadar had said to me about talking to a Child of Chaos face-to-face, the way folks used to. If my mom wanted me to be backwards, abiding by the old ways, then this was the perfect compromise. For my first act as Grimoire-writer extraordinaire, I would write a spell to summon a Child of Chaos.

I had no idea how to even start writing a spell like that, but determination was a pretty damn good motivator. I'd find a way to attain the right knowledge and the necessary Chaos juice to get it going, and with a little help from a certain Ms. Merlin, I knew we might be able to get it on its proverbial feet.

I also knew it could end up being my first and last spell in the Grimoire. But it seemed like a risk worth taking.

THIRTY-FIVE

Harley

I crouched in front of the glass box and tapped gently. The feathered serpent slithered toward me, its violet eyes peering at me with curiosity. Its tongue lashed against the smooth interior, and a soft hiss formed condensation on the glass. I smiled as it ruffled its white-and-violet feathers, its bright-blue-and-fuchsia scales rattling together in something like contentment.

"How can you gawk at that thing like it's anything close to cute?" Wade asked, pulling a face.

"Because it *is*. This thing is adorable!" I glanced at him, amused by his aversion. "What's got you so creeped out about it? Not a reptile fan?"

"Not a Purge beast fan."

"Are you saying you'll just ignore yours, when it comes?"

He shrugged. "I wouldn't get attached to it, that's for sure."

"Looks like you're in the minority here," I said, nodding at Quetzi, who was nudging the partition between his box and Santana's Purge beast. "Quetzi loves it, I love it, and Tobe is head over heels. And here you are, terrified of a little snake."

"They're just not my thing. Plus, you've got no idea how powerful this snake is."

"What is your thing?" I asked, my cheeks suddenly burning as I realized what I'd said. *He's not going to say "you," you sap. A romantic comedy this ain't.* After all the babbling I'd been doing lately, he probably already thought I'd lost my marbles.

He seemed oblivious to my embarrassment. "I'm fine with Purge beasts like Tobe. If they could all be like that, things would be so much easier. Instead of guessing whether they're going to attack you, or paralyze you in your sleep, or rob you of your life breath by breath, they could just tell you."

"Where's the fun in that?"

"You've got a weird attitude toward danger, Harley," he said with a smile.

"When you've lived on the mean streets of Mount Hope, nothing seems dangerous anymore. Put a gun in my face and I'd just shrug and give you my money," I replied. "I think Katherine might be the only thing that actually one-hundred percent terrifies me. Give me a thousand car-jackings instead of her."

Quetzi shuddered, his tongue flicking out of his mouth as his feathers ruffled. I frowned at him through the glass. *What have you got going on under those shiny scales of yours, huh?* Clearly, there was some reason the serpent didn't like Katherine, not that hating her guts was anything new; I had a feeling we could all get on that particular bandwagon. Still, the mere mention of her name made Quetzi mad. Whatever beef they had with one another, it ran deep.

I wondered if Quetzi would help us fight Katherine. If he had a grudge against her, maybe it'd be a win-win for all of us. Right now, we could definitely use all the help we could get.

I was still pretty shaken up after my first encounter with the Big Bad. It seemed impossible that we'd somehow managed to escape with our lives, though I guessed we'd only made matters worse, in a lot of respects. I'd pissed her off, big time, by trying to bury her alive, and put massive targets on our backs as a result. She'd already been after me, but we might've had a bit more time if I hadn't made her extra mad. Now, there were no more *ifs* regarding her, only *when*.

"How're you feeling about her after the factory thing?" Wade asked.

"Even more freaked out."

He nodded. "I didn't expect her to be so… I don't know. It's hard to put my finger on, but she wasn't what I expected."

"She's got the Merlin-Shipton sense of humor, that's for sure," I muttered.

"When you were down in that hole, what did she say to you?"

"It wasn't what she said down there that scared me," I admitted. "It was what she said before, when the rest of you were running for it. She said she'd kill me last. She said she'd make me watch you all die, slowly and painfully—and creatively, since that seems to be her speed—and I really think she meant it." Bitter tears sprang to my eyes, though I quickly forced them back. I wasn't going to shed tears over Katherine's threats. No way.

To my surprise, Wade crouched down beside me and put his arm around my shoulders. "We won't let that happen, Harley. We know what she's up to, and we'll fight her tooth and nail until she surrenders or we kill her. She isn't getting her hands on any of us, I promise you that."

"You can't promise that," I murmured, my heart racing at his closeness. I could smell the spicy scent of his cologne and see the faint graze of stubble that ran along the edge of his strong jaw. *Damn, you're a handsome bastard. Ugh. Why'd you have to be so freaking cute? Seriously, it's not cool, man.*

He flashed me a smile that made my insides *squee*. "I just did."

With him being so close to me, my mind turned to Stella and the way she'd jumped fearlessly to protect Channing from Katherine's magic. She loved him so intensely that she'd nearly sacrificed herself, even though he didn't love her back; it was kind of awe-inspiring. *Do I feel that way about you, Crowley? Would I save you from a ball of destruction? Yeah, probably.*

Realization dawned. Wade had done the same thing for me, in shielding me from the debris of the collapsing factory.

Wait... does that mean... no, it can't, can it?

I had no idea what to do about it. He'd given no thought to his own life when he'd knocked me to the ground and covered me like that. He'd thought only of my safety. Surely, there was only one reason he'd have done something so insanely stupid.

This is your moment, Merlin. You're all snuggled up, he's being charming, and he saved you from a cave-in. It's now or never.

"Wade… can I tell you something?" My heart was hammering a mile a minute, my palms clammy and gross. If he'd reached out for my hand, he'd probably think he'd touched an eel instead.

He looked down at me. "Sure. What's up?"

"I… I'm getting really frustrated with these restrictions," I said. "Like, I want to be satisfied with the way things are, but I can't. There's so much more that I could explore, and I feel like I'm being held back—like I can't just reach out and grab what I want, you know?"

Smooth, Harley. Way to chicken out by chatting all vague and stuff. He's not going to have a clue what you're talking about.

"With the Suppressor, you mean?"

"Uh… yeah," I replied, my heart sinking. "Like, if I could just let it all out at once, then maybe I wouldn't have to feel this… this all-consuming *whatever* inside me, all the time. It's messing with my head. It's making me act all crazy, and it's getting to the point where I'm not sure how much longer I can go on without… uh, letting it all out. Or, at least, getting it to come out. How do I even do that? I don't have a clue."

Harley, you bumbling coward.

"That sounds like... a lot is going on," Wade said, his brow furrowed. He looked even more adorable when he was completely baffled by something, and I was clearly confusing the heck out of him. Despite my best efforts, he didn't seem to be picking up on the subtext. I just looked like a babbling idiot, and he looked like a beautiful, bemused, gorgeous creature that I wanted to smooch the face off of.

Enough with the mush! I'm about to barf. Now, if he'd stop blinking those deep green peepers at me, maybe I could get a grip. Lovesick puppy dog was not a state I'd ever thought I'd find myself in. The hard-as-nails Harley I knew would have kicked my ass for getting this way, yet here I was, melting into a puddle of adoration, waving goodbye to tough-guy me.

Fortunately for my self-respect, Tobe appeared, interrupting Wade's and my weird moment.

"Sorry to disturb you," he said in his signature growl, "but Alton has asked me to pass on a message. He wishes to see you in his office, Harley, at your earliest convenience. I believe he meant now, but I think he was being polite."

"Thank you, Tobe. I'll head there right away." I sounded a little too eager, jumping at the chance to leave the awkward conversation with Wade. He was confused; I was confused; we were all confused. It seemed better to leave the situation to stew for a while, until I could muster the balls to admit how I felt. Stella's warning rang in my head—that I should probably come clean while I had the chance. *Yeah, but not now. I look like a beet and it isn't cute.*

"See you later, maybe?" Wade asked.

I nodded effusively. "Yeah, sure, absolutely, love to."

Wishing I'd stopped at "Yeah, sure," I hurried out of the Bestiary and headed toward Alton's office. By the time I got there, my cheeks had just about cooled and my heartrate had returned to a normal pace. Rapping on the hefty double doors with their ominous lion-knockers, I pushed through into the office beyond. Alton sat behind his desk, and he looked up as I entered. However, he wasn't the only one in the room. Sitting in one of the high-backed armchairs was a bald teenage boy.

I frowned. "Sorry, am I interrupting something? I can wait outside until you're done."

"Not at all. In fact, we were just waiting for you," Alton replied, gesturing for me to sit. "Harley, this is Tarver. He's new to the San Diego Coven, recently moved here from—where did you say you were from?"

The boy smiled nervously. "Iowa."

"Yes, Iowa, of course. Anyway, I was wondering if you might do the honors of taking Tarver on a tour around the coven." Alton looked to me with a steady, slightly weird gaze.

"Me?"

He nodded. "Yes, I'm sure you know enough of the coven by now to show him the ropes." He smiled a secret smile that kind of creeped me out. All of this was unsettling, but what could I do? I didn't want to seem rude to this kid.

"Um… okay?" Confusion fogged my brain. I was still fairly new, too; I hadn't even known there was a pool here until a couple of days ago, and I still doubted I'd seen everything this place had to offer. Wade had given me the quick tour, or so it seemed. There were probably a bunch of rooms and cool things that I'd yet to discover, so why did Alton want *me* to take Tarver around?

"Off you go, then," Alton instructed.

"Okay… uh, let me show you what this place has to offer," I said, putting on a smile. Tarver practically leapt out of his seat with excitement and followed me out of the office and into the labyrinth of the SDC.

I took him to all the usual places first, like the banquet hall and the Main Assembly Hall, and explained the points system to him. I tried not to make us sound too lame, but we were still lagging way behind the other covens without any sign of a boost to our ranking. Even battling Katherine Shipton face-to-face hadn't won us any favors with the Mage Council. Apparently, according to Alton, it "was still undergoing further verification, as to whether it could qualify as a viable means of awarding points," as they could only take our word for it. Even with the bolstering witness statements of Channing and Stella, Levi was being a complete tool about it. They'd given us an extra hundred for rescuing Micah, but that still left us with a long way to go.

Still, Tarver didn't seem to mind. He walked along happily enough, taking in all the sights and sounds of the coven. He seemed nice, though a little quiet. I'd tried to make small talk throughout our tour, but he hadn't bitten. Instead, he'd grown more and more fidgety, to the point where I was starting to wonder if he was the mole and I was about to get attacked.

As we reached one of the empty training halls, Tarver looked around surreptitiously.

Is this it? Is this the moment when you're going to strike?

I prepped my palms for any eventuality, tensing my muscles in readiness. After my fight with Katherine, I was exhausted and completely spent in the magical sense, but no mole was going to take me down today. No chance. I had to have reserves somewhere.

"There's something I need to tell you," he said, turning back to me.

I frowned. "Oh, yeah?" This guy and Alton were acting really strange, and I didn't like it one bit. With Shapeshifters and curses like Krieger's being bandied about the place, nobody could be trusted.

Tarver reached up to the underside of his jaw and pulled away his skin in one horrifying movement. I nearly screamed, clamping my hand over my mouth as I saw the face underneath. I couldn't quite believe it.

"Jacob?" I whispered, before leaping forward to hug him, gripping him tight. "You're safe, you're safe, you're safe. Isadora said you were, but I didn't know what to believe. You're here—you're here and you're safe!"

He chuckled. "Yep. Thanks for the warm welcome."

"What's with the Scooby-Doo mask trick? You've got to warn a girl before you go tearing your face off in front of her. And why didn't you just tell me who you were in Alton's office, you dope?"

"Alton said I should try and see if the mask fooled you," he replied, grinning. "Looks like you're the benchmark for this working."

"Yeah, it worked!"

"Well, that makes me feel a little calmer about all of this," he said. "I was really worried back there, sure you'd realize it was me. See, I'll be staying incognito at the coven and helping Alton out with a bit of spy work, so this disguise *has* to be flawless." He took the mask and put it back on, the fleshy material melding perfectly to his face. Creepy didn't even begin to cover it.

A sad thought then crossed my mind. "Did Alton tell you about Isadora?"

He nodded. "Yeah, he filled me in on everything."

"I tried to rescue her, but she wouldn't come with me," I said, my voice catching in my throat. The image of her on the ground at Katherine's feet, being forced to do things beyond her control, was a vision I couldn't shake.

"That sounds like her."

"There's a spell on Isadora," I explained. "That's why she refused. She said Katherine would kill her if she came with me."

"I know," he said. "But we're going to get her back, one way or another."

I smiled proudly. "You read my mind."

"I knew you wouldn't abandon her. That's why she worries about you—she knows you'll do whatever it takes to protect her, which is why she's been protecting you all this time. Keeping her distance to stop you from becoming a target."

I chuckled wryly. "It didn't do much good, in the end. I think I've had a target on my back since birth." Shaking off my gloomy state, I patted Jacob on the back. "In the meantime, before we can go after her, we'll need to find out as much as possible about Katherine's plans and locate the rest of the missing kids. We got pretty lucky with Micah, and I know we can do better."

Jacob gasped, startling me. "I almost forgot something!" He reached into his jacket pocket and took out a letter, handing it to me with a shy smile. "It's from Isadora."

I glanced down at the envelope with wide eyes. On the front, written in elegant cursive, were the words *"As promised."* I realized the letter must contain everything Isadora knew about Hiram, Hester, and Katherine—the trifecta that had brought us all to this point. The full truth about them, finally.

But Isadora had also mentioned something else. A secret I might not want to hear. Something dark, that might even have to do with me, instead. Her vague statement had been lurking at the back of my mind ever since she'd given it. Now, she was delivering the choice she'd promised—to discover the matter for myself, whether I liked the outcome or not.

Given how anxious she had been about telling me, a part of me wondered whether I was better off not knowing. I didn't have to open the envelope. I could bury it under my mattress and forget it existed. But then I'd never know my family's story. Or mine.

Clutching the letter closer to my chest, I nodded stiffly. "Thank you, Jacob."

Sometimes the truth could be more painful than living a lie, and maybe this truth was something I would regret discovering. But in the end, reality had to be the wiser and saner path.

At least, I hoped so...

Ready for the next part of Harley's story?

Dear Reader,

Thank you for reading Book 3 of Harley's journey. I hope it entertained you!

As for Book 4: **Harley Merlin and the First Ritual**, it releases **November 30th, 2018**. Things are hotting up!

Visit: www.bellaforrest.net for details.

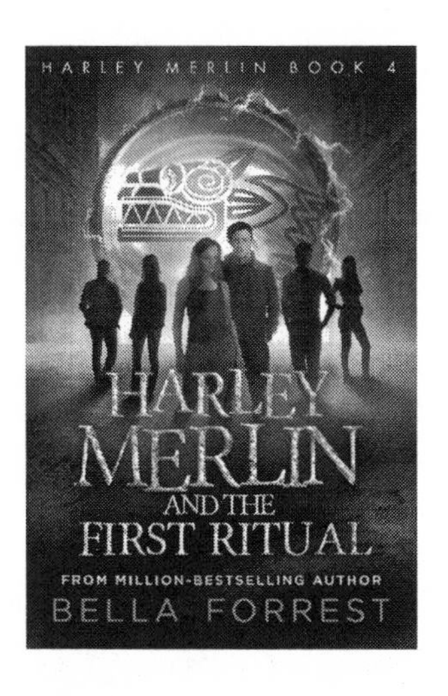

I'm excited to continue Harley's journey with you!

See you on the other side…

Love,

Bella x

P.S. Sign up to my VIP email list and you'll be the first to know when my next book releases: **www.morebellaforrest.com**

(Your email will be kept 100% private and you can unsubscribe at any time.)

P.P.S. I'd also love to hear from you. Come say hi on Facebook: Facebook.com/BellaForrestAuthor. Or Twitter: @ashadeofvampire. Or Instagram: @ashadeofvampire.

Read more by Bella Forrest

HARLEY MERLIN

Harley Merlin and the Secret Coven (Book 1)

Harley Merlin and the Mystery Twins (Book 2)

Harley Merlin and the Stolen Magicals (Book 3)

Harley Merlin and the First Ritual (Book 4)

THE GENDER GAME

(Action-adventure/romance. Completed series.)

The Gender Game (Book 1)

The Gender Secret (Book 2)

The Gender Lie (Book 3)

The Gender War (Book 4)

The Gender Fall (Book 5)

The Gender Plan (Book 6)

The Gender End (Book 7)

THE GIRL WHO DARED TO THINK

(Action-adventure/romance. Completed series.)

The Girl Who Dared to Think (Book 1)

The Girl Who Dared to Stand (Book 2)

The Girl Who Dared to Descend (Book 3)

The Girl Who Dared to Rise (Book 4)

The Girl Who Dared to Lead (Book 5)

The Girl Who Dared to Endure (Book 6)

The Girl Who Dared to Fight (Book 7)

THE CHILD THIEF

(Action-adventure/romance.)

The Child Thief (Book 1)

Deep Shadows (Book 2)

Thin Lines (Book 3)

Little Lies (Book 4)

Ghost Towns (Book 5)

HOTBLOODS

(Supernatural romance. Completed series.)

Hotbloods (Book 1)

Coldbloods (Book 2)

Renegades (Book 3)

Venturers (Book 4)

Traitors (Book 5)

Allies (Book 6)

Invaders (Book 7)

Stargazers (Book 8)

A SHADE OF VAMPIRE SERIES

(Supernatural romance)

Series 1: Derek & Sofia's story

A Shade of Vampire (Book 1)

A Shade of Blood (Book 2)

A Castle of Sand (Book 3)

A Shadow of Light (Book 4)

A Blaze of Sun (Book 5)

A Gate of Night (Book 6)

A Break of Day (Book 7)

Series 2: Rose & Caleb's story

A Shade of Novak (Book 8)

A Bond of Blood (Book 9)

A Spell of Time (Book 10)

A Chase of Prey (Book 11)

A Shade of Doubt (Book 12)

A Turn of Tides (Book 13)

A Dawn of Strength (Book 14)

A Fall of Secrets (Book 15)

An End of Night (Book 16)

Series 3: The Shade continues with a new hero...

A Wind of Change (Book 17)

A Trail of Echoes (Book 18)

A Soldier of Shadows (Book 19)

A Hero of Realms (Book 20)

A Vial of Life (Book 21)

A Fork of Paths (Book 22)

A Flight of Souls (Book 23)

A Bridge of Stars (Book 24)

Series 4: A Clan of Novaks

A Clan of Novaks (Book 25)

A World of New (Book 26)

A Web of Lies (Book 27)

A Touch of Truth (Book 28)

An Hour of Need (Book 29)

A Game of Risk (Book 30)

A Twist of Fates (Book 31)

A Day of Glory (Book 32)

Series 5: A Dawn of Guardians

A Dawn of Guardians (Book 33)

A Sword of Chance (Book 34)

A Race of Trials (Book 35)

A King of Shadow (Book 36)

An Empire of Stones (Book 37)

A Power of Old (Book 38)

A Rip of Realms (Book 39)

A Throne of Fire (Book 40)

A Tide of War (Book 41)

Series 6: A Gift of Three

A Gift of Three (Book 42)

A House of Mysteries (Book 43)

A Tangle of Hearts (Book 44)

A Meet of Tribes (Book 45)

A Ride of Peril (Book 46)

A Passage of Threats (Book 47)

A Tip of Balance (Book 48)

A Shield of Glass (Book 49)

A Clash of Storms (Book 50)

Series 7: A Call of Vampires

A Call of Vampires (Book 51)

A Valley of Darkness (Book 52)

A Hunt of Fiends (Book 53)

A Den of Tricks (Book 54)

A City of Lies (Book 55)

A League of Exiles (Book 56)

A Charge of Allies (Book 57)

A Snare of Vengeance (Book 58)

A Battle of Souls (Book 59)

Series 8: A Voyage of Founders

A Voyage of Founders (Book 60)

A Land of Perfects (Book 61)

A Citadel of Captives (Book 62)

A Jungle of Rogues (Book 63)

A Camp of Savages (Book 64)

A Plague of Deceit (Book 65)

An Edge of Malice (Book 66)

A Dome of Blood (Book 67)

A SHADE OF DRAGON TRILOGY

A Shade of Dragon 1

A Shade of Dragon 2

A Shade of Dragon 3

A SHADE OF KIEV TRILOGY

A Shade of Kiev 1

A Shade of Kiev 2

A Shade of Kiev 3

THE SECRET OF SPELLSHADOW MANOR

(Supernatural/Magic YA. Completed series)

The Secret of Spellshadow Manor (Book 1)

The Breaker (Book 2)

The Chain (Book 3)

The Keep (Book 4)

The Test (Book 5)

The Spell (Book 6)

BEAUTIFUL MONSTER DUOLOGY

(Supernatural romance)

Beautiful Monster 1

Beautiful Monster 2

DETECTIVE ERIN BOND

(Adult thriller/mystery)

Lights, Camera, GONE

Write, Edit, KILL

For an updated list of Bella's books, please visit her website: www.bellaforrest.net

Join Bella's VIP email list and she'll send you an email reminder as soon as her next book is out: www.morebellaforrest.com